Raves for
A Rather Lovely Inheritance

"A spirited heroine." —*Publishers Weekly*

"An entertaining yarn with family drama and intrigue aplenty."
—*Booklist*

"Utterly charming . . . excellent characterization and dialogue [with] a sweet touch of romance. If a novel can be both gentle and lively, surely this is one . . . *A Rather Lovely Inheritance* tantalizes and entertains with its mystery and skullduggery . . . Penny [is] a perfectly lovable heroine. It's a rare gem of a book that leaves behind a feeling of pure pleasure. I'm awarding it a Perfect Ten!" —*Romance Reviews Today*

"I haven't read anything like it in quite a while, and I thoroughly enjoyed myself . . . Penny is a delightful heroine . . . Who wouldn't enjoy the unexpected chance to rattle around London and then fly off to the sunny Côte d'Azur?" —*DearAuthor.com*

"Combines suspense, romance, and crafty wit. The protagonist is a character to cheer for, and the mystery subplot will keep readers turning the pages." —*Romantic Times*

"[Penny] hooks everyone . . . with her klutzy optimism . . . Fans will enjoy the lighthearted breezy storyline as the Yank takes England, France, and Italy." —*Midwest Book Review*

"[Has] everything—mystery, romance, [and] a whirlwind tour of Europe's hot spots." —*Kirkus Reviews*

"A return to the golden age of romantic suspense! *A Rather Lovely Inheritance* weds old-style glamour to chick-lit flair. You just want to move into the novel yourself—on a long-term lease, with hero and snazzy sports car included (villains sold separately)."
—Lauren Willig, author of *The Secret History of the Pink Carnation*

ALSO BY C.A. BELMOND

A Rather Lovely Inheritance

A Rather Curious
Engagement

C.A. Belmond

 NEW AMERICAN LIBRARY

New American Library
Published by New American Library, a division of
Penguin Group (USA) Inc., 375 Hudson Street,
New York, New York 10014, USA
Penguin Group (Canada), 90 Eglinton Avenue East, Suite 700, Toronto,
Ontario M4P 2Y3, Canada (a division of Pearson Penguin Canada Inc.)
Penguin Books Ltd., 80 Strand, London WC2R 0RL, England
Penguin Ireland, 25 St. Stephen's Green, Dublin 2,
Ireland (a division of Penguin Books Ltd.)
Penguin Group (Australia), 250 Camberwell Road, Camberwell, Victoria 3124,
Australia (a division of Pearson Australia Group Pty. Ltd.)
Penguin Books India Pvt. Ltd., 11 Community Centre, Panchsheel Park,
New Delhi - 110 017, India
Penguin Group (NZ), 67 Apollo Drive, Rosedale, North Shore 0632,
New Zealand (a division of Pearson New Zealand Ltd.)
Penguin Books (South Africa) (Pty.) Ltd., 24 Sturdee Avenue,
Rosebank, Johannesburg 2196, South Africa

Penguin Books Ltd., Registered Offices:
80 Strand, London WC2R 0RL, England

First published by New American Library,
a division of Penguin Group (USA) Inc.

First Printing, July 2008
10 9 8 7 6 5 4 3 2 1

REGISTERED TRADEMARK—MARCA REGISTRADA

LIBRARY OF CONGRESS CATALOGING-IN-PUBLICATION DATA:

Belmond, C.A.
A rather curious engagement/C.A. Belmond.
p. cm.
ISBN 978-0-451-22405-7
1. Americans—Europe—Fiction. 2. Inheritance and succession—Fiction. I. Title.
PS3602. E46R36 2008
813'.6—dc22   2007052514

Set in Simoncini Garamond
Designed by Ginger Legato

Printed in the United States of America

Pour mon copain

Part One

Chapter One

The auctioneer raised his gavel in a practiced arc that crested like a wave and then began its inevitable descent.

"Fair warning!" he cried in his crisp French-accented English. "Going for five hundred thousand to the man in the last row. Five hundred twice—"

But the gavel didn't come down. The auctioneer caught it in mid-swing on its descent, and held it aloft as he cocked his head to one side like an insect whose fine antennae had picked up a subtle vibe, a tremor of hope. Then, very dramatically, he swiveled his gaze attentively toward a young woman standing at one of the phone banks on the right side of the audience. He leaned toward her, peering over the tops of his metal-rimmed eyeglasses.

"Five-fifty?" he asked.

The slim young woman was dressed in a narrow black suit, with flame-red lipstick on her thin mouth, her hair pulled tightly into a very severe bun which somehow implied that she worked only for clients with serious money. She gave a brief but vigorous nod.

"I have five-fifty!" the auctioneer cried triumphantly. "Five-fifty against the room."

It wasn't a room, exactly. We were all sitting under an enormous blue-and-white-striped tent, specially pitched just for this occasion in the front courtyard of a chic Art Deco hotel situated right on the Promenade des Anglais in Nice, smack-dab on the glorious French Riviera.

Directly across the street was the sparkling blue Mediterranean Sea. To our left was the half-moon shaped "indoor/outdoor" swimming pool, where guests could actually swim from outside to indoors via a pass-through draped with strips of heavy waterproofed fabric which reminded me of—well, the dangling fingers in a car-wash. But that's the kind of mind I have. One thing invariably leads to another, no matter how incongruous.

Some of the world's wealthiest jet-setters had converged here, occupying fifteen rows of white folding chairs, divided by a center aisle. Every seat was taken, and there wasn't even any space available in the standing-room zone at the back, where onlookers were restlessly jockeying to get close enough to hear the results. Since this auction had been organized for an English charity, the audience was comprised mostly of Brits, with a good representation of Germans, Russians, Chinese, Indian, but not as many French as you'd think. Lots of Americans, too.

There was no apparent dress code: some women wore formal Chanel suits with white gloves and pumps; other very tanned ladies wore expensively casual white linen shirts and matching white pants; and a few daring souls wore long diaphanous flowered dresses with pashmina shawls and gold sandals. As for the men, they were mostly divided up between those dapper blades who wore navy-blue blazers with light-colored trousers; or the touristy type in leisure suits, or golf jackets and pale blue pants.

The only people dressed in formal plain dark business suits were the auction-house "reps" who stood behind long, very narrow tables on either side of the tent, facing the crowd, manning the banks of telephones to accept bids from anonymous buyers who couldn't—or wouldn't—show up. The "reps" all knew one another, like members of a mysterious college fraternity, and the auctioneer called on them by first name. Martin. Sophie. Gemma. Nick. Some, seated in the front rows, were working with computers instead of telephones.

I had an aisle seat, so I found myself eavesdropping on the phone reps whenever there was a lull in the crowd. They were very discreet, but now, for instance, I could hear one young man murmuring, "We'd have to go to six. What do you want to do?" followed by a long pause.

"Six hundred," said another young man in the first row, looking up from his computer.

"Six from the Internet," purred the auctioneer, pouncing on the number.

"This one's going to hit a million," Jeremy muttered to me now, as he eyed the other auction reps who were frantically speaking into their telephones or clicking their computers to warn the anonymous collectors that they worked for.

We'd been keenly watching the auctioneer deftly manipulate the audience. He was a consummate actor with expert timing—switching seamlessly from joy to sorrow, sympathy to contempt—and he was part-magician, too, for he could bend a moment so that it lasted longer than it should, or he could snap it back like a rubber band. He had only stepped up to the platform about ten items ago, replacing the previous auctioneer just as the crowd was getting used to her, effectively changing horses in midstream, as casinos do with blackjack dealers.

Was this to make sure that no one was cheating? Well, antiques can at times come accompanied by a fair share of shady goings-on.

Paintings that aren't entirely authenticated but "thought to be" a master's work. Golden goblets being auctioned on behalf of an anonymous collector who'd "found" them in an attic. Cases of venerable old wines that may or may not have been cellared properly; golf clubs studded with emeralds thought to have once belonged to an English earl (what caddy would you trust with that?); and even a baby horse whose lineage was purportedly of good racehorse stock. At the moment, people were bidding on a garish pearl and yellow-diamond brooch set in gold, shaped like a giant bug. After that, there were about ten more items to go—before we got to the big one that Jeremy and I had come here for.

"One million euros!" someone shouted, leapfrogging ahead of the other bidders to make sure nobody beat him to it. I gasped at how high the stakes could easily become.

"One million, going once . . . ?" said the auctioneer. This time, the bidding reps shook their heads in defeat. "Going twice . . . going three times . . ." moaned the auctioneer in ecstasy. Bang! The gavel finally came down with such finality that some people physically jumped in their seats. "SOLD to the man in the third row! Please pay the cashier on your way out."

I glanced apprehensively at Jeremy, who was waiting patiently, with his usual calm English poise. When we'd first arrived, I had seen more than a few women, both old and young, glance up speculatively at his handsome face with his blue eyes and dark, wavy brown hair; and some of these women actually gave him a wide, inviting smile, which, in his usual preoccupied way, Jeremy failed to notice. He sat quietly, his auction catalog all rolled up in one hand. His bidding paddle—which looked like a table-tennis paddle except that it had a three-digit number on it, indicating that he'd pre-registered to be a bidder—was lying in his lap. Nothing in his manner betrayed his feelings; unless you were in love with him and were learning, day by day, to read the subtle signals in his expressions.

You know you really love a guy when you suddenly feel a little sorry for him for loving *you* so much that he's now doing something he might not ordinarily do. I felt a bit guilty; I'd pestered and badgered him until I finally got him to tell me the one item in the world he'd actually care to splurge a chunk of his inheritance on.

Jeremy must have felt me looking at him, because he glanced at me and gave me a reassuring smile. The sweet guy. I fervently made a wish that, whatever happened—whether we won or lost—it would turn out to be a good thing, and not a bad thing. I felt a clutch of excitement in my stomach, and my mouth was dry. After all, I'd soon have a dog in this race.

But to understand how a couple of dogs like us ended up on the Riviera ready to bet a flock of euros on a dream, you'd have to know about a few things that happened to us, not so very long ago.

Chapter Two

AMERICAN HEIRESS TRACKS DOWN
PRICELESS ENGLISH LEGACY

*An American girl has become the recipient of an
English inheritance that amounts to a windfall of
European real estate, a classic 1930s auto, and vintage couture ball gowns. But it was the digging up
by the intrepid American heiress of an extremely
rare work of Renaissance art (in the garage of a
French villa) which made up the lion's share of
the legacy claimed by Miss Nichols, bringing the
honeypot to a total of, insiders say, at least fifty
million euros . . .*

Y ou get a rather odd feeling when you spot something in the
newspaper about yourself. The news was always about other
people in the world-at-large; now suddenly it's you that they're
dissecting. Then you actually read the darned thing, and it's not
entirely wrong but it's definitely not right. It's a small shock, this aura
of unreality, so your mind does something weird, thinking that it must

be someone else they're talking about. You peer at the accompanying photograph. There you are, all right. But if that's really you in there, well, since you can't be in two places at once, then maybe you aren't really here, right? That's how my mind dealt with it, at first.

This article appeared months ago, as a feature profile in the Money section of a big London newspaper, and it got picked up all around the world, even on some TV news. To this day, it still pops up in a magazine or news bit. And people believe it, too, because if it weren't true then they wouldn't print it, right? Humph. Life isn't all black-and-white.

Let's start with that headline, for instance. I think it makes me sound like a St. Bernard dog who sniffed out a pot of gold under an avalanche in the Alps, especially with that business about my "digging up" some extremely rare Renaissance art. Yes, I had to do considerable research to find that little painting. Great-Aunt Penelope didn't leave it out in plain sight. Actually, she hid it in the door of her antique car, and smuggled it out of Italy in the 1940s, so the Nazis wouldn't get it. But she had all the proper paperwork of ownership. And then, just before she died, fearing that the family "vultures" would get their talons on it, she put it back in its hiding place in her old auto, which was housed in a dilapidated garage at her villa in Antibes; and she wrote a letter which the judge deemed an airtight will, leaving it to me.

You'd never know it, to read the newspaper story. You'd think I'd pulled a fast one and nabbed it away from the French and the English, who think all works of antiquity are best kept in their hands. The English especially harbor the dire expectation that American girls come to London specifically to carry out their dastardly gold-digging, outrageously buccaneering, socially interloping schemes to get their mitts on helpless English bigwigs and their money.

Penny Nichols—her real name—is a former tele-
vision movie actress. She received this bequest
from her English Great-Aunt, one Penelope Laid-
ley, a grand 1920s flapper, dance-hall artist and
consort to some of the biggest names in finance,
politics and entertainment.

Yes, I work in TV movies, but not as an actress, even with my ridiculously theatrical name. My French/American father couldn't help giving me that last name, and my English mother blithely named me after her eccentric Aunt Pen. When I was a kid I actually met Great-Aunt Penelope, and she seemed like a marvellous old lady; but it wasn't until after her death that I found out astonishing things about her. She was indeed a fabulous flapper, although I do believe that Aunt Pen would have objected to the words "consort to some of the biggest names." She was, er, a mistress to *one* financier, but that was before she met the great love of her life, who died in the second World War, so she never married.

But these tabloid facts just don't begin to do justice to her personality and life. To read the papers, you'd never know about her warmth, her compassion, her sparkle, and her generous heart, which had room even for her shady nephew, Rollo; and for me, her little namesake; and Jeremy, for whom she had a special affection because he's a direct descendant of the man she'd loved.

The jaunty brown-eyed copper-haired heiress,
Miss Penny Nichols, took London by storm last
year, swooping into town for the reading of her
Great-Aunt's will just in time to walk off with
most of it, including a Belgravia bolt hole which
Miss Nichols took immediate possession of. Penny

*Nichols' detractors accuse her of having scooped
nearly all of the entire family inheritance away
from her English relations, who contested the will
but lost.*

For the record, I didn't "swoop" or "scoop"—I was formally invited to the reading of the will, to represent my mother. And frankly, her cousin Rollo made out quite all right, inheriting all Aunt Pen's English bank assets plus lots of fancy, expensive furniture from France. But, Rollo's mother, Great-Aunt Dorothy (otherwise known as the Head Vulture, and no doubt the "detractor" the news story alluded to) convinced Rollo to contest the will for a bigger share, and he fought dirty.

In the end, however, we all cut a deal: He quit fighting to get more than he was supposed to, and the rest of us didn't press charges for the shameless shenanigans he pulled—including breaking and entering, theft, and transporting stolen goods across the border, which could have resulted in him being chucked into the Bastille. (The French do not take kindly to the pilfering of priceless art.)

Now, about that "Belgravia bolt hole" I'm living in, technically, my mother was the one who inherited Aunt Pen's London apartment, but Mom said she "had no use for it" and therefore gave it to me (and if you saw the New York City crackerbox I'd been living in, you'd understand why. Also, my folks are happily ensconced in Connecticut, and they winter in Florida, so nobody will ever convince them to move away and live somewhere else, ever again. They come to Europe once a year to see me.)

It's astonishingly true that Jeremy and I, together, inherited millions of euros, though, all totalled, it was closer to half the amount the newspaper said we did. Maybe it wasn't so astonishing for

Jeremy, who was pretty much born to be rich—he's the stepson of Uncle Peter, my mother's brother, and his mum's family is quite wealthy, too. Anyway, Aunt Pen left him the villa in Antibes. I got the garage . . . and the car inside the garage . . . and the painting inside the car.

The photograph in the newspaper was snapped on the day I sold the painting to a fine little museum in Italy that I knew would take proper care of it. The photo shows the museum director, an alert-eyed, slightly balding but very dignified man, standing to the right of the beautiful little painting of a Madonna and Child, done by a female student of Leonardo. Yup, da Vinci. To the left of the painting is Jeremy, standing protectively beside me, with just a hint of mistrust in his eyes as he gazes at the photographer. And then there's me, looking slightly dazed.

I still can't quite believe it, even now. I keep expecting to wake up back in New York, scraping by as an historical researcher for romantic bio-pics shown on cable-TV movies-of-the-week. I continue to do some consulting for my friends at Pentathlon Productions, but it's different now. (I can't be the first to notice that work is more fun when you aren't threatened with starvation if they fire you.) Sometimes I even have dreams that gremlins or police or my old grammar school principal is chasing after me for impersonating an heiress, telling me I'm now in big trouble and will be punished for it. Yet day by day, waking up in the dramatic big canopied four-poster bed in Great-Aunt Penelope's London townhouse, I am discovering that this new life of mine is, after all, very real.

> *Another heir to this fortune is Penny Nichols' distant English cousin, Jeremy Laidley, who also inherited some of the property—and who recently*

divorced his wife. The barrister Jeremy Laidley is
rumored to be a love interest of Miss Nichols. Do
we hear wedding bells? Don't forget that pre-nup!
The couple are considering spending part of their
inheritance on a flight to the moon as one of the
world's first space tourists. What else will a gal so
young do with all that lovely cashola?

Thanks a lot, boys. To this day I still get weird calls in the night from strange men who would love to "share my world" and help me handle all that "cashola." Jeremy, too, has been constantly buttonholed (over at the watercooler in his law firm) by females who seldom before had reason to talk to him, but, upon hearing of his "windfall", suddenly announced, abruptly and without prelude, that they wished to "bear his child." (And these women are law partners. The secretaries just want him to either marry them or else buy them a car.)

Now, as for that ridiculous bit about space tourism, well, believe me, there is just no way that either one of us would blow off any part of the inheritance on a trip to the moon. What happened was, I was sitting in a restaurant minding my own business when some hyper-friendly salesman actually plunked himself in the empty chair opposite me and unceremoniously proceeded to make his pitch to sell me a ticket to the moon. I politely declined, insisting I'd feel claustrophobic in a space capsule, so he bowed, got up and left, and I thought that would be an end to it. Instead, he told the press that I was on his list of upcoming space tourists, and so they printed it. This then opened the floodgates to all manner of salesmen and phony investors. I thought I had junk mail and telemarketing problems before. Phew! My parents still get surprise visits (at dinnertime) from people who claim that they went to school with me (they didn't) and loaned me money that was never reimbursed (no way).

Money really can do odd things to people, and Jeremy and I are trying to make sure that it doesn't do strange things to us. Yet, obviously, the games have already begun. In a way, it's like winning a lottery; if you're not careful, pretty soon you only know two kinds of people in the world: 1) those who want to take your money away from you, and 2) those who say they want to help you get more money . . . and guess what? More often than not, those two types of people are actually one-in-the-same.

But, much more important than all that finance stuff, I'd like to clear up one other little personal matter in that news story. I don't care for the insinuations that I'm some kind of homewrecker. Jeremy was divorced long before I came on the scene, and before the inheritance. Also, technically, he's not my cousin. His stepfather is my Uncle Peter (Mom's brother) but there's no blood connection to my family at all. None of us knew this until Great-Aunt Penelope's will brought the whole thing to light. As kids, Jeremy and I had simply thought of each other as distant relatives, because he lived in England and I grew up in America. The inheritance brought us together as adults, amid wild circumstances that made it necessary for us to team up just to figure it all out. We rode that roller coaster together . . . and discovered how we really felt about each other.

As for the bit in the article about wedding bells, well, that's rushing things. Love is spectacular enough for the moment! Also, regarding the sneery talk about pre-nups, the fact is that Jeremy and I have already figured out a way to pool our inheritance so that we can make the most of it.

So life is perfect and I toddled off to live happily ever after, right?

Erm. Look. I'm not complaining. How could I?

But even when you've fallen into good fortune and feel like you're in heaven, you know, there's always a snake in the garden. Our garden was no exception, and our snake was named Lydia.

Jeremy's first wife.

Chapter Three

I can remember that day with crystal clarity, even though it happened months ago. There she stood, right in the middle of Jeremy's living room, holding a drink in her hand, wearing a low-cut black-and-red chiffon dress, and diamond earrings almost as big as those ice cubes clinking in her cocktail. Her hair was expensively coiffed, and her skin and body had that highly polished, smooth, glossy, pampered glamorous look that requires a woman to spend all day allowing strange doctors to do fearful things to her.

She looked me over once, twice, thrice, and then had the nerve to tell me, in her high-rent accent, "I'm afraid you'll just have to go." Funny thing is, she meant it.

I'd known about her, of course, but this was the first time we came face-to-face. Blonde, beautiful, posh and totally batty, she'd been out of his life for several years, but she apparently reads the newspapers, too, or else she'd heard about the inheritance on the grapevine from Jeremy's friends, but in any case—and, here I do not exaggerate—the ink had barely dried on the French judge's settlement of Great-Aunt Penelope's will, when Lydia turned up that day, having got Jeremy's doorman to let her into his spiffy modern bachelor's apartment in South Kensington.

Naturally, with feline cunning, she'd managed to pick the night that Jeremy and I had just flown back from France and were planning to plot our future together, over a champagne supper. I'd gone to pick up some groceries, then returned to his apartment, while Jeremy was finalizing some stuff at the office before meeting me here for a night of wine, food, and . . .

Lydia.

Well, of course, I stood my ground. I plunked myself right there on his sofa, and Lydia and I stared at each other, motionless, like two lionesses. And that's exactly how Jeremy found us, moments later. I heard his key in the lock, and his footsteps, and I turned around just in time to see the expression on his face.

He had been looking down, engrossed in thought, carefully juggling his keys, briefcase, champagne, and a big bunch of fragrant wine-red roses wrapped in blue tissue paper. He glanced up, saw me first, and gave me a smile that went right to my heart. Then he saw Lydia, who had sidled off into the shadows and fixed him a drink to match hers. She floated toward him as if they were still married, and she was the lady of the house, ready to give her hubbie a great big kiss and hug . . .

Look. I very rarely take an instant dislike to someone. But when a perfect stranger turns a high-beam glare of pure hatred on you the minute you walk in the door, and then tells you to shove off while she makes a play for the man you love, well, frankly, I just wanted to choke her, then and there. But, you've got to be careful, where men are concerned. The minute you show your claws, they think you're the Bad One.

At the sight of his ex-wife, Jeremy's expression went from happy to shocked dismay, then polite recovery, ending with a guilty, apologetic look. "Lydia!" he exclaimed. "What on earth—!" When she kissed him, he didn't kiss back, I noticed, but he didn't fling her off, either. I'd rather hoped he would.

"Hello, darling!" she cried, and she actually took the flowers and champagne from his hands, as if he'd bought them for her.

I abandoned all pretext of being civilized, and I leaped off the sofa, positioned myself between them and said rather pointedly, "How beautiful. Are those for me, Jeremy?"

Jeremy stepped back from her now, and said, "Yes, of course," at which Lydia, without ever taking her eyes off Jeremy, passed the flowers and champagne to me with the careless gesture of a woman who's asked the maid to take care of them for her.

"Penny," Jeremy said, "this is Lydia—"

"Yes, your ex-wife, right?" I said bluntly, putting the flowers and champagne on the hall table. He looked like a trapped animal that didn't know which way to bolt. Then he recovered, and took a step toward me and held out his arm to put around me.

Lydia immediately grasped the meaning of this gesture. I could see panic register in her hazel-colored eyes, which then narrowed in ill-concealed fury. Quickly, she said in an urgent tone loaded with meaning, "Jeremy. Might I have a word with you?"

Jeremy said knowingly, almost as if talking to a naughty school-girl, "Lydia. For God's sake. What *are* you doing here?"

"I'm afraid it's very serious," she said, looking tragic, "and very personal. I really do need your help, Jeremy, or I wouldn't have come. I've no one else to turn to. Obviously."

She didn't look at me, and she didn't exactly say, "So let's toss this other woman out the window," but she might as well have. I knew what was coming next. I guess I've known one or two neurotic types well enough to understand that she will next insist on sequestering the man for a private conference, that would lead to talking on the telephone at all hours of the day and night. This poison flower had to be nipped in the bud, right now.

"Why don't we all sit down and sort this out?" I said helpfully but crisply. "Lydia, if you need our assistance, we will do what we can. Please speak freely in front of both of us. But I'm afraid we must be quick, because we have plans for tonight and we are already late."

Jeremy's jaw dropped. Frankly, I don't even know where my words came from. I just sort of made them up as I went along. But hell, if she was going to act so dramatic about it, then I could be cinematic, too, and let them both see how absurd she was being.

Because not for a minute did I believe that Lydia was in any real jeopardy. I had already studied her quite carefully, looking for telltale clues, Girl Detective that I am. No bruises, no trembling, and she appeared perfectly healthy and clear-eyed and determined, and even remarkably well-rested, not at all like a damsel-in-distress.

Jeremy recovered a bit, and grinned at me. "Yes, a good idea, let's sit down," he said hastily. "Certainly, Lydia, whatever you have to say to me, you can say freely in front of Penny. I take it you two have been introduced?" he asked dryly.

"Not exactly," Lydia said, a bit crossly. "Is *She* your fiancée?"

I really hate when women refer to other women as *She*. You know the tone. You know what it means. And then there's that phony fiancée question, as if to imply that if you aren't engaged, then he doesn't really love you.

Jeremy ignored the question and asked, "What's up, Lydia?"

And, I swear to God, she burst into hysterical sobs. I watched in utter admiration of how such a woman could go from haughty bitchiness to pathos, right on a dime.

I looked over at Jeremy and I said, "Oh, hell. Ten minutes, okay? I'll go chill the champagne." And then I murmured so that only he could hear, "And don't you dare let her put her head on your shoulder or use your handkerchief."

He didn't object to this; he even patted my shoulder consolingly, which at least indicated that he understood the impact on me of her crummy timing.

I stalked off into his kitchen, and put the champagne in ice and salt and water, and snipped off the ends of the roses and put them in a vase of lukewarm water. I never left Jeremy and his "ex" entirely alone, however, because Jeremy's kitchen has an open section that looks right onto the living room. So, as Lydia spoke to him, he could see me balefully watching him. He and Lydia spoke in low voices, and then he rose and came into the kitchen, looking worried.

"I know you think she's shamming," was the first thing he said.

"Call it a woman's intuition," I said airily.

"I know, I know," he said. "She's always been given to high nerves. And believe me, nobody's more aware than I of how adept she is at manipulating people." He paused. "But be that as it may, it does sound as if she's had a bad time." And he told me her indisputable tale of woe, in a nutshell. *After* she ran off with Jeremy's best friend from work (a liaison which didn't work out), she then "fell in love" with a wealthy Bolivian boyfriend who had grown up so spoiled that he wasn't accustomed to ever being told "No."

"Apparently," Jeremy said, "he was a cruel bastard, took money from her and cheated on her, and yet when she wanted to break up, he rather ominously told her that he would 'never let her go' and even went so far as to lock her in his hacienda or whatever, and had his bodyguards spy on her. But somehow she managed to evade them, and got on a friend's private airplane and came to London."

"Swell," I said. "So now she'll lead her boyfriends' thugs straight to your doorstep. And don't tell me, let me guess. She wants to stay right here, in your apartment."

"Don't be ridiculous," Jeremy said. "She wouldn't do that."

"Good," I said, feeling momentarily ashamed.

"Apparently she's found an apartment," Jeremy said. He paused. I knew.

"Where, exactly?" I said in a deadly tone. He just looked at me.

"Right down the street?" I asked in disbelief. Silence.

"In *your* building?" I exclaimed. Jeremy flushed guiltily. "What floor?" I asked.

"This one," he said, then added hurriedly, "way on the other end, though."

"No," I said. "No, no, a thousand times no."

"What can I do? I don't exactly own the whole building, you know," he said in the tone of annoying reasonableness that a man uses when he suspects that your instincts are totally justified, but if he says so, it will then require him to do something difficult which will undoubtedly cause a ruckus. "She says she got a good deal on the place, and had to act fast."

"She sure did!" I glanced over at Lydia, who had gone to the window to strike a wounded pose. "What exactly does she want from you, apart from being jolly neighbors now?" I asked.

Jeremy sighed wearily. "Nothing, really. Just moral support, I suppose."

"Piffle," I said.

"Penny," Jeremy pleaded, "you must trust me on this one, I think there's enough truth to this story so that I can't just turn my back on her."

"I trust you," I said. "I just don't trust her."

"She didn't manage so well when we split up," Jeremy said, looking upset. "She tried to commit suicide, even." Normally, this would have given me quite a pause, but then I recalled a conversation I'd had with Jeremy's mother, in which she confided about how much neurotic stress this woman had inflicted on him, so that Jeremy never really had a day's peace in their one-year marriage.

I peered at him keenly. "Lydia's managed to make you feel guilty and totally responsible for the divorce all along, hasn't she?" I asked gently.

"It's just that we had so much bitterness at the end," Jeremy said. "I do feel that I could have managed it better."

"It takes two to tango," I pointed out. "It couldn't have been all your fault."

"I know that," he said. "But look, you and I are so happy, and so fortunate, that we can afford to be kind. Can't we? Because I'd like to take this opportunity to end this chapter of my life peaceably, now that I have the chance."

Privately, I observed that Lydia didn't appear remotely ready to "end" anything. But, as I said, I was not about to let some woman trap me into being the Bad One. Nor was I going to be played for a sap, either.

"Fine," I said. "I'll be as kind and civilized as is humanly, and womanly, possible." He smiled wryly. "Just do me a favor, willya, pal?" I asked as charmingly as I could with Lydia prowling around. "Will you get rid of her so we can drink our champagne and start having fun?"

Jeremy kissed me quickly. "You bet," he said. I waited in the kitchen, watching, and I don't know exactly what he said to her then; however, it worked, because she got up and waved gaily to me and went out.

Sure, I thought miserably. Tootle-oo to you, too. I've won the battle tonight, but she's ready for war. She'll be around him day and night. Bumping into him in the hallway whilst collecting her newspaper in her nightie. Riding down the elevator to do laundry together, can I share your suds? Stopping by on Saturday morning to borrow the proverbial cup of sugar. Inviting him in for a drink on New Year's Eve and acting drunker than she really is, so she can kiss and seduce him at midnight. Oh, please.

After she was gone, we went ahead with our plans. Jeremy seemed philosophical, in that thoughtful way of his, as we unpacked the groceries, and he recovered from it all when he started busily chopping vegetables and sautéing them in a pan. He'd clearly planned the whole meal in his head beforehand, so he wanted to cook the entire thing himself. I could tell that it was going to be wonderful.

"You sit down, put your feet up, relax and let's have some of that champagne," he said enthusiastically. Just before he popped the cork he said, as if making a wish, "To our future, and thank you, Aunt Pen!" The cork made a fine vigorous *Pop!* and I watched him pour the champagne, which was full of perfect small, lively bubbles.

"I'm not as good a chef as your Dad, of course," Jeremy called out from the kitchen, "but I'm going to ask him to teach me. After all, you are a girl raised on *gastronomie* dinners. I love the way your parents cook and joke around together." He glanced up through the pass-through window, then said, "What's the matter? Why are you opening all the windows out there?"

"Hmmm? Oh, just felt like some fresh air," I said innocently from the living room, having tried yet failed to do it surreptitiously.

"Don't like the smell of onions?" he asked, peering.

I didn't want him to get the wrong idea about his nice cooking. So I admitted, "It's just her perfume. The whole room reeks of it."

Jeremy, carrying the champagne glasses, came out, sniffing. "I don't smell it," he said. I couldn't imagine how he could miss it; it hung in the air like a lingering cloud.

"Well," I said lightly, "perhaps I'm better at scenting trouble than you are."

Jeremy ruffled my hair affectionately, but then said what no gal wants to hear: "Women!" As if we were all created equal. But then he led me to the window and we clinked glasses and sipped the champagne, and he kissed me, before he went back into the kitchen. That particular kiss helped a lot.

So, that evening, neither one of us mentioned Lydia again. But of course, we both knew that she was sitting over there in her new apartment, just like a snake behind a rock. As I continued opening windows and lighting candles and setting a romantic table and doing whatever spell-casting I could to erase Lydia's presence, I realized that, from this moment on, I'd have to find a way to put some distance between her and us; so that Jeremy and I could have a fair chance to carry out the great Plan that Jeremy came up with, back in Italy after the inheritance had been settled: he'd said we should take the time to imagine, and then create, the independent life we always wanted, now that Great-Aunt Penelope had given us her blessings.

Chapter Four

But life in London in those following months was like being twirled up in a tornado and deposited on another planet. The world seemed to be coming at us from all directions, and even now as I try to sort it out, it's like giving somebody a tour of a fun-house, where the angles of the room are all distorted by crazy mirrors and tilting floors, and doors and windows that lead to nowhere.

Every week the postman deposited a full sack of mail filled mostly with letters from people I'd never met, some totally bonkers, some with truly heartbreaking stories of personal tragedy, or worthy charities. My answering machine logged an average of forty-five messages a day, no matter how many times I changed my phone number. My e-mails kept hitting overload—and so did I. People sent me whole narratives of their lives and woes, and I just wanted to rescue everybody, but Jeremy and I had hired an accountant to help us figure out the money and taxes, so we agreed not to commit to any expenditure before we met with him.

Once, when I opened the front door to collect the morning paper, I found a strange man with a handlebar moustache, his hand poised over the doorbell, who wanted to sell me a "gen-yoo-wine" dinosaur skull for several hundred thousand pounds.

"I don't own a museum," I told him, feeling confused.

"Your friends will die of envy," he promised. "I dug it up myself."

It's not impossibly hard to tell strangers to back off, but friends and colleagues are another matter entirely. Take, for instance, my old client, Bruce, who owns Pentathlon Productions, the company that had kept me gainfully employed . . . more or less . . . as a free-lance set-design researcher. In the past, we hardly spoke, because I was hired through my friend Erik, the production designer. But one night, Bruce telephoned me and told me all his hopes and dreams of expanding his company so that he could do his own projects instead of just the romantic dramas he directed for cable TV.

"I never told you this," he said, "but I wasn't always a nighttime historical soaper hack. I used to shoot good documentaries, and damn it, they won awards—*real* awards. Revolutions, wars, hostage crises, election fraud. I was there, baby. Did I ever tell you about the time I went to Panama?" He sighed heavily. "But then the kids were born, and, well, Cheryl's a great scriptwriter and these historical romance movies pay the tuition. But," he added hopefully, "documentary films are making big money now in theatrical re-lease. It would be a good investment, Penny. I'd make it pay."

"Aw, gee, Bruce," I said with genuine regret. "It sounds like a great idea. But Jeremy and I have been getting so many requests like this, that the accountant won't even release the money till we sit down with him."

"To protect you from shameless slobs like me," Bruce said in his self-deprecating way. "I understand." For a moment his tone turned unexpectedly fatherly. "That's exactly what you should do. Well, if you decide you're interested, will you call me? I'll present it to you in a way that your accountant will like, with all the marketing research and data I've got, so he can show it to anybody he wants, to verify that it's solid."

"Of course," I said, genuinely touched by his sincerity.

Erik telephoned shortly afterward; he had his spies and he'd found out what was afoot. When I told him how badly I felt about putting Bruce off, Erik was outraged.

"Don't you dare give Bruce or anybody else a chunk of your inheritance!" he admonished. "Nobody cared about *your* welfare when you were scraping by with barely enough money for rent and canned beans! Penny, sweetheart, mark my words: Life doesn't often give you a chance like this, to do what you want. *Take* it!"

For every "friend-who-need-lots-of-money" tale I had to tell, Jeremy had six. Guys at the office wanted him to invest in their Internet brainchild. Others simply wanted to advise him where to invest; and more often than not their advice conflicted with one another. Gold. Biotech. Blue chips. The Thai stock market. Biofuel. Futures. China. We telephoned the accountant, and his instructions were, "Pick one thing you want to invest in that you really feel strongly about, perhaps something that matters to you personally. Do the research, but make no promises. See you on Monday at ten."

Well, to tell an historical researcher to "do the research" is a big mistake. Within a week my head—and my computer—were filled with far too much information about the world. But the accountant had said to pick something that mattered to us "personally", and one day, I finally figured out what that was.

Our own little business enterprise. I didn't know exactly what it would be yet, but I knew I had to find it a home. So, that Sunday just before our meeting with the accountant, sitting in Great-Aunt Penelope's second-floor apartment, I presented my brainstorm to my pal.

"Jeremy," I announced, "I have the perfect investment for us. It's right here, under our noses . . ." and here I paused dramatically—"We should buy up this entire townhouse!"

The sun was pouring in through the big windows that fronted on to the street, overlooking a lovely green square with great old trees. We were sitting in Aunt Pen's cozy library, in the small wing chairs opposite the bookcases, with the pretty round table between us, and a fire in the fireplace crackling away.

Jeremy looked suitably impressed. "That's quite ambitious," he said.

"Well, I had a little talk with Doris, the elderly lady who lives on the third floor," I said in a low voice, even though I couldn't possibly be overheard. "She told me that she and her husband have decided to sell up and retire to Spain. They have a little house there, and they're ready to make the break, she says. Asked me if I knew anybody who'd want to buy."

"Careful," Jeremy cautioned. "There's been all that press about us, and I'm sure she's heard of the inheritance. If she knows you're the buyer, she may expect more than a fair market price. Maybe you should consider letting my office handle the transaction. It's possible we can pull this off without the sellers knowing who bought it."

"Um," I said. "I already told her I was interested."

Jeremy sighed that light, ah-well sigh that an Englishman uses when he's trying to disguise how badly he really thinks you screwed up; yet at the same time he's telling you in that maddening way of his. I ploughed on, anyway.

"Well," I added boldly, "there we were, standing in the hallway talking, when in comes Gladys, the old lady from the first-floor apartment. So of course she hung around wanting to know what Doris and I were up to. So then Gladys said wouldn't it be nice if

I bought her place, too, because her daughter had already invited her to come to Canada and live with them, and she could see her grandchild be born and grow up, and her husband loves fishing there . . ."

"Good God," Jeremy groaned. "Why didn't you just announce the whole deal on the evening news?"

"Well, Gladys said that she and her husband would be willing to consider 'a good offer,'" I amended lamely. "And everybody liked the idea of one person owning the whole house, and restoring it to its former glory."

"We'd have to check the freehold, for one thing," Jeremy said. Now I groaned. England has this archaic way of sometimes leasing London houses for 99 years instead of selling it to you outright. It was all very complicated, but the fact that Jeremy was thinking in these terms meant that he thought we might actually pull it off.

"They showed me their apartments," I said. "They've lived in them forever, and you know how old people are, they don't like to change things unless something breaks and can't be held together with Scotch tape anymore. So both apartments need updating. Which they admit, and that might keep the price manageable."

"I suppose the basement could be converted into a garage," Jeremy said thoughtfully. I perked up. I knew that launching an independent career would be a much bigger leap for Jeremy, so I thought that creating a tangible workplace would make it more desirable and real.

"And here's the best part," I said, now that I had him hooked, "I'm thinking that we can convert the first floor of this townhouse into a suite of beautiful offices, where we could start up our new consulting firm. You know, like you said in Italy. Remember?"

He smiled wryly at me. I'd been trying to nudge him along with this; after all, it was his Plan. Jeremy had said that we should first take a hiatus from work, and travel a bit, taking time to think about how we might pool our talents and create an enterprise of our own—so that we wouldn't just be ships passing in the night in our respective careers.

"You said, that with *your* legal expertise, concerning international law and personal estates," I reminded him, "combined with *my* historical research expertise—"

"I believe I called it your 'natural-born snooping ability,'" Jeremy corrected.

"Can't you just see it?" I rhapsodized. "The ground-floor apartment is actually much bigger than this one. Your office could have one of those world-map globes, the kind that opens up and turns out to be a fully stocked bar. You can have drinks with your best clients there. A beautiful Persian rug in front of the fireplace, with a loyal Great Dane asleep on it, and a desk with antique paperweights and leather pen cup and . . ."

"Penny," Jeremy said in amusement, "you forgot the pipe rack. You and your old movies! Who am I supposed to be, Sherlock Holmes? All of that is very well—although the Great Dane might be a bit dubious—but I want state-of-the-art Internet access and computerized files and worldwide video phone conferencing . . ."

"And you shall have it!" I exclaimed, making a flourish with my arm.

"We'd have to put in better security," he added. "I always worry about you being here like this, with only old-fashioned technology standing between you and the nutters. Not even a peephole in the main door to see who's out there!"

"Fine, fine," I said. "Get all the security you want. But let's also have a set of elegant, old-time intercoms from my office to yours. For when all that computerized messaging fails."

"All right, fine. Fixing up the townhouse is a good investment," Jeremy said. "Let's run it by the accountant."

"Oh, Jeremy!" I cried, flinging my arms around him. "What a great time we'll have now!" I was glad we'd hatched this plot right here, with the aura of Great-Aunt Penelope's spirit hovering. I figured she'd watch out for us now, just in case we ran into any, ya know, trouble.

Part Two

Chapter Five

Now. If you ever come up with a great big beautiful dream, and you want to see it shot down right before your very eyes, why, just take it to a professional. Take it to a lawyer, a shrink, or, as we did, to a high-powered accountant.

Martin-the-accountant's office was in the financial heart of London that has all kinds of crazy new buildings, shaped like giant pickles or glass pyramids or dazzlingly reflective gold bouillon.

Jeremy and I entered a building with a lobby full of gigantic real tropical trees, and we rode the glass elevator to dizzying heights. All the while, I had one person's advice still ringing in my ears. Believe it or not, it had come from cousin Rollo's mother, yes, the awful Great-Aunt Dorothy. She had contacted first Jeremy, and then me, and told each of us to please remember one thing: *"Capital, my dear child, must never be invaded."*

"What's that supposed to mean?" I asked Jeremy as the glass elevator took us sailing up into the stratosphere.

"It means you should never spend the original sum," Jeremy explained. "Just live off the interest and dividends."

"Wow," I asked in a hushed voice. "Can we actually do that?" In the past, any interest I earned in my pitiful savings account was so tiny that the guy who did my taxes used to laugh himself into fits in April, when I gave him my annual total in scant dollars and cents to report as "additional income."

"We'll see. I must admit, the old crone gave us good advice," Jeremy said wryly.

"Why should Dorothy suddenly take it into her head to give *us* good advice?" I asked suspiciously. Dorothy was the "blue-blooded American" who'd married Great-Uncle Roland, the brother of my Grandmother and Great-Aunt Penelope. She was hanging on to every tuppence she had, even refusing to give any to her own son—so Rollo was "running through" whatever he'd inherited from his father, which was doled out by an estate lawyer in controlled monthly payments.

"She probably wants to make sure we don't spend all that lovely money before she can figure out another way to siphon it off into Rollo's treasure chest," Jeremy replied. He turned to me now, very serious. "Penny," he said, "you can change your mind about sharing everything we inherited fifty-fifty. By rights, most of Aunt Pen's estate is yours."

"No," I said positively. "You read her letter. She clearly wanted us to put our heads together and figure out what we thought was best. And after all, the painting originally came from your ancestors, before it was entrusted to her. Obviously she wanted us to *trust* each other, so it makes sense to put it all into a joint *trust*." I grinned. "Unless you want to renege on sharing your villa with me."

"Idiot," he said. "All right, then. We'll put everything together and reap the rewards. We'll just make sure we protect you. I have some ideas."

The elevator glided to a stop, bounced a bit, then really landed. The glass doors parted, and there was a whoosh of air that seemed to propel us forward.

The receptionists gave us dazzling smiles and acted as if we were visiting royalty. I could see how an heiress could easily be fooled into thinking she's really as important as all this cooing, delightful fanfare implied. Personally, I found it slightly alarming. Jeremy and I were ushered down one long corridor after another, until we found the accountant in his glass-and-mahogany-and-leather lair.

Martin was an owlish fellow who gazed at us from across his enormous, glass-topped desk that had nothing on it but a pad of lined paper and a ballpoint pen. Here was a man who moved billions, yet all the computers and faxes and files were buried in the offices of his underlings, which we'd just passed through. He gestured for us to take the two seats on the other side of his desk. These were like huge black leather mitts. I immediately got lost in mine, until I figured out how to skitter myself forward, and perch only on its edge. Jeremy sat in the one next to mine, with each of his arms resting on a colossal leather arm of his chair.

Martin had very cropped light-yellow hair with matching eyebrows. He was Scottish, older than us but not that old, certainly not old enough to be as punctilious as he was. He was given to single-word sentences followed by long, empty pauses. He'd say, "So . . ." and then make some rapid notes for long moments, during which I tried to read them upside down, but couldn't. Then he'd say, "Now, the total net worth of your share, Penny, combining the London flat and its contents, the sale of the painting, and the car in Antibes . . . and the garage . . ." and he'd scratch out some more, "less the death taxes . . ."

Sheesh, I thought as he scratched away. I knew perfectly well that he already had these figures somewhere on a computer, because he'd e-mailed it to me, but he seemed to think he had to spell it all out to us, personally, in terms any idiot could comprehend, by showing the math worked out right before our eyes.

"And yours, Jeremy, for the villa in the South of France..." Scratch, scratch, scratch. This man, believe it or not, was rumored to be a genius with handling large investments and estates. Only somebody that important would dare to make everything sound so simpleminded.

Jeremy tolerated this for a brief bit before he jumped in impatiently and said, "Martin, we know what we've got. Let's talk turkey, okeh?"

Martin smiled broadly at him, then at me. Oh, I realized. It's about me. There are some men who will never admit that women are born with brains, too.

Somehow Jeremy managed to speed him up a little. Not a lot, but we got past the almighty boring taxes, and when Martin asked, with a slight gleam in his eye, "Now how risk-averse are you?" I simply couldn't wait for Jeremy to give him our prepared answer.

"We like to sleep nights," I said bluntly. "We're not looking for any strange ways to shelter the money, no offshore stuff, no funny business."

He smiled tolerantly, glancing infuriatingly at Jeremy for verification before saying, "All right then. What I suggest is that, apart from certain expenses which I'll elaborate on in a moment, you each invest your money for a period of one year, during which you hold off on making any major commitments to family members and friends. This will give you time to assess what you really want to do." He again turned to Jeremy. "Shall we deal with Miss Nichols' inheritance first, or—?"

"We're going to share it," I said. Martin raised an eyebrow, and the pencil stopped. ·

"We want to protect the whole estate," Jeremy explained. "We want to create a joint trust in both our names—"

"Oh? How much of the inheritance do you wish to—combine?" Martin asked.

"All of it," I said.

Martin actually sat back in his chair, stunned.

"But—my records show that you are not, married, is that correct?" Martin asked, looking genuinely confused.

"That's correct," Jeremy said.

Martin cleared his throat and looked apologetically at Jeremy. "I must ask this. Do you plan to marry in the near future?"

We had been asked that question so many times lately and, when it came from strangers, we had a stock answer. "Our plans on that score," Jeremy said, "are private at the moment."

"I see," Martin said briskly, visibly adapting. But he glanced at me warningly now, in a tone indicating that he'd seen more than a few relationships go down in flames, and said, "But, Miss Nichols, you do understand that, in the event that in the future this situation, ah, changes; you may want things spelled out clearly now, as to how the money should be, er, divided in the event of an, um, irreconcilable dispute."

I knew that he was trying to protect me. Still, the last thing I wanted right now were visions of romantic misery—the cheating, lying, abuse, betrayal and general torture that men and women can inflict on those they once claimed to adore. I felt it was tempting fate, to conjure up these images in the face of our shining future.

Then Jeremy did something truly heroic. He said, "We do not expect that sort of eventuality, but, should it occur, since Penny's share was initially larger than mine, if the trust should ever have to be divided, she should get three-quarters."

Martin raised an eyebrow. "Ah," he said. "Well, I'd be comfortable with that."

I turned to Jeremy, astounded. "You didn't tell me you had that up your sleeve," I said.

"It's the only way I'll agree to combining it into a trust," Jeremy said gently.

And somehow, after that little exchange, things took off from there. Martin got on board now, and was ready to discuss investment and savings ideas. "Is there anything in particular you'd like to invest in, Miss Nichols?" he asked.

So it was then that we proposed our trial balloon about buying up the townhouse, and Martin prepared his little pin to pop it. His first and immediate response was, "Mmmm. Real estate. Been going through the roof, so to speak, in your area, but been falling in others, so it's hard to say . . ." Insultingly, he didn't even write it down on his pad. His pale brows furrowed.

"This is the building you are in now, Miss Nichols?" he asked. I nodded.

"Well, if you're keen on the property market, quite honestly, there are better options than London right now for tax savings. Dubai and Hong Kong, for instance. I could check around—"

"No!" I said, a bit panicked at where this was going. "It's not just any old property we want. It's more personal than that."

"Call it our little enterprise," Jeremy said firmly.

Martin looked at us from one to the other, and, I think, it began to dawn on him that we were not the usual type of customer who unsentimentally wants to just increase the coffers. One good thing about having lots of money is that it seems to give you a license to be eccentric.

"All right," he said briskly, "I'll look into it. I can even help handle the purchase of it, if you wish." He turned a page in his pad. "Anything else?"

"The trouble is, there are so many things," I said. I told him of the ones I'd been considering: plant a forest, save the fish, build a whole new town that was totally environmentally good, help a children's wing of a hospital, fund archaeological digs and start a museum that would rescue fragile artifacts . . . I had already set aside those correspondences I'd received, as the ones I cared about to show the accountant.

"I would put those under the category of charities-and-philanthropy. A charity is an excellent idea, and one that I was going to recommend," Martin said. "You should decide this together, by picking one or two worthy causes that you really think you'll want to continue contributing to over time, and I will look into them for you and advise you. You needn't make this decision right away; in fact, I encourage you to wait until you're certain. You have time. But I wasn't asking you about philanthropy at the moment. I just want to know if there are any stocks that you are interested in. I can always recommend some to you, of course, but—"

Jeremy mentioned a few stocks, and then they both looked at me.

"Well," I said boldly, "I want to invest in our own business. Once we figure out what we want to do. That's what the other townhouse apartments are for. Our offices."

Martin looked a little flummoxed, as if I'd suddenly starting speaking in an obscure, foreign language that he was unfamiliar with. "Do you plan to start a company?" he asked. I turned to Jeremy for help.

"We think we might," Jeremy said. "We have not developed a business plan yet."

"Then here is what I suggest," Martin said. "Make an estimate of your upcoming year's expenses. Think about if you have any other repairs or purchases, large or small, plus whatever you both think you'll need to live on. Eventually, this will settle into a fairly consistent category each year of general upkeep and living expenses. We'll make sure that you always have enough cash available for this. But, apart from such regular expenses, let's say that this year you will also have three major expenditures."

He actually held up three fingers to tick them off visually. "One, your 'Business Development' idea, which is the purchase of the other apartments in the townhouse. We'll put some extra money aside here for operating expenses in case you want to open home offices there this year. Two, your Charity; I'll set aside a reasonable deduction for that, and I won't need to know which one you want to do until the next tax time."

Jeremy and I were both waiting for the third item. Martin had filled his pad with tons of notes, but now he put down his pen and said something unexpectedly human.

"And three, you might allow yourselves one big Personal Splurge," he said, smiling, "because it will make it easier to stick to this plan. That will leave the bulk of your inheritance to be locked up for a year in safe investments; I'll put together a recommendation for a one-year portfolio. After a year, you can reassess and decide what you want to do long-term. But," he added, rising now to see us out, "I won't lock anything away until I hear from you on just how much you'd like to set aside for—fun."

Chapter Six

"Martin had some good ideas, overall," Jeremy said as we went back to my flat. He looked at me searchingly, and I knew that he was feeling responsible because we'd found the accountant through Jeremy's connections.

"Yeah, I guess in the end, Martin's a good egg," I said, as we went upstairs. "He warmed up at the end. I loved his idea of the Splurge. But geez, he acts like we're little kids. He wasn't exactly explaining the theory of relativity, you know."

"Yes, well, you'd be surprised at what he has to deal with every day," Jeremy explained. "People get windfalls and within a year it's gone, to family and so-called friends. Sports figures and actors who have more money than they know what to do with, but plenty of people telling them to buy a bigger wristwatch and a car and a house for everybody they ever knew. Or brokers with big city bonuses at the end of the year who blow it all on nights out with champagne, *foie gras* hamburgers and, er, worse."

As we walked in the door, the phone was ringing. I let the machine answer it, but when I heard my father's voice, I picked it up. My parents wanted us to know that they'd be coming to Europe soon, and I wrote down the dates.

I told my dad that we'd just been to see the accountant, and planned to set up a trust, to squirrel away the money until we really knew what to do with it.

But even before I could tell him about Martin's suggestion that we pick one Splurge, my father, who seldom butts in to give advice, said, "Fine, this is all very sensible. But remember that life is also meant to have some *luxe, calme et volupté.*"

I knew that this expression meant a lot more than just the sum of its parts of luxury, serenity and sensual joy. "Too much austerity is not good for the blood," Dad went on. "Very hard to sustain because it's so extreme. You should have *une petite indulgence*," he said. "Some-zing you've always wanted to have."

It was the very same advice as Martin's, only my dad, being French, made it sound more thrilling, and as soon as he said it, I felt that life was handing me one of those messages from fate, where you could almost hear a bell ring.

"I agree," said my pragmatic English mother, having picked up the extension. "It should be a real indulgence, something truly exciting and out of the ordinary. You and Jeremy should sit down right this minute, and brainstorm until you come up with it. Run out and get two pads of paper and two pencils."

"What am I, six years old?" I groused.

But after I handed the phone to Jeremy, who wanted to say hello to my parents, I went off and did just as I was told, rummaging around for pads and pencils, and putting the kettle on to make tea. When Jeremy rang off the phone, he said, "Your mother is right, we shouldn't wait to think up our Splurge. Let's do it right now."

"I already got the pads and pencils," I said. "Here they are."

So we plunked right down on the sofa, each gazing at a blank page, and looking off into the distance, dreaming. It took longer than you might guess, narrowing it down to one splurge that we'd ordinarily never dare think of doing. It wasn't as easy as I expected. Sure, I could imagine everyday indulgences: walk into a jewelry store and nab whatever struck my fancy, buy new clothes . . . I started scratching these things on my pad, just like Martin, but I was vaguely dissatisfied. After all, I truly felt that life had given me more than I ever dreamed. Whatever we chose should really mean something.

I glanced up to see how Jeremy was doing. He was very, very quiet, gazing out the window. His handsome face, with those blue eyes and dark lashes and dark hair, looked quite serious. And I realized that while I had been scratching away on my pad, he had made barely a sound. I surreptitiously craned my neck to steal a look at his pad. Not much written, indeed . . .

"You're not supposed to peek," came his scolding voice, even though he was still looking out the window.

"Aw, c'mon, let's compare," I said.

"I'm not ready yet," he said.

So I waited. And I waited and I waited. I made tea. I made a nice tray of little sandwiches with no crusts, and cookies, and a few slices of the miniature orange pound cake we'd picked up on the way home, and little dishes of jam. And then we nibbled on the food and drank the tea. And the sun started to slip down in the sky, casting a burnt-orange glow across the room. And still, he didn't write.

"Jeremy," I said finally, in what I thought was a tone of infinite patience, "time is going by. Our *lives* are going by. It's fish-or-cut-bait time. Let's compare."

"You really are a nosey woman," he said, but he put his pad down on the table. "You go first," he insisted.

"The best I could come up with," I admitted, "is that I definitely want to fix up the Dragonetta." That was the vintage 1930s auto that Great-Aunt Penelope had bequeathed to me. "After all," I explained, "it got her safely out of wartime Italy, and it's where she hid the painting. She said it brought her luck. And Denby says it has a great engine . . ."

Denby was the mechanic on the Riviera who had assessed the car as valuable and certainly worth fixing up; he was just waiting for me to give him the go-ahead.

"Of course, that would also mean repairing the garage," I warned. "That roof is askew, and there are holes in one of the walls; you saw what mice did to the car's upholstery."

"Fine, fine. You don't have to convince me," Jeremy said approvingly; he'd been an auto buff since he was a boy, and he loved that car so much that he even had a modern replica of it. "What else did you come up with?" Jeremy inquired.

I blushed a little. "Um, clothes," I said. "Nothing hysterically expensive. I just want to have enough well-made, beautiful items, so I can actually wear them instead of just saving them for special occasions."

"Perfectly all right," Jeremy assured me. "Clothes make the woman. But I consider things like the car and clothes just upkeep. What Martin called our year's expenses."

"Right," I agreed. "We should set aside money for them, but I don't really think it's what Martin and my dad meant about our great Splurge."

Jeremy leaned forward, and actually took my hands in his.

"Penny," he said in a serious tone. "I just want to say one thing. I know that we agreed to make this little hiatus of ours an experiment, to see what we really care about in life, and what we want to do with our future. Well, I want you to know that, sure, as far as career and all that are concerned, yes, I am exploring my options. But when it comes to love—"

He paused here, a trifle embarrassed, but then he pressed on resolutely, "When it comes to *you*, well, I'm not feeling experimental at all. I know how I feel about you, and that won't change. I just don't want to rush what I feel is happening naturally all on its own, between us."

He said this so earnestly, so gently, that I could scarcely believe such a beautiful moment in my life had come so effortlessly, as if we'd been flying on the back of a white swan that just made the downiest, softest of landings. I was actually choked up, and I couldn't speak right away. When I did, all I could say was, "Ah, babe . . ."

"I told your father so, too," he said, "when you were in the kitchen."

I was shocked. "You told him what?"

"That we're not fooling around, that we're serious," he said matter-of-factly, picking up his pencil again and squinting at his pad. "He knew what I meant. He also knew what it meant for me to say it aloud, to him, especially."

"My God," I said, awed. "How very medieval, yet chivalrous of you." I kissed him, then peeked at his face teasingly. Now he did become self-conscious and a bit stern, as if dealing with an unruly student.

"Chivalry, nothing," he said briskly. "Fact is, I was merely getting my dibs in early. No other man will stand a chance with you now, at least where your father is concerned. Can we put these pads away?"

"No way, pal!" I cried. "What's *your* big wish?"

He cleared his throat, trying to look casual. "Well, along the lines of fixing up the estate, I, too, would like to make some repairs. On the villa in Antibes."

"Definitely," I said. "Repairs and upkeep for living expenses. What else?"

"A wine cellar," he said, looking a little sheepish. "I always wanted a good one. Not the ridiculously expensive ones that investors buy. Just good wines to drink over time, so I can be a generous host and we can have great parties. Remember that wine cellar in the basement of Aunt Pen's villa? Empty racks now, but it looked like she kept plenty of good stuff down there. I'd like to fill it up again."

"Fine. Also goes into the year's expenses," I said, because I suspected that there was a much bigger fish lurking in this pond.

"Good, done," Jeremy said briskly, moving as if to put his pad away, as if the meeting was adjourned.

"Wait a minute," I said. "You've got something else on that pad."

I craned my neck, trying to read what it was. He'd written it so faintly, and it had a big question mark after it.

"I haven't finalized this one," he said, looking a bit panicked.

"Oh, come on," I said.

"No, really," he said.

"Jeremy!" I coaxed in my sweetest, most supportive, most soothingly feminine voice. "I won't hold you to it, if you change your mind. But it's 'no-fair', not to tell."

I could swear he held his breath for a minute, like a pearl diver about to leap off a cliff and plunge to great depths below, into a churning sea where most mortal men dared not go.

"We-e-ell," he said uneasily.

"Jeremy, *What-is-it?*" I almost whispered.

And that was when he confessed about the Big Splurge, the Toy, as he called it.

"A yacht," he mumbled. "And if you laugh, I'll wring your neck."

I wasn't even sure I'd heard him correctly. "A yacht?" I asked sincerely. But Englishmen always think you're laughing at them, even when you're not. I don't know what they do to kids in those boarding schools, but his ears turned bright red.

"I am not talking about some run-of-the-mill, show-offy monster tub made of stainless steel and epoxy and loaded with plasma screens and jacuzzis and strapped with jet-skis," he said defensively. "The one I want is a classic motor yacht, built in 1926, an absolute beauty made of teak and mahogany, totally dignified, I assure you."

"The 'one'?" I echoed. "You mean, you have a specific yacht in mind?"

"Well, of course, my dear girl," he said. "I am not given to idle dreams."

"Where is it?" I asked. "Can I see it?"

"You can. And, more immediately, I can show you a picture of it. Would you like to see a picture?" he asked. I picked up a small pillow from the sofa and threw it at him.

"What do *you* think?" I shouted. He grinned, got up, went out of the room and out the front door and down into the street. Mystified, I went to the window, and watched him go to his car at the curb, open the trunk, rummage about and then return with what looked like a thick glossy magazine. When he came back into the apartment, he tossed it on the table next to me, laying it open to a dog-eared page. It was actually a fancy catalog for an upcoming auction to be held in Nice, France, for the benefit of an organization that raised money to protect the world's oceans and marine life. The catalog had been well-thumbed, and the page he pointed to was for: *Lot #28. A "classic motor yacht."*

"Oh, Jeremy!" I breathed, examining it closely. "It really *is* gorgeous!"

That's all I had to say to encourage him to plunge ahead enthusiastically. "It's 35 meters long . . ." he began.

"I can't do meters," I complained.

"Really, what's so complicated about counting in tens?" Jeremy countered. "As opposed to twelves, what's the good of that?"

"Just translate," I ordered.

"All right, it's—" He took out his mobile, did a calculation, and said triumphantly, "It is one hundred fourteen point eight-two-nine feet. Say 115 feet. Anyhow, its weighs 170 tons, and can do a maximum speed of 15 knots—which is about 17 miles per hour," he translated, seeing the blank look on my face.

"And," he went on, "it's already been refitted with new 250hp engines. The cockpit can seat eight people comfortably, and the cabins can accommodate six guests, still leaving room for five crew members. Which is just about right, so that you still have plenty of privacy. Of course, it does need some upgrading; but the great thing about it is that it's had the same owner for years and years, and he's just feeling too old to keep her anymore. He's got a berth in Nice for it, which he's selling along with it."

He'd been reeling off numbers and speaking so quickly that I could barely keep up, but it was plain to see that he'd harbored this passion for some time, keeping it hidden while he turned it over and over in his mind, in that eager but self-controlled way of his.

"Does it have a name?" I asked, looking closer. I read it aloud. "Oh . . . *Liesl's Dream.*"

"We could call it anything we want," Jeremy said absently. But looking at the catalog brought him back down to earth. "Except . . ." His voice trailed off.

"What?" I prodded.

"Well," he said, resuming his old cautious tone, "it's just that we haven't a hope in hell of getting it."

"Why not?" I asked.

"Because people get crazy at auctions, and sometimes, just to keep the other guy from getting it, they drive the price up. I don't want to throw our money away if that happens. There's only one thing worse than chasing a dream, and that's coming really close, only to watch somebody else take it away from you."

"Oh, swell!" I exclaimed. "Following that philosophy, Columbus wouldn't have sailed the Atlantic, and Babe Ruth wouldn't have hit a single home run, and Noah wouldn't have built his ark . . ."

"Do stick with baseball, and stay away from the nautical motifs," Jeremy suggested. "Anyhow, this is supposed to be something we both want, and I'm not sure I should drag you into it—"

"*I'm* sure! It's a great idea. Come on, brace up!" I said, imitating my English mother's pull-yourself-together scolding tone. "If you don't take a chance on this dream of yours, I guarantee you that you will spend the rest of your life wondering what would have happened if only you'd showed up for this auction. Where are they holding this clambake, anyway?"

"At an hotel in Nice," Jeremy said. "It's a charity auction, which means there will be all kinds of politicians, collectors, celebrities, you name it."

"Perfect! It's all for a worthy cause. Are they selling other yachts? And don't holler, I know this is the one you want," I said hastily.

"It's the only yacht in the auction," Jeremy said darkly. "They're selling a lot of other fancy stuff, none of which interests me in the least."

Then I said the magic words. "Hey, this would be just the right way to do our 'time off' that you wanted. In a yacht! Travel all round the ports and islands of the Riviera. Imagine how liberating it would be for us to see the coast from a boat, just like the ancient Greeks! We could go in the summertime."

Jeremy looked intrigued. "You could look the yacht over," he said thoughtfully. "With your expertise on history, antiques and art, you could tell me if it's really as good as they say it is. They allow viewing of it before the auction, by appointment, of course."

"Fine," I said briskly. "We're going. Buy your ticket or do whatever you have to do, and get two, because I'm going with you to the auction. It gives us a target date for you to wrap up all your business and get us out of London."

Chapter Seven

Well, getting The Lawyer Who Never Takes A Vacation to arrange for time off is a job for Wonder Woman. I got some unexpected help from Jeremy's mother (she's my Aunt Sheila, because, after Jeremy's father died, she married Uncle Peter, Mom's brother).

Aunt Sheila lives in a pretty, modern apartment in Chelsea, and one evening, when we stopped in to see her, Jeremy told her he'd just been accosted outside his office by a guy who tried to convince him to spend his money taking "gladiator lessons" (very expensive, and requiring one to wear a toga.) It was then that Aunt Sheila offered her advice about how to put some distance between us and the aggressive salesmen who accosted us on a daily—and nightly—basis.

"Become a moving target, darlings," she said. "Take the *whole* summer off. You'll always remember having had a few months of being fancy-free, while you're young enough to really enjoy it. Don't tell anyone where they can find you. Let the office field your calls."

"We're not students anymore," Jeremy reminded her. "Taking a 'gap year.'"

He always pretends to faintly disapprove of his mum, who grew up in the music scene of the Swinging Sixties, and who nowadays still manages to look top-drawer yet bohemian, her hair and figure still pretty much as it was circa 1964. She still wears the style of moderately short, A-line dresses and pale stockings and flat shoes of that era.

"All I'm suggesting," she said mildly, "is a gap *summer*. If you can't spare a whole summer at this juncture of your life, more's the pity."

I think it was the idea that he'd reached a "juncture" which finally got Jeremy on board, as if the whole world was telling him that he'd come to an important crossroads. So, Jeremy said that if summer was our target gap time, then in the springtime months before it, he'd work like mad to clear his schedule, preparing his clients to work with Rupert, the young guy in his office who was being groomed by Jeremy anyway.

As for me, I was the kind of freelancer who invariably ended up working when other people didn't want to, like holidays and summers, so the idea of actually having a whole, luxurious summer vacation really was a grand indulgence.

"I think it fits right in with the Plan," I said.

"And at the summer's end," Jeremy said, warming to the idea, "we can sort out all the other things we need to decide."

Now, I want to say, here and now, that I was all for getting away from London and taking time off, even before Lydia appeared on the scene, literally darkening Jeremy's doorstep. But now that she'd shown up, I figured we had all the more reason to vamoose.

Fortunately, since Jeremy was clearing the decks to take this time off, his work required him to do even more of those quick business jaunts to Brussels and Frankfurt and Antwerp, to schmooze his clients and prepare them for his hiatus. This kept him out of his bachelor apartment, and out of Lydia's reach; and whenever he was in town, we always met at my flat. I was managing the trust when Jeremy was away, and I was counting the weeks until the auction.

I began to feel that we were on a lucky streak. The townhouse deal wasn't easy, but Martin and I managed to pull it off with just a few minor skirmishes involving other buyers who finally backed off. The other apartments weren't really filled with the kinds of "mod-cons" that buyers in this part of town expect. Doris and her husband, who lived upstairs, had such a small kitchen, and a leaky roof, that we were able to get a good price for it rather quickly. And downstairs, Gladys and her husband, inspired by the sale of Doris' place, were now eager to sell and then move into their daughter's house, rent-free, in Canada. Gladys' ground-floor flat had old-fashioned plumbing and fixtures, which desperately needed updating, so this kept the selling price a bit lower than it might otherwise have been. The accountants and lawyers were actually a big help here; I think they felt protective of us now.

Jeremy and I e-mailed each other and commiserated over what needed to be done to bring the townhouse into the twenty-first century. To me, the house represented our future careers, and I sensed that, in launching an independent enterprise, how you end up depends a lot on how you begin. Therefore I wanted to make the place really work for us, by reviving the lovely, old-fashioned period detail yet making certain it had all the vital things we'd need to work from there. The wiring was ka-fluey, for instance. (All of it. Phones, electric, Internet.) And of course, whenever you're remodeling, sooner or later somebody suggests knocking out a wall.

In this case, it was on the first floor, and it would combine two small rooms into one nice large sitting room, perfectly positioned between my office and Jeremy's. I envisioned this big room as the place where we'd catch up with each other at the end of the day, as a bridge between our work and our personal life. And finally, Jeremy could have his garage in the basement, so he wouldn't have to park on the street anymore. The house was solidly built and could take this level of renovation.

Good, I thought, that meant we had a strong foundation—metaphorically as well as concretely. Because it was clear to me that at summer's end, we would be coming back here to make big decisions, not the least of which was whether our working and personal relationship was going to really last.

So. I guess you could understand why, just days before we were going to depart for the auction in Nice, I, still immersed in paving the way for our future, got a bit of a shock when I telephoned Jeremy at his apartment (where he had stopped off to unpack his business-travel suitcase and pack up his things for our summer off)—and, a woman answered the phone.

"Hall-ooo?" she said in her posh, well-rested way. I tried to tell myself that I'd dialed the wrong number, and got someone else's high-end, neurotic ex-wife. But I knew it was her.

"Where's Jeremy?" I said brusquely.

"And who may I say is calling?" Lydia said, and then giggled helplessly for his benefit. I heard him call out, and she said, "I think it's a wrong number, darling," just to stick it to me.

"Lydia," I said in my best worldly-heiress voice, "this is Penny. Put Jeremy on."

"Ooh, can't do it," she said. "He's in the shower. But I'll tell him you called."

I won't even mention all the expletives that ran through my mind. Fortunately I didn't have to say them, because I heard Jeremy say plaintively, "Lydia, who is it? The office?" Then it dawned on him. "Is that Penny?"

" 'Bye now," she was saying, but Jeremy must have made a grab for it.

"Penny," he said, quickly and contritely. "Is that you?"

"You've got ten seconds to tell me why you're in the shower with That Person in your apartment," I said calmly.

"I was not in the shower," he said indignantly. "Is that what she told you?"

He must have made a face at her, because I heard her giggle again.

"Yes, we've been having oh-so-much-fun playing cat and mouse over you," I said. "Why is she there?"

"She wanted some legal advice," he said, sounding as if he knew perfectly well what I thought of that.

My voice took on a phonily casual tone. "Oh?" I said, still trying to sound like the sort of elegant woman who's so confident that nothing threatens her. "And did you 'recuse' yourself, and refer her to another lawyer?"

"Well, I had to hear her out first, to see who to refer her to," Jeremy said, a shade irritated with her, or with me, or with both of us, or women in general.

"She must have been frustrated all these months while you were away on business trips," I said with a light laugh. "She must have been crouched over by the elevator waiting for you to show up again." I expected him to reproach me, but when he didn't, I knew that I'd guessed fairly correctly. "God, she did, didn't she?" I marveled.

"Just about," he admitted.

"My advice is, pack your duds and shoo her out of there and bolt the door and don't look back," I said crisply.

"Yes, ma'am," he said meekly, dog that he was. Then I had a horrid thought, imagining his open suitcases lying about, a telltale sign for Lydia to see that he was going on an extended trip.

"You didn't tell her where we're going, did you, Jeremy?" I asked pleadingly. "You didn't tell her about our Plan, with our future enterprise and the yacht, and our great gap summer and . . . ?"

"No, of course not," he said. "She did notice the suitcases, and asked for a number where she could reach me, because of this on-going legal matter she's got—"

I didn't even wait for him to finish. I snapped, "Let her call through to your office, like all your other clients!"

"I did better than that," he said in a low voice. "I'll tell you when I get there."

At his surreptitious tone, I had the creepy idea that she might be listening, and that he suspected this, too. "Please hurry out of there," I said, as winsomely as I could. "For my sake, all right?"

"I'm coming on wings," he promised.

I braced myself for a delay, and excuses about London traffic. But Jeremy arrived pretty quickly, with all his suitcases stuffed in the trunk of his car, and he came bounding up the steps.

"So," he said without ceremony, "want to know how I brilliantly handled the whole Lydia debacle?"

"Brilliantly?" I said as lightly as I could. "You let her into your apartment; you let her answer your phone. Brilliant? Hmmm . . ."

"She's got some legal tangles about money and property with that Brazilian dude," Jeremy explained.

"Did you refer her to Harold or Rupert?" I asked. Harold was a senior partner in Jeremy's firm, and Rupert was Jeremy's right-hand man.

"Neither," he said. "I asked a mutual friend of ours, who works for a completely different firm, to look in on her."

"Our friend?" I asked. "Who?"

"Not you-and-me ours," he said hastily. "A close friend of mine from university. Bertie. Lydia knows him and trusts him, because he's her crowd."

"Did she go for it?" I asked, trying not to feel excluded by this "our crowd" business, yet I felt my heart bobbing up and down as if it had suddenly been chucked overboard and was clinging to a lifesaver to stay afloat.

"Yes, and she had to admit it was the perfect solution."

This did nothing to allay my suspicions of Lydia's motives, but I didn't comment.

Jeremy added teasingly, "I thought I'd get heaps of praise for the way I handled this thing. Feel free to shower me with adulation anytime now." He peered at me. "You're upset," he noted. (Genius.) "Darling," he said softly, "I can't go around acting like I don't know Lydia, or am afraid to be near her."

"Why not?" I said in a small voice. "I have forsaken all my previous beaux." I hesitated. "Jeremy," I said, "It *is* really—over between you two, isn't it?"

He said, very honestly, "Yes, of course. But somehow, you have to work at divorce almost as much as you worked on the marriage. To make a real break of those emotional bonds, not just a fake one."

"Bonds?" I asked faintly. "Do you still have them?"

By now I'd begun to recklessly break all my rules about dealing with men. For instance, Rule Number One: Never ask a question that you think you don't want to know the answer to.

"It's just that, you know the other person's vulnerabilities, so while they're driving everyone else crazy, you know that they're suffering," he explained. "At first, everybody, including me, thought Lydia was so sure of herself when we were all still in school—she seemed to have it all—beauty, breeding, charm. She always said I was her 'rock,' so everyone told us that we were perfect together."

Aw, nuts, I had to ask, I thought to myself. Jolly school memories. What fun.

"But out in the real world, she was more fragile than most people realized," Jeremy was saying a bit guiltily. "We all took our time getting married—everybody was just having fun, starting up with our careers—and I had been living in Paris, working with a firm there for years. When I came back to London, I was weary of the single life, and Lydia was especially unhappy with it. I thought if she had another 'safe haven,' as school was, then everything would be all right. But it never was. It turned out that we were not really compatible at all. But even now, when it's clearly over, it's hard not to care when that person seems to be in trouble. I can't just treat her as if she's dead. It kills something inside you when you do that. Something you want to keep alive for, well, a certain redheaded person, for instance."

Oh. That would be me, I guess. I'm quite susceptible to this sort of talk, but I wanted to be sure that I wasn't being a gullible little dummy. Jeremy had never been this forthcoming about his past before. I gazed searchingly at his face, looking for any telltale signs of duplicity, deceit, or general dastardliness, but found none. I supposed I could, after all, trust this man I loved so much. Maybe. The trouble with loving a good guy is that he wants to be straight with everyone, so you feel like a rat when you wish he'd be a tad hostile to his "ex."

"So. Let that be an end to it. And, I could do with a kiss now, as a reward for being a good, faithful dog," Jeremy said.

"Hold on, dog," I said. "I just want to know one thing. You didn't give her *any* information at all about where we're going to be . . . did you?"

Rule Number Two: Don't interrogate. But I'm only human. This was no longer about whether Lydia still loved, or wanted to possess,

Jeremy. I only cared if *he* still cared for her in some old-times'-sake way that she could exploit. And somehow it would have felt like a violation if he had told her of our Splurge.

"Look," Jeremy said. "I'm weary of talking about Lydia. But the answer is: No, I did not tell her where we're going. I said I'd be out of the country on a private sojourn. Well, I didn't say it quite like that. But she got the picture." Then his expression changed, as if he felt he'd just been enlightened.

"So that's the whole reason you want the yacht and our summer off? You just want us as far away from Lydia as possible, don't you?" he said with a knowing smirk.

"May I remind you," I loftily told him, "that, originally, it was your idea that we take a sabbatical from work? Remember, when you chased me down at the museum and told me that you loved and adored me?"

"And I do," he said, "despite your occasional skullduggery."

"*My* skullduggery!" I said. "How about Lydia's? Sneaking into your building, and then breaking into your apartment, lying in wait for you while drinking your whisky! You must admit, her timing is mighty suspicious."

"No, no, really, it's not about us," Jeremy insisted. "It's about her breakup with that guy, and she got homesick for London."

"Pshaw!" I cried. "And I can prove it to you. I'll wager five cents that the minute you leave London, she will, too. If, however, she is sincere, she'll stay put even if you're not around. But she won't."

Rule Number Three: Avoid saying anything bad about another woman, even when she appears to be exploiting everyone's better nature for her own wretched purposes.

"You really don't think she's got a sincere bone in her body, do you?" Jeremy asked.

"It's not about bones," I said stubbornly. "It's about tactics."

"Well, not to worry," Jeremy said reasonably. "In a couple of days she'll set her sights on bigger fish than me. London is full of rich billionaires."

I suddenly realized that we had just spent all this time talking of nothing but Lydia. If I wanted to dispel her influence, then I would have to stop worrying about her.

"All right, then," I said in a more playful tone, "I am bound to conclude that you actually did, in difficult circumstances, acquit yourself admirably and loyally, and I do, indeed, wish to kiss you."

Jeremy brightened immediately, and he leaned toward me expectantly for a reward of a kiss. And, I just can't help it. It's really quite alarming, the effect that man has on me. The moment I felt him coming closer, and caught a whiff of that nice Jeremy-smell, well . . .

And, thankfully, after that, the conversation went in a much better direction. He asked for news of progress on the townhouse, and, feeling much more cheerful, I said, "Wait here. I want to show you something." I jumped up and ran off and then returned with a folder containing some sketches on tissue paper, sandwiched in cardboard.

"Take a look at these font samples and tell me which one you like best." I held out a sheet of paper.

"But what's it for?" he asked, mystified.

"An engraved brass plaque for the townhouse, to go right next to the front door," I said eagerly, "you know, like they use for landmark buildings." I showed him a sketch. It said:

Nichols and Laidley, Ltd.
Discretion guaranteed.
Inquire within.

"Good Lord," Jeremy said, astonished. "You really do think that life is just like a 1930s movie, don't you? What's that supposed to mean, 'Discretion guaranteed'? What sort of dodgy business do you think we're going to end up in?"

"Oh, relax," I said airily. "I had to write something down, for the engraver, just to see what the fonts will look like. Plenty of time to finalize the details, my good man."

Jeremy paused, then gazed at the paper again. "Who says your name goes first?" he demanded with a mock challenge. "It's perfectly obvious that 'Laidley and Nichols' has a much better ring to it."

"Beauty before age, chum," I said wickedly.

Later, when my bags were all packed and we were ready to head out to France, we went downstairs, and looked in on the first-floor apartment, where renovations were just beginning. Jeremy's secretary would supervise for us while we were gone. A room in the back of the house which overlooked the garden, already came with built-in bookcases and a working fireplace. This was where the wall would be knocked down to merge it with a smaller room next to it. When we pulled up the ragged old carpeting, we found beautiful hardwood floors. I planned to furnish this room with the kind of leather chairs and ottomans and lamps and all that stuff men like. And there would be a sideboard and a window-seat.

Jeremy said enthusiastically, "You were right. This place has great possibilities."

"At the end of the day, we can have a glass of wine and compare notes about how our workday went," I suggested.

"Fine. Your mythological Great Dane can snooze on a carpet in here, instead of my office," Jeremy said, carefully stepping around the carpenters' tools and electricians' wires with a pleased look.

We locked up carefully; Jeremy's secretary had another key.

Then we stepped outside, and headed for his spiffy modern forest-green Dragonetta. As he held the passenger door open for me, I exhaled a loud, involuntary sigh of relief, which he didn't miss.

"Not to worry," he said reassuringly. "We are, as my mum advised, a moving target, 'Footloose and fancy-free.' And, just to show I'm a good sport, you can put your name first. *Nichols and Laidley* it is." He went around to the other side of the car and slid into his seat, and, looking a bit relieved himself, started the car, and off we went.

The trunk was full of our suitcases; and on the back seat was a cooler with food and wine. I told myself that I could finally relax now. We were heading out for the ferry to take us across the English Channel to France. Then we'd drive down to the gorgeous Mediterranean, and Great-Aunt Penelope's beloved villa in Antibes. With the wind in my hair, I started to feel better already, visualizing the pleasures that lay ahead. We'd settle into the villa, fill the swimming pool, eat fresh fish every day, build Jeremy's wine cellar, and scoot around the winding roads of the Riviera . . .

. . . and bid on *Liesl's Dream*. With a bit of luck, it would become our dreamboat.

Part Three

Chapter Eight

The Riviera was still there, waiting for us. I'd begun to wonder if I'd simply dreamed it up. But as we drove along the winding corniche road, I found it even more lovely than I remembered, and I was astonished all over again at the sheer breathtaking swoop of those staggeringly high cliffs, with clustered hotels and villas impossibly built right into them. I kept admiring the view of the sea and the sky, which was like a watercolor painting done in three distinct shades of blue: near-turquoise for the endless sea; deeper azure for the broad horizon; and a soft pale baby-blanket blue for the wide-open sky.

I breathed it all in, watching the way the gently bright sunlight kisses everything in sight, illuminating the glowing colors within the puffy white clouds, the terracotta roof tiles, the pink stonework, the lush greenery and the riotous color of each flower. The sea sparkled as if it were flecked with diamonds, and the salty air made me want to swim with the little golden fishes that dart around in small coves all along the coastline.

In order to be on time for our appointment to view the yacht, we actually drove straight to the harbor in Nice, even before going to reopen Great-Aunt Penelope's villa. Jeremy was already pre-registered as a bidder, and the organizers of the auction were smart enough to make sure that they spaced the appointments well apart, so that we never saw anybody else who was interested in bidding on it.

We pulled into the parking area that lined the harbor, which was shaped like a horseshoe. Ringing the harbor from across the road were picturesque three-story pastel-colored buildings with cafés and bistros at street level. At the far end of the quay was a yacht club. The boats were all either berthed at the pier or, as with the bigger ones, anchored farther out in the harbor.

When I opened the car door and inhaled the scent of the sea, I felt the immediate urge to jump aboard a boat and be a part of the nautical fun and frolic. All along the quay, the atmosphere was festively clubby, as if everyone here was in on a great secret about belonging to the world of the sea. Just the sound of the waves splashing against the hulls, and the seagulls cawing, and the shouts of men who were hosing down their decks, filled me with anticipation of great voyages and adventures.

A tall, very elegant Frenchman who represented the auction house was waiting at the yacht clubhouse to show us around. He was dressed in a simple, well-cut sleek blue suit, and he greeted us with an impeccable French politeness that had an easy, human undertone which could elevate any task into an important achievement. He told us that his name was Laurent.

"This way, please," he said in a well-modulated voice. As he led us past the other boats, I noted all the different fanciful names, and the flags from countries far and wide: from Norway, England, the Netherlands, the Caribbean, Argentina and of course, France. And then, there she was, tucked snugly into her slip between two larger boats—*Liesl's Dream.*

In a way, I kind of wished I hadn't seen her before the auction.

Because, right at first sight I could tell that *Liesl's Dream* was the perfect boat for two romantics like us. Even from a distance, its old-fashioned design gave it an instant, cozy charm, and, though sleek and seaworthy, she had an air of being not just a boat, but a home. The sun glowed warmly on the elegant burnished-wood exterior and gleaming brass rails, making the yacht stand in quiet contrast to all the large modern silver-and-white aluminum and plastic that surrounded it. The decks on both the main and the upper levels had chairs and tables stacked and arranged as if politely awaiting the order to cast off; the pilot house—a cute, boxlike structure sitting on the top-level deck—had spanking-clean windows from which to view your path to the wider world; and the French flag fluttered in the breeze.

As we walked up the gangway or *passerelle*, I had that brief delicious feeling of being suspended between land and sea, wobbling a little until I hopped onto the boat, which felt substantial and welcoming. Laurent led us around, explaining that this beauty had been built in Italy, and he paused to point out the many excellent features. Jeremy would look to me for affirmation, and I nodded to confirm that everything was authentic, including the precious teak and mahogany that gave the yacht such an old-fashioned elegance. I could see that it had been lovingly furnished and carefully tended to meet high standards of excellence. As I assessed each piece I knew that the praise for *Liesl's Dream* certainly was not exaggerated, and it might even be a bit under-valued.

We examined the yacht from front to back—no, wait, that's "fore-and-aft." Since the boat was parked with its back-end (er, "aft", also known as the "stern") to the shore, we began with the "aft deck" which was a casual outdoor lounging area with teak steamer chairs covered with striped cushions, and matching little teak tables. A sliding mahogany door led us inside to the dining room—oops, dining "salon"—which was dominated by a large oval table whose surface was a painted, glazed "celestial map", with all the stars and planets to guide you. A sideboard worked as a storage cupboard for the boat's patterned silverware, and for the china dinnerware which was cream-colored, trimmed with maroon and gold, all securely nestled and strapped down in green felt padded pockets.

From there, charming French doors opened onto the living room or "main salon" where we admired the wine-colored carpeting, mahogany cabinetry and panelling, and luxurious upholstered and leather chairs in shades of pale butterscotch and deeper caramel. This was the most elegant yet eccentric area of the boat, with 1920s light fixtures, including hurricane lamps mounted on the walls. Jeremy, fascinated, nudged my arm when he saw two matching wood-and-glass cupboards that were filled with an eclectic mix of seafaring items.

"They're called 'cabinets of curiosities,'" I said. "They were all the rage in the 1700s among learned gentlemen who wanted to display their knowledge of botany and science and art, and show off what they found on their worldly travels."

The curio cupboards were illuminated with special lighting, and held a collection of maritime collectibles: a white and silver-plated cocktail shaker, shaped like a lighthouse, circa 1928; a model ship that was a replica of a Napoleonic prisoner-of-war vessel; a mid-eighteenth century pocket world globe "with fish skin case"; a compass in a leather pouch; a turn-of-the-century hourglass; vintage binoculars; an antique chess set carved out of wood; a Chinese figurine of a sailor's head with a small clock in his cap; and a document box, with old seafaring maps.

The main salon also had a low oval coffee table, its surface painted and glazed like the one in the dining salon, only instead of a "celestial" map, this one was a "terrestrial" map with an old-fashioned depiction of the earth's seas and continents. And over in the corner was a wonderful antique gramophone mounted on a cupboard containing old records, mostly classical. This fascinated Jeremy, who loves music. "Is it a working Victrola?" he asked.

Laurent nodded. He had been smiling indulgently at me and I realized that I had tarried among the little collection of antiques. He explained that the main salon was really the heart of the boat, with exits on all four sides. From here, you could go out sideways through either of two smaller "wing" doors that led to narrow decks called "side galleys" which ran along the boat, one on the "port" side (left) and the other on the "starboard" side (right). These narrow galleys made it possible to walk all around the perimeter of the boat from outdoors, circling along all its decks without ever coming inside.

Or, you could, as we now did, proceed farther forward, through a door leading to the cocktail bar, which was fully outfitted with glasses, a small sink, a nicely polished bar and six high bar stools padded with faux zebra skin—the one funny touch to an otherwise subtle design. And from the bar, you could go out to the "fore deck" at the very front of the boat (a.k.a. the "bow" or "prow").

"Would you now like to go below and see the kitchen and cabins?" Laurent asked politely. He showed us the two staircases in the bar area: a very beautiful, dramatic curving one with mahogany banister; and a much narrower, functional one for the crew. I pictured the crew nimbly scurrying up and down their own staircase, and I imagined that the two separate staircases were as much to keep the owners and guests out of the way of the busy crew, as it was to provide privacy for revellers.

The master "cabin" (bedroom) was truly luxurious, having a

great bed with matching walnut tables and 1920s lamps, a bookcase, an armoire with drawers beneath it, and a chest of drawers
with an adjoining vanity table and mirror. There was even a private
bathroom with a triangular-shaped shower in the corner. Laurent
showed us that all the doors down here slid open and closed along
tracks that took them into the walls, rather than swinging open
into a room and taking up valuable space. It made for a neat, compact "ship-shape" sleeping level. The guest rooms had a shared
bath, and smaller beds, but plenty of drawers and cupboards.

The crew had bunk beds and footlockers in a room off the
kitchen. The kitchen was the most modernized, with brushed aluminum cabinetry and a stove that was "gimballed" which meant
that when the sea acted up and the boat tilted, the stove would
maintain its balance, to prevent having the cooking food slosh over
and scald the cook. I noted that everything was either mounted or
anchored in some way, a constant reminder that you were on a boat
which could pitch, roll, but hopefully not overturn. To me, these
signs of the very changeable aspect of travel were a reminder of the
impermanent nature of the voyage of life itself.

When we climbed back up to the main level, Laurent then let
us scamper up a ladder-like stair to the smaller topmost "bridge
deck," which had a little sunbed area in the rear. In the center was
a lifeboat (another reminder of life's little emergencies). And at the
fore was the boxlike "pilot house" where you steered the ship. Or,
your captain did. I admired the lovely antique fittings such as the
ship's wheel, bell, compass, clock, and chronometers.

Finally, our tour was over. But I didn't want to go. The whole
thing felt like the ultimate dollhouse. I wanted to plunk right down
in that cute furniture and have dinner on those adorable dishes,
and then wash the cups in the tiny sink, like a little girl playing
house. Then I wanted to tiptoe into the bedroom and pick out a

book from the glassed-in bookcase, and turn on one of those quaint lamps and fling myself down on the grand bed in the master cabin, and read about historical expeditions while Jeremy mixed me a cocktail upstairs in the bar. There were even charming little curtains at the portholes.

While I was mentally playing house, Jeremy went over the listed details about the engine and all that necessary nuts-and-bolts stuff. He'd already gotten Denby, the expert who repaired high-end and vintage cars, to visit earlier with an engineer friend, to assess the boat's engine. Denby's report indicated that the engine had passed inspection with "flying colors."

Laurent informed us that the captain and crew who had worked on this yacht for many years were still available and willing to continue working for the new owner. Apparently, the current owner was an elderly gentleman who was well-known and respected, and had taken part in annual boat races, so everybody knew it was a good boat. But the poor man was not in the best of health, so he had finally decided to part with it.

"Have you had many interested viewers?" Jeremy asked as casually as he could. Laurent said, suavely and carefully, "A bit. Yes. But not too many. Some think it old-fashioned, because they want only the big boats with all the modern conveniences, you know, radar, GPS, VHF, satellite TV, stereo system and DVD player."

The fact that he was not afraid of discouraging a sale indicated to me that he was confident the boat would sell well. Jeremy waited till Laurent's back was turned before he exchanged a significant look with me. We both still hoped that the lack of modern amenities would at least discourage a number of bidders who'd prefer a state-of-the-art boat. But to me, such conveniences could always be added to an antique boat, more easily than the reverse of trying to spruce up a modern boat with these impossible-to-get precious wood and fixtures.

I tried to play it cool as we said goodbye to Laurent, even when he smiled and wished us *"Bon chance."* But the moment we were back in the car and Jeremy said, "Well? What do you think?" I couldn't control my enthusiasm.

"It's fabulous!" I squealed. "Jeremy, this is *perfect* for us! It's just the right atmosphere for taking the summer off and carrying out our Plan."

"Ah," Jeremy said, "I was rather afraid you'd say so. Now all we have to do is win it."

Chapter Nine

When we finally arrived at the villa in Antibes, we were hot and dusty from the road, and dying for a swim. Jeremy had already arranged for the pool to be filled, by a company that specialized in salt water without too many chemicals. So it was like seeing an oasis. The fountain in the front drive had also been filled, and it gurgled and splashed as if anticipating our arrival. The gravel drive had been raked by a gardener whose father had worked for Great-Aunt Penelope. The garage was refurbished and expanded now, to house two cars, and its roof was fixed at last. But it was empty because Denby, who'd recently returned from the Caribbean, was still working on restoring my vintage auto in his shop.

"Which side do you want to reserve for your car?" Jeremy asked as we pulled up.

"The left," I said. He pulled his forest-green modern Dragonetta into the right slot. I pictured my cobalt blue old-timer snuggling up alongside his, and I giggled.

"It's going to be so cute when mine's ready," I said. "His-and-her Dragonettas."

"We'll toot around town and honk our horns at each other,"

Jeremy said, amused. "We'll become the town eccentrics here, too."

The villa itself lay beyond, standing in dignified, meditative quiet, waiting for us to put the key in the lock. Jeremy pushed open the front door and I listened to our footsteps echoing as we went back and forth, bringing in our suitcases and setting them down in the front foyer. From the main level, two curving staircases led to the open second-floor hallway above, which overlooked the circular foyer below where we were now standing. Straight ahead, a door under the stairs led to the main-floor drawing room. We went in.

"Hallo-ohh!" Jeremy exclaimed, and his voice bounced hollowly off the empty rooms. We knew, of course, that cousin Rollo had removed all the furniture from the villa, as he was entitled to do for his inheritance. This had been carefully supervised by our French lawyers. Still, there was something innately shocking about the empty, naked drawing room. The baby grand piano, the clock, sofa, chandelier—which had all been covered with dust-sheets, like friendly ghosts—had vanished. In the dining room, the big table and chairs were gone; so were the heavy drapes that once cloaked the French windows.

"Old Rollo even took the nails from the walls where the pictures were hanging," Jeremy observed wryly, as we toured the villa. "If there were mousetraps lying about, I'd bet he took those, too."

"With or without the dead mice?" I asked, deadpan. I'd never seen any mousetraps.

"You don't want to know," he replied.

A girl from town, Celeste, who'd worked for Aunt Pen right up to the day she died, had prepared the house for us this week, cleaning up the dust and cobwebs, airing it out, turning on the electric and water; and meeting the furniture guys, because I'd ordered

new kitchen appliances (to replace the old ones that Rollo had unceremoniously yanked out) and a new bed for the master bedroom.
There were repairs to make on this place, too, but we'd decided to
wait until the townhouse in London was ready to be occupied before starting work here.

Meanwhile, the villa was habitable in the rooms that Celeste
had cleared out for us: kitchen, master bedroom and bath, and the
patio chairs and table outside where we would dine. (Rollo was
only entitled to the indoor furnishings.)

"Look, Celeste put milk and bottled water in the refrigerator
for us!" I said. "And a fresh baguette and a can of coffee in the
pantry. And, a basket of fresh fruit with big purple plums, and
green grapes, and cute little oranges," I noted. "That was thoughtful of her."

"Great. Let's go for a swim," Jeremy suggested. We bounded up
the stairs like schoolkids turned loose on summer vacation, jumped
into our bathing suits, and then clattered back down and outside
for a swim in the pool that lay beyond the patio.

I greeted the terracotta pots all around the pool as if they were
old friends. Some curious birds swooped dramatically overhead,
diving and rising daringly, as if to inspect the new owners. I swam
and swam and swam, admiring the way the dappled sunlight reflected in the pool; then I flipped over and inhaled the scent of
jasmine which wafted with unexpected intensity when the wind
shifted. Far off in the distance, I could hear a church bell singing
its solemn bittersweet tune of time. At that moment, I felt intensely
glad to be alive.

Floating there, released from gravity, I thought of Great-Aunt
Penelope, who was my grandmother's sister. I'd seen the photographs of her in her glorious youth, at elegant parties around the
grand piano in this villa. Aunt Pen had never married, but she'd

been a popular young hostess who spent many summers here before the second World War broke out. She'd fallen deeply in love with a man who died in that war—Jeremy's Italian great-grandfather. But this little family secret had only recently come to light, because of the inheritance battle. It was why she left this villa to Jeremy, in a letter exhorting both of us to enjoy the good things in life.

Almost as if reading my mind, Jeremy swam up to me and said, "I keep expecting Aunt Pen to pop her head out of one of those windows and call out to us. Absurd, isn't it? We never came here as kids. Yet, I feel she's watching over us." He smiled. "I think I just heard her say, 'Care for a cocktail?'"

So we jumped out, toweled dry, and unpacked the bottle of wine and the roasted chicken we'd picked up en route for our supper, together with the bread and fruit from the pantry. We ate at the cast-iron table on the patio, until mosquitoes hummed ominously. Then we went inside, upstairs . . . and finished our wine by candlelight.

The next day, we drove to the open-air markets for supplies. I loved the stalls where fishmongers and bakers and farmers and flower-growers and butchers and poulterers (because yes, in France you may actually have a separate butcher who deals only with birds and game), all proud, professional people who had been up with the morning dew—were ready to sell us the freshest food I'd ever seen in my life. Cheese still warm from being finished, vegetables and fruit so sweet and succulent I just wanted to pop them into my mouth like candy; and beans and nuts and coffee that were sitting in burlap sacks, and got weighed up for us and put into little sacks of our own; and heirloom flowers that actually smelled the way they're supposed to.

"Jeremy," I said jokingly, after tasting the cheese and buying three different kinds, "I have made a terrible mistake. I can't stay here. I will spend my days only wanting to go from one meal to the next until I've eaten everything in sight, and I will get fat."

"No, you won't," he said, "because for one thing, you burn up all the calories with that brain of yours that's always collecting rare information about everything. And secondly, we're going to bike and swim and dash about having the time of our lives. Look around you. Nobody's fat."

We carried everything back to the car. Jeremy announced, "And now, the wine."

I glanced about. "Where? I don't see a wine store," I said.

"Not a shop!" Jeremy said scornfully. "We're going direct to a couple of wineries. I already did the advance work, my dear girl. Just sit back and enjoy the ride."

Well. I only sipped a bit from each sample glass. Really. I never drank a full glass. And still. Suffice it to say, Jeremy got a good start on his wine cellar. Ruby reds, crisp clean whites, sparklers, aperitifs, dessert wines, and that *l'eau de vie* which is supposed to be the "water of life"—a clear, nearly colorless brandy that's been spiffed up with essence of raspberries or cherries or blackberries.

"I'm just not sure I can stand it," I mumbled as we drove home, my nostrils still sniffing the cool wet scent of the cellars we'd visited and the wines we'd tasted.

"Stand what?" Jeremy inquired.

I glanced at his elegant face, and then I looked away quickly, having one of those shy moments when merely experiencing his presence—his maleness and his sweetness—gave me a ridiculously simple thrill. Being in love—really in love—seems to be a remarkable combination of both excitement and yet a profound peacefulness.

"All this happiness and pleasure," I replied, managing to sound as if I was just talking about the day, and not our lives and our destiny and the whole ball of wax.

Jeremy kissed me. "You'll be surprised at how quickly we'll get used to it," he said.

Chapter Ten

And so, the big day dawned. There we were, seated in the front courtyard of that Art Deco hotel on the Promenade des Anglais in Nice, patiently waiting for all the other stuff to be auctioned off before *Liesl's Dream* came up. The suspense was nearly unbearable. The only way I could keep myself from chewing on my handbag, was to watch the parade of people who arrived, ready to fling tons of money away on toys yet still feel virtuous because it was for a charity. (Actually, the owners of the items would retain a pretty decent profit from the sale.)

Everyone chatted and waved at one another as they took their seats under the white tent that occasionally flapped like a sailboat in the Mediterranean breeze. I was Jeremy's expert on antiques and history, but he was my guide to High Society, explaining who all these people were. Turns out, the rich come in an assortment of sizes and shapes. The brazenly suntanned ones who arrived loaded down with enormous jewelry and heavy perfume were what Jeremy called The New Arrivals. These had made their money quite recently, through investment banking, steel and other industry, supermarket or clothing chains, even garbage collecting. No matter how old the guy was, the girl who accompanied him was younger—with exaggeratedly enormous breasts and a hard, doll-like painted face. But both seemed please to show off that they were with the other.

Then there were the Celebs, so easy to spot because of the flash-bulbs popping around them; they usually paused obligingly to allow photographers to snap them, and fans to admire them. Politicians also got photographed, but they were less relaxed about it than the Celebs, because they were always grabbing someone's hand to shake, to drag them into a photo op. I recognized a few TV, Hollywood and Internet moguls from their pictures in the newspapers; and Jeremy pointed out a couple of high-flying celebrity lawyers who made an outrageous living defending wealthy clients who, as he put it, "*will* keep trying to overthrow the governments of smaller countries." There was one guy whom Jeremy had seen on TV but couldn't identify until I recognized the fellow as a Big Lottery Winner from the States. He was the only one in this crowd who looked baffled instead of purposeful.

With the bang of the first gavel, my heart revved up and I watched alertly as each item was auctioned off. I tried to guess which bidders might come up against us for the yacht, but it was impossible to tell. One by one the items were sold off: first, an assortment of framed paintings of English country houses and land-scapes, French châteaus, huntsmen on horseback, and dogs. Funnily enough, the more popular dog portraits went for more money than some of the higher-quality portraits of humans. Several fairly good pieces of small furniture came next. Then a few oddball items, like a first-prize trophy in a bear-hunting contest, which was a loving-cup studded with meteorite fragments, who knows why. And then some vintage jewelry.

As the bidding heated up, I began to notice what sore losers certain rich people can be. Some of them actually cursed aloud as they left, or threw their catalogs in the garbage bin on the way out, like people who'd bet on a bad horse at the races. I guess they were accustomed to getting what they want, whereas regular folks are so familiar with disappointment that they take it more philosophically. But think about it. When was the last time you actually heard a multimillionaire say, "Oh well, you win some, you lose some"? Practically never.

I was just getting lulled to a peculiar suspended state of passivity that bore a small resemblance to sleepy relaxation, as the auctioneer was saying, "We will proceed with Lots Number 18 through 27, a collection of fine antique musical instruments and memorabilia which were graciously donated by . . ."

And then, a strange thing happened, a quirk of fate that led to many others.

He stopped, having been interrupted by a young woman in a pale green suit and a pale green headband, who had come hurrying over to him and now whispered in his ear. He frowned, and leaned toward her to urgently ask her something; she listened alertly, but she shook her head.

Then both of them turned to the audience with the identical false smiles of people who don't want you to notice that there's a problem. The auctioneer said briskly, "Very sorry, but there has been a slight mix-up with the tagging of Lots 18 through 27, so they will be delayed."

A murmur of surprise arose, but he quenched it quickly and firmly, saying, "So, we will move on to . . . Lot Number 28." This meant that the yacht would now be auctioned much earlier than originally planned. I gulped, and glanced at Jeremy. He was ready.

"Lot Number 28," the auctioneer repeated with more firmness. I heard Jeremy let out his breath in a puff of anticipation. Already, my toes were curling and my fingers were crossed. "*Liesl's Dream . . .*"

the auctioneer intoned, and then he said each word as if were worth its weight in gold: "a-classic-1920s-motor-yacht."

He paused for effect. "Let's begin the bidding at 300,000 euros, shall we?" he said crisply. I didn't see who bid on it, but immediately the auctioneer lifted his eyebrow, nodded and said, "I have 300,000 euros on the telephone."

Nuts, I thought. The phones were always a bit mysterious, and it wasn't uncommon to have anonymous bidders, holed up in their chalet in Geneva or somewhere, who could fling money from afar at something they wanted badly.

"Three-fifty!" said a very blowsy woman in a pink-striped chiffon blouse and orange pants. She had dyed blonde hair pouffed up in a high beehive, and twinkly blue eye shadow. Her arms were loaded with gold bracelets that made a tinkly sound when she waved her hand to bid, like the rattle of loose change.

"I have three-fifty, do I have four?" asked the auctioneer politely.

"Four," said a firm masculine voice, calm and clear. That was Jeremy. He held up his paddle to show the auctioneer his bidding number. I was so thrilled that I froze like a deer—didn't blink, didn't move a muscle for fear of betraying our hopes, because now people were twisting around in their seats to stare at us. This was far, far worse than playing poker or betting at a casino. It took all my willpower to keep a blank face.

"I have four to the tall man in the room," the auctioneer said. "Do I hear four-fifty?"

"Four hundred and ten thousand euros!" cried a man a few rows ahead of us. He had a scraggly moustache, and his clothes, though fine, looked a bit shabby. To my surprise, the auctioneer ignored him, until the man repeated his bid.

"I'm asking four-fifty," the auctioneer said rather snippily.

"Four twenty-five," the little man suggested.

"Four-fifty!" the woman with the beehive hairdo shouted impatiently.

"Four-fifty to madame . . . do I hear five?" The auctioneer aimed his gavel at each bidder like a circus lion-tamer managing the lions—one here, one there. Somebody from the front row of online bidders murmured something, and the auctioneer picked him off with a triumphant, "I have five, to the front of the room. Do I hear five-fifty?"

There was a sudden drop, a moment of silence. "Five going once," the auctioneer said. More silence. "Going twice—"

Wordlessly, Jeremy held up his paddle. The auctioneer practically winked at him.

"Five-fifty to you, sir," he said respectfully. Holy cow, I thought. Jeremy had set his limit for 800,000 euros. Now I could swear that the two of us were breathing in tandem, in-out, in-out, be-cool, hang-on.

"Five-sixty," said the little man in the shabby suit.

The auctioneer shook his head patronizingly. "I'm sorry, but I can't accept bids in smaller denominations," he said, as if the poor guy was trying to pay with pennies. "The bid stands at five-fifty. Do I hear six hundred?"

A young Asian man in a sharply cut suit nodded to him from the phone bank. "Six!" the auctioneer cried out triumphantly. "Looking for six-fifty . . ." he said swiftly.

Jeremy lifted his paddle. I felt dizzy, as if we'd just parachuted out of an airplane and I was in free-fall, doing that agonizing count before you're allowed to open your chute. Not that I ever sky-dived. But my stomach was surely doing something like it, right now.

"Six-fifty!" the auctioneer said, accepting his bid. "I have—"

"Seven!" said the beehive-bun woman crossly.

"I have seven! Do I hear seven-fifty—?" The auctioneer was pirouetting on his toes now, to keep up with the bidding. The shabby man, seeing how fast the bidding was going and how he'd been shoved out of the competition, got up in a huff and charged down the center aisle, his feelings hurt. I saw Laurent, the Frenchman who was organizing the event, go out after him, and they went into the hotel's glass corridor. From their gestures it was obvious that Laurent was soothingly smoothing the guy's ruffled feathers, and it must have worked, because in the end they exchanged business cards and shook hands.

Jeremy held up his paddle.

"Seven-fifty to you, sir!" said the auctioneer. He raised his gavel like a music conductor bringing on the finale. "Fair warning! The bid is seven-fifty, going once . . . Go-ing twi-i-ice . . ." he said, drawing out his words like taffy to elasticize the last moment. "Do I hear eight-t-t?" he drawled. He was deliberately playing the comedian now; I'd seen him do it before, skillfully, to break the tension and embolden someone to bid. I'd found it mildly amusing then, but now I was thinking, *Oh, shut up, shut up, just take Jeremy's bid and let's swing on outa here, okay?*

"Seven-fifty . . . for the last time . . ." the auctioneer conceded. Yet even as the gavel descended with the weight of inevitability, I could hear a ruckus in the back. At first, I didn't know what it was, but it sounded fairly violent and dangerous. A last-minute bidder was trying to fight his way in, and some hotel bouncers were struggling to keep him out and quiet him down.

But he was too late. Wham! The gavel came down in a sharp rap of finality.

". . . sold to the tall gentleman! Please pay the cashier on your way out!" the auctioneer cried.

Now I let out my breath all at once, no longer needing to hide my emotion. I turned to Jeremy. He gave me the sweetest smile, which, I instantly realized, was not about the boat. It was about a dream of the future for the two of us. "Let's go," he whispered, and we got up as people in the crowd gave us the bright, encouraging smiles they reserve for young people who've won something that nobody thought they would.

Well. Except the beehive lady, who followed us out. I was careful not to catch her eye and give her any openings, but I could feel her gaze boring holes into my back, and I knew she was going to say something, I just didn't know what.

We stepped into the cool, air-conditioned glassed-in hallway that led to the hotel conference room where the cashiers were busily taking payments from bidders, when the woman suddenly grabbed my arm in a pinch that felt as if a lobster had seized me, and she spat out, in a spiteful hiss, "It's not *that* great a yacht, it doesn't even have a Jacuzzi!"

She gave me a triumphant smirk before stalking off, as if she thought she'd just ruined my day. That, apparently, took away the sting of defeat for her.

Jeremy had reached the booth where cashiers were cheerily collecting the money from successful bidders. "Congratulations, sir!" said the man who accepted Jeremy's check. Two other female cashiers looked up and beamed at him, too. At our right, there was a guy in a black suit and dark sunglasses, his face impassive, standing with his hands folded over his crotch in that strange way that security people sometimes do.

As Jeremy dealt with the necessary paperwork, I glanced ahead and saw that a little reception had been set up, outdoors, just beyond the auction tent. There was a bar-cart that resembled an ice-cream stand, with a small yellow canopy of its own, attended by five bartenders; and lots of people were milling around, drinking cocktails and nibbling on canapés. A few had the look of happy winners, but many were simply curious, admiring charity-benefit attendees, and some were hoping to spot famous people.

When we stepped out into the sunlight, I said "Phew! I'm glad we don't do this sort of thing every day. My nerves can't take it."

There was, undeniably, a certain high that came from chucking a ton of money out the window. For the first time in my life I began to understand how gambling could become addictive, and I thought of all the stories I'd heard about fortunes made and fortunes lost, all in one night, at casinos here on the Côte d'Azur. I looked at Jeremy, proud of the amazing self-control he'd displayed.

"Congratulations!" I cried. "You handled yourself beautifully."

"What say we have a drink to celebrate?" Jeremy said happily.

But before Jeremy could even take a step toward the bar-cart, a big tall guy swooped down on us, carrying a giant bottle of champagne. He was a very broad-shouldered man, dressed in a black leather jacket despite the mild weather. He wore a black shirt, a grey tie, and the biggest gold wristwatch I've ever seen in my life. I recognized him as the guy who'd tried in vain to fight his way into the auction just before the gavel went down on our yacht.

I noticed now that he was flanked by three Amazon-sized women—one blonde, one brunette, and one red-haired, all with yards and yards of flowing locks, and all of them long-waisted and long-limbed, like fashion models, with sharply chiseled facial bones that made them look like Nordic goddesses. They wore staggeringly high heels, and their bodies were decked in blindingly bright jewelry. All three of them smiled at us with dazzling white teeth, turning on the charm full-wattage.

Behind them were three tough guys in dark suits and dark reflecting sunglasses, and I realized that one of these was the thuggy-looking man who'd been watching us at the cashiers' booth. I had assumed that he was with hotel security, but now I could see that he'd been planted there to stake out and identify whoever had won the yacht. Us.

The main man in leather stepped ahead of his entourage, moving deliberately toward us in a smooth, sleek way.

"Jeremy," I whispered warningly. "He's the guy who . . ."

"I know, I know," Jeremy said. The guy extended a hand to Jeremy to shake.

"Congratulations," he said in a Russian accent. "It's a marvellous little boat." He was still holding the champagne bottle, which I could see was frosty-cold. He snapped his fingers, and a waiter appeared as if by magic. "Glasses," the Russian said. The waiter signalled another waiter, who speedily arrived with a tray of empty champagne flutes.

"Let us drink a toast to *Liesl's Dream*," the man said, handing the bottle to the waiter, who swiftly wrapped a towel around it and popped it open, then began to pour. As each glass was filled, the Russian handed them out, and he gave the first glass to me, and the second to Jeremy. Then the Goddesses.

Something floating in my glass, glinting in the sunlight, caught my eye. It was bigger than the bubbles. I peered closer. There was more than one funny flake tumbling around in my glass, like tiny glimmering fish. "What's in there?" I asked Jeremy in a low voice. The Russian heard me, and he laughed with delight.

"Gold, darling!" he said. "32 carats. Don't worry, it's fine to eat."

Edible gold flakes. Well. I found it hard to believe that you could really drink it without dying of poison or setting off some metal detector somewhere in the distant future. But the Goddesses were tilting back their long necks and quaffing it down. Cautiously

I sipped, just to say I'd done it. I'm not sure I swallowed any. Frankly, I hope not.

"I am so disappointed that I miss the bidding!" the Big Guy exclaimed. "My ladies kept me waiting today, but I thought we'd make it on time except for this peculiar change to the schedule. Something very unusual happened today, did it not?"

I glanced at the Goddesses, and I wondered if the guy meant that they'd all been—well, in bed together this morning—or if it was something as mundane as waiting for three women to finish dressing and primping for an event. I was even a little afraid for them, as if he might later have them whipped for ruining his shot at the yacht. But the Goddesses looked blank, unworried, untroubled, and just stood there glancing away vaguely, smiling when they caught the eye of another admiring male (if he looked rich and handsome and powerful enough, that is.)

Jeremy took one polite sip, then set his glass down definitely on a table, so I followed his lead and did the same. I saw that the Big Guy had been studying Jeremy, perhaps to figure out if we'd deliberately tinkered with the auction schedule to make the yacht come up earlier. Something in the Russian's lean, handsome face revealed that he decided we weren't clever enough or connected enough, and he relaxed a bit. Jeremy had quickly signalled the valet who stood at the front driveway of the hotel. Within minutes they brought his Dragonetta around. Laurent, who'd given us the original tour of the yacht, now strode up smilingly to Jeremy, gave him some information about the crew, and handed him the key.

As Jeremy took it, I saw the Russian fellow's gaze pick up the glint of gold sunlight that reflected off the key. Then the guy caught me watching him, and he stepped up to me in a powerful, commanding way, murmuring with hot breath in my ear, in a way that tickled the hair on my neck.

"Tell your boyfriend I will give him three times what he paid for it," he said in a rich, deep voice. "Then you can come and sail away with me on it. I take you all around the world and show you all the wonders." I found myself involuntarily shivering from the expert way he aimed his breath—and seductive words—at my neck.

"Um," I said. "That's very nice, thanks, but—my boyfriend and I are already booked on a different sort of cruise. Together."

This was one of those little bits of movie dialogue that I must have heard while nodding off to sleep at night in front of the TV's late-late-late show. These arcane expressions just pop out of my mouth from time to time, usually when I'm in tricky situations with men.

"But I'll be sure to give him your message," I added meaning-fully, as if to imply that he'd better back off or Jeremy would have thugs of his own beat him up. The Russian stared at me to see if I could possibly be so innocent, then he laughed good-naturedly.

Jeremy returned, took my hand firmly, said to the Russian, "Cheers, thanks," and yanked me away toward the car. We had scarcely roared off when Jeremy said to me, not without a slight ac-cusing tone, "So. How much did he offer you?"

"For the boat, or for me?" I countered.

Jeremy said, "Hah. Both!"

"For the boat, three times what you paid for it," I admitted. Jeremy made a snort of derision. "For me," I added loftily, "he 'vants to sail me around the world and show me all its vonders.'"

"And what did you say to him?" Jeremy asked.

"I told him I'd meet him down by Pier Six," I said with a straight face. "I said I'd have the keys to the yacht between my teeth."

"This Riviera is having a mighty bad influence on you," Jeremy scolded. "I suppose I'm lucky you weren't carried off by an Arab prince."

I reached into my pocketbook for my sunglasses. The purse had come unsnapped, I noticed. And sitting there, right on top, was a cream-colored business card with only one line of text on it: *Andrei Gaspar.* "Huh," I said, reading the words aloud. "How did this get here—?"

Jeremy whistled. "So that's who he was," he said. "You almost got shanghaied by one of the richest blokes in Russia. *Out* of Russia, actually. Lives in London now."

"That guy?" I asked, astonished. "Wow. When did he manage to drop his card in my . . . ?" Then, remembering his hot breath tickling my neck, I blushed. I felt indignant, and quickly rummaged through my purse to make sure nothing was missing. It wasn't.

"Well, darling," Jeremy said with a sideways smirk, "you've met your first oligarch."

Chapter Eleven

In the next few days, Jeremy and I became absorbed in all things nautical. I couldn't believe how much there was to learn about a boat. And instead of experiencing "buyer's remorse," I found that everything we learned about the yacht made us happier and happier, with pleasant surprises about how lovely it was. Jeremy had contacted Claude, the captain, who in turn would arrange to reassemble the crew, which included Brice, the first mate; Gerard, an engineer; and François, the steward who would do a little cooking.

The captain met with us at the yacht to go over some preliminary details. Claude was an attractive, athletic-looking Frenchman in his mid-fifties, with neatly clipped salt-and-pepper hair, a rugged tan, and a taut, muscular body beneath his impeccably pressed clothes. He possessed a skillful combination of both nautical authority, and deference to Jeremy, the new owner. All of this inspired confidence in having him as the man who would literally steer our ship.

He shook hands with Jeremy, and nodded respectfully to me with the kind of politely approving smile that Frenchmen, regardless of their age, give to a woman to acknowledge her female presence.

He told us that a boat, no matter how beautiful, was only as good as its upkeep. Fortunately, this one had been well cared-for, and operated every summer until very recently when it sat through a few seasons and then was suddenly, unexpectedly taken out in stormy weather.

Although he would not recommend a major refitting, he would still like to hire some day workers to paint, repair, and give the cabins and salons a thorough cleaning. He would also advise putting some of the modern safety and security equipment aboard. He suggested I select some bed linens and bath towels from a store that catered to yachts, and would monogram everything for us. He thought we should pick out a monogram for the crew's uniforms, too.

"See?" I told Jeremy. "Another reason to select fonts. I'm a pro by now."

"And you said you wished to change the name, sir?" the captain inquired, consulting his notes. "You wish to call her *Penelope's Dream*, is that correct?" he asked.

"Yes," Jeremy said firmly.

"Very well, sir. It shall be done." The captain smiled at me, because Jeremy had already introduced me as "Mademoiselle Penelope Nichols."

I couldn't even trust myself to speak until we had clambered down the gangway. My eyes misted over when I said, "Who did you name that boat for?"

"You, of course, you fool," Jeremy said.

"Well," I said, "it could have been for Aunt Pen."

"Sure, her, too," Jeremy said. "Claude says we should come back in a week and look over the boat. He says we can christen her and take a couple of friends out on a trial run which he would do anyway to see what needs to be done on her engine. Then he'll need another few weeks to put in all the modern equipment and finish spiffing her up."

"Jeremy," I said, bursting with enthusiasm, "why don't we hold a little cocktail party when we go for our test run? You know, invite our parents and maybe a few close friends."

"Sure!" he said. "I'll stock the yacht's wine cabinet, too."

Well. If you buy a fancy boat, there is no such thing as a private little party. Because apparently, it was big news among the yachting set that *Liesl's Dream* had changed hands. The original owner, it turned out, had cut a dapper figure and was beloved by many, and had raced her and won trophies, so people were curious about who the new owner was. News items showed up in papers with names like *The Yachting Gazette*.

People who weren't involved in yachting were also interested, because, I soon realized, it's very common for onlookers to gather round marinas whenever a new boat pulls into port or gets christened; everyone's hoping to spot a famous guest, like a rock musician or a fashion model or a Hollywood actor or sports hero or some international tycoon. Even if it's just plain folks like us, the photographers snap away anyhow, in case we turn out to be more important than they guessed . . . or if we crash the boat on a drunken spree and drown in the deep . . . thereby becoming newsworthy after all.

And the press, whilst snapping away, aren't the least bit shy about sidling on board for a free drink and snack. Actually we had quite a few uninvited guests that night, but Jeremy and I were initially too preoccupied to notice.

When we first came aboard, Claude and the crew, looking sharp in their new uniforms, had lined up to formally welcome "the new owners." Jeremy looked ever so nice in light-colored trousers and dark jacket; and I wore a navy chiffon dress with white piping and white sash, white ballet flats and a white scarf on my hair.

My parents were in Europe now and they turned up spiffily dressed, with Mom in a pale pink linen pantsuit and Dad in light grey pants, a white shirt and navy cashmere sweater. Dad is one of those Frenchmen who looks fit and trim no matter how much butter he eats. I inherited my brown eyes and delicate pale skin from him. Mom has copper-colored hair like mine, but she's adorably petite, and her face has that wry, watchful look that intelligent English women have. They were as eager to see us again as they were to view the yacht, and they listened, wide-eyed, when I regaled them with the story of the auction. Jeremy and I took them on a tour; my father was fascinated by the kitchen stove, and would have liked nothing better than to test it out, right then and there, but he behaved himself by going back up on deck to mingle with the other guests.

When we returned, Aunt Sheila, Jeremy's mum, had arrived. She was positively stunning in a violet-grey dress, seeming perfectly at home at a yacht party, youthful as ever, with blonde straight bangs across her forehead and a cool Britannia attitude. She and my parents settled in together on the teak steamer chairs on the aft deck, and François brought them champagne.

Jeremy had not invited office friends from London, but one of our guests was a young French lawyer from the Parisian branch of his firm, who'd originally helped us with the settling of Great-Aunt Penelope's will, and was now handling the legal transaction of the boat. This was Louis, an impeccable fellow with curly dark hair. He told me that the vivacious—and slightly rapacious—Severine, the inheritance lawyer who'd once been after Jeremy, was not only married now but was expecting her first child.

"I'll bet she still looks great," I said in a low voice. Louis smiled.

"But you look radiant," Louis said diplomatically. "It's nice to be happy, yes?"

"Penny Nichols!" cried Erik as he came aboard. My former boss, a terrific set designer, still looked like a big Irish wolfhound even though he'd cut his wild white hair shorter now. Right next to him was his partner, the wiry, dark-haired Tim. They were already in town to pick up a TV award for one of their movie sets.

"Darling, you look positively chic," Erik said approvingly. "Let's sit down this week and have a real chat. Bring Jeremy. Lunch, day after tomorrow?" And he gave me the name of a place where he'd be meeting all day with movie and TV people.

"Need someone to spin records for you tonight on that marvellous Victrola?" Tim offered, as we moved into the main salon. I wasn't sure if Jeremy would let anybody handle that particular toy, but Jeremy said magnanimously, "Sure, that would be great."

Lest you think we were the only ones playing music and making noise and being snapped by photographers, let me tell you, there were plenty of other parties in the harbor that night. In fact, some revellers were making a night of hopping from one boat to another because they'd lined up four boats in a row for their big bash. It was a little raucous at first, like a posher version of, well, tailgating at a football game. But it was fun to watch so many people having a good time, as if the whole jaunty yachting culture was at play, with boats coming and going, and big ships dropping anchor farther out to sea, sending their guests zooming into shore on zippy little "launches" so that they could dine at restaurants on land.

All in all, we had a good crowd of about twenty-five people . . . not counting the press and a few other strangers. Our guests were milling around the boat, some congregating on the deck, others hanging out in the main salon. As Brice and François moved about carrying drinks and canapés on silver trays, I noticed, over by the cocktail bar, a rather sad-looking, handsome man who stood alone, gazing at the crowd, and speaking with a German accent when he accepted a glass of champagne. He was in his mid-to-late thirties, with wavy yellow-blond hair, and greenish-blue eyes that glanced around the room as if taking in every detail. He wore a suit of fine linen woven in various shades of green and blue and brown, with a soft beige linen shirt.

At that particular moment Claude and Jeremy summoned me to christen the boat. As I walked toward them, the sad-looking German saw me glance at him and he nodded, bowed slightly and said, "The very best of luck to you."

I nodded uncertainly, then reached Jeremy and the captain, who handed me a bottle of champagne.

"Oh, God," I said, stricken, thinking of everything that could possibly go wrong and somehow be a bad omen. What if the bottle wouldn't break? Or, suppose it shattered in a million pieces and sent shards flying everywhere to cut up the guests?

"Don't be shy," Jeremy encouraged. "Go for it."

So I marched right up, leaned over, squinted in determination, wound up like a baseball batter, and said boldly, "I christen thee *Penelope's Dream!*"

And . . . *Thwack!* It was kinda tricky, but I managed to crack that bottle on the first whack without slicing myself to ribbons or making any horrible dents in the boat. Everyone broke into applause, and the press even took pictures. So then I felt like Queen Elizabeth. Nothing to it.

"Whew!" I said under my breath. "Glad that's sorted." I beamed back at the smiling crowd, and noticed that the sad-looking German had vanished.

Then I spotted a familiar but uninvited face in the crowd—a man coming purposefully toward me with a broad grin. "Holy smokes, Jeremy, look who's here," I said under my breath.

Jeremy looked up sharply as good old cousin Rollo loped toward us, reaching out to shake Jeremy's hand; and he gave me a wet kiss on the cheek, acting like a long-lost friend instead of the relative who'd tried to swindle our inheritance right out from under our feet.

"Congratulations!" he exclaimed, then roared with laughter at the expression on our faces. He hadn't changed a bit. Wealthy as he is, his suits always look as if he slept in them on a park bench. His pouchy face still had the look of a burnt-out con man, and when he leaned near me I caught that whiff of stale tobacco, spilt whisky, and late nights in seedy bars with dubious women. Rollo is actually my mom's cousin. He is what you might call a man of leisure. This leaves him lots of free time to collect various antiques and artifacts which have more than once been of dubious origin. It crossed my mind that Rollo was just the sort of fellow who'd read up on the latest yachting and auction news.

"I was over at Monte," he said easily, "and heard all about it. What fun, eh?" he added genially as he snatched a drink from the steward's tray. He was already holding a small plate piled high with assorted canapés from the sideboard in the salon. There wasn't a single bit of food he'd missed.

"Monte, eh?" Jeremy said, and I knew that we were both picturing Rollo at the roulette table in Monte Carlo, already gambling away his portion of the inheritance. And when he ran out of dosh, well, guess who he'd come to for more?

Yet, there is something oddly vulnerable about him, despite his weaseliness, which makes all of us feel that when he stumbles too hard, he'll need the family to protect him. And, I have to admit, there wasn't a trace of rancor or ill-will in his face, voice or gestures. He seemed genuinely pleased . . . at least, to have relatives that he considered well-heeled and able to offer him even more of the finer things in life. It was as if we had suddenly become people worth knowing.

"Penny, my dear, I hope you have many pleasant voyages aboard this vessel," Rollo said enthusiastically.

"Sir?" Claude said to Jeremy. "We are ready to embark on our trial run."

Rollo respectfully backed away, but I kept an eye on him and noticed him studying all the little trinkets and fancy items aboard. I even saw him pick up the little antique hourglass and study it, and I half-expected him to slip it into his pocket, but he put it back, very reverently, exactly where it belonged.

Jeremy, seeing that I was eyeing Rollo, whispered to me, "Don't worry. I told Brice to keep an eye on Old Sticky Fingers."

And suddenly the crew was rapidly hauling up the funny balloon-like bumpers that keep your boat from knocking into other boats or scraping against the dock, and the deck hands were tossing up the ropes that tethered us. The ship's bell clanged and the engine cleared its throat and everybody clapped for it, and the whole boat rumbled a bit.

"All ahead!" cried the captain. Jeremy led me to the front deck, which faced out of the harbor, because it was berthed with its back-end at the dock. Our guests all congregated on the decks, clinging to the rails expectantly, and, in a moment of unparalleled magic, *Penelope's Dream* went chugging out toward the sea.

Other boats parked beside us seemed to float into retreat, in that funny way where at first you're not sure who's moving, you or them. Then you realize it's you who are going forward, not they who are going backward. A few curious ducks paddled alongside us but soon gave up the chase. At first, we moved slowly, until we were clear of the harbor. Then, we picked up speed. Now the whole coastline began to rapidly recede as we pulled out into the wider sea. The beautiful Mediterranean opened her great blue arms in welcome.

Jeremy squeezed my hand and I squeezed back. Still standing on the fore deck at the railing, I could feel the salty spray rising up in a joyous mist as we sliced through it. Within minutes, it seemed, the harbor had completely retreated into the backdrop, and as the boat turned slightly to the right, I saw that everything on the coast's rising cliffs looked doll-like in miniature. The pocket of sea that surrounded us seemed to expand and grow wider, and wider still, until we had the delicious, heady experience of being released from the land, set free upon the open sea and open sky with nothing to hem us in, tie us down or hold us back. It was almost like taking off in a balloon, with the wind pushing us along in a great big *pouff* of good luck.

Other boats passed us and honked their horns, and their passengers waved. We saw the slow, purposeful ferry that goes out to the island of Corsica, painted a gay yellow. As we sped along, we passed a monstrous megayacht followed by a fleet of its accompanying little adjunct boats, which trailed after it like ducklings following a mama duck. Claude, our captain, seemed to know about every yacht in the bay. He told us that the whole entourage belonged to an oil baron, and actually had a helipad and small chopper on board.

Jeremy and I walked back along the side galley to the aft deck, where most of our guests were relaxing. I found my parents still tucked up happily in the steamer chairs, chatting with Aunt Sheila. Jeremy went to get their drinks refreshed. My father rose, stretched his legs and came up to stand beside me at the railing.

"Well, little Penn-ee, how does it feel to have your very own boat?" he asked teasingly.

"A bit scary, but wonderful," I admitted cheerfully. "No matter how comfy a yacht is, the sea is always bigger." I had suddenly realized that my compact little personal universe was just bobbing along on the surface of a globe that itself is whirling around in the vastness of time and space.

"In life, it is good to take chances on a dream," Dad chuckled. My father had spent his youth in France taking care of his mother until she died, but he'd managed to get his university degree while working as a chef; and he'd pursued his dream by coming to the States, where he met Mom, who had also made a break with England to seek her future abroad. When they told stories of their courtship days, it was almost like listening to a bedtime story that grows sweetly familiar as you hear it repeated. I'd felt protected by their cozy stories; but I wondered if I'd ever have stories of my own to tell. Now, as an adult, it was fun to offer my father a chance to relax, lean his elbows on the railing and tilt his head up to the sun. The nice thing about chasing a dream is that you get to share it with people you love.

As the wind rippled around us, Dad told me that he and my mother would be visiting friends in France, then they'd head back to London before flying home to the States. We both glanced at my mother, just as Rollo came over to talk to her. Mom smiled politely, but I could tell that she was rather alarmed at the sight of him.

"Rollo invited himself," I told Dad.

"Ah. Then I had better go rescue your mother," my father drawled. I moved along the decks, stopping to make sure that I'd spent some time with each guest. Jeremy was doing the same, and now and again we'd look up at each other and smile.

Since this little maiden voyage was a trial run to see what things worked properly and what needed tinkering, we trailed along only about as far as Antibes, then turned to head back. On the way, majestic sailboats appeared suddenly from around the bend, their sails flapping like proud swans. By now our guests had gathered together on the aft deck, and people began singing, in harmony and counterpoint, applauding anyone whose voice was especially entertaining. Sometimes I'd see a member of the crew, stopping to assess if things were going all right, and then he'd smile in amusement at the guests' evident pleasure.

Finally, the now-familiar harbor at Nice came rising up into view, and *Penelope's Dream* slowed her speed. Soon we were gliding past the boats that were too big to park at the dock. As we passed an enormous anchored yacht, I heard a strangely familiar sound which at first I could not identify because it seemed so out of place.

Ka-thunka thunka. Ka-thunka thunka. I peered at the boat.

"Is that a basketball court on the aft deck?" I asked in utter disbelief.

Ka-thunka thunk. "Yep," Jeremy said, shaking his head. He thinks Americans will put a basketball net on anything, everywhere they go. (Maybe he's right.)

Then *Penelope's Dream* backed right into her snug berth. Lots of other people on the quay stopped by to admire her, too, and to wish us well. The sun, which made the sea sparkle like a movie star's sequined blue gown, had become a flaming red-gold ball, that made the wood and brass fixtures on the boat just glow with polished glory; and, while the sky was still blue, the moon shot up out of the sea as if it had been fired from a cannon, rising high against the velvet backdrop of the sky, and hanging there like a great big pearl.

Our guests began to drift away, calling out their fond goodbyes, until it was just Jeremy and me (and the crew). Slowly, the stars came out, one by one at first, and then more, as if a magician had taken a magic wand and was lighting lamps for those at sea. The old-fashioned music playing from our Victrola echoed along the harbor like ghostly voices from the past.

Standing at the fore deck, I heard recordings of lilting singers from long ago, like Caruso and Chaliapin, floating toward me from the gramophone. Soon Jeremy came and stood by my side.

"We got an amazing collection of old classical records with that Victrola," he enthused. "Claude says the owner used to just sit on the boat in the harbor, smoke his pipe and listen to Beethoven. People could hear the symphonies wafting out across the water at night." He breathed deeply. "That's exactly what I'm going to do. Just sit on deck and listen to the Victrola and chill out." It was the first time I'd seen him look really happy at the prospect of kicking back and taking time off.

We stood there, side by side, a bit longer, watching as the stars intensified. The captain wished us good-night as we finally left the boat and climbed into Jeremy's car. Claude had told us that the trial run was very successful. Once the final tweaks and upgrading were done, we would lay in food, water, and supplies. The boat would be refueled. And then, as Jeremy said, *Penelope's Dream* would be on her way. And we would embark on our very special summer.

Part Four

Chapter Twelve

At five-thirty the next morning in the villa, we were awakened unceremoniously by a loud, startling *Oooo-ooo-wooo-WHOOSH!* sound that rattled the entire house, and even caused the chirping birds to shut up and listen in dread. It had begun as a low rumble, which crested in a loud boom, as if someone had beat a gong . . . in the basement.

Jeremy was already out the bedroom door before I could exclaim, "Oh my God, what was that?" We tore downstairs.

"It came from the cellar," I said unnecessarily. He picked up a flashlight and shone it ahead of us, down the basement stairwell.

"Oh, bloody hell," he said wearily. I peered around him.

Ahoy, mate. The entire basement was flooded, and anything that wasn't nailed down was floating merrily by. Empty cans and bottles (Great-Aunt Penelope had been a saver of "useful" things) and ancient packets of garden seeds and even a punctured bicycle tire.

Jeremy, a man of few words (particularly when he hasn't even had his morning coffee) was already on the telephone with Denby, who, in addition to fixing up my auto, now turned out to be a useful resource for getting workmen to show up in a hurry. He suggested a plumber and said, "Mention my name, I fixed his Ferrari."

As Jeremy dialed the plumber's number he muttered, "A plumber with a Ferrari. That will surely bankrupt us."

The plumber was actually a very cheerful fellow named Jean-Paul. He arrived in thigh-high boots, a pair of overalls that were stained with grime and that orange stuff that collects in pipes, and he had a toolkit in hand. He sloshed around downstairs while I made coffee with hot milk in big cereal-bowl sized cups which the French use for their morning *café au lait*. I offered Jean-Paul a cup, which he accepted, as he explained that something had plugged up a pipe and caused it to burst. It could be anything, including a snake or animal that had nested, having assumed, since nobody was occupying the house, that we wouldn't be needing our pipes.

"C'est normal," Jean-Paul said, "these things are bound to happen when you start really using a house that has been asleep so long." He gave us his estimate and explained that the work ought to be done right away, so that the water didn't soak the wood and require *détermitage* (termite control).

"Okay, okay," Jeremy said hastily. Since he had the plumber here, he asked the guy to take a look at the bathrooms and toilets upstairs, which he suspected required work. Jean-Paul made his assessment; one of the toilets needed replacement, and there were a few pipes that looked suspicious.

"Know what I think?" Jeremy told me as Jean-Paul set to work. "We might as well have the renovations done all at once, right now. The plasterer, the electrician, the carpenter, everybody. Remember those loose floor boards on the upstairs landing? You nearly killed yourself on those the first time we came here."

"Pardon me," I reminded, "but where are we going to live?"

"On the good ship *Penelope's Dream*," Jeremy said enthusiastically.

"Could we really do that?" I asked, intrigued.

"Why not?" Jeremy said. "Once the upgrades are done. You said we should cruise around the Med, stopping at all the places we've always wanted to visit. We can always do an overnight in an hotel."

"That sounds great!" I cried. "Saint Tropez, Monte Carlo, Portofino, Amalfi . . ."

"I'll make the phone calls for some of the repairs now, while I might still catch these guys. Then, let's go down to the harbor and plot our course on the maps," Jeremy said. "We're supposed to meet Claude at noon anyway."

"Okay, but don't forget, we've got lunch tomorrow with Erik and Tim in Nice at the Negresco," I reminded.

"The Negresco! Why'd they pick that?"

"Erik's got all kinds of meetings lined up there. But you have to come, they're dying to chat with you because they didn't get to really talk to you at the party," I added.

"These are the guys you worked with on those movies, right?" Jeremy said warily. "Erik's the set designer and what does Tim do?"

"Practically everything else on the set—he's the prop-master, but he coordinates stuff with the wardrobe people, and with me, so that it's all historically accurate."

"They want to find out if I'm worthy of you. Okay, I can do it," Jeremy said cheerfully. Then he asked curiously, "Do you miss the work?"

"It hasn't been *that* long," I said. "I'm not a workaholic, like you. But you're improving, now that you've won your yacht and have taken your first class at 'The Riviera's Training School for Bon Vivants.' "

"Very funny," Jeremy said. "Finish your breakfast and let's go."

Chapter Thirteen

Looking back on it now, I feel kind of sorry for us. I mean, we started out happily tooling along the *moyenne corniche* road from Antibes to Nice, the wind in our hair, the sun at our backs, the sea sparkling to our right, the sky overhead a soft, encouraging blue. On such a morning you want to sing with joy, and we actually did, tootling along, singing every song we could think of that had boats or the sea in them. It started with the radio, when we found an English-language station that was playing *By the sea, by the sea, by the beautiful sea . . .*

And then we swung around the curve of the harbor, parked the car and headed for our boat's little parking slot . . .

. . . and stopped dead in our tracks. I turned around in confusion, mentally retracing my steps. For a moment I completely lost my bearings. "Hey, that's weird," I said. "We must have passed . . ."

"No, we didn't," Jeremy said tensely. We stood there, rooted to the spot. Where *Penelope's Dream* was supposed to be berthed. The parking space in the harbor. For our boat. Which was not there. Gone. Vanished. Zippo.

At first we just couldn't believe it. Surely there was some mistake. Were we standing at the wrong end of the pier or something?

Totally flummoxed, I stared at the yawning slot of blue sea that was gently rocking to and fro. A terrifyingly empty slot. Nothing there except for an occasional swan paddling contentedly through it, and some seagulls overhead, circling and swooping and keening sadly. But as far as classic yachts were concerned, well, there was none. Just Jeremy, me and the empty patch of sea.

Plish, splish.

We were silent, for what seemed like a very, very long time.

"But . . . but . . ." I spluttered, still unable to believe it. "Whah—where—what happened to it?"

Jeremy swallowed hard, then said the dreaded word. "Stolen."

"Maybe Claude took it out for a test run," I said. "Sure, that's it."

"No," Jeremy said positively. "He said it had to be refueled and the engine would need a tuning that will take all day. Claude is out picking up equipment to update the boat with all those safety features which . . ." The irony of all this dawned on him, ". . . help prevent theft. This—is—a disaster."

"Maybe the harbormaster had it moved," I suggested.

Jeremy considered this and said, as if he hoped but remained unconvinced, "Let's look around." We got back in the car, and he rapidly drove around the harbor. I could tell how upset he was by the way he took the turns more rapidly, cutting it closer than usual. He stopped abruptly at the harbormaster's booth, went inside, then rapidly returned.

"We'd better go alert the police," Jeremy said in a dry, cracked voice.

At the far end of the harbor, two uniformed marine gendarmes were sitting in their office, which was just beyond the yacht club-house. Their headquarters was a fairly large room with two desks and computers, and lots of file cabinets. A middle-aged policeman with a small moustache and a barrel of a chest, and grey hair at the temples, was on the telephone when we came in. A younger one, who was very tall, thin and alert, looked up at us immediately. He had a sweet boyish quality of wanting to help you stop being unhappy. So his smile of welcome faded as he saw the stricken looks on our faces.

Jeremy grimly told them what had happened, and the older man, who hung up the phone, listened intently, asking the usual preliminary questions such as who else had access to the boat—friends, family, crew, perhaps—and might have taken it out for a morning spin, etcetera, etcetera. We explained that the yacht was still being worked on, and the man began nodding before Jeremy finished explaining.

"Mais oui," he said with a heavy sigh, "I am afraid we have seen it before. 'Le boat-jacking,' " he said, in that way that the French will use English words which do not have a French equivalent, usually reserved for things that are too dumb or awful to be French.

"Does this happen a lot?" I asked, aghast. The older man shrugged. I turned to the younger one, and tried again, in French, first asking the young one's name.

"Moi? Je m'appelle Thierry," he said. And he explained, very sympathetically, that as yachts were becoming bigger, more ostentatious and more expensively equipped with priceless items, the Côte d'Azur, which had long been a playground for the rich, was a prime target for professional thieves seeking such enormously tempting floating treasure chests.

"Unfortunately, it's not too hard to do," Thierry remarked. "Some yachts are easier to steal than a car—or even a parked motorbike! Because the owners are often absent, so a thief could watch, and plan, and calculate when to strike. All he has to do is break the lock on the cabin door, and *voilà!* It's done."

This was too much for Jeremy. He had been silently stewing,

and now he was totally incensed. "Well, if it's such a bloody common occurrence, why can't you put a stop to it?" he exclaimed. "Doesn't anybody watch these harbors, for Christ's sake?"

The older man, who had quickly reported the theft into a radio, turned around slowly in his chair. "It is usually the custom for the owner to keep a man aboard his boat overnight to watch out for this sort of thing, now that the season has begun," he said.

"My captain is on his way over and you can ask him," Jeremy said testily.

The older cop turned to Thierry and said something rapidly in French, and they had a brief conference *sotto voce,* during which I heard the older guy mutter that he surely didn't need *le rosbif* to tell him how to do his job, and would Thierry please get him out of his office while they tried to locate our boat.

Once a Frenchman makes reference to an Englishman's fondness for roast beef, well, the diplomatic thing to do is to hustle said Englishman out of the office. Thierry saw Jeremy's thunderous expression, turned to me and said apologetically, "We will try to find it, I assure you. When your captain arrives we will question him about everything, all the crew members, everyone. We know these men very well, so we do not really suspect them, but perhaps they have heard something that may be useful."

"Is there anything else that we can do with you, together, to help?" I asked quickly. "Right away, before it's too late?"

Thierry looked at me sympathetically, then turned to the older man and spoke quickly again in French as if asking permission for something. The older man grunted.

"Come. I take you out in the patrol boat," Thierry said brightly. "We will check the coves and see if we can find anything." It was a good thing that Jeremy was out the door before I heard the older man mutter, *"Impossible."*

Despite his misery, Jeremy was temporarily impressed with Thierry's patrol boat, equipped with an actual machine gun. It was a white boat with a blue and a red stripe on the side, like the French flag. It must have had a very powerful engine because we roared out of the harbor in no time at all. Sailboats floated by us, and fishing boats which had cast their nets; many of their owners waved at Thierry, who waved back. Thierry called out to some of the fishermen, and slowed down to pull alongside them and lean over and ask them if they'd seen anything, regarding a boat *classique*. Each time, they shook their heads, then looked at Jeremy and me.

Thierry acted personally sorry for the whole matter, just out of common human sympathy. He kept assuring us, over his shoulder, that they would do all that they could to find it. Jeremy was mute as a stone the whole time, so Thierry found himself talking to me instead, his brown eyes warm and expressive.

"It's difficult, you know," he said, expertly steering the patrol boat, with strong, tanned forearms. "With stolen yachts, there is no formal international roster listing those that are missing, the way that there is with stolen art. Some of the newer boats have the tracking systems on board, but many, like yours, do not."

I held my breath at this, and heard Jeremy growl unintelligibly.

"Don't you have video cameras watching all the piers?" I asked.

Thierry coughed delicately, having to explain to me what was already obvious to Jeremy. "In some, but not all places. You see," he drawled with a touch of irony, "at night, people like to be happy on their boats. They do not like so much to be watched in their comings and goings, and to have all the world know about how they spend their leisure time."

Although Thierry was speaking perfect English, Jeremy now translated what he meant.

"It means they don't want their wives to know about the girls they bring on board when the wives are back home," Jeremy said gloomily. "Plus other questionable pastimes, like drug-dealing, art-smuggling, trading in stolen stuff from unauthorized archaeological digs, exchanging political favors, and top-secret business deals. They don't want a record of those goings-on. They'd rather take their chances, and use their own private security."

"Oh," I said, feeling suddenly very unworldly. "Huh."

"We once stopped a boat that was full of exotic pets," Thierry agreed. "Giant turtles. Big, big snakes. Endangered birds."

I started thinking about all those awful stories about under-aged girls kidnapped into prostitution, and desperate boat people from poor African countries packed onto flimsy boats that capsized and left them trying to swim to shore in an ill-fated attempt to get past immigration officials. There was, after all, a shady side to the sunny Riviera.

Thierry very matter-of-factly told me about all the priceless treasures that people kept on their yachts, such as expensive wine collections. This made me cringe, thinking of all the wine that Jeremy had just last night put aboard the boat. I glanced apprehensively at Jeremy's profile, which remained stony as he stared out to sea, pretending he hadn't heard.

Thierry continued, unperturbed at Jeremy's silence. He explained that another reason the Riviera was a prime target for rings of professional yacht thieves was because they knew that all they had to do was to take a boat a scant twelve miles out to sea, and then it was in international waters, beyond the jurisdiction of the local police.

"So they take the boats to Tunisia or Malta," he explained, "and they register them with a fake offshore company, because they have repainted and disguised them. Then they might take a boat to, say, the Black Sea, and sell it to a buyer who isn't too fussy to know the details."

"Or who commissioned the theft in the first place," Jeremy said dryly.

"It's possible, it's possible," Thierry said.

The mention of the Black Sea made me prick up my ears, and I must have glanced at Jeremy, because Thierry looked up alertly and said, "Do you have any enemies? Is there anyone you think might want to steal your boat?"

We both hesitated. Then Jeremy told him about the Russian guy with his entourage of glamour girls and tough guys, and the lady with the beehive hairdo at the auction who was bidding so vigorously against us, and even the poor guy whose smaller bids were refused by the auctioneer. Thierry asked about what they'd all said and done. When I explained that the Russian guy had offered to buy the boat, Thierry asked me to tell him, word for word, exactly what the man had said to me. So I told him. When I got to the part where the guy suggested that I dump Jeremy and sail away with him around the world, Thierry grinned.

"Wait a minute," Jeremy said. "I thought you were kidding about that. Did he actually *say* that to you?"

"I *told* you that," I said.

"No, you didn't," Jeremy said. "Not in those words. I'd have remembered, if you'd told me those exact words."

"I certainly *did* tell you!" I said, feeling cranky myself. After all, we'd been awakened at an ungodly hour by that burst pipe. And our plans of living on our yacht for a couple of weeks had just been torpedoed. Plus, I was touchy because I had the feeling that Jeremy was looking for somebody to blame for this rotten mishap, and there I was, the gal who told him to go ahead, live a little, chase after his dream boat.

Our bickering didn't seem to disturb Thierry, who appeared to take a philosophical attitude toward lovers. He just grinned, and kept his speedboat chugging around in the inky Mediterranean Sea, until a police helicopter came flying overhead. Thierry waved to its pilot. It transpired that the grumpy older gendarme had actually swung into action and sent the chopper out to look for our yacht. The pilot would pick up where we left off, so it was time for us to head back to shore.

I thanked Thierry and we returned to his office, where Jeremy filled out some paperwork. Then Claude, our captain, showed up, looking utterly aghast, and the whole thing started all over again. It was horrible. Jeremy tried gamely to be calm and English and civilized about the whole thing, but I could tell that it was just tearing him up inside, and by now, his face was ashen.

"They can't have gone far!" Claude exclaimed, genuinely distressed. "There simply wasn't enough fuel." But we all knew that a boat could be towed by a determined, professional thief. Claude told Thierry that one of the deck-hands was supposed to have stayed aboard overnight to avert exactly this sort of catastrophe. Claude had called the man's mobile, and found out that the guy had indeed strayed away last night because he'd met a woman from the bar at the harbor, and gone to her place for a little supper, and . . .

Jeremy looked like he wanted to choke somebody. I have to admit, I almost dreaded going back to the villa with him. We drove home in utter silence, except for one stupid remark he made in response to me, when I'd said, "Well, at least we've got Thierry on our side. I know he'll try."

To which Jeremy responded, "Well, he's on *your* side, for certain. You two were jolly mates today, I must say." He was only half-joking.

"Don't be daft," I chided. "I was only playing good cop to your bad cop." I craned my neck and peered at him, and ordinarily, he would have smiled. The worst part was, he tried to smile. And failed, miserably.

When we got home, the villa was a fine mess, with the plumber and his men hammering and banging about. Even if our nerves weren't already shot, this would have done us in. "It's probably better if we stay out of their way, go outside for a swim," I suggested quickly. "They'll be gone by suppertime. The bedroom looks okay. Just don't get up in the middle of the night to go to the bathroom without your shoes on. I saw pipes and screws all over the floor."

"Fine, whatever," Jeremy said listlessly.

Outside by the pool, it seemed to me that the birds were chirping mournfully for us, and the squirrels were clicking their teeth, *tsk tsk tsk*. Jeremy must have heard it, too, because later, as he wrapped himself in a towel and sank onto a lawn chair, he muttered, "That's what I get for putting my heart and soul into a fool's dream. Never again," he vowed. "Serves me right."

"Aw, come on," I said, "don't go all Puritanical on me now. Where's that hedonist I know and adore?"

"Sunk, off the coast of Nice," he said morosely.

Chapter Fourteen

It wasn't any better the next morning. Not at all. We were up early, to have breakfast before the carpenter arrived and the plumber returned, and as I staggered into the kitchen to make coffee, Jeremy was already on the telephone, and kept taking calls all through breakfast. While I was clearing up the kitchen, he came in and announced with spookily cheerful gallows humor, "Well, just when you think it can't get worse . . ."

"What now?" I asked in dread.

"There was a delay back at the home office, and the insurance papers haven't been fully processed and signed," he announced, with horrified mirth. "If we play our cards just right, we might manage to be entirely, totally out of luck."

"Harold will sort this out for you," I said.

But Jeremy looked slightly alarmed and said, "The last thing I want is for the office to find out about this." He added gloomily, "I suppose we'll hang about here for a few more days, then head back to London."

"London!" I exclaimed. "What for?"

"What else can we do?" he said. "We can't stay here inhaling all this sawdust and plaster while the villa is being repaired . . ."

At the mention of London—and the image of Lydia still ensconced in Jeremy's building—my mind started whirling rapidly.

"I think that would be a mistake," I said quickly. "We should
stick to our plans of travelling, so we can keep checking in here to
make certain they're still looking for the boat. Somebody's sure to
have seen something." Then I added, "Wow, I almost forgot. We
have a lunch date with Erik and Tim today."

"Can't we postpone it?" Jeremy asked. "I'm not very good company today. Or else, perhaps you should go alone—and at least get
a breather from me," he said, as if he felt a little ashamed of himself
for losing even a modicum of self-restraint.

"I'm afraid to leave you alone," I said, only half-joking.

But Jeremy rallied enough to give me a firm nod and say, "No,
no. I'll be fine. I have to straighten out this mess, and that wouldn't
be any picnic for you. Go, and give them my apologies, and tell
your friends I look forward to seeing them next time. I'll drop you
off at the hotel on my way to the harbor."

Actually, I was glad to go alone, so I could blurt out the whole
disaster and soak up all the sympathy I could get. Whereas when
you're with a boyfriend, he never wants you to tell other people
about your troubles because he thinks it reflects badly on his male
competence. But as a woman, I knew that life is full of screw-ups,
and the only way to get on top of them is to rip 'em apart in conversation and cut them down to size.

I found Erik and Tim sitting beneath a white carousel pony
with a blue saddle, in a famously eccentric bar/restaurant in one of
the most elegant and expensive hotels on the Promenade des Anglais.
The dining room was completely decked out with rows of vintage
merry-go-round ponies and decorations. Amid walnut panelling,
velvet armchairs, low-key lighting, fascinating tapestries, and portraits of famous people, the booths were a raspberry-colored pink

with yellow trim and yellow-and-white tablecloths. Erik and Tim had been holding court here all morning, meeting with colleagues and friends.

We had worked together for years, in fact, Erik was the one who launched me in my career as an historical researcher for films. So he took one look at my face and said instantly, "Oh my God, what *happened?*"

"Somebody stole our boat!" I cried, slipping into my side of the booth.

"What!" Erik and Tim chorused. At their sympathetic clucking, I felt like a little kid who's been very brave up till now, but at the mere sound of paternal comfort, becomes ready to bust out bawling. I told them the whole sorry story of how *Penelope's Dream* was rapidly turning into Penelope's Nightmare.

The waiter, at first attentive, saw that something was amiss, and politely backed off. But now Erik said, "You poor baby. You need sustenance. Here, I'll order for you. Let's see, some white asparagus salad and then something hot for nourishment, like grilled fish with fennel." He signalled the waiter and gave him the order.

"Thanks. Well, anyway, Jeremy and I are now homeless," I announced dramatically.

"You mean you are 'all at sea'?" Tim couldn't resist punning, and I groaned. "I suppose you have no idea who stole the yacht," he mused, more seriously. "But are you sure you haven't missed any clues?"

Erik was gazing upward at the sky, as he does when he's thinking deeply. "It seems to have been outfitted carefully, with no expense spared. Who was the original owner?"

"Some old guy that used to race it," I said. "He's well-known around here, but I don't know much about him."

Tim declared that the French police were efficient and effective, so we surely had not seen the last of *Penelope's Dream*. This made me feel enormously better, as did the excellent lunch.

Then, ready to abandon the whole miserable subject, I was grateful when Erik regaled me with stories of the latest fiascos, as he called them, on the sets of the historical bio-pics that they produced with Bruce for cable TV. They had now branched out into "historical" stories of ghosts, witches, séances, and other tales of the supernatural.

"Which, to my humble prop-master's mind, go beyond the realm of 'history,'" Tim said.

"But, you'd be surprised at how many generals, kings, and politicians believed in the power of tarot cards and tea leaves and astrology," I said.

Erik sighed tragically. "We miss you dreadfully! I don't know what to do with these new kids out of college, they are so careless with the facts. Not at all like you, Penny dear. You were so blissfully meticulous. When you go back into business, whatever you choose, please leave room for a little consulting for us. We are merely floundering without you."

"So is Paul," Tim added slyly, referring to the cable network executive who'd been a former boyfriend of mine, "why, he's had a broken engagement with a gal from Scarsdale who met somebody else—apparently more important than Paul—at a health club. Well, honey, she dashed away with him a mere *two weeks* before she was supposed to tie the knot with Paul."

The waiter smiled in relief at us, seeing that things were going better, as he deposited the check. Erik was the only person I know who, since the inheritance, still offered to pay for lunch instead of automatically expecting me to do it. He insisted today, and I tried to argue, but I somehow knew that it was best to let him do it. However, I made him promise to let me pick it up next time.

"By the way, what happened with Jeremy's ex-wife?" Erik asked.

I filled them in, and explained that Jeremy was already threatening to go back to London. They both shook their heads vehemently. "Well, don't *let* him!" Erik exclaimed.

At that moment my mobile phone rang. I answered it, spoke briefly, then turned to my two friends, wide-eyed.

"Oh, dear," said Erik. "This looks serious. I sense there's more trouble ahead for the Homeless Heiress and Her Hero."

"That was Jeremy," I said. "The gendarmes have just found *Penelope's Dream*."

"What!" Erik and Tim chorused. Then, "Where?"

"Sitting in the harbor at Villefranche." Thierry had been out in his patrol boat, and spotted it.

"Villefranche!" Tim said, intrigued. "Isn't that where the Rolling Stones hung out to record *Exile on Main Street*?"

"That's a spooky place," Eric warned. "All those dark, narrow streets. I was once accosted by gypsies there, too. I'm not kidding!"

I rose quickly. "I have to go," I said. "Jeremy's going to pick me up on his way from Antibes." I turned back to kiss Erik and Tim goodbye.

"Beware London," Tim whispered to me.

"Good luck, and when you get home, *call me*," Erik said, looking amused. "I want to hear every last word!"

I went outside, where the cabs and doormen were busily orchestrating the arrivals and departures of hotel guests. Jeremy came motoring up to the front door and just barely stopped the car long enough for me to hop in. Then we roared off to Villefranche.

Chapter Fifteen

Villefranche is indeed an intriguing corner of the Côte d'Azur. An old military port, it's a very deep, natural harbor with a forbidding stone fortress and an antiquated, scary-looking eighteenth-century building that was once used as a prison for galley slaves. From the main, corniche road we had to drive down, down, down, spiralling along hairpin turns with very narrow, walled roads that eventually took us to sea level. With its sheer height and old stone architecture, Villefranche is breathtakingly beautiful, yet on its labyrinthine roads, one wrong turn can send you into a walled-in, deserted cul-de-sac, gloomy in the shadows of mysterious old houses packed in cheek by jowl, so that it can be dark even in daylight. I could see why Cocteau used it as a setting for the underworld in his film *Orpheus*.

And Erik was right; when we paused at a traffic light, aggressive gypsy girls wearing tank tops and jeans that left their midriffs bare, accosted us. They were carrying buckets of dirty water, and brandishing squeegees, trying to intimidate every alarmed driver who stopped at the light into paying for their dubious windshield-washing.

When we reached the quay, Thierry looked very excited as he

stood on the deck of *Penelope's Dream* waiting for us, just like a hunting spaniel who has been keeping his eye on a pheasant, and is very proud of having found it for you. I praised him to the hilt, whether Jeremy liked it or not. Thierry explained that the boat-jackers had apparently dropped anchor to hide it between some bigger boats. But, he warned us, the boat had been "deeply disturbed."

From a distance, the yacht appeared virtually untouched, unmolested. Inside was another matter entirely. The boat had definitely been ransacked, including Jeremy's new wine collection—several bottles were shattered as if they'd been hurriedly shoved aside. Yet, after a thorough search, we found nothing missing. All the little treasures were still there in the curio cabinets and china cupboard.

Thierry explained to us what he thought had happened—that the boat-jackers had taken the boat out, discovered that there wasn't much fuel, and hastily pulled into the nearest harbor. He pointed to the shore, where our little lifeboat was beached. He thought it would have taken two men to haul it off the yacht. "They took the lifeboat to shore, and left it there. They probably ran away or had someone pick them up. We are checking with local bars and cafés."

"Those jackasses," Jeremy muttered in disgust when he saw our little emergency boat lying where it had been hastily abandoned.

Claude showed up, and at first he whistled when he saw the damage. Then he walked up and down the boat with an incredulous look on his face, the expression of a captain who took great pride in the boat he was skippering, and was personally offended by what had been done to it. He'd brought Gerard, the engineer, with him. Gerard was a big bear of a fellow from Wales, with tattoos on his arms, and he went right to work to silently appraise the situation. Claude retrieved the little emergency boat, and they hoisted it back on the yacht.

When Gerard finished his assessment he told Jeremy reassuringly, "It's not too bad. They damaged the engine some. I'll bet the noise it made was what scared them off. But it can be fixed." He surmised that the thieves had been amateurs. Claude concurred, and guessed that it was probably kids who had taken it out for a joyride.

Thierry said, "A terrible prank, but alas, we, too, have our share of destructive hoodlums." Thierry turned to me and said, "Try not to become too jaded by all of this."

"I'll refuel it here so I can get it back to Nice to work on it," Gerard said. He added that the repairs must be done before we could even think of taking her out to sea on an extended voyage. So he and Claude stayed behind with *Penelope's Dream*, and Thierry took off in his patrol boat.

Jeremy and I got back in his car and drove to the maritime police station in Nice, where the older gendarme was preparing new paperwork for this latest twist of events. While Jeremy was finishing up with him, Thierry returned. I stood gazing out at the harbor, waiting for Jeremy, until I recalled what Erik had asked me.

"Thierry. Who exactly was the original owner of this boat?" I inquired.

"I show you," Thierry said. He led me to the yacht club next door. The bar area was filled with patrons, many in nautical gear with white trousers, navy blue jackets and gold braid, and spiffy caps on their heads. They were jocular and talkative, but there was a light drop in the conversation level as we entered, the way regulars do when somebody new arrives. They knew Thierry, and probably assumed I was a lady friend, judging by their grins. Thierry acted proud to have me as his companion in public, but was at all times very elegantly deferential to me.

He led me to a bunch of framed photographs on the wall to the left of the bar. These were pictures of prize-winners, whether they were holding up big fish that they had caught, or trophy cups that they'd won in a car or yacht race. He pointed to a photograph of a very dapper man wearing elegant nautical attire and an ascot at his throat, and holding a trophy cup. Thierry told me this was an old German aristocrat, the Count von Norbert, well-known as a kindly, generous, courteous gentleman. But nothing much was known of the man's personal life.

"He is older now than he was in this picture," Thierry said. "Alas, he does not show up so much these days. The yacht just sat here, winter and summer, kept up but seldom taken out, until that last time, which was quite out of season and *pas normal*," he said, sounding puzzled in the way a Frenchman can't figure out why someone's behaving irrationally. "We were not entirely surprised to see him put his boat up for sale."

Over the next couple of days, Jeremy and I regrouped at the villa, discussing our options amid all that banging, hammering and sawing that the workmen were doing. By now Jeremy had recovered his old can-do, warrior spirit, since the boat was back where it belonged and the insurance papers had come through.

While he worked out the boat repairs with Gerard and Claude, I borrowed his car and went to local libraries to do some fast research and mighty nimble footwork. Killing two birds with one stone is a dreadfully strenuous activity: I had to dissuade Jeremy from going back to London and giving up on our Plan; and, I simply had to get the bottom of Le Boat-Jacking. The police had already investigated the crew, and the other bidders, but turned up nothing, so the trail went cold. Therefore, I felt I must find out all I could about the history of *Penelope's Dream*.

Because not for a minute did I believe that we had simply been the victim of a delinquent's prank. And, much as everybody wanted to just put the whole thing behind them, I couldn't shake the feeling that the story wasn't over. So I wanted to be ready when the next shoe dropped. And I wanted Jeremy aboard.

"Come on," I coaxed, trying to engage his curiosity about the theft. "Dontcha wanna find out who took our boat?"

"Penny," Jeremy said in a strained voice. "We told the police everything we know. We even told them about Rollo, just in case he had anything to do with it, which I doubt."

"Yeah, and did you see their faces when we described Rollo?" I said. "The older cop especially. He started looking at us funny, as if *we* were a bit fishy."

"My point exactly," Jeremy said. "It's a great big world out there, little girl, and the cops have seen and heard it all—money-laundering, insurance scams, you name it. If *you* start acting peculiar, they'll soon be giving us the fisheye."

This intrigued me momentarily. "You think the cops are now thinking, *Perhaps this couple isn't as dopey as they look. Perhaps Penny and Jeremy are really the brains behind a ring of con artists?*" I asked.

"They will if you keep acting like a Girl Detective," Jeremy cautioned. I could sort of see his point. You know how it works. The minute you start telling people about your strange relatives, well, *you* start to sound strange for having them. And there is just something about Rollo that actually does make you end up doing things that technically you shouldn't be doing, like sneaking into hotel rooms and crossing the border with priceless art.

"So just let the police do their job," Jeremy said. "And stay out of it. Don't go looking for trouble, because if you do, you will surely find it."

"But now we've got *our* reputations at stake—" I objected.

"Leave it to the cops," Jeremy said firmly. "I want to put this whole mess out of my mind for awhile. Then I'll figure out what to do."

That sounded ominous to me. "What do you mean?" I prodded.

"I mean, I might just sell this damned unlucky boat and go home," he said.

"Back to your old life?" I said, as if I could not believe my ears.

"Yes, my dull old life," he retorted. "Where I may not have had a yacht, and a flooded-out Riviera villa, a townhouse in Belgravia and huge investments . . . but, on the other hand, at least I used to have a job, a purpose in life, and, most magnificently of all, my sanity."

I knew he was just letting off steam. Surely. But, I couldn't take any chances.

"Oh, come on, brace up!" I said, invoking his staunch English heritage of sailors and pirates and explorers and empire-builders. "When the smoke clears, you'll see that there are great adventures to have, and many pleasures ahead."

"Fine," Jeremy said, "I'll keep the Victrola and sit in my parlor on Sundays, listening to Mozart."

I seized this opening. "Would you settle for Beethoven?" I asked eagerly, knowing it was his favorite composer. I saw the gleam of interest in his eyes.

"Oh?" he said idly. "Where?"

I bounced onto the seat next to him. "Lake Como," I proclaimed, emboldened.

Jeremy looked startled. "Lake Como! Great," he said, "we can extend the wreckage of our luck to yet another country now." I ignored this.

"They're having a classical music festival featuring Beethoven this year. Plus, I heard that Lake Como is just beautiful, a really enchanted place," I said.

"I *know* Lake Como is beautiful," Jeremy informed me. "I went there as a little boy. By any chance have you been talking to Mum?"

"Nope," I said. "I just heard it's a secluded, perfect spot to chill out."

"It is indeed," Jeremy admitted. "Especially on an island there, the Isola Comacina, with just a restaurant and the ruins of old churches, and old olive trees. Nobody really lives on it. I pretended I was a castaway, on my own island. I remember feeling as if no harm could come to us because nobody would ever find us there, hidden among the mountains."

"Boy, that sounds great," I said. "Frankly, I could use a little calm and beauty."

He looked at me with affection and said, "Yes, if you've never been, then you should see it sometime. You would love it, too."

"Not sometime, this time," I pressed. "We have bigger things to figure out besides the yacht alone, you know. We can't let day-to-day events pull us back into old habits."

"You're right to say that we need to gain some perspective," he admitted. He looked at me and said with self-reproach, "This hasn't exactly been a picnic for you, either. Here I am so busy feeling sorry for myself that I failed to notice. After all, it's Penny's Dream, stolen from you as well as me. You could use a breather yourself."

"Exactly!" I cried. "The cops will keep an eye on the boat, and so will Claude and the crew, now that they're working on it. When the repairs are all done, we'll let cooler heads prevail. Then we can decide whether to keep the yacht or sell it. In the meantime, a little Beethoven music ought to improve our brain cells."

"Yes, well, I must be losing my mind," Jeremy said slowly, "because what you say is actually making sense to me."

"Great!" I said, pouncing on the idea before he could change his mind. "Let's leave tomorrow! I'm really looking forward to taking a break from all this."

It wasn't a lie, exactly. I mean, there actually was a Beethoven music festival going on at Lake Como. And I have always wanted to go there. And it made sense, really, to get away from the Riviera for a bit. However, I had one other teensy little reason for wanting to go there. I would certainly share this with Jeremy. But first I wanted to be sure that I was on the right track, and that my info was correct and up-to-date . . . and that the Count Hubert von Norbert, previous owner of our yacht, was still currently residing in a castle near the Alps . . . at Lake Como.

Part Five

Chapter Sixteen

L ake Como was unlike any lake I'd ever seen. I think of lakes as . . . well, round. But Lake Como is shaped like a dancing frog, as if Matisse had painted it. It's the third largest lake in Italy, but you'd never know it because of those long skinny legs; and even at the "torso," or widest part, it's only about three miles across, yet it's also one of the deepest lakes in all of Europe. It is surrounded by magnificent Alpine mountains, and its shores are covered with evergreens and great big blossoming shrubs, which are reflected by the lake, giving the entire place a glowing emerald color. Green lake, green pine-covered mountains rising like protective walls, their peaks shrouded in misty, milky-white clouds at whose summit one might suppose that Zeus and all the other gods of Olympus were enthroned.

The town of Como itself sits at the "toe" of the left "leg." It is a busy, bustling city that we drove beyond, because we had booked into a Grand Hotel at a quieter town farther up this leg. The beautiful old hotel seemed to be waiting just for us, perched high up above the lake. Our taxi pulled into the gravel driveway on the left side of the road. As we climbed out, I saw that, to our right, directly across the street, our hotel had a wooden pier extending out on the lake, with an outdoor restaurant on it. Beyond this was a gangway leading to a big "float" with a sizeable swimming pool atop it, so the whole pool just sat there serenely bobbing on the lake.

The bellhop waited patiently as I stopped in my tracks and gazed, open-mouthed, at the way the late afternoon sun was reflected in the swimming pool and the beautiful outstretched lake, and beyond, at the stunning view of the other coastline across the "leg" with its matching mountains, villages and hotels.

"Oh, Jeremy!" I breathed. "Let's sit here and watch the sun set over the lake!"

"Erm, mind if we see our room first?" Jeremy said with amusement. We crunch-crunched across the brief gravel driveway, went into the hotel, and entered a glass elevator that took us up to the beautiful golden Belle Epoque lobby.

"You know, they shot the movie *Grand Hotel* right here, with Greta Garbo and John Barrymore!" I enthused, as we made our way to the front desk, which had a fleet of pretty Italian women wearing identical scarves made of the silk that Como is famous for. The receptionists were busily checking their guests in and out. When our turn came, they handed us a big heavy gold key with an enormous gold tassel. Then we went in another glass elevator, which was flanked by dramatic curving stairs . . . in case you felt like floating down in a chiffon gown to meet your date like a movie star.

Inside our room was a narrow hallway with a closet to the left, and a marble bathroom to the right. Beyond this was the main part of the room, with shuttered windows, a great big bed, a chest of drawers, and comfortable armchairs. The bellhop quietly brought in our bags. I flung open one of the shutters, and stared rapturously at the picture-book view of the mountainous sky, with its soft mysterious clouds, the lovely lake beyond, and, in the gardens below, some big green shrubs that were covered with giant rhododendron blossoms in pink and blue, practically the size of a cheerleader's pom-poms. There were slender gnarled trees that attracted swooping, chirping birds, whose balletic moves made the whole place look like a garden from a fairy tale.

We went downstairs again, and entered the bar, which had outdoor tables on a balcony. You could gaze over the wrought-iron railing at the street below, and the lake and the floating pool beyond, which rocked and tilted gently like a swimmer's float whenever a passing speedboat ruffled it or whenever the wind rippled its tides. We ordered *bellinis*, a cocktail made of champagne and the juice of fresh peaches. We smiled at everyone, and they smiled at us, because there was something about the nature of the place that made people happy and relaxed, as if they'd found a sheltered little corner of paradise, attended by waiters who had the calm courtesy and patience of angels.

Across the lake, we could see lights coming up on the beautiful town of Bellagio, so named from the Latin "Bi-lacus" which means "between the lakes" because the pretty town sits right at the—well, the lake's crotch of the frog's legs. Just north of Bellagio is the "torso" of the dancing frog.

And as we sat gazing out, the breeze stirred our senses and there seemed to be a whiff of magic in the air, because the wind had made its mysterious daily shift—from the afternoon *breva* which comes upward from the south to north—to the *tivà* which does the reverse at night. The waiter explained this matter-of-factly to us. But if you happen to be sitting there just at the moment when the wind makes that shift, you could swear that the spirits are speaking to you, ushering in your deepest wishes, or foretelling a great change in store for you.

"Mmm," Jeremy said, sensing this, and closing his eyes. "Wonderful."

"And tomorrow," I said enthusiastically, "we can go exploring the lake by boat. There's plenty of ferries to take us anywhere we want to go."

"Fine. I'll take you to my secret island for lunch," Jeremy promised.

"The Isola Comacina?" I asked eagerly. He looked surprised.

"How did you remember that name so easily?" he asked.

"I looked it up," I said quickly. "This place is so rich in history," I enthused. "Prehistoric bears used to roam around this lake. And later, royalty from ancient Rome on up to Victorian England, had villas here where they threw wild parties and had secret escapes from their castles. And Lake Como inspired so many great artists—Shelley and Wordsworth and Verdi and Liszt all created masterpieces while hanging around here."

"And don't forget the infamous guests as well—like Mussolini, who very nearly escaped over the mountains into nearby Switzerland . . . almost," Jeremy said, his eyes still closed. But then he opened one eye and peered at me knowingly.

"So. Are you going to tell me now or later?" he inquired.

"What?" I asked innocently.

"Why are we here?" Jeremy asked firmly. "And don't tell me it's to relax. That's all very well, but I know how that head of yours works, and you wouldn't haul me all the way up here just for Beethoven. You're no ordinary tourist, at least, not when you've got that look in your eye. You've picked up the scent and you're on to something. So, what is it?"

I wasn't entirely sure I liked having a man getting to know me so well that he could see through my best nonchalant act. I mean, I thought I'd been pretty discreet. But, since it was clear that the jig was up, I told him. "It just so happens that the guy who owned *Liesl's Dream* lives on Lake Como," I announced. "In an old castle somewhere around here. His name is the Count von Norbert. The lady at the front desk told me everyone knows him, because he's been here a long time, ever since he came over from Germany during World War Two, to escape the Nazis. They say he's old and frail now, and is a bit of a recluse."

"Aha!" Jeremy said. "I just knew it somehow had to do with the yacht."

"Wait a minute," I said, slightly insulted. "If you knew that, then why did you go along with me?"

"Because I also know," Jeremy said, "that if I didn't, you'd try to pull this off yourself. And somebody has to keep an eye on you."

"What am I, some doofus or something?" I demanded.

"No, it's merely that you always think the best of people," he replied. "Therefore, someone has to be on hand to think the worst."

"Are you saying you suspected this all along?" I asked.

"I was fairly certain you were up to no good when we left Antibes," he said maddeningly, "but I knew for absolutely sure just now, when I went to get smaller change to tip the porter—and I saw you over at the front desk gabbing with the older lady receptionist. She gave you maps and she circled things on it."

"Boy," I said indignantly. "You're a bigger snoop than I am."

"I learned from the master," he replied. "So, what else have you got?"

"Well," I said eagerly, "the Count comes from a very old aristocratic family in Bonn. He was only eighteen when he married his childhood sweetheart—named Liesl. Ya get it?"

"Yes, yes, as in *Liesl's Dream,*" Jeremy said. "Go on."

"She was studying to become a concert pianist. But she caught polio and became crippled. Hitler didn't have much tolerance for people with disabilities, you know. And the Count thought the fascists were ruining Germany, so he and Liesl decided to hightail it out of there. So they came here, to Lake Como. Liesl gave music lessons for many years after that, and the Count helped other war refugees who barely escaped with their lives."

"Where'd you get all this gossipy, personal stuff?" Jeremy asked.

"Turns out the receptionist was once a pupil of Liesl's," I said. "She adored them. Says the Count and his wife were *molto generoso*, even after the war, supporting local charities and orphanages, making donations to fix the church bell, all that kind of stuff."

"Sounds like a nice dapper sort of fellow," Jeremy commented, intrigued.

"Yeah, she said he always cuts a *bella figura* in town, even after Liesl died in the 1970s, when her youngest child was only a couple of years old. The Count still made public appearances to keep up their charities and stuff . . . *Until,*" I added mysteriously, "very recently, when something went wrong. All they know around here was that he went off on his yacht and came back 'a changed man.'"

"Blimey," Jeremy said warily. "What's that supposed to mean?"

"Well," I went on dramatically, "nobody really knows. All she said was, 'Alas, the Count suffered a stroke. He is more frail these days, a bit forgetful. He does not make so many public appearances anymore.' From the way she said it, I gathered that he's now a bit—senile or something." I paused for breath.

"Wow," Jeremy said. "That's some story."

"You haven't heard the best part," I said. "True, he doesn't get out much anymore, *but* in honor of his wife, he always attends the annual music festival. In all these years, they say, he never misses. As in tomorrow night."

"Good God, the audacity!" Jeremy marveled. "Luring me in with Beethoven, you treacherous female."

"Well, it's taking place right here in our hotel," I continued, undaunted. "In one of those gorgeous old salons on the lobby level," I said eagerly. "You know, the ones with antique wallpaper and golden trim, and those sofas that make you think of kings and queens with powdered wigs, throwing music soirées. I saw the waiters setting up rows of extra seating already. And there was a platform for the string musicians and pianist. And tables full of champagne glasses. It's going to be wonderful. So," I said briskly, "that gives us all day tomorrow to find out more about the Count, maybe see where he lives."

"You'll have to take me to my island and feed me a magnificent lunch," Jeremy warned. "I can't snoop on an empty stomach."

"Why, naturally," I said.

"Good," Jeremy said briskly. "Because I already made the reservations."

Chapter Seventeen

Well, we overslept a bit. But it was all part of the enchantment. The shuttered windows kept us in such a spellbound slumber that only the sound of the maids hoovering the hallways finally stirred us. I suppose, too, that the strange stress of the last week had caught up with us. So we gulped our coffee and rushed out of the hotel to catch our ferry, which we just barely made, jumping aboard seconds before it began ploughing across the lake.

I was glad to be out on the water, inhaling the invigorating air and finally getting my bearings. I soon realized that travelling by boat was absolutely the only way to really gain a perspective on Lake Como, with its string of pretty little towns. The mountains rose all around us as we flirted past the little coves and promontories with their villages, lovely churches and splendid villas, jewel-like in the soft morning sun, in colors of yellow and pink and ochre and terracotta. The Count's castle was supposedly not very far from here, high up in the hills above a small town called Ossuccio. I figured we might get a glimpse of it from the little island that Jeremy loved.

"Ready for a little history lesson, Miss Researcher-Slash-Spy?" Jeremy asked with a cunning look.

"Why do you look so smug?" I asked.

"Because for once *I've* got some history tidbits for *you*," he crowed. "Looked it all up when I was a kid hanging about here. For starters, the Isola Comacina is the only island on Lake Como. It's tucked into a cozy nook of a peninsula—"

"Halfway down the left thigh of the frog's leg!" I cried. I'd already spied it on the map.

"Frog's leg?" Jeremy inquired. "Perchance, do you mean the Lake?"

"Yes, go on," I urged.

"Well, the island is quite small—you can hike from one end to the other pretty easily. Even so, armies have fought over the Isola Comacina for centuries. When the Romans occupied it, the island was prized for the valuable olive oil from its trees," Jeremy explained. "Then the city of Como teamed up with the notorious Barbarossa—"

"That means the 'red-bearded' one, doesn't it?" I asked.

Jeremy said, "Yes, but he was actually Frederick the First—a German king from the 1100s. Nowadays the island is practically deserted," Jeremy said, "except for some old churches and ruins, and, of course, the restaurant, which has been around since the 1940s and hopefully will be here until the end of time."

"Is it run by the original owner still?" I asked.

Jeremy shook his head with a sly smile. "Nope. The very first owner was one of Mussolini's captains, who ran away and used this place as his hideaway; then he opened this restaurant. But don't worry. Far as I know, nobody's hiding out there now. You are in for a treat. Here we are."

I leaned forward, eager to catch my first glimpse of the Isola Comacina, which now appeared to drift magically into view as our ferry rounded the corner and pulled up to its shores. It was a tiny floating world unto itself, lush and green. We walked from the pier along a footpath, up to a high promontory, atop which the restaurant was perched. Other diners were arriving in their own little speedboats.

The proprietor, a tall, tanned handsome man, stood at the entrance to greet each guest with a very natural attentiveness. He led us to a table laid with white cloth and pink napkins, perfectly situated in the shade of a leafy tree, where we had a view of the approaching boats.

A round-faced waiter with a businesslike manner plunked down a carafe of sparkling water, and a bottle of chilled white wine, and two short, stemless thick wine glasses—the kind that resemble whisky tumblers. I glanced around, looking for a chalkboard or something with the day's special on it.

"Psst," I said to Jeremy, "where's the menu?"

"This is one restaurant where you don't have to even think about what you want to eat," Jeremy said, unfolding his napkin and dropping it in his lap. "They always serve the same one basic menu, because they do everything utterly right. Just sit back and be glad."

This mystified me at first, until suddenly a flock of waiters arrived and began placing, in rapid succession, an array of pretty white-yellow-and-purple flowered bowls filled with appetizers, on the smaller serving table on my right.

"Go ahead," Jeremy said, "pass it round." I picked up one bowl after another, took some for my plate, then handed it to Jeremy. We tasted the various incredible *antipasto,* each served in its own vinaigrette. It was like being introduced to every vegetable for the very first time, and being transported by its perfection: tomato topped with a sliver of lemon; small, nearly seedless zucchini; enormous yet delicate white beans; succulent red beets; sweet carrots, and some delightful greens I'd never had before. And somewhere along the way, a big fresh loaf of bread had been placed on the table; and, there was now a platter of plump round onions that had been baked whole, to a soft and incredible sweetness. This was followed by little plates of tender prosciutto—the kind you can only get in Italy—accompanied by a delicate bit of melon that I popped into my mouth and realized, oh, *that's* what melon is supposed to taste like.

All the while, the elegant owner, with his alert, intelligent eyes, was assessing the progress of everyone's meal so that no one was ever left wanting. The effect of this careful attentiveness was that all the diners settled into a contented hum of dignified conversation.

Seated under the tree with a breeze ruffling my hair, I felt a contented calm, and yet a heightened awareness of the sensual delights around me—the sun, the sky, the sea, the food, the pleasant company. I couldn't help becoming fascinated with the other diners, most of whom were Italian, grouped around long tables for entire families whose children behaved phenomenally well, even when they had finished eating.

One little boy, dressed in formal white pants and white shirt, tiptoed around the perimeter of the restaurant beyond its railings, but his mother, elegantly dressed in a cream-colored suit, only had to call out his name once to make him come hurrying to her side.

"So this is where you came on vacation as a kid?" I asked Jeremy, picturing him as a sweet, earnest English boy sitting in one of these chairs, swinging his legs, those blue eyes of his taking in everything around him.

"Yes, for several years in a row, in early summer," Jeremy replied.

"You and your mum, and Uncle Peter?" I asked. Jeremy's English stepfather was Mom's brother.

"Peter came once with us," Jeremy said. "He loved it, too, but was always busy at work. He told me that someday I'd come here with my own wife and kid. Mum took me back here a couple more times after that."

Jeremy had never known his real father, an Italian-American who came to London in the late 1960s for the music scene and fell in love with Jeremy's mother; but ended up being drafted into the Vietnam war and died a few years later, not long after Jeremy was born. I wondered if Aunt Sheila had deliberately brought Jeremy here as a boy so that he'd become familiar with his Italian heritage.

The next plate arrived with a subtle flourish—a cold meat platter consisting of a slice of "English" ham and paper-thin shavings of a tender roast beef called *bresaola*. All the food was served in just the right amounts so that you could eat everything without over-doing it.

"Jeremy," I said after we'd devoured it, "this is heavenly. I am never going to leave this place. I am going to stay in this chair until they fling me into the lake."

"I won't let them," he promised.

I gazed across the lake at the mysterious shores opposite us. Small towns nestled at the foothills, looked like little villages from a long-ago world of make-believe. Somewhere across the lake was the coastal town where the Count lived in his castle. But there were so many intriguing châteaus and villas dotting the landscape, I couldn't tell which one belonged to him.

"Looking for your Count?" Jeremy asked, amused. "I don't know what you expect from the guy. He doesn't sound like he's in very good shape. He might be mad as a March hare, for all you know."

"Maybe. But I just can't help feeling that he might help us figure out what happened to *Penelope's Dream*."

"Well, what's the bloke look like?" Jeremy asked.

"Elegant. Aristocratic. A big intelligent head. The kind of profile you could put on a monument," I said. "Blond hair. But that picture was taken years ago." The image of the Count from the photograph in the yacht club was fading fast in my memory, but I still thought I might recognize him.

The older waiter arrived with a very serious-looking platter that he placed on a temporary serving table which a younger waiter had set up for him in advance. A big, cooked trout that had been grilled over charcoal, was now being cut in half for us. The older waiter worked expertly with his cutlery, and lifted the fish right off the bones, placing one half on my plate first, then the other half on Jeremy's.

"Mmmm," I murmured. I sighed happily. "A fresh fish makes you feel like you're going to live forever." We gazed in amusement at the occasional boat passing by, whose driver and passengers waved or peered curiously at us. A man at a nearby table picked up his pink linen napkin, stood up and waved it like a nautical signal to his friends so that they'd know where he was sitting and they could join him. Small speedboats here were like taxicabs. Everyone looked happy.

"I love travelling by boat," I said. Then I added, "You're not really thinking of selling *Penelope's Dream*, are you?"

"No," Jeremy said. "I mean, I considered it. But I guess I was just blowing off steam. I felt a bit of a fool, having it stolen right out from under us. Being here on the lake has reminded me why I wanted a boat in the first place."

Score one for Lake Como so far, I thought to myself.

After we'd finished off that fish, the next course arrived: we each got a half of a free-range chicken that had been slightly crushed and cooked in an iron pot with oil. It came with a green salad. Which was followed by a little chunk of parmigiano cheese that the waiters carried over in a giant wheel, spearing our chunks with the tip of a knife. And finally, just before the coffee, came a dessert of fresh ice cream called *fior di vaniglia.*

"Flower of vanilla! But they're cutting up something to go with it," I whispered.

"Oranges," Jeremy whispered back. "Sliced not a minute earlier than when you're ready to eat them. And I think they pour some kind of liqueur around it."

I tasted the elegant combination, and then I laughed. "Oh my God," I said. "Now I know what a creamsicle is trying to be."

While Jeremy paid the bill, I excused myself to go the powder room, which was just off a big echoing room that served as an indoor restaurant during inclement weather. Nobody was eating there now. On the way back through this room, I noticed a whole wall of framed photographs of celebrities posing with the proprietor of the restaurant, taken over many, many years. He looked the same, handsome and smiling with his guests, but it was like being in a time tunnel, with faces and figures from many years gone by. Actors, musicians, all manner of famous folk, some who'd autographed the picture.

Then I saw it. I wasn't sure at first, because the Count was even younger in this picture than he'd been in the photo at the Riviera yacht club. Here, he was very trim, handsome and, well, sexy. He had a wry curl of a smile that indicated a man who saw the ironic humor in life, and although his gaze was level and sharp, there was a twinkle of mischief in his eyes. The restaurant owner stood at his left; but on the Count's right was a beautiful woman, with a 1940s hairdo—the kind with a big roll of a curl on her forehead—and that dark red lipstick and nail polish that you can spot even in a black-and-white photo. I peered at the signatures. *Count Hubert von Norbert.* And, right next to it, his wife had scrawled only her first name. *Liesl.*

I glanced up at the proprietor as he came out of the kitchen, where he'd gone to check on something. He smiled, and came over to see what I was looking at.

"Ah, the Count von Norbert!" he said. "Many, many years ago."

I asked him about what had become of the Count, and he told me that indeed, the Count still resided on Lake Como, and had dined here for many years with his lovely wife. "Er, do you have any idea where, exactly, he lives?" I queried. "A castle near a town across the lake, right?"

He led me back outside, and pointed at one of the villages nestled near the shore; then, he raised his finger higher, higher, higher, up into the green hills, where, half-hidden from view by the clustered pines, was an old grey castle, tall and narrow, with a tower and turrets. It was such a natural color, blending in with the cliffs, that it appeared as if it had simply sprung up out of the rocks.

Jeremy had been watching us from the table, while he was taking care of the bill. Now he sauntered over to see what I was up to. The proprietor shook hands with him in that easy, generous way, and Jeremy thanked him for the meal, telling him that the place was as charming as he remembered it. The man received this compliment with dignified, modest grace. Then he excused himself to go and tend to some newly arrived guests.

"Jeremy!" I said. "Look. That castle. It's where the Count lives. And, I found a picture of him! Come and see." I dragged him back into the dining hall, and over to the photo of the Count and his wife posing with the owner.

Jeremy peered closely, intrigued in spite of himself. "So that's him," he said.

"And that's Liesl," I said. "Isn't she glamorous? Oh, Jeremy, I hope he shows up at the concert tonight. Come on!" I cried. "I don't want to miss our ferry back."

"Hold on," Jeremy said calmly, checking his watch. "We still have time to show you a great spot you shouldn't miss."

He led me along a path that wove around and up a grassy hill. We paused at its crest, to look at the ruins of churches whose stones lay about in the tall grass. We stood in a hushed quiet, broken only by the occasional soft scurrying of a lizard who was probably hurrying off to vespers. There was something about the silence, and the air, and the heightened feeling you get from having had good food and wine, and being greeted and treated like a human being when you arrive. I felt open and happy, wanting to be *molto generoso* to the whole wide world.

I glanced at Jeremy, who was watching me as if quite pleased that I had responded so warmly to these surroundings. I suddenly felt that sweet joy of one's first childhood love, when, as a little girl, you'd be thrilled when a boy you liked took you to his favorite place, as a token of his devotion to you. "This was your hideaway as a kid, right?" I said.

Jeremy said nothing. He just leaned over and gave me a long, lingering kiss. There was something different in it this time, something very intense, and it left me shaky inside. For a moment, neither of us could speak. Even later, when we turned and began our descent down the hill, we moved in silence, listening only to the rustle of our footsteps walking through time.

Finally, holding hands, we went to the dock where the ferry

would come. There were a lot of people waiting. Jeremy saw a water taxi that had just dropped some people off. He went up to the driver, and I saw them bargain back and forth. Then Jeremy held out his hand to me, and I climbed aboard our private little taxi that would carry us back to the Grand Hotel.

It went much faster than the ferry, which was an unexpected thrill. The boat sliced across the lake, sending powerful waves rushing behind us to the shore. I sat close to Jeremy, snuggling in his arms. We were quiet for a long time, all the way until we saw the lights of the dock again.

Chapter Eighteen

The Grand Hotel was already abuzz with music-lovers when we returned. Many had come to the hotel's formal dining room to eat, and now were eagerly anticipating listening to a fine string quartet and pianists play an evening of Beethoven. We went upstairs to spruce up and change clothes. Jeremy put on a nice blue linen suit, and I dressed in a bright pink frock, which had tulip-shaped short sleeves and the dropped waist of a flapper. It was one of Great-Aunt Penelope's vintage party dresses. I'd carefully sorted them, saving the most exquisite for a museum display I was planning, for the benefit of a children's charity. But this 1920s charmer actually fit me well, so I simply couldn't resist. I wore it with a pair of delicate gold sandals.

As we descended, I could hear that the violinists had begun to tune up. Slowly, the audience drifted into their seats, and the conversational buzz gradually dropped in volume. I kept a sharp lookout, but there were so many white-haired older gentlemen at this gathering. I did not see anyone that reminded me of the photographs of the Count, but it was hard to tell in such a crowd.

Jeremy and I took our seats on the aisle. These were nicely padded armless dining chairs in a style similar to Louis XVI, that had been assembled in theatrical rows. A very elegant lady who represented the hotel stepped forward and announced that the program would commence. A tall, middle-aged woman in a long black gown took her position at one piano, and a bearded man took his at the other.

Hearing Beethoven in this European setting, with the mountains all around us and the lake lapping at the shores, I felt a deeper understanding of music I'd heard all my life. The spirited, galloping passages made me think of hunters racing their horses through these dark, deep forests. The towering, sonorous peaks were like the mountains speaking; and the sweet, heartbreakingly delicate interludes were like the flight of the birds that I had seen swooping in the gardens here in perfect arcs. The music wove around us mysteriously, taking us to depths of great sorrow and heights of joy, and all the labyrinthine passages that connected them. At the very last, Beethoven brought us back down to earth so gently, and so softly, that there was an awed silence before the applause, as if the audience could not bear to break the spell.

After several selections, the performers took numerous bows, and were presented with bouquets of flowers. Then everybody rose and began rapidly pouring out into the lobby, where there was a festive atmosphere as the hotel guests and concert-goers were milling about holding glasses of *spumante,* looking slightly flushed from their cocktails and the contagious excitement as they responded to the sight of one another dressed up in celebratory evening finery. Attractive women fluttered by in long, wispy dresses, light summer shawls and high heels and sparkling jewelry; and their exclamations mingled with the deeper roar of the elegantly-suited men's jocular voices.

"Any sight of the Count?" Jeremy whispered.

"Nope," I said gloomily, "and I'm not even sure I'd recognize him if I saw him. For all I know he could have come and gone already."

"I'll get us some sparkling wine," Jeremy said.

"Okay," I said distractedly as he headed toward the bar where white-coated waiters were pouring it into flutes.

I prowled around the lobby, peering at any possibility. People were waiting for taxicabs or boats to take them away. I watched every one who was preparing to leave. One very tall, elderly man was seated on a small striped sofa. When I glanced at him I caught his eye, and he smiled broadly and encouragingly.

"Count?" I asked, half-under my breath.

"Count what?" he asked delightedly, rising. He came closer, very close, and I could smell whisky on his breath. "Did you enjoy the concert tonight, young lady?" he asked, leering closer.

"Oops," I said, backing off. "Sorry. Thought you were someone else."

"Maybe I am!" he said. "Don't I know you?"

A touristy-looking woman, loaded down with a colorful beaded necklace and matching bracelets, was talking to her friends a few feet away, but now she looked up knowingly. "Bob," she said sharply, as if speaking to an unruly child, and the man looked sheepish.

I moved away hastily, and drifted around the exits, searching, but mostly I just got in people's way as they were leaving. Dejectedly, I turned back to the lobby.

Then I noticed a bent old man in a wheelchair near the lobby door, quietly waiting for his car to take its turn to pull up into the gravel driveway. There was something in his shriveled little face that rang a bell—those blue eyes and elegant profile. But I couldn't be sure, certainly not from this distance.

His minder, a middle-aged nurse, had stepped away from him and was peering out the door to see if she could spot their car in the procession of headlights. So she did not notice when the poor guy dropped his pipe and could not reach to retrieve it.

I hurried over, picked up his pipe and handed it gently back to him.

"Yours?" I said with a smile. He turned his face upward and gave me a delighted, beatific smile. "Do you speak English?" I asked.

"Of course, of course, thank you, my dear girl!" he said in a charming German accent. He peered at me as if he thought he should remember me, but couldn't. I realized that by wearing Great-Aunt Penelope's vintage 1920s dress, I probably looked as if I'd stepped out of another era, perhaps even his own past. I knew that the nurse would be back at any minute and whisk him right out from under my nose. I had to take a chance, fast.

"Are you the Count von Norbert?" I asked lightly. He beamed.

"I certainly am!" he chuckled. "And what is your name, my child?"

I told him, and then he said, "So, you are a fellow Beethoven lover?"

"Oh, yes," I said, "and my boyfriend is, especially."

"Really?" he asked. "And how did you come to know my name?"

Something made me tell him the whole truth. "We fell in love with your yacht and bought it at the auction in Nice," I said, very directly. Then I held my breath, watching him to see if his face would betray cunning, wariness or anything else to connect him with the shenanigans on *Liesl's Dream*. But his face had a pure innocence, and he looked genuinely happy to meet me.

"Isn't that nice?" he said in a way that made me wonder if he'd really understood what I'd just said. I looked up and saw that Jeremy had observed what I was doing, and he'd managed to detain the nurse, to buy me more time. From the look of things I think he was pretending to ask her directions, because she was gesturing toward the road.

"I would love to talk to you about the boat," I said quickly.

"Talk? Why, my dear, then you and your boyfriend must come to have cocktails with me and tell me all about it!" he exclaimed. "Tomorrow night, promptly at five. I must dine early these days, you see."

The nurse was marching back toward us now. Jeremy trailed behind, watching the whole thing. The nurse glanced at me, and she looked a bit wary, but the Count told her firmly, "Clara, give this delightful girl our address and tell her how to find us."

Clara, not betraying any surprise, told me where to find the Count's castle, then she hurried off to speak to his driver, who came out of the car to take care of the Count and his wheelchair, while the nurse prepared the backseat of the car for him, adjusting blankets. Jeremy had come to my side now.

"This is my boyfriend," I said hastily to the Count as he was about to be steered away. "Jeremy Laidley. Jeremy, this the Count von Norbert," I added significantly.

"Pleased to meet you," Jeremy said to the Count, who nodded and extended a shaky hand which seemed so frail that Jeremy grasped it carefully.

"Five o'clock sharp!" the Count reminded me as he was wheeled into the elevator and then disappeared below.

Jeremy gave me one of those scolding looks. "So," he said slowly, "after first accosting every old man in sight and getting yourself picked up by a friskier member of the geriatric set—yes, I saw that previous little escapade—you now have indeed managed to find your Count. What kind of caper are you sending us on this time?"

"You and I," I said triumphantly, "have just been given a rare invitation. We're having cocktails with the Count up at his castle in the mountains tomorrow night."

Chapter Nineteen

"I hope you brought a bag of cookies with you," Jeremy muttered as he drove a rental car up the steep, narrow, winding roads to the Count's castle. The farther up the cliffs we went, the thicker the lush gardens and forest all around us, which made the roads even darker.

"I brought a little basket of fruit," I said. "Why do I need to bring him cookies?" I asked, thinking there was some posh tradition I was unaware of.

"So that we can leave a trail of crumbs on our way through the forest and find our way home from this Bavarian castle," Jeremy said wickedly as he steered around a hairpin bend in the darkening road. "Otherwise, you know how these stories end. Two little kiddies go up to the wizard's castle and he serves you milk and butter biscuits—but then you find out you're going to be roasted over a spit for dinner. After he chops off your head."

"I think you've just mixed up sixteen different fairy tales from five countries," I said, but I had to admit that this part of the country did look a bit Hansel-and-Gretel-ish. Beyond the Alps, after all, were Austria, Switzerland and Germany, not so very far away.

"That guy looks like a little gnome from a Bavarian fairy tale," Jeremy continued.

"Can you believe he and his wife had to escape across the border?" I asked, awed.

"Penny," Jeremy said as we made our ascent up a steep gravel driveway, "from what you told me, this guy won't even remember what you just said to him yesterday, much less what happened to him years ago. I don't know what the poor fellow can tell you. Previous owners of houses and cars and boats seldom want to chat about it after the sale."

"Look at it this way—at the very least, we'll have cocktails with an interesting man," I said. We had reached the top of the driveway now, which opened onto a flat turnaround that formed a perfect circle and was ringed with stone parapets.

" 'At the very least,' as I pointed out to you, we'll disappear and never be seen or heard from again," Jeremy said, as the car crunched over the gravel and he parked it under a very large chestnut tree growing right out of the center of the circle.

For a moment, we just sat there, gazing at the castle. Up close, it was tall, vertical but very narrow, with a tower on the left, and a small staircase and a moat on the right side. It was set upon a clearing, but beyond the gardens it was surrounded by a dense growth of shrubbery and thickets and very tall evergreens, and this made a backdrop of many varying shades of green—pale yellow-green for leafy trees, deep blue-green for the pine, and an almost black-green for the ivy that crept along one side of the tower and some of the surrounding garden walls. We were up in the hills that I'd seen reflecting on Lake Como when we arrived, which had made me think of the lake as a shimmering emerald.

As we got out and walked toward the front door, I realized that the back of the castle faced the lake. I could glimpse part of a garden, and a terrace trimmed with elegant balustrades. Because we were so high up, the entire property had a view of a great expanse of sky and mountains. However, many of the castle's windows were extremely narrow, with iron grillwork over them, which I thought could make you feel like a prisoner from the inside. I fleetingly pictured Rapunzel in that tower, letting down her hair, desperate to get out.

As we drew even closer, the wind made a low moaning sound when it blew around the corners, whistling through narrow arched passageways. Approaching the square, biscuit-box main part of the castle, I saw that it was a beautiful and yet a rather forbidding place; fortresses, after all, are meant to discourage invaders with unscalable walls, inaccessible windows and nothing in the way of a welcome at the heavy wooden front door, which had iron hinges and was shaped with a curve at the top that made me think of Robin Hood and Ivanhoe clanging in to visit a medieval king. Jeremy rang the bell, which chimed dolefully. A few moments passed. Then I heard heavy, slow, deliberate footsteps.

"Fee, fi, fo, fum," Jeremy muttered.

"Shut up," I hissed back. The door was opened by a man almost as old as the Count, and when we told him who we were he said, "Yes, you are expected," and he led us into a reception foyer right off the brief entrance hallway. The foyer was surprisingly cheerful and bright, with walls painted a pale rose, and its molding in a deeper magenta, patterned in the French *trompe l'oeil* fashion, with heavy gilt-framed mirrors on either side.

"The Count wishes you to wait in the smoking room," the butler said, and he led us through a doorway off the hallway. Jeremy perked up immediately when he saw this room, which was outfitted expressly for men: satisfyingly deep armchairs in leather, flanked by tables set for a game of chess on one, a deck of Victorian cards on the other, and, against the wall, a gun-rack with antique guns enclosed in a locked glass-and-wood case.

In one corner, on a large English desk, was a sterling silver "sleeve" that held a box of cigarettes upright. On the wall across from the desk was a bookcase whose lowest shelf was an open drop-leaf affair containing a row of colorful pipes arranged on a pipe-rack. Straight before us was a fireplace, and its cast-iron log-holder had two carved iron cherubs on either side, holding out their angelic hands as if they were warming them by a fire. Upon a big table in the center of the room were giant curved candle-holders, made of silver and—walrus tusks.

"Wow," I said, wandering around the room, peering more closely. "These walls are made of white oak. They did that because this kind of wood not only absorbs smoke well, but it's known to 'give back' the smell of oak, so it actually perfumes the room."

"This is how I want my study to look back at the townhouse," Jeremy proclaimed with a straight face.

"You don't smoke," I objected, slightly alarmed.

"I will now," he said.

He pointed to a chinoiserie that had a row of very tall, slender red-and-gold identically-bound volumes on it. "I read, don't I?"

"Not those," I said, "because if I'm not mistaken, they are not books. They're secret boxes, that are used to hide documents in."

"I'd open them and look," Jeremy said, "but if they have sur-veillance cameras in here, we might get thrown into the moat for spying. Think he's got sharks in the moats?" he teased.

"Is James Bond your only cultural frame of reference?" I in-quired.

"I'll bet the Count's got a pair of pit bulls prowling around here," Jeremy insisted.

The butler reappeared at the door, and led us back out into the foyer, to the far end this time. He touched one of the wall panels which, in the true spirit of *trompe l'oeil*, was actually a hidden door that opened into a narrow, dark staircase which corkscrewed around and around to an upper floor. A brief hallway led to quite a beautiful study, dominated by an incredibly large window with a breathtaking view of the sky above and, far below, Lake Como. Light came from a large chandelier overhead made of wood, smoked quartz and rock crystal. The walls were covered with floor-to-ceiling bookshelves that had braces holding all kinds of ancient volumes.

"Are *these* books real?" Jeremy whispered as we walked through it.

"Yes," I murmured.

Jeremy paused to look at several framed pictures grouped on one wall.

"What kind of paintings are these?" Jeremy asked, as the butler departed.

I stopped to get a closer look. They were portraits and landscapes, very workmanlike in their painterly style, except for one extraordinary technique. "Why, these are reverse-glass paintings," I said. "They're actually painted backwards, right on the glass, before they are flipped around, mounted and framed."

In fact, this room held all kinds of treasures, obviously furnished by a playful personality who had enough funds to have spent years and years becoming a significant collector. I pointed to a wall of illuminated shelves built just like the "curio cabinets" on the boat.

"Now I know we've come to the right place," I said, gazing at the collection of rare and whimsical grown-up "toys": elaborate medieval clocks, Victorian mechanical games, and vintage model trains with dining cars outfitted with miniature passengers and furniture and lamps.

"Jeremy, look!" I said, pointing to a round table in a corner by the big window. Mounted on a mahogany block was a model ship that absolutely resembled the yacht. "It's *Liesl's Dream*!" I said. "I mean, *Penelope's Dream* now."

There was a very large wingchair beside this table, set right before the big window so that you could plunk yourself down and gaze out at the view. Only, I couldn't plunk myself in it just now. Because at the moment, it was occupied. By the Count, who sat there in a gold and russet smoking robe, his feet thrust into Oriental slippers, his eyes shut, his head tilted slightly, resting on his left hand, his elbow propped on the wing of the chair. A soft blue and black plaid cashmere blanket was tucked across his lap. I gestured quickly to Jeremy, who came to my side, did a double-take, and then stood gazing in fascination.

"Count von Norbert?" I said quietly. Nothing. Jeremy raised his eyebrows incredulously. Finally I bravely reached out, and gently touched the old man's shoulder. He didn't jump or recoil. He just opened his sleepy, watery blue eyes. He gazed at me without expression, at first; then his eyes focused, took in my face, and he smiled.

Chapter Twenty

"Hello, little girl," the Count said in his elegant German accent. "Who might you be?" He had a rather intelligent charm beneath his fuddled gaze, and I got a hint of his former self, a man who perhaps possessed a fairly high degree of wit and sophistication. This unexpected radiance shone in his face until something like a cloud passed over it.

"I'm Penny Nichols and this is Jeremy Laidley," I said. At his utterly blank look, I didn't know what to say, so all I stammered out was, "We've come for cocktails."

"Have you?" said the Count forgetfully, sounding intrigued and more awake now. "How delightful." He reached out to the table at his side, pulled open a small, curved drawer, and took out a box of long matches. These he handed to Jeremy, and gestured toward something on the window-ledge. It was a miniature cannon.

"Go ahead, young man. You do the honors," he said. Jeremy took the matches but hesitated. "That's right, that's right," the Count said more loudly and encouragingly.

Jeremy went over to the cannon, peered at it, then turned to us and said in a strange voice, "I suppose I'd better open the window first."

"Naturally!" boomed the Count. Jeremy reached for the iron handle that made the window open outward. The cannon's little snoot was pointed toward the lake.

"A moment," said the Count, fumbling inside his chest pocket for a gold watch on a chain. He popped it open, then held it out as if it were a stop-watch.

"Ready, and . . . fire away!"

Jeremy lit the match and then the fuse. Instinctively, he backed off. I heard a slight hiss, then a small but sonorous *BOOM!* which echoed all through the house, slightly rattling the chandelier. There was a tiny scent of gunpowder in the room.

Jeremy and I looked at the Count. He smiled with benign magnificence. A moment later, a cuckoo clock in the far corner of the room woke up, thrusting its little wooden bird out of his tiny door and proclaiming the hour. The Count frowned slightly.

"That clock has always been ever so slightly late," he sighed.

I thought I heard footsteps. Yes, somebody was definitely scurrying around the castle somewhere. One hoped it was a butler, and not a great big rat.

"Cocktail hour!" the Count proclaimed joyfully as the doors were flung open and the butler came in wheeling a cocktail trolley. "Do you prefer gin or whisky or sherry?"

"Gin," Jeremy said quickly.

"Me, too," I said, before they could stick me with the ladylike sherry.

"And a whisky for me," said the Count happily. The butler mixed them quickly and handed each of us a thick, needle-etched crystal glass. The thought occurred to me that this expensive leaded-crystal glassware was now known to make people a little nutty, because of the lead, but I resolutely put this tidbit of knowledge out of my mind.

"Cheers," Jeremy said, as the butler left the room and closed the doors.

"Salutations!" said the Count. He took a big sip and then his face lit up with delight. He gestured out the window. "And how do you like Lake Como?" he asked.

"It's heavenly," I said fervently. Feeling a bit like Little Red Riding Hood, I handed the Count the basket of fruit we'd brought.

"For me? Ah. So nice to have young people around," said the Count, taking the basket and placing in on the table near him. "Much better than staring at all these old faces," he said, gesturing at the portraits on the walls. "My family from Bonn, going back to my great-great-great-grandfather Sigwald in the 1800s, and his son Rolf . . . Or, was it the 1700s . . . ?" His voice trailed off and he shook his head, as if trying to get rid of the cobwebs. "I am afraid my memory is not quite what it used to be," he said sadly.

Very carefully, I pointed to the model ship. "What a beautiful boat," I said. The Count smiled with a bittersweet expression.

"It is *Liesl's Dream*, isn't it?" I asked.

"Have you met my wife, Liesl?" he said, looking confused. "I have not seen her today. Is she in the garden?"

Jeremy looked faintly alarmed, and shot me a warning look.

"No, we've never met," I said softly.

The Count must have felt our apprehension, because he got that wary look in his eyes which forgetful people do, as if he sensed from our reactions that something was wrong, yet he didn't really want clarification—especially about a beloved person from his past who, in his mind, had never quite left him. Hurriedly he added, "My wife loves the sea. I bought the yacht for her. Such adventures we had aboard it! But my children do not like the sea, they get sick! I got sick, too, the very last time," he said, his blue gaze clearing a bit now as he recalled something which made him visibly upset.

"That terrible voyage to the island that nearly ruined my health and sealed my fate!" He gestured toward his legs. The stroke he'd suffered, of course.

"What island?" Jeremy asked.

The Count, lost in thought, seemed not to have heard him.

"The mistral came up!" said the Count, with a searching, faraway look, as if he were peering through a telescope of memory, and trying to bring the view into focus. "It fought us all the way! And I was so close, so close! To think that, after all this time, I found the Lion, only to lose it again! Do you believe in fate? An old beggar woman on that dock put a curse on us that night. I could swear Poseidon himself wanted to stop me! And what did he do with the Lion?"

He turned his bright blue eyes on me beseechingly. "Where is my Lion?" he asked in an endearing, childlike way. "Have you seen it? Where could it be?"

"What Lion?" I asked softly.

"You are a curious young lady, aren't you?" he asked in amusement. "Are you a collector, too?" There it was again, the way his gaze would clear as if the world had come back into focus. When this happened, he seemed more sharp, energized, even more virile.

"I'm an art historian," I said.

"Ah! That explains it. Then you will appreciate my treasures," he said gleefully, as if glad to show them to someone who might comprehend their true value. Yet he was also like a little boy showing off his toys.

"Come, you will see," said the Count, setting down his empty whisky glass. "You steer the ship, young man," he said to Jeremy, gesturing to the back of his wing chair. Jeremy went over to it, mystified, then realized that there actually were handles at the back, almost like bicycle handles with brakes, so the upholstered chair was actually a very elaborate wheelchair.

The Count reached into another pocket and pulled out a big iron key, which he handed to me, and he directed us to steer him down a long corridor leading to a tower room. The heavy wooden door creaked complainingly when I shoved it open. It was quite dark inside. After fumbling about, I found an electric light switch, but even so, there was no overhead light. Instead, it activated numerous display lights within glass shelves from floor to ceiling all around the circular tower room, including some freestanding tables of glassed-in display cases, as in a museum. Everywhere you looked, lights were illuminating small metal figures of art.

Jeremy and I gazed about, dumbstruck, at what appeared to be a great copper zoo. The entire room was filled with a collection of strange medieval-looking cast-metal objects, each standing about a foot high, all different from each other yet somehow similar. It was a metallic bestiary of centaurs, horses, griffiths, dragons and other creatures.

"Oh!" I cried. "Aren't they all amazing? What are they?"

"Aquamanilia," said the Count, and I repeated it, rolling the syllables off my tongue, *Ah-kwa-man-eel-ee-ya*.

"They have been in my family for years," the Count said proudly.

Jeremy and I moved from item to item. I kept exclaiming at each figure, saying, "Look! Here's a knight on a horse, isn't he excellent! And see this one, Jeremy. A unicorn. And this, a dragon with a snake on its back, riding it like a little jockey! And . . . whoops!" That last one was a bearded, moustachioed figure— labelled "Aristotle"—bent over on all fours with a voluptuous woman astride him. And right next to that was a wife spanking her husband with a ladle . . .

"Yes, well, humph," Jeremy said, steering me away from the erotica shelf. (He didn't, as he told me later, mind me looking at them, but he'd be damned if he'd let the old man watch me looking at them.)

I moved along to the other shelves, admiring the clever ingenuity and design of each metal figure. But as I looked at one big wall of shelves I realized a strange thing about these particular artifacts—so many were lions. Lions here, lions there. Lots and lots of lions.

That left only one display table, right in the center of the room, which appeared to be the seat of honor for a major piece in the collection. But there was nothing inside it.

"What is this for?" I asked.

The Count let out a heartbreaking cry of frustration. "For the greatest Lion of all!" he exclaimed. "The Beethoven Lion!"

I heard Jeremy's sharp intake of breath. Whereas I hardly dared breathe at all, for fear of breaking the spell. Instead I listened, wide-eyed, as the Count continued fretfully, "He rightfully belonged to my family, centuries ago, but he was stolen away from my ancestors! My grandfather almost got it back, but then those thieves took it away again."

I glanced at Jeremy, wondering how much of this was real, and how much was, perhaps, a fantasy in the Count's mind from his childhood.

"Your grandfather?" Jeremy repeated.

"Yes, at the auction in Frankfurt," the Count said. "Only to have it disappear yet again."

I perked up. "Recently?" I asked.

"No, no, it was when Grandfather was a young man," the Count said fretfully. Jeremy sighed lightly at this, but fortunately the Count didn't hear it.

"All *his* life, Grandfather kept searching. Yet he never saw it again. But I—I—" the Count held out a hand, palm upward, fingers closed. "I went all the way to that abominable island! I got there first. I had it in the palm of my hand. Yes, I tell you, the Lion was mine!" He opened his fingers apart now, and said dramatically, "Yet, somehow it slipped through my fingers. He would have been the triumph of my family's collection, restored at last."

"The Beethoven Lion!" I murmured, entranced.

And then, I nearly jumped out of my skin when a deep voice came out from the darkness behind us, saying, "Father! What are you doing here at this hour of the night?"

There was a figure of a man in the hallway, and he was coming toward us rapidly. The Count looked suddenly like a naughty little boy, caught with his hand in the cookie jar. But as the man moved toward him, the Count tilted his head back and smiled at him affectionately.

"Kurt, I have some new friends today," he said. "You must come and meet them. This is—" and he paused forgetfully.

"Penny Nichols," I said quickly. "And Jeremy Laidley."

"And this is my son, Kurt," said the Count, then he said, "Good heavens, Kurt, stop scowling there in the dark. Come and say hello."

Kurt stepped out of the shadows and expertly grabbed the handles of his father's chair, turning it around to pilot him out of the room. "Pleased to meet you," Kurt said.

I stared at him. It was the young German guy on the boat. Surely he knew who we were, yet his face did not betray that he'd ever seen us before.

"My boy is quite an adventurer," the Count said proudly. "He studies the climate all around the world! He climbs high mountains and lives for months and months in the big trees, to make a study. He is very smart. But always he is far away. Except this summer when he has come to visit me."

Kurt just said, "Let us go back now, Father. It's too drafty in this room at night."

Jeremy and I followed them back to the Count's study, but I managed to mutter into Jeremy's ear, "That's the sad-looking German guy I told you about, who came to our cocktail party!" Jeremy had to think a moment to remember, then nodded.

"You must introduce these nice people to your mother," the Count said happily. Kurt appeared visibly pained by this remark, and it was clear that his father's condition deeply troubled him.

The Count looked up at me now. "Old age is a shipwreck," he said plaintively. "Know who said that?" I shook my head.

"General Charles de Gaulle!" the Count said, and then laughed uproariously at a German Count quoting a hero of the French Resistance.

"Your supper awaits you, Papa," Kurt said, as the butler arrived to wheel him away.

The Count, looking a bit dejected, bid us farewell in a sigh, "Ah, well, *adieu!*"

Chapter Twenty-one

"I hope you will join me for bit of cold supper," Kurt said in the easy way of a man accustomed to luxury in all its incarnations, both formal and relaxed. He led us down the dramatic wood staircase, across a brief landing, to a large, bright room on the right side of the castle, which he called "the master's kitchen."

"The cook will send it up from her kitchen," Kurt continued. "I thought we'd be more comfortable here, rather than the dining hall, which is very big and very dark and a bit gloomy for a small party."

"What do you think he wants from us?" I mumbled to Jeremy.

"The boat," Jeremy mumbled back, as we followed him.

This master's kitchen was really an informal family dining room, with a polished terracotta floor, sparkling white cabinets, a metal sink, a simple stove, and a narrow refrigerator. A big dining table took up most of the room, its surface made of individual squares of tile, each being a replica of a page from an antique botanical book, with colorful illustrations of fruits and flowers, all labelled with their Latin names.

A young servant girl in her early twenties, with a flat, round cheerful face and two long braids tightly plaited down her back, dressed in a blue-and-white-checked uniform and a spotless white apron, was taking plates and cutlery from the cabinets and laying them out on the table for us. The "cook's kitchen"—where the real food preparation was done—was apparently downstairs in the basement, because very soon we heard a rumbling sound behind one of the cupboards, and when the servant opened the cupboard I saw that it had a dumbwaiter inside. The girl reached in and lifted a large platter with a silver dome. She staggered under the weight of the platter as she placed it on a sideboard, took off the cover, and carried the tray around to each of us. She served the men first.

"You were on the boat the night of our party," Jeremy said. Kurt nodded without the slightest trace of guilt on his face.

"*Ja*, it's true," he said cheerfully. "I wanted to make sure that my father hadn't left his little trinket behind on the boat. Night and day he asks me where it is, I couldn't stand it any longer, so I went to take a look."

"Why didn't you introduce yourself and just ask us about it?" I said.

"I saw that you had your family and friends there," Kurt said. "I did not wish to intrude on a family party." He sighed. "My foolish sister should have checked before she sold the boat," he said, sounding irritated. "She has taken over the family finances ever since father had his stroke; she's like his secretary. Too efficient and too quick. She convinced him it was best to sell it, to help pay for his nurse and the medical expenses, which have been considerable. But father did not remember to tell my sister that he left his dearest treasure behind. If she'd known, of course, she would not have included it in the sale. Just a sentimental trinket, you understand, but—" Kurt sighed in a melancholy way, "he is *so* fond of it."

When the girl with the tray came to my side, I nodded toward what I wanted from the platter of cold meats, sausages, and cheese as she held a serving spoon and fork expertly in one hand and made the selections for me, while still balancing the platter in her other arm. After she served us, the girl went back out and then returned with a tray of glass steins of beer for each of us. A little sandy-haired boy toddled in, carrying a basket of bread which he very seriously offered to each of us. I had to smile at him, but when I said, "Thank you very much," he looked suddenly shy, and quickly bowed and hurried out of the room.

"He is the cook's grandchild," Kurt said tolerantly. "She cares for him when the mother is working in town. They are Polish, but the boy's father is English. The young girl is his sister. They are very hardworking people." We ate in silence for a moment. Then Kurt looked inquiringly at Jeremy, giving him an opening to broach the subject on everyone's minds.

"Are you aware that someone stole the boat the night of our party, and ransacked it?" Jeremy demanded, watching Kurt's face for his reaction.

Kurt was still unperturbed by the implication. "The marine gendarmes told me about it," he said, calmly but sympathetically. "Well, they have to question everybody, don't they? It's the law. But of course, we had nothing to do with this, I assure you. I had planned to return and ask your permission to search the boat for the aquamanile."

Hmm, I realized distractedly. Aquamanil-*ia* was the plural, meaning a bunch of them, as a general category; whereas aquamanil-*e* is for just one of them. "What are these things, actually?" I asked. "Bronze sculptures? From what period and country?"

Kurt turned his full attention to me in a charmingly accommodating way, as if delighted to have piqued my curiosity. "Oh, they date back to ancient times! They were made all through the Roman empire and the Dark Ages, too. Many of the later ones are of Germanic origin."

"*Aqua* is water," I mused aloud, "and *manile*—?"

"From the word for 'hands,'" Kurt said. "To wash your hands with. Or, to pour oil. They were used for religious rituals as well as for hand-washing at the table. You see, they are not mere sculptures. They are actually hollow metal vessels, with a spout—usually in the animal's mouth—for pouring it out, and another hidden little hatch on top—usually in the animal's head—to fill it with water or oil."

"How amazing!" I said, at the thought that those finely detailed figures of fanciful and mythological animal shapes were actually functional objects, like a teakettle.

He added proudly that German workshops were important in the making of aquamanilia, because of their proximity to the mines that provided the copper alloy needed to create them, in a very complex process that involved many stages, not unlike an alchemist.

Jeremy had been patiently taking this all in, but now he spoke boldly. "What about the Beethoven Lion?" he asked. "That's what your father is looking for, right?"

Kurt looked momentarily thrown, but he recovered. "Have you seen it?" he inquired. "Is it true the damned thing really exists, and that Father was not just—er—dreaming about it?"

"I don't know," Jeremy said. "We saw nothing like these objects on the yacht."

"What's it got to do with Beethoven?" I asked, intrigued.

"Why, because it looked like the great composer himself," Kurt said, as if it were the most obvious reason in the world. "Or so they say! The Lion's head, with that great mane and its ferocious scowl, you know—" Kurt screwed his face into a frown—"supposedly resembled Beethoven's fierce face and all that wild hair of his."

"Your father said something about an auction," Jeremy prompted.

Kurt sighed an existential kind of sigh. "Oh, that old chestnut is a legend in my family by now! Papa says the Lion was stolen from our family hundreds of years ago, and my grandfather sought to retrieve it when he thought he came across it—only to have it disappear yet again."

"And now your father says the same thing," I said. A shadow crossed Kurt's face. I realized I might have inadvertently suggested that craziness ran in his family.

"Is this object very valuable?" Jeremy asked.

Kurt shrugged, "To my family, of course, for sentimental reasons. Perhaps to music fans, because of the possible Beethoven connection—which is questionable."

"I'd love to see it!" I exclaimed.

"Yes, well, so would Father," Kurt said ruefully, as the servant girl came in again, opened the dumbwaiter and pulled out another platter, this time with a silver coffee service and a pot of whipped cream.

"Is that why there are so many lions in his collection?" I asked.

Kurt, looking embarrassed, said, "Obviously this is not the first time that my father has gone out on a wild chase, thinking he'd found it. Come, see for yourself."

He led us back into the smoking room, and he marched right up to that bookcase with those tall skinny things that looked like books, but which I'd suspected were hiding-boxes. When Kurt pulled down one box and opened it, revealing that there were large envelopes hidden in them, I smirked triumphantly at Jeremy.

"Take a look," Kurt said, opening the envelopes and spreading their contents out on the table. These were X-rays of several lion aquamanilia. He held them up to the light, so that we actually could see the interiors of the animal figures, and their clever construction, with holes where gas escaped as the molten metal was poured; and you could also see the iron rods inside that held the figure of a knight upright on one of them.

"It is a way of verifying the authenticity, I suppose. Father hired so-called experts to track down his lost treasure, and whenever they thought they'd found it, he authorized them to buy it for him. But not one of these turned out to be the Beethoven Lion," Kurt said dolefully. "My father even went so far as to install his own X-ray machine upstairs which his nurse knows how to use. I wish I could make him give this up."

"What happened to your father when he went out on the yacht?" Jeremy asked.

"Ah, that's the question!" Kurt exclaimed. "Did he really get his hands on the Beethoven Lion? Father insists he did, and believes he left it on the boat; which is why I'd like to see for myself if perhaps he hid it in an odd place, or if he was merely—dreaming again. Sure, it would be marvellous if we found it, but even so, it would probably turn out to be just another mistake," he said, gesturing at the X-rays as he put them away again. He really did look dubious. "However, if I find no lion at all on the yacht, at least I can tell Father that I searched with my own eyes and it simply is not there. Maybe then he will stop asking me over and over about it."

"But whoever took the yacht may have already stolen it," Jeremy said.

Kurt said, "Of course, that's entirely possible."

Jeremy had been sharply sizing up the situation. Now he said, very neutrally, "We will be happy to search the yacht with you, to see if it was somehow overlooked. If the Lion turns up, then of course we'll make some arrangement. But you do understand that the yacht was sold to us with its contents, so everything else on that boat must stay on it. Agreed?"

"Yes, certainly." Kurt made a small, polite bow, and Jeremy told him when to meet us at the yacht in Nice. Then Kurt walked us to the front door, and we went out into the cool, mysterious night.

"Boy, you were pretty tough," I observed as we got into the car.

"I wanted to make sure that he doesn't show up and try to claim half the stuff on that yacht," Jeremy said in his lawyerly way.

"He won't."

"Well," Jeremy said as he started the car and we headed out into the cool, dark night, "these guys must know more than they're telling us."

"You don't trust the Count?" I asked incredulously.

"Did it ever occur to you that your nice little Count might just be the mastermind behind 'Le Boat-Jacking'?" he inquired.

"Oh, please," I scoffed. "That sweet old bean? He's barely got all his marbles in place."

"Those are the ones," Jeremy said darkly. "A father-and-son team of con artists."

"You don't really believe that," I observed, "or you wouldn't have agreed to this. You know as well as I do that there's no Lion on that boat."

"Says who?" Jeremy demanded.

"I say," I said. "I can just feel it isn't."

Jeremy groaned. "Then why didn't you 'feel' that the boat was going to be stolen?" he said. "That would have been useful."

"I didn't say I was a soothsayer," I said huffily. "I merely said I could tell that the thing isn't on the yacht. But of course, we should look."

"Exactly. I'll call Claude and make damned sure he doesn't let anybody near that boat until we get there," Jeremy said.

"Maybe we should also ask Louis to keep an eye on everybody

down there," I pointed out in a rare burst of pragmatism. "Louis did a great job protecting our interests with the French part of Great-Aunt Penelope's estate. After all, Claude may still be loyal to the Count. And even Thierry and those gendarmes like the Count. So I say, let's put a man of ours on the case."

"What?" Jeremy said with mock surprise. "You mean to say you don't trust your little French cop boyfriend?" He had been regularly teasing me about Thierry, saying that the guy had a crush on me, and implying that it was somewhat mutual (it wasn't) or that at the very least, I was enjoying it (I was) and therefore possibly encouraging it (I wasn't. Well. Not really.)

"Ho, ho," I replied. Then I said more soberly, "Oh, Jeremy. I hope neither one of us ends up like the poor Count. 'Shipwrecked,' as he said. Isn't life so sad in the end?"

"Well, if I go a bit senile someday, just park me in the corner like him," Jeremy said, "but be sure to hire somebody to fire off the cannon every evening for the cocktail hour."

When we returned to our room at the Grand Hotel, and Jeremy put the gold-tasseled key into the lock, we found that the maids had made up our room again with fresh towels, and had laid white linen squares on the floor along each side of the bed, atop the rug, so that, if we got up in the middle of the night and couldn't find our little terrycloth slippers, we could step on something clean and gentle. On each pillow were little wrapped candies and chocolates (that actually were worth unwrapping), and our bathrobes had been hung up; but my half-filled bottle of water and its glass remained on the nightstand, politely unmolested. Jeremy flung open the window and we gazed out at the beautiful mysterious lake, and inhaled the night scent of flowers as the moon sent its shimmering glow across the water.

Yep. It was going to be awfully hard to say goodbye to Lake Como.

Part Six

Chapter Twenty-two

The repairs on our villa at Antibes were coming along nicely, but the workmen were still at it, and they acted as if we had no business being there, getting underfoot on their work site. We didn't linger; Jeremy and I were in a tearing hurry to get to the yacht in Nice. But now we had my little chariot awaiting us. There it was, sitting in its parking slot on the left side of the garage—Aunt Penelope's 1936 Dragonetta, all spruced, repaired, shined up and ready to go.

I almost didn't recognize it, because when it was first bequeathed to me, it was perilously on its way to becoming a rust-bucket, with upholstery all torn up by those disrespectful mice. But Denby had lovingly repaired it all, being careful to use materials that were natural to its period, and avoiding turning it into one of those cars that have been so completely overhauled that they bear no real resemblance to their original glory. He'd left a note on the windshield. *She's a real beauty, Penny, and she's ready to rock and roll. Enjoy!*

"He did a great job," Jeremy commented as I ran around squealing over every beautiful restoration. "Let's go to the harbor in this car today," he suggested.

Dare I drive it? I did. Fortunately, when I was sixteen my father had insisted that I learn to drive a manual as well as an automatic. At the time, I suspected him of dark motives, like trying to postpone my inevitable freedom on wheels. But now I saw the wisdom of it. I hopped in the driver's seat, Jeremy slid into the passenger seat, and I tentatively started her up. The motor purred promisingly. Very carefully, I backed it out of the garage and turned around in the circular drive. Smooth as silk, with an engine worthy of a great little airplane. Halfway down the driveway I carefully tested the breaks.

"Nice and easy," Jeremy observed approvingly. Confident, I began to pick up speed. I liked the way she responded, and it was a thrill to feel so connected to the road, hugging the turns and emerging from them with pinpoint control. Finally, I set that cobalt-blue baby loose on the main corniche road of the Riviera. And I could swear that, like a horse, it was happy to be back on familiar turf. It was light, fast, and powerful. Every time we passed through a village and I paused at a light, people came out of shops and cafés to admire it.

"You're a natural in this car," Jeremy said in amusement. I felt I was travelling in another era, and yet, I knew that this little auto would always be a part of my future, having been the instrument that first set me on the path to our inheritance, and the wider, more exciting realm of chasing after one's destiny.

Penelope's Dream was sitting serenely in the harbor. One of the day workers was hosing down her decks. Yachts, as Claude had warned us, require constant care—washing, polishing, tinkering, fussing—because one is always fighting the elements of salty sea and air that want to corrode and rot and wear the thing down and take it back to the sea. Gerard, the engineer, was busy in the engine room. He nodded and grunted to us but went right back to work.

Louis, our French lawyer, was waiting in the main salon for us. He had taken seriously his assignment of watching out to make sure that nobody, not even the crew, disturbed anything from the curio cupboards or anywhere else.

He conferred with us in a low tone. "Nobody's touched anything since you called," he said. "The captain isn't here yet. He'll come later. But the German gentleman has arrived. I told him to wait on the forward deck so I could keep an eye on him."

Louis went now to invite Kurt to join us. Kurt seemed to understand the situation, and did not look offended at being kept waiting out on the deck. He and Louis both had that old-world courtesy which goes a long way when dealing with a situation requiring diplomacy. (Like, when nobody really trusts anybody.)

Jeremy explained that Louis would supervise the searching of the yacht.

"Perhaps," Jeremy suggested to Kurt, "before we begin, you could fill us in on this trip that the Count says he took when he was searching for the Lion."

"I have been trying to get my father to do just that," Kurt said ruefully. "Claude can tell you the details, but here's the important facts: My father thought he tracked down the Beethoven Lion to a dealer in Corsica. Papa didn't want to let it slip through his fingers, so he immediately went to meet with the man. Papa returned to the boat with a wrapped parcel that he took aboard. The whole crew saw the package, but he never let them touch it or unwrap it. They hit bad weather on the way back to Nice, and my father fell ill and had a stroke. It was many months before he could recover his speech and other faculties, and we had to keep him in the nurse's care. His memory came back, slowly, but in patches. And he told my sister it was all right to sell the yacht, for he seemed to know that he would never race her again."

Kurt had been looking off in the distance, remembering. Then his gaze settled on the boat as if he were returning to the present. "Later, Father began to remember buying the Lion, so he searched the castle for it. But when the news reached him that the sale of his boat at auction had gone through, this apparently triggered something in his mind. He now seemed to recall that he'd left the Lion behind on the boat. He described getting up out of bed in the night to check on it, in a suitcase in a linen closet just outside his cabin."

Kurt looked up at us now. "You can see why I would like to lay this story to rest," he said. "Father gets agitated every time he remembers it."

I'd noticed that Kurt seemed genuinely pained at the picture of his father conducting this odd transaction. His father's mind had been intact then, so I wondered if Kurt's discomfort was due to the possibility that his father had been conducting business that may not have been entirely on the up-and-up. This is a real hazard for collectors. When they want something badly, it's too easy to cross the fine line between "found" and "stolen" goods, and a buyer might end up commissioning an art "dealer" who thinks nothing of looting an archaeological site and smuggling the treasure out of the country illegally.

From the look on Jeremy's face, all this had crossed his mind, too. "Okay," Jeremy said to Kurt. "Let's take a look."

Louis conducted the search. He started with the dining salon, the bar, and the main salon. Initially, it seemed a perfunctory exercise. Jeremy and I had been through these cupboards over and over, first when we explored the boat upon buying it, then to assess what supplies we needed, and again after the boat was stolen. I knew darned well that there was no Lion here. This was merely for Kurt to see for himself.

But then, he casually dropped a bombshell. "My father, like many collectors, has special hidden compartments for his greatest treasures," Kurt said. "Even I did not know all his hiding places on the boat until just yesterday when he told me where they were. May I?"

He returned to the trophy shelves in the bar, and began tapping on wall panels alongside them, which opened to reveal hidden cupboards.

"Secret compartments!" I cried. "Wow!" Kurt and Louis smiled in amusement, then glanced at Jeremy as if to say *And where did you find this slightly naive, wildly enthusiastic American girl?* Jeremy allowed himself a pleased but complicit Euro-smile. I ignored them, fascinated with all the compartments, which were like miniature versions of the secret doorway in the castle. I kept trying to guess the next little hideaway; it was like staring at a drawing and looking for all the hidden faces imbedded in the artwork. We found a hidden drawer beneath the mini-refrigerator under the bar; and, in the main salon, there was a false bottom in the side-table near the sofa.

When we went down below, Louis began with the linen closet, sliding the door open so that we could see it had only towels, sheets, blankets, napkins and tablecloths in it. Then we tried the master cabin, where Kurt found a drawer beneath the bed-table, and a cupboard behind the vanity mirror, and even under the wash-stand in the bathroom. But, every single cupboard was empty.

"You see," Kurt was saying, "when Father was a younger man, and went on expeditions to dangerous places, these secret drawers kept things safely hidden, both at sea and when the boat was docked." And, I thought, in case the police took it into their heads to board the boat and search for stolen antiquities.

"They were for father's guests, too," Kurt continued, "so the ladies could hide their jewelry in these secret places, when they swam or bathed or slept at night, or went ashore to shop."

Which meant that they didn't trust the hired help, either, I mused. Another hazard of wealth. You buy too much stuff, and then you have to be suspicious that everyone on earth—including friends and servants—wants to steal it from you.

"Well, that's that," Kurt said as he stood up, having examined the last hiding-place in the guest cabins. "I can tell Father that there was no sign of the Lion aboard this boat. Either he never had it—or somebody stole it off the boat—that is what Father will say."

He looked at us now as if he'd just made a decision about something that had been hovering over the whole discussion. "I would like to make a proposition. You see, my father is unlikely to abandon his pursuit; he's already been talking about hiring another investigator to find his Lion. When I pointed out where this has led us—to that menagerie of wrong lions—he said, 'Why not ask that delightful girl and her young man who came to visit? She is an expert.'"

"Us?" I said in surprise. Kurt nodded, and turned to Jeremy now.

"I hope you do not mind, but I did some investigating of my own," Kurt said. "It wasn't hard; many museum people are talking about the American heiress and her English lawyer who work as a team. They say you tracked down a hidden, priceless painting that had been in your family's possession for a long time, but which everyone else had been unable to find. And that you took great care in choosing the museum you sold it to. Everyone said that you kept your head, and conducted this fairly, taking time to verify your find, with a meticulous attention to detail."

He had turned back to me now. "The other investigators were—clumsy—with my father's feelings, getting him over-excited for nothing. I saw how gentle you were with him. And so I wonder if you would allow me to engage both your services to look for this little treasure? Do you think you would possibly accept such an engagement?"

I stifled a gasp. I was thrilled. Our very first commission for the firm of Nichols and Laidley. Or Laidley and Nichols. Whatever.

But Jeremy, cool hotshot lawyer that he is, said very calmly, "Well, that is an interesting proposal, I must say. But we will have to give it some thought."

I surreptitiously pinched Jeremy's arm to communicate my opinion on the subject. Being English, he didn't even say "ouch."

"It would be great if you could find out, once and for all, if the damned thing ever really existed," Kurt said.

"In that case," Jeremy said, "you must tell us all you know about the Beethoven Lion."

"Ah," Kurt said. "Not very much, I'm afraid. But I do know that most aquamanilia made during this period, though valuable to collectors, are not usually as prized as the ancient and the medieval ones. You see, the Beethoven Lion was supposed to have been made in the 1800s. In those days, it became a real vogue among the wealthy to collect aquamanilia. Only, there wasn't enough of the real antique stuff to go around. So metalworkers began to make copies of the medieval ones—and sometimes they actually sold such copies as genuine originals, but they were outright fakes! Very ingenious what they did, even deliberately putting a false patina on them to convince buyers that they'd bought bona fide antiques."

"But the Beethoven Lion, surely, was considered a genuine contemporary item at the time, right?" I asked.

"If it actually existed at all!" Kurt said. "My father always believed so. But many collectors and music experts began to doubt it, and the story died down. Until, very recently, a picture was published by an English travel photojournalist who claimed to come across it. That got everyone looking again. Then, supposedly, this antiques dealer got his hands on it."

"What was the dealer's name?" Jeremy asked. Kurt shook his head.

" 'Jones' somebody. He was English. That's all Father could recall. But I am beginning to suspect that the whole thing was a hoax, and the dealer tricked him. I've been unable to locate the man. He has apparently vanished into thin air."

This wasn't much to go on. But I found it fascinating. Yessir. Digging needed to be done. I was surprised at how happy I was to be back in the saddle again.

"What did your father pay for the Lion?" Jeremy asked.

"Now *that* he remembers!" Kurt exclaimed. "He says he paid a hundred thousand euros." Kurt sighed. "So, if you think you might take this on, then perhaps you could tell me your fee . . ." he suggested.

To my delight, Jeremy, Louis and Kurt skillfully discussed what sort of terms we would consider if we took on this engagement. Jeremy suggested that, if we actually found the Lion, and there was a conflict about ownership, it could be sold to a museum and the proceeds would be split, just as we did with Great-Aunt Penelope's painting; and that way, our fee would come from the sale. It was a way of our not taking a salary or any money up front, which Jeremy thought would protect us from being the kind of hired guns who'd end up worrying more about covering the client's—er—butt—than about finding out the truth. Louis said that he could draw up proper papers to make the agreement legal, without in any way impinging on our ownership of the yacht and its other contents. Kurt actually seemed not only comfortable with this, but, somehow, relieved. I realized that he had been burdened with the task of finding out about the Lion, and he seemed cheered to have lucid company with whom he could talk about it freely. He thanked us politely, then went off and climbed into a black BMW and drove away.

"How do you like that?" Jeremy demanded, once Kurt was gone. "*He* checked *us* out!"

"But this is fantastic!" I cried. "It's the beginning of our new enterprise." I peered at Jeremy. "What made you agree to do it?"

"Well, it came down to this," Jeremy said. "I knew that you'd go investigating this thing anyway. I figure if we make it official, then at least you'll have a legitimate reason for sticking your nose where it doesn't belong. But you have to promise me one thing."

"What?" I asked suspiciously.

"You have to run everything you're going to do by me first, to make sure you don't do something that will make me, your partner in this absurd enterprise, have to pay ransom to some kidnapper or go searching for you on the shady side of the Riviera."

"Huh!" I observed. "Could it be that you're just as excited as I am about this? It's because it's got to do with Beethoven, right? That's the part that intrigues you. Admit it!"

"Promise me what I just asked you to promise," Jeremy said firmly.

"Oh, that, sure, okay," I said evasively. Louis smiled.

Jeremy said wearily, "I could do with a cuppa."

"What? Oh, tea," I said. "Wish you'd speak English now and then. I'd love to make us some tea!" I enthused, remembering the adorable tea service on board. It had been so securely fastened to the china cupboard, which was lined with felt and had special indentations for the cups and saucers and plates to rest in securely, that the vandals didn't bother to destroy them.

"Are you sure you know how to make tea without the bags?" Jeremy asked mockingly.

"With *my* English mother?" I said, offended. "Surely you jest, m'boy. Sit down and relax while I play house with this cute little kettle and this adorable stove. Fortunately for us, François went ahead and bought us some fresh tea and coffee. You guys go sit in the salon."

Louis and Jeremy went off, and I put the kettle on and arranged the tea tray. But then François, the steward, came aboard, horrified that we had to prepare our own food. I couldn't shoo him away. Being French, he was appalled to find me doing something un-scheduled or *pas normal*, like showing up with guests without giv-ing him advance instructions. He'd arrived with a shopping bag full of sandwiches, fruit and lemon, to make lunch for the crew.

"But if only you had told me you were coming, I would have gladly prepared something really special for you to eat!" he cried, in genuine distress.

"No prob," I said, hurriedly trying to find a way to get him out of my hair. "We only want tea." But he insisted on making it for us.

So I went into the salon and sat down next to Jeremy on the sofa. Louis's mobile phone rang, and after he took the call, he said that he must return to the office on another matter. He apologized profusely to me for having to miss my little tea party.

After he'd gone, Jeremy said teasingly, "Why is it that we are suddenly surrounded by young French men instantly smitten with the American heiress? Thierry was nuts about you. Now Louis and François blush when you look at them. Even Kurt loves it when you ask him questions, and he's not even French!"

"Are you implying that men like me for my money?" I de-manded, "and not my beauty, charm, wit, and innate loveliness?"

"On the contrary, my dear," Jeremy assured me. "What they like about you, money could never buy."

François arrived, and set the tray down in front of us, with cups for three people. When he saw that Louis had gone, I said quickly, "It's okay, I'm sure Claude will want a cup when he arrives."

After François left us, Jeremy raised his teacup to clink with mine, and I said, "To our first 'engagement' . . . and the Beethoven Lion!"

But then, what could have been a perfect moment aboard our yacht, was ever-so-slightly altered. "Yoo-hoo!" came a dreadfully familiar voice, instantly breaking the spell. We both looked at each other in dismay.

"Lord, no!" Jeremy groaned.

A moment later, Rollo's head popped around the corner with a searching look. Then he saw our expression, and he broke into a wide grin.

Chapter Twenty-three

"Well, cheers!" Rollo cried, ambling toward us without waiting for an invitation. "What's this—a real English tea? Splendid! Wouldn't mind a cup myself." And he settled himself on the other side of the sofa, sinking in with a relieved, weary *"Whuf!"*

"Been looking for you all week," he said, taking off his Panama hat and dropping it on the table. "Heard about the theft of *Penelope's Dream* and the wreckage! Bad luck, old boy," he said, turning to Jeremy. "Terribly sorry to hear it."

"Everything's fine now," Jeremy said, tersely and gruffly. Rollo turned to me with a gimlet eye.

"Don't wish to intrude," he said, "but did I hear you say something about the Beethoven Lion? How extraordinary. I say, my man—" he addressed François, who had returned to see if we needed anything, "have you got any more lemon for the tea?"

I glanced up apologetically at François. "We have use for that third teacup, after all," I told him. François observed that I had been as inconvenienced as he, and he nodded as if he'd do his best to lighten my load. He poured tea for Rollo before leaving again.

"Rollo," Jeremy said warily, "what do you know about the Beethoven Lion?"

"Why, it's a curious piece of aquamanilia," Rollo said eagerly. "Prized more for its legendary aspect." He turned to me. "Are you fond of aquamanilia, my dear?"

"I don't really know much about it," I admitted. It dawned on me that this sort of stuff was right up Rollo's alley. He'd once tried to engage me in a discussion of the arcane items he collected. I wasn't very receptive at the time; nobody was, not even his own mother, who had a sort of impatient contempt for his preoccupations. He now looked genuinely pleased to have a family member finally listening to him showing off his expertise.

"Aquamanilia were made with a complex metal-casting technique that medieval monks even wrote treatises on. It's a real art form, but it takes the brawn and skill of a blacksmith to do it! Very complicated indeed," Rollo explained. He paused to study—and appraise—a soft white linen napkin with navy monogram that said *Penelope's Dream* on one side and *N&L* in smaller lettering on the reverse side. Then he set it in his lap, helped himself to the little *petits fours* cakes, and began to eat hungrily. He turned to me with a look of appreciation.

"Well, this is marvellous, sitting down to table with family," he said. "Much, much better than eating in a restaurant or an hotel."

Jeremy growled into his teacup, but I had seen something in Rollo's face that I found oddly touching. Sure, he was still appraising everything in sight—like the silverware, for instance; yet, he also seemed like a kid who'd never had a cozy family meal around the table together. I could imagine that as a boy it would have been mighty hard for Rollo to snuggle up to his mum, because Great-Aunt Dorothy had all the warmth of a cobra.

"But this Beethoven Lion," I prompted, "what's so special about it?"

"A gift to old Ludwig," Rollo said. "But it was lost. Or stolen. Some sort of feud, I think. Went back and forth for years. Are you in the market for this rare item? It will cost you a pretty penny—if you'll pardon the pun."

I looked him squarely in the face and said, "Rollo. Just tell me something. I will only ask you this one time, so I want an honest answer from you, because sooner or later, you know, the truth will out. Did *you* have anything to do with the ransacking and hijacking of our yacht? And did you by any chance find the Lion yourself, that night of the cocktail party or any other time?"

Even Jeremy gaspèd. He'd been thinking the same thing all along, of course, and watching for the slightest telltale sign. After all, Rollo had once had no qualms about stealing Great-Aunt Penelope's painting from us. There was a moment of silence that hung in the air as heavily as a giant rock. Rollo's pouchy eyes registered both pathos and craftiness. Finally he sighed aggrievedly and spoke.

"Child, you wound me to the quick!" he said. "Here I am, trying to assist you with all my might. And, I might add, at no possible gain to myself. Well, if you must ask, then I must answer. And the answer is, *NO-Sir!* I had nothing whatsoever to do with what happened to your boat. I swear on the soul of my mother."

I kicked Jeremy before he could snort at this. Rollo revered his mother—and her money—with utter devotion. Rollo now seemed to have recovered his good humor, but he was still very solemn when he said, "You have many fine treasures aboard this boat, but I did not see a Lion on her. Did someone lead you to believe that it was here?"

He glanced from me to Jeremy and back to me again, and when we didn't answer his question, he said stoutly, "Well, you can believe me or not. When things go wrong in this family, I'm always the one people look at cross-eyed, understandably so, I daresay. But for what little it's worth, I did not steal your Lion or anything else aboard this boat."

I'd watched him searchingly, and I thought I saw the gleam of something genuine, under his usual flinty, jaded demeanor. "Okay," I said finally. "I believe you."

Rollo beamed, then jerked his head towards Jeremy, saying wryly, in a stage whisper, "*He* doesn't quite believe in me, but perhaps he'll come round, eventually."

There was a noise from outside, and Jeremy said in brisk relief, "Ah, here comes the captain now." A moment later, Claude entered the salon with his usual athletic, easy gait. Jeremy asked Claude, in low tones, about the fateful night that the Count said they'd taken the boat to Corsica and found the Lion.

Claude's dark grey eyes registered all the nuances, and he nodded vigorously. "Yes, we did make that trip, exactly as he says," he told us. "And I do remember that a man met the Count at the quay, and they went off to a dockside bar together."

"That has to be the art dealer!" I exclaimed to Jeremy. Turning to Claude I asked, "Was he English?"

Claude shrugged. "I couldn't say for sure, but I think so. Yes, I believe he was."

Jeremy eyed him, looking for signs of perhaps too much loyalty to the Count. "What did he look like?" he asked.

"Oh, blue blazer, tan pants, dark sunglasses, brown hair," Claude replied.

"Geez, that could be anybody," I said. "And with a name like Jones. That's as bad as Smith."

"Huh!" said Rollo, interested. "Jones, you say? Why, I'll bet it's old Mortimer Jones. Antiques dealer, right?"

"Does he live around here?" I asked eagerly. Rollo chuckled.

"One might say he operates around here," he said. "In Corsica these days, I'm told, but he gets around. He's based in London, though."

"What happened after they went into the bar?" I asked Claude.

"I don't really know," Claude replied. "The Count was gone for about an hour. When he returned to the boat to go home, he was alone. He was extremely agitated, and in a hurry to go, as if his life depended on getting away from there. But he was carrying a wrapped package in his arms, like a baby."

Jeremy, having decided that there was no point now trying to keep this from Rollo, asked the captain point-blank, "Claude, did you see what it was?"

Claude shook his head. "He never unwrapped it in front of us. It was very strange, because he would not let any of us touch it, not even to put it away for him. It was not like him to be that way, so secretive. He had trusted us to look after his daughter's children many times! Anyway, he took it into his cabin and I never saw it after that. We had very bad weather going home, and the Count became very sick. It was all we could do to get safely to port, and the ambulance met us at the dock. We feared for his life, and that was all that mattered."

"Have you ever seen a metal sculpture of a Lion, here on the boat or anywhere else?" I asked.

Claude said, "No. Soon after he went into the hospital, the Count's daughter came to collect his things. She was very thorough, and removed everything she thought was important—his luggage, clothes and personal effects. I was with her when she did this. There was no Lion aboard."

"And no one else saw or removed anything else from the boat?" Jeremy asked.

Claude reminded Jeremy that Thierry and the older gendarme had thoroughly questioned the entire crew and found them blameless, even the unfortunate young man who'd left his night watch here, who was so penitent he'd even offered to pay for damages from his paycheck.

"Impossible, of course," Claude said. "He'd be paying you back for longer than he imagines. He's just young, that's all." Claude now informed us that Gerald had said he'd need more time to get the engine back in shape; and the security equipment was still being installed. Then he excused himself and went below.

As we walked outside to the main deck with Rollo trailing behind us, Jeremy muttered, "I still say that the Count and Kurt know more than they're telling."

Rollo said, "Afraid you're not going to get very far with this line of thinking, dear boy. Kurt and the Count are fairly well-known in these parts. Impeccable reputation and all. However, I've a notion about that dealer who may have sold the Lion to the Count."

Jeremy gave him a weary expression, but I said eagerly, "What?"

"Well, if he's who I think he is, he's a bit of a bad hat," Rollo warned. "You don't want to just stomp around asking for him, because he'll find out you've been nosing about, and he'll keep away. The island has a reputation for being rather kind to fugitives, no questions asked. If you like, I can make some discreet inquiries among the sort of people I know who can get information quietly."

"That's all we need," Jeremy said. "Perhaps somebody has already tried to warn us off, by molesting the boat."

Rollo nodded. "I will be careful, I assure you."

"Personally, I think we should take the boat straight out to Corsica the minute Gerald is finished with the repairs!" I said. "Retrace the Count's trip. Find this guy—"

"If it's old Mortimer, then he won't be hanging about Corsica now. He always vanishes at the first sign of trouble," Rollo said.

"That's just what Kurt said, that the guy has disappeared," said Jeremy.

"Laying low," Rollo said sagely. "But he'll pop up again, as soon as he thinks the coast is clear. Always does."

"Really?" said Jeremy. "And how do you know so much about this guy?"

With a straight face, Rollo said, "I hear tell." Then he turned to me and said, "The minute I get the word, I'll let you know."

"Or," Jeremy said, "we could try a truly novel approach, and leave it to the police. Thierry must have police contacts in Corsica."

"My dear fellow," Rollo said, "historically, the Corsicans are a proud people who would prefer not to be ruled by the French. I don't think your French police will get very far. But it's up to you. Meanwhile, I'll let you know whatever I find out," he promised.

He picked up his Panama hat, tipped it in the air in my direction, and shambled off to his silver Mercedes.

Watching Rollo drive away, Jeremy shook his head and said, "Well, there he goes, to sell the Count's Lion on the black market, I suppose. He's probably had it hidden in the boot of his car the whole time."

"Oh, come on," I chided him. "If Rollo had the Lion he wouldn't bother hanging around here."

"Sure he would," Jeremy said, "just to see how much we know, and how much we'd pay to get it back."

"Well, if you don't trust Rollo and you don't trust Kurt, how come you essentially took them on as partners in our little engagement?" I asked.

"You know the old saying. 'Keep your friends close, and your enemies closer,' " said Jeremy. He exhaled deeply, then turned to me and noted, "There are storm clouds over there. They look bad. But we might have time for a swim back at the villa, or—"

I never heard the rest, because at that moment a shiny, showy Range Rover came roaring into the parking lot and pulled up very aggressively alongside my Dragonetta. The driver was honking his horn like a schoolboy, and the woman in the passenger's seat was hanging out her window, blonde hair trailing in the breeze.

As soon as the car completely ground to a stop, the woman hopped out as if she couldn't bear to wait another second, and came tripping toward us on the highest strappy-sandaled heels I'd ever seen, and a daringly gauzy orange dress through which you could, well, see a lot of her. She was carrying an open bottle of champagne in one hand, and two glasses in the other; and she marched right up the *passerelle* and on deck, straight to Jeremy, and flung her arms around his neck, and planted a great big wet kiss on his lips.

"Lydia!" he said in a choked voice. "What on earth are you doing *here*?"

Chapter Twenty-four

T he driver of the Rover came stumbling up after Lydia, moving with a rolling side-to-side gait like a bear who'd had too much to drink.

"Jerry, old boy!" he cried out.

"Darling, we've got the most wonderful news!" Lydia cried, still with one arm around Jeremy's neck. "Congratulations are in order, and you've got to make a toast and wish us well," she exclaimed, pouring champagne into one glass and handing it to him, and pouring some into another glass for herself, and then clinking them and saying, in an intimate tone as if telling him a secret, "Bertie and I are engaged to be married!"

Bertie had staggered up to us now. "Hullo!" he said suddenly, stopping in his tracks at the sight of me. "And who's this adorable creature?"

"Bertie, meet Penny," Jeremy said in a slightly strangled voice, "and Penny, this is Bertie, a longtime friend of mine."

Lord love a duck. The old school chum. The lawyer from another firm who was supposed to be keeping an eye on Lydia for us. In case she wanted to kill herself. Or something.

Bertie was a portly fellow, very tall and good-looking, with a long big-cheeked face and a big thick jaw and a good-natured expression that never seemed to leave him. There was something instantly affable and benign about him, although his eyes were sharp enough to comprehend someone else's irony or disapproval. He wore an elegant tan-colored suit and white shirt, but his tie was loosened away from his neck. And one of his plump cheeks had a lipstick smear on it.

I was watching Jeremy now, to see how he handled it. Jeremy, sensing this, had gone all stiff and formal, and he did not invite them to come below deck. So we just stood there the whole time, a *long* time, talking like people who've bumped into one another in a supermarket aisle, frozen in their tracks, pretending to be great chums but stuck at some sort of social impasse.

Bertie and Lydia were so preoccupied with their own news that at first they didn't notice that they hadn't been invited to sit down and hang around. Then, at one point, Lydia did say, "Jeremy! Aren't you going to show us around your lovely yacht?"

And Bertie chimed in, "Right—give us the royal navy tour!"

But Jeremy quickly dissembled, saying that the boat was under repairs, and he'd promised the captain that he wouldn't bring anyone inside to get underfoot just yet. They didn't really care. They had too much exciting news to tell about their wedding plans.

"And we owe great thanks to *you*, Jeremy," Lydia exclaimed, "for bringing me and Bertie together again." Her voice was excited and high-pitched, with a jarring false note at the end of it.

Even though I wanted to believe that she was being sincere (and finally out of Jeremy's hair), I couldn't. I glanced at Bertie, who beamed so happily that I actually felt a little sorry for him. I looked at Jeremy, and he appeared quite uneasy, which only confirmed my suspicions that Lydia was still working on him.

Lydia was prattling on now about how she'd finally realized

that she and Bertie had really *always* been in love with each other but had been committed to other people, the timing had never been right, when one was available, the other wasn't . . .

I was actually rather horridly fascinated by this. I'd never seen anyone spend so much uninterrupted time talking about herself, in that breathless neurotic way. Nobody could get a word in edgewise, except Bertie now and then, when his participation served to enhance Lydia's story. Over and over again she impressed upon Jeremy that she was *so* happy now.

I'd even begun to feel a bit anxious for her because she seemed so terribly agitated . . . until she lobbed another conversational grenade aboard. Guess what? Not only was she getting married, but she'd also reclaimed her passion for decorating, and after talking to some other school chums and their wives, she was convinced that now was the perfect time to set up her interior decorating business in London.

At this point, she turned to look at me directly for the first and only time on this visit, and she widened her eyes when she said, "You've been *so* nice. I'd like to offer you my services to redecorate your villa in Antibes—for *free*," she declared, grasping my forearm with her long-nailed hand. "Bertie and I just drove over there today, and already I have so many great ideas! You won't believe how terrific we can make that place look—and when we're done, I can arrange to have my friend, who edits a decorating magazine, come down and shoot the whole villa for a multiple-page spread in her magazine, you know, 'a makeover for your second home on the Riviera!' It will be great publicity, and it could help my new business really take off! And your villa will be the talk of the Riviera. Won't that be *fun*?"

She said all this girl-to-girl, as if we were old sorority sisters or something. But even though most of her face was smiling widely, her eyes were hard and cold, so angry, in fact, that I fought off the urge to shrink from her. And suddenly, the thought that she had, this very day, gone traipsing around Great-Aunt Penelope's villa, freely poking her nose in all the rooms because the distracted workmen wouldn't know enough to stop her as she went about plotting with her mental measuring tape ... well, it made my blood run cold. Something fierce and protective rose up in me, some instinct I didn't even know I had, when it came to defending, not only Aunt Pen's memory, but the legacy she'd given to me and Jeremy, and the sweet future we were trying to carve out for ourselves.

I said firmly, "Thanks very much, but we have already hired someone else."

"Oh, you can always tell 'whoever' that you've had a change of heart. Think it over," Lydia said, to Jeremy, not me.

I shot a warning look at Jeremy, as if to say, *There is no way in high heaven that I will let this broad get her mitts on my Great-Aunt's villa, you can take that to the bank.*

And Jeremy gave me an imploring look, as if to say, *Whatever we do, please let's not have a scene, I know these people are jackasses but they're old friends and well-connected so if we ever show our faces in London again we may need them someday.*

And my face said, *Then that makes this your party, Bub. Get them out of here.*

Mercifully, Bertie's slightly fogged-out brain cleared a little as he remembered something, looked at his watch and said, "Hang on. We're going to miss our plane if we don't skedattle."

"How long have you been down here?" Jeremy asked.

"Took a long weekend," Bertie said. From the look on his face, and Jeremy's, I could tell that we all simultaneously realized that Lydia had deliberately dragged him all around the coast looking for Jeremy. Thankfully we'd been at Lake Como.

Lydia turned to Jeremy now and said, "Darling, Bertie is having a great big party in London next week to celebrate, and you know how much he adores you, and now that we're all dear friends again, and everyone's finally happy ever after, you *must* come! Bertie will call and give you all the details!"

"Right," Bertie said, unexpectedly serious with Jeremy. "You've got to come. No more excuses. I'll telephone you straight away, once I have all the particulars." And they all hugged one another, and then Lydia went tripping off with Bertie into their Rover, which roared away, leaving a cloud of dust in their wake.

I just stared at Jeremy.

"What? What?" he said defensively. "I didn't promise them anything. And I never gave her our address down here, nor the harbor where we were, nothing. I don't know how she tracked us down. Unless, I suppose, she got Bertie to do it. I mean, Rupert knows him, so . . . But, look on the bright side," he said cheerfully. "At least I'm off the hook! She's finally found a husband who wants to watch over her. He really does. And Bertie's always wanted to meet you, so you ought to see him when he's less—er—celebratory."

Jeremy looked unmistakably fond of his school chum when he said, "Bertie was a good friend, he really was. We lost touch socially, because, well, his wife didn't really care for Lydia."

That I could believe. But I said nothing. I supposed that Lydia could have read, online, about the christening of our yacht in that boaters' gazette.

"Bertie and I got each other through university, and he's one person I've always known I could really count on, even though we used to compete over girls in our school days," Jeremy explained.

"Oh, *bingo!*" I said wearily. "Well, I have to hand it to Lydia, she knew just which cards to play, and which buttons to push."

Jeremy, intelligent man that he is, actually looked genuinely bewildered. "What are you on about?" he asked. "Did it ever occur to you that you can sometimes be wrong? For instance, you thought Lydia was after me! See how mistaken you were?"

"Piffle," I said. "Did it ever occur to *you*," I went on to explain with infinite patience, "that Lydia is trying to make you jealous by evoking your old rivalry with Bertie over girls?"

Jeremy's eyes narrowed. "Oh, I don't think so."

"In any case, you owe me a nickel," I said. At his blank look, I said, "The Sincerity Test I told you about when we left London. Remember our bet? I said that if Lydia was really trying to start anew, she'd stay put in her nice new apartment, soberly assess her life, and get on with it. But if she was after you, then she wouldn't be able to stand being in London when you weren't there. She even found an excuse to come chasing after you in the Riviera and check out your boat. And she snooped around our villa! Damn it, Jeremy! She might have been trying to assess your inheritance to figure out what you're worth."

"She's had that one all figured out, ages ago," Jeremy protested, "and Bertie is a fine catch, believe me. He stands to inherit a great deal, and he's already made millions."

"Nevertheless," I continued, undaunted, "I do NOT want that woman dogging our path down here for months on end with her brilliant ideas to make the villa look like some horrible magazine spread. And, I might add, the last thing we need right now is publicity. Showing the whole world—all those crazy people who want to sell us things or want us to pay for their kids' college tuition— exactly where we live and what we've got. Including whoever it was who vandalized the boat—I mean, suppose there were really drugs hidden in that Lion and smuggled onto the yacht? Happens all the time. If they couldn't find it, they might think we've got it stashed at the villa. And Lydia will give them a road map straight to us."

"Hold it right there," Jeremy said, sounding annoyed now. "Before you go off the deep end with drug smugglers and axe-murderers."

"All I'm saying is, we need our privacy, and we can decorate our own home, ourselves, thank-you-very-much," I said hotly.

"Really, Penny, I thought you were bigger than all this silly female competitive stuff," Jeremy said, annoyed.

Now, no woman in love wants to hear even the tiniest bit of disillusionment in her man's voice, particularly when he's just had his ex-wife hanging about with her arms around his neck. But I was feeling a tad let down, too.

"Well, *I* thought I'd found the one man on earth who was above being duped by manipulative women like Lydia," I retorted. "And P.S., I am not competing with her. She is competing with me! There's a world of difference . . ."

"Penny," Jeremy said slowly, "I don't care a hoot about having Lydia decorate the villa. I frankly think she'll forget all about it when she gets back to London, because she's got a rather short attention span."

"Hah!" I said darkly. "She won't forget."

"If she persists," Jeremy said, "you can tell her again that you don't want it. I leave it to you. Only, please, do it with dignity. Above all, I don't want to quarrel with her—or you—anymore. It's not about an ex-wife. It's about Bertie. One has to be careful with friends, especially when you don't like their choice of spouse. Once the women get catty with each other, things can get very ugly very fast. Everybody starts trading insults, and the resentments can fester for years and years. And I don't want to be put in the position where I can never talk to Bertie again. I like Bertie. I've missed him. And life is too damned short to forget about your friends. I know he's an ass sometimes, but so is everybody. Including me."

"No, you're not," I said in a small, distressed voice, then amended it with, "except when you let your ex-wife touch you as if you still belong to her."

I frankly felt, at this point, that Jeremy should have woken up and realized that all I needed was a little reassurance on his part. But he was too upset to notice. He was saying, "You have my permission to tell Lydia to bug off about the decorating, but just don't do it with ill will. Can we even do it with some grace? Is that possible?"

I thought I detected a teeny tiny bit of the old class prejudice, as if somehow I'd been raised without his snotty attitude which passed for good breeding.

"Oh, gosh, gee, let me see, I *guess* I can figure out a way to be gracious," I said, "even though of course it goes against all my principles. Just who do you think raised me, anyway?"

"Good God," Jeremy said, amused now, "how did this turn into a quarrel about upbringing?" He sighed heavily. "Penny, we don't have to go to Bertie's party. This is our summer break, and we've got plenty of excuses to beg off. There will be other parties, anyway. But do let's be careful with people, all right?"

I suddenly got a terrible, awful, rotten vision of what my future could hold. I thought of having to chum around with Bertie and Lydia for the rest of our lives. The curse of a working imagination is that suddenly you can conjure up the most vivid pictures even before you've given your mind permission to do so. I saw Lydia in ski-bunny costume, forcing us to go on winter vacations with her. I saw her in a teeny bikini, jumping into *my* pool at the villa. I saw shooting parties in country houses where I'd get stuck with the females while the men went out and hunted poor little foxes and pheasants. And everything, no matter what we'd do, would become a competitive sport: who's got the bigger car, the better apartment, the trendiest kitchen, the nicer clothes, the prettier figure, the smartest babies, the most sought-after nanny, the richest husband, the sexiest wife.

But I realized that there was a lot I didn't know about Jeremy's circle of friends, and, therefore, a few things I didn't know about him. I loved him enough to want to find out what they were, and to consider that, if he cared about Bertie and his crowd, then there were probably good things I'd overlooked or hadn't yet discovered about them. I certainly didn't want to add to his stress, nor make him feel he had to choose.

We drove back to the villa quietly, very quietly, more quietly than ever before. Then Jeremy reached out and squeezed my hand.

"Don't worry," he said. "Once *Penelope's Dream* is up and running, and we're no longer a captive audience sitting there in the harbor, then nobody will be able to find us and we'll always have a ready-made excuse—as Mum said, we'll be a moving target. Meanwhile, you and I have gotten ourselves a little assignment. What do you say we get cracking on it?"

Chapter Twenty-five

The best thing about the next couple of days was that I discovered how much more delightful it was to have a partner in my eccentric career. Until now I'd always done my research alone, working for days, even weeks without talking to a solitary soul, except for the occasional curator or librarian. I don't know if I started out in life with the personality of a hermit, or if I developed it of necessity, because of my job. Sometimes you think you're a certain type of personality just because your life circumstances didn't offer you much choice.

But now, I had Jeremy to commiserate with. We camped out in the living room of the villa, because it was the one room that the workmen were done with. We dragged the furniture off the patio and set ourselves up there. At least we were now wired for high-speed Internet, so we set up our computers and sat, head-to-head, digging up whatever we could that was pertinent to the case. We were so engrossed that we scarcely noticed when it began to rain, until it started coming down in sheets, and the workmen told us they'd have to knock off till it stopped.

Well, to slightly alter a well-used expression, when it rains on the Riviera, it pours. Cats and dogs. And those charming, breathtaking corniche roads that make hairpin turns around the stunning cliffs, suddenly turn into a scary roller coaster. You don't want to go for a drive anymore. You just want to stock the house with food and coffee and wine, and snuggle under a blanket until the sun comes out again.

And that's exactly what we did, for several days, sitting there clicking away on our computers. Every now and then one of us would shout out some new information, and print it and put it in a file marked "Lion" or the one marked "Boat." And, Jeremy kept making jokes. Bad ones, at times. And I kept laughing at them, even though I knew I shouldn't encourage him. But he was working seriously, too, and at lunchtime we'd take a break and compare notes.

"What have you got?" he'd say briskly, looking up.

I said, "Remember the Count said that some beggar woman had put on a curse on him—as if she'd even caused that storm that made him ill?"

"Of course," Jeremy said.

"Well," I said excitedly, "he may not have been totally bonkers. In Corsica they have these local shamans called *mazzeri*. That's the plural. It's 'mazzer-*u*' for a guy and 'mazzer-*a*' for a woman. Anyway, they conduct their magic at night, in their dreams. During the daytime, they are fairly ordinary citizens, but are known for their strange, hypnotic stare."

"Like vampires or zombies?" Jeremy asked, fascinated.

"No, not at all. Being one of the *mazzeri* is considered a higher calling. *Mazzeri* could be anybody—the butcher, the baker, the farmer's wife, the mayor. Ordinary by day; but in the parallel world of dreams, they are 'spirit-hunters.' "

"And how exactly does *that* work?" Jeremy inquired.

"Well, since the *mazzeri* operate in the dream world, they know that, at night, the souls of living people take the form of animals, and roam the woods," I replied. "So the *mazzeri* must attack the first animal they come upon, even if it's the soul of someone they know or love. They hunt with sticks and stones. If they wound that soul in their dreams, then, in real life, that person will fall ill. If they kill the animal, then the person will die—but not immediately—so, back in the real, daytime world, the *mazzeri* are able to foretell death or tragedy, see how it works? It's because they know what happens to people's souls at night when we're all asleep, and they know which animal represents the soul of which neighbor."

"Pretty spooky," Jeremy commented. "I imagine nobody wants to get on the bad side of one of these shamans, day or night."

"Yeah, and it's supposed to be a very stressful job," I explained. "The *mazzeri* often try to warn people and save them from their fate. This stuff dates back to Paleolithic times. You know, all those beautiful cave paintings of human figures with animal heads, like bison and boar?" I took a deep breath. "And that's not all. The spirits of the dead come back periodically to visit, or have battles with each other. You don't want to get caught in the middle of one of those ghost battles, they say."

"So," Jeremy said thoughtfully, "you think some local woman was trying to warn the Count that disaster awaited him?"

"Yes," I said. "And it spooked him."

"But," Jeremy said slowly, "why should it spook him?"

"What do you mean?" I asked.

Jeremy said, "The Count is a man of science and art. Why should he care what a superstitious local woman said, unless he'd done something to feel guilty about?"

"Like?"

"Like dealing in stolen artifacts," Jeremy said. "Like grave robbers."

"Wait a minute," I said suspiciously. "What have *you* got?"

Jeremy said loftily, "It just so happens that I think I may have turned up the photograph that got the Count, and all those other crazy collectors, thinking that the Lion still existed somewhere. Look."

He turned his computer screen so I could see it. The photo was very blurry, and it looked as if it had been part of a newspaper feature. "It's from Corsica."

"What is it?" I asked, squinting. "It looks like some sort of festival."

"You might say," Jeremy said. "It's a ritual for the second day of November."

"All Souls' Day," I said, enthralled.

"Right-O. Every year, the Corsicans light torches and have processions, and they visit the family tombs and light candles and put out food and milk, to try to appease their dead relatives, who come back to inspect their graves and make sure you're doing good upkeep," Jeremy said. "Anyway, the next morning, the family checks the fireplace hearth to see if they spot any footprints of the dead."

I shivered. The rain was still pelting against the windows and making sighing sounds as it whooshed around the villa. "But why did the photographer—?"

"Oh, he was just a travel photojournalist who was taking pictures of the procession because he liked the local costumes and color," Jeremy said. "He had no real idea what he was dealing with. But look in the far left corner of the picture. See that metallic thing glowing in the candlelight?"

I peered closer. "Hey," I said. "That *could* be a lion."

Jeremy said, "Apparently, when this article was published, it set off a little firestorm among collectors. A museum director spotted the photo, and hurried down to Corsica to check it out—but by the time he got there, it was gone."

"Gone!" I said. "As in stolen?"

"As in pilfered, pounced-on, pocketed," Jeremy said emphatically. "Nobody knows who, in that stampede of collectors, took it."

"Wow," I said, impressed. "Do you think it was the Count?"

"Or that dealer. Jones."

"But if this thing was in Corsica," I said, "what's it got to do with Beethoven?"

"Ah," Jeremy said. "Beethoven. I've been checking him out, as well."

"Me, too," I said. "What have you got?"

"Nothing about the Lion whatsoever," he said. He flipped over a page of his notepad and read off the things he'd jotted down. "Beethoven was a short fellow—under five foot four. He had a pretty wretched childhood—a terribly abusive teacher who beat him, and an alcoholic father who used to throw him in the cellar without food for punishment, and then wake him in the dead of night and make him practice the piano till dawn."

"He was born in Germany but he lived most of his life in Vienna, didn't he?" I asked, looking at my own notes.

"Yes, he *had* to live there—it was part of the deal he made with his Viennese patrons. Some of them paid up, but some didn't," Jeremy said. "So he had money problems."

"Did he ever marry?" I asked, enthralled.

Jeremy shook his head. "He had affairs with high-society women, and proposed to a number of them, but they turned him down. Well, he had a violent temper and, sorry to say, he was a bit of a slob. Or, to put it more kindly, 'preoccupied.' He'd leave food lying around, stale beer and all, when he was composing. And he'd get so absorbed that he'd forget about his appearance in public," Jeremy explained. "He had all these aristocratic students, including young ladies, like this princess who lived across the street from him. But he'd show up for her music lessons dressed in his pajamas, slippers and little pointy nightcap!"

"But one of his students said he was a very patient teacher," I noted, "who would seldom scold you for hitting wrong notes or missing a passage, because Beethoven figured these were accidental errors; but he would be furious if a student failed to play with the right 'expression' because this showed a lack of attention, feeling and knowledge."

"Right. Even when he was deaf, he could tell if they were doing it correctly by 'sight-reading' the notes and watching the way a pianist moved his hands as he played," Jeremy marvelled. "Kept composing right to the end. They say he used to walk around town humming to himself and gesturing, figuring out the next symphony, dressed like a bag man. Rotten little kids used to taunt him."

"Poor guy. He had awful stomach trouble," I said. "Possibly from lead poisoning. He died when he was only fifty-six." I sighed. "How *could* he write all that beautiful music in so short a time, and without hearing so much of it? Maybe *he* had special powers and could hunt men's souls in his sleep, too—with music."

I was still looking at the notes we'd made when the telephone rang. Jeremy went to answer it. I didn't start paying attention until I heard his tone, and then the words, "Where is she now? Is she out of the hospital?"

I stopped what I was doing, and looked at him. He tried to signal but was too busy getting the details. Finally I heard him say, "I see. Tell her I'll be there as soon as I can."

He hung up, looking troubled. "Mum's had a fall," he said.

"The cleaner found her, and took her to the hospital, but they say it's not bad. They were afraid she might have broken her hip, but they're telling me now that it's a broken ankle."

I realized that Aunt Sheila, although so chic and young-looking, was really old enough to be concerned about ordinary falls causing serious trouble.

"She's home now. I really ought to go and look in on her," Jeremy said. "She told the cleaner not to upset me, and to tell me she's fine; but she's on her own there, and I want to see her for myself."

"Of course," I said. "I'll go with you."

"You don't have to," Jeremy said. "This is not such great weather for flying."

I glanced out the window, and saw that the rain was letting up a bit, and there was even a small, promising patch of blue in the sky. "No, it's looking better out there. I'll go with you," I offered.

"Well, actually, it might not be a bad idea for you to come," Jeremy agreed, looking at his notes. "That photographer is English, and so is the museum director. We could look them up and see if they have any more info about the Lion."

Then a horrible thought crossed my mind, and either Jeremy read my face or else he had the same thought.

"Oh, God," I said. "This doesn't mean we have to go see Lydia and Bertie, does it?"

"No," Jeremy said. "We can stay at Mum's and never set foot in my apartment. We'll skulk in and out of town and nobody will know or care. Besides, aren't your parents going back to the States soon? We promised we'd catch up with them before they leave."

So. Like it or not, I realized, London was calling.

Part Seven

Part Seven

Chapter Twenty-six

We found Aunt Sheila at home, sitting in bed, with a bandaged foot propped up on its own little pillow. She had a bruise on her cheek, too. She looked embarrassed when she saw us.

"I told you two you didn't have to come!" she protested. Jeremy, carrying pretty flowers which he placed in her hands, bent over to kiss the other cheek.

"Penny, darling, really, I'm all right," Aunt Sheila said. "Tell my son I'm all right."

"I did," I said, "but he loves you. Can't help it."

"What happened, Mum?" Jeremy asked, sitting on the end of the bed.

"The silliest thing! I was rushing about, and I missed that step-down in the bedroom, just missed it completely, and I went down rather hard," Aunt Sheila replied.

"Did they do X-rays?" Jeremy asked.

"Of everything! The hip is all right, which is what they were worried about, and no concussion. I'm fine."

"How long were you alone before the maid came?" I asked.

"About twenty minutes, I think. I may have blacked out briefly.

Don't worry. Matilde is looking out for me," Aunt Sheila said. "She stops in once a day to see if I need anything."

"But how can you get around the apartment?" Jeremy asked, gesturing toward the bathroom. Aunt Sheila pointed to a pair of crutches.

"That's not going to work," Jeremy said briskly. "You need somebody here full-time."

"What, to take my temperature and blood pressure and all that bother?" Aunt Sheila said, looking horrified. "I don't want a stranger in the house."

"We thought we'd stay a couple of days," I said. "We're going to visit my folks. They're holed up in some hotel here. I wanted to see them before they head home."

"Oh, dear, I'd hoped to take them out to dinner," Aunt Sheila said.

"We'll figure out something," I said. "Meanwhile, Jeremy and I are going to cook you some supper. Jeremy's getting really good at it, because we've been to these terrific local markets in France, and he's charmed the people who sell the groceries into telling us all about how they like to cook it."

"So, no arguments," Jeremy said. "You're stuck with us."

"You might have let me know," Aunt Sheila said reproachfully. "I'd have had the guest rooms specially made ready for you."

"That's exactly why we didn't tell you," Jeremy said, "but we let Matilde know."

I followed Jeremy out to the kitchen. "She's all right, I think," he said. "But I'm glad we came, just to look after her for a few days. Meanwhile, we still have time to make some research calls. You phone the curator, and I'll call the photographer. Let's see if we can get appointments for tomorrow morning."

Well, the next day, it was actually fun, skulking around London. Jeremy said he felt as if we ought to be dressed in disguise, each wearing a nose and glasses, so that nobody he knew would recognize us and find out that we were temporarily back in town. But the photographer's studio was way out on a fairly seedy side of London, where there were lots of big warehouses that offered comparatively lower rent for audio recording, TV studios, and artists' lofts. I didn't think anybody from Jeremy's posh crowd would be hanging around here.

We went up a creaky old freight elevator—the kind that has only an iron grate for a door so that you can actually see every floor you pass—to the third floor. The door to the photographer's studio was ajar, but Jeremy knocked on it anyway.

"Come in," called out a male voice. We entered, into a spacious one-huge-room that held a very large table, near floor-to-ceiling windows that looked out onto the street; and, on the other end, a bed, a flat-screen TV and DVD center and a kitchen comprised of sink, stove, small refrigerator and oven. The door to an adjoining bathroom was open, and a young female assistant was hanging up wet pictures. The photographer himself, whom Jeremy recognized from his research, was seated at the big table, which was heaped with stacks of enlarged photographs and three giant computer monitors. There was a radio playing somewhere, broadcasting the news in a low, barely audible murmur.

As we moved closer, Jeremy introduced me to the photographer, whose name was Clive.

"Right," Clive said, nodding, looking me up and down. He was a very tall, thin guy with a mop of ash-brown hair. He had lively grey eyes, and wore the kind of khaki shirt, pants and vest that have lots of pockets, which photographers often wear.

"What can I do for you?" he inquired, sitting back in his office chair.

When Jeremy reminded him why we were here, Clive said, "Oh, right, the Lion."

Clive's chair had wheels, so he just rolled himself over to a nearby file cabinet and rummaged through it. He pulled out a file and slapped it on the table. He smiled at me, but spoke to Jeremy.

"Unbelievable ruddy big deal about this thing," he said. "Here I thought I was doing a nice little tourist piece, but I've had my old studio broken into three times before I pulled up stakes and moved here. Did Beethoven put this on his piano or something?"

"That's what we're trying to figure out," Jeremy admitted. "As I mentioned on the phone, we're assisting an old duffer who's a Beethoven buff, and he heard you got near it."

Clive gestured to two folding chairs on the other side of the table, inviting us to sit. Then he handed us the file. The top photo was the one we'd seen on the Internet, but now I could view the details more easily, because the print was larger and sharper. Clive had obviously focused on the memorial procession, following it from the church to the grave, of old men and women, and children dressed up in native costumes, holding candles and torches. Behind them was a grassy hill, and what looked like an open cave all alight with candles.

"What is that?" I asked, pointing to the cave.

"It's a shepherd's hut, built into the hillside. Very old; the family that you see in front of it has made it into a family crypt," Clive said. "It is kept closed all year, except for this feast day when people lay wreaths of flowers and offerings to their dead ancestors." He flipped the photo over so that we could see the next ones, which were of the church procession. Finally, we got to the last picture.

This was a blow-up of the metallic item that had been in the background of the first picture. It was still blurry, so I supposed you could imagine it to be what you wanted. But I did think it looked very much like a metalworked piece, and a lion standing on all fours with a great big mane.

"That's the best shot I've got of it," Clive said, reading our minds. "The rest underneath are just copies."

"Has the Lion been actually verified by anyone?" Jeremy asked.

Clive shook his head. "The museum bloke who was supposed to do that simply didn't get there in time," he said hurriedly. "And to tell you the truth, I'm sick of the whole thing. People think I saw it and can identify it, so they bring me all sorts of lions, believing they've recovered it. I never even noticed the damned thing. There was so much else to look at that night. But once the collectors saw the picture, well, that really set the cat among the pigeons."

I stared at the photograph of the festival, with all those faces glowing in the candlelight. "Which of these people are related to the one in the—grave?" I asked.

"All of them!" Clive said. "They have a large family. I asked about the Lion. They didn't really want to talk about it. Said it had been in their family for centuries."

"I don't suppose they could explain the Beethoven connection?" Jeremy asked.

"Bah," Clive said. "I think these antiques boys make up this guff to drive up the price."

"Who do you think stole it?" I asked boldly.

Clive shrugged. "Could be any number of brokers or traders in this stuff," he said. "Some of them think nothing of walking off with treasures from graves or digs. But personally, I think it was a rival family. I heard that there had been some kind of feud going on, and the thing changed hands and went back and forth and blood was spilled."

"Like, a *vendetta*?" I asked, wide-eyed.

"The word itself was invented in Corsica, they say," Clive replied. "Their history is full of revenge stories. Whole towns carried on for centuries."

"Can I make a copy of the first and last pictures?" I asked.

"Take one of each, love," Clive said. "I've got plenty more. Just do me a favor. If you write an article about it, *don't* credit me as the photographer. I've had enough of it. I used to like Corsica. Rented a nice little place, but now I can't get a moment's peace."

He shook his head wearily. "I've published thousands of pictures," he said. "War zones, sweatshops, drug lords. But have you ever seen antiques collectors when they've got their sights trained on something? They just won't listen to reason."

Jeremy asked if the museum director we'd planned to talk to was indeed the one who had come down to verify the Lion. "Yeah, Donaldson. He just missed it," Clive said uncomfortably. "Wasn't fast enough. Supposedly an expert on that stuff, but I wouldn't bother with him. Don't think he'll have much to add for you. Pissy kind of fellow, very imperious. I must tell you that lots of people have been after this Lion, but the trail went cold almost as soon as it heated up. I heard there's a curse on the thing, so frankly, I'd like to see an end to it."

We thanked him and headed out. "Right, cheers," he said.

Chapter Twenty-seven

"Well, that wasn't much help," I said as we went out onto the street and climbed into the rental car. "Poor guy, he's sick of it."

"I'd say it's a bit more than that," Jeremy said. "I'm not sure what ails him, but maybe the museum expert can tell us."

The traffic in London was nearly hopeless. It took us forever to get across town to the higher-end section where the small, elegant museum was situated in a narrow brick house on a quiet, leafy street. As we climbed the white stairs to the front door, I noticed a surveillance camera just above the entrance, which was unlocked. But as we stepped into a small foyer, there was an inner door which was locked; and we had to be buzzed in by the tall, dark security guard at the front desk. I could see him through the window. He looked up when we rang, sized us up, and let us in. There was a young woman with her hair skinned back in a tight ponytail, standing alongside him. Both wore black suits.

"Would you like a catalog?" she asked. I saw a banner for the current display, which was *Swords and Shields of the Middle Ages.*

"No, thanks," Jeremy said easily. "We have an appointment with Mr. Donaldson," he explained.

The girl picked up the telephone, and spoke in a low voice. When she hung up she said indifferently, "Please wait here. He'll be out presently."

We drifted around in the lobby, waiting interminably. During the whole time, no visitors came in or out of the museum.

"Why does this place look like a 'front' for something?" I whispered to Jeremy. "You know, where some spy comes in from the cold." I sighed. "I suppose we could have done all this by phone," I said gloomily.

"No," Jeremy said, "because we couldn't look them in the eye on the phone. At first, I wasn't entirely convinced that this Lion is the same one everybody's been chasing after for centuries. But now I think it's a distinct possibility."

"Why?" I asked. He grinned at me.

"Oh, call it a hunch," he said. "Think you're the only one who gets them?"

The ponytail girl saw us laughing, and she looked unamused. I was glad when a tall, slender man came striding into the lobby. He wore an expensive blue pin-striped suit, very shiny black shoes, a blue and white silk tie, and a white silk handkerchief in his pocket. His very air of importance, and the sudden deference of the guards, told me that he was our man.

Mr. Donaldson shook hands with Jeremy and said, "Follow me, please," and led us down a marble-floored corridor, past a back workroom where two men in white aprons were sitting on stools at a table with small paintbrushes, delicately cleaning and restoring antique figurines. He ushered us into an office at the back of the building, overlooking a small walled-in garden. The view was of carefully tended shrubs, trees and flowers, and a gravel path with large modern metal sculptures—one resembling a bent-over tulip, another a very long-legged bird.

Donaldson's office was neat and fastidious, just like him. In fact, Donaldson looked as if he'd be right at home inside one of those Magritte paintings, of men going to work with an umbrella and a bowler hat. However, he possessed a certain twenty-first century slick salesmanship which incessant fund-raising required; he knew who we were, having read about us in the art press, so he immediately asked about the painting we'd inherited, and then he did a pitch for his own museum, asking to be the first to show "anything else amusing that you recover."

I was getting accustomed to such sales pitches by now, and I no longer panicked at the thought that people whom I'd just met, urgently expected me to give them money and endorsements; for I'd discovered that initially, nothing more was required of me than an attentive expression and a pleasant smile. Jeremy and I took the seats he offered us.

"You're here about the Beethoven Lion," Donaldson said.

"Yes, we've just spoken to the photographer," Jeremy said, watching for Donaldson's reaction. The man snorted in disgust.

"Clive? Yes, well, we have him to thank for the loss of it," he said.

"Why?" I asked.

"Why? Because five minutes after I'd told him I wanted to see it with my own eyes, he went to his favorite bar in Corsica and got drunk, and told everyone about it," Donaldson said, shaking his head. "When I got there the place was already over-run with dealers, tourists, and press." He sighed. "Travel journalists. Can't keep their mouths shut about anything."

"Could you explain the Beethoven connection to a lion aquamanile?" Jeremy asked.

Donaldson cleared his throat. "Well, there are very few hard facts to go on. If indeed it is the actual Lion in question," Donaldson said, "then it would date back to the early 1800s, when

Beethoven was in Vienna. There was a certain German aqua-manilia craftsman who set up a workshop outside Vienna, and he produced some fine pieces, during the era of Napoleon. I'm afraid at this point we leave the realm of known fact and enter the world of legend. There are actually many variations on the story of the Beethoven Lion, but this is the one I find most credible, and the one that most people in this field tell."

I had to clasp my hands firmly together in my lap to keep from squealing with glee, like a little kid who's demanded to hear a particular bedtime story and is finally going to get to hear it. *The Tale of the Lion*, I thought.

"The legend goes that the origin of the Beethoven Lion dates back to a wealthy German family who were friends with Beethoven, and they commissioned it as a birthday gift for him." He paused, allowing this to sink in.

"How old was Beethoven?" I asked.

"Well, let's see, this was in 1804, so he must have been—" Mr. Donaldson glanced skyward, trying to recall, "in those days they recorded the day that you were baptized, but actual birth dates are not always known. Even Beethoven himself didn't know his own birth date, though he tried throughout his life to find out! However, since it was the custom to baptize an infant within twenty-four hours of its birth—in case it died, you see, they wanted to be sure of the safety of its soul—that would put Beethoven's birthday at, say, December 16, 1770. So at the time we're interested in—the spring of 1804, he would have been 34, no, actually, 33 years old."

I realized that every question I asked was going to involve a long, complicated answer, so I decided not to interrupt the flow of his explanations unless really necessary.

"So, you were saying, that this aquamanile was commissioned as a birthday gift?" Jeremy prompted.

"What?" he asked, blinking. "Oh, yes." He stopped.

"And who was this German family?" Jeremy asked.

"It's only a story, nobody really knows. More like a fairy tale, really. Various people who knew Beethoven have told different fragments of this story, and it's been pieced together with gossip and innuendo."

"But why did this wealthy family want to give Beethoven a gift?" Jeremy prodded, on the verge of conducting one of his lawyerlike interrogations.

"Why, because their eldest daughter—who was very intelligent, well-educated and her father's pet—was a piano student of Beethoven's. Her father commissioned a young artisan from this aquamanilia workshop, to make something special for the great Master. But I'm afraid the father got a bit more than he bargained for.

"You see, at the time, the man's daughter—now I think her first name was—Gertrude, I believe, or Gerta, perhaps—anyway, she was engaged to be married off to a wealthy but much older man. Most young girls of this time understood their parents' expectations of them, because a good marriage was very much a family affair in those days—and parents married them off fairly young, when they would make obedient wives. Quite often the bridegrooms were nearly old enough to be their fathers.

"This girl probably would have done what her family asked," Donaldson went on, warming to his subject as if it were contemporary gossip about living people, "but, unfortunately for all concerned, she fell in love with the young man who made the aquamanile. Well, after all, he kept coming to the house to consult with the father, and the father would include his daughter in these discussions because she knew the Master better than any of them. So. The romance went on secretly for a time, but eventually, the impetuous boy declared his love for her and proposed marriage. Rather a romantic sort of fellow, you know, honest and all. So he put on his Sunday best, and went to see her father and declared his intentions.

"But of course the father was furious, and shouted that a marriage of that sort was completely out of the question, that the boy was considered quite beneath them, and in any case the girl was betrothed to another man, and you just didn't go round disgracing your fiancé and your family by marrying a fellow from the working classes. There was quite a row."

"What about Beethoven?" Jeremy prompted. "And the Lion."

"Beethoven, meanwhile, was having problems of his own," Mr. Donaldson said wryly. "He was already going deaf by this time. However, this was of course a very important period for him, very productive, and he was creating masterworks that would break with the very formal conventions of classical music at that time. He was finishing his great Third Symphony."

"The 'Eroica,'" Jeremy said, totally enthralled now.

"Yes, but, well," Mr. Donaldson said, with a sudden glint in his eye, "that was not the original title of the work. The original title was 'Napoleon Bonaparte.'"

Not being a music buff like Jeremy, I asked, "Why did a great German composer want to name a whole symphony after Napoleon, a French emperor who conquered everybody in sight?"

"Well, you must understand the times," Donaldson replied. "You see in those days, many people were chafing under the thumb of hereditary kings and despots and even religious leaders. People craved reform, hoped for release from all the corruption and tyranny. Artists in particular were at the forefront of pushing for 'modernity,' as they always are, and the notion of the rights of the 'individual.' Along came Napoleon, and, you know, aside from his great conquests, he made stirring speeches and actually did make some reforms—after all, the French Revolution was not so far from memory."

"Right," I said, excitedly remembering my Napoleonic history from the sudsy cable-TV movie I'd been involved in, on the romance of Napoleon and Josephine. "They say Napoleon declared that 'only hungry people make revolutions' so he proposed to do things that would benefit everyone—build roads, schools, reform the inheritance laws . . . People really had high hopes for Napoleon, didn't they?"

"Quite so," said Donaldson. "And men like Beethoven believed that a self-made man like Napoleon was just the right new, modern sort of leader who would, unlike the kings, be a defender of the 'Rights of Man.' Some say that Beethoven had even compared Napoleon to the greatest of the ancient Roman consuls."

"'Eroica' means hero," Jeremy said. "So it was meant for Napoleon—but it never quite came off, did it?"

"It very nearly did," Donaldson said. "By this time, some say, plans had progressed so far forward that the French ambassador was ready to personally deliver a copy of the manuscript directly from Beethoven to Napoleon, as a gift. And people who knew and visited Beethoven at this time do claim that they saw the name 'Bonaparte' at the top of the manuscript."

"So what happened?" I asked breathlessly.

"Well, unfortunately, Napoleon chose this time to declare himself emperor. The story goes that when Beethoven heard this, he was furious, declaring that now Napoleon would trample on those rights of man and become simply another tyrant. It is said that Beethoven then flew into a rage, took hold of the title page of the symphony, and tore it in two and cast it to the ground! And then he changed the name of the work to 'Sinfonia Eroica.'"

"Wow," I said.

"Wait a minute," said Jeremy. "I've heard about some of this. But, Beethoven didn't tear up the original title page. He erased the title! So violently, in fact, that it left a hole in the paper."

"How do you know this?" I demanded, impressed.

"I've seen the manuscript," Jeremy said. "It was on display in a museum in Vienna. And he wrote the new name on it instead."

"Ah," said Mr. Donaldson, pleased, "you are thinking of the copyist's draft! That is the one which Beethoven erased, and made a hole in." At my perplexed look, he added, "The copyist's draft is a cleaner version of the original. Of course, Beethoven would also have to hand-write corrections to the copyist's draft, because they didn't always get it right. In fact, sometimes Beethoven got quite exasperated with such errors, and he'd write *You damned fool!* along with his corrections in the margins. What you saw, young man, was Beethoven's handwritten corrections on a copyist's draft."

"Oh," Jeremy said. "Okay."

"Anyway, the original handwritten manuscript is called an 'autograph' you see, because it is written completely in the composer's hand. Now, Beethoven was known to be quite casual about leaving the discarded pages from his 'autographs' hanging about his workroom—with all his scribblings and doodlings on them—all scattered about, crumpled on the floor, where anyone could walk away with them. Some people say that, in his fury over Napoleon's audacious betrayal, Beethoven tore up the title page of his *original* draft of the 'Eroica' and cast it on the floor, amid all the other scraps from his manuscripts. So, we know what happened to the copyist's draft; as you say, it ended up in a museum."

I got that thrill of a chill at the back of my neck, and I felt a shiver of expectation.

"However, the original manuscript," Mr. Donaldson said, leaning forward a little in his chair, even lowering his voice slightly, "the one written in Beethoven's hand, has gone missing. Nobody knows what happened to it."

"But," Jeremy said dryly, "I'm sure there are theories."

Mr. Donaldson nodded and his voice dropped lower. "What I am about to tell you is not commonly said to the general public, so please keep this under your hat. There are many rumors, of course. But the one that obsessive collectors tend to believe is this: that the female student had come to visit Beethoven that day, and that in all the fuss, she managed, unseen, to pick up a fragment of his original manuscript. And she kept it, and took it to her lover, that boy who was making the Lion aquamanile.

"The girl told her boyfriend, 'We must keep it in a safe place,' for she cherished Beethoven's work and believed that the fragment would surely be of historical value some day. Someone—either the girl or one of her servants—later claimed that the young artisan put the autograph fragment into a metal tube, which he then inserted into the Lion aquamanile, through an opening in the head of the Lion which would have ordinarily been stoppered so that you could fill and refill it. But something went wrong, and the gift of the Lion was never delivered to Beethoven. That we are fairly certain of. And there the story ends."

"Wait!" I cried. "It can't possibly end there."

He sat back in his chair, smiling regretfully. "Well, the girl married the man her father wanted her to. Nobody knows what became of the young man."

"Holy smokes," I said in a low voice. Mr. Donaldson didn't really know what I meant; he just thought I was reacting to the story in general. But Jeremy knew what I was thinking. Maybe the Count had really found the Beethoven Lion, after all.

"What's this Lion actually worth?" Jeremy asked. Mr. Donaldson smiled.

"Oh, it's hard to put an exact price on these sorts of things," Donaldson said maddeningly. "Aquamanilia can range from twenty thousand to a million euros."

I always hate it when these guys hedge, with such a wide berth. "Could you narrow that estimate a little?" I inquired.

"Well, a lion aquamanile from this period, of this quality, could probably fetch about fifty thousand euros," he said. I was baffled at first, because Kurt had said that the Count paid a hundred thousand euros for it. Donaldson saw my expression and said, "You see, the nineteenth-century ones are generally less valuable than the medieval ones."

"But," said Jeremy alertly, "if it's the Beethoven Lion—"

"Obviously that's another story," Donaldson said quickly, as if the idea excited even an old hand like him. "Why, then you could be talking about one and a half million euros or more, I should think."

I gasped. Perhaps the Count was craftier than I'd realized. He'd paid the dealer what might have appeared to be a really good profit—the price of a medieval piece for an item from a later, lesser period—when in fact the Lion could well turn out to be worth millions.

"May I ask," Donaldson said carefully, "what has prompted your interest in this piece? Has something new come to light?"

"We're not sure yet," Jeremy said. "We'll let you know if it does."

"Please do," Donaldson said. There was a knock at the door, and a silver-haired secretary entered, reminding Donaldson of an impending phone call. She glanced at us curiously before she left.

Jeremy rose, ready to go. Mr. Donaldson took out a business card and wrote something on the back. "Here is my private number and e-mail address," he said. "Only whatever you do, don't talk to the press until you've got it safely in your hands."

Chapter Twenty-eight

When we left the museum and were out on the street, the lunchtime crowd was already out and about. We had planned to be long gone before lunch, but the earlier traffic jam had delayed us.

Jeremy was saying, "I'd like to get back and see how Mum is doing—" when we were interrupted by a shout from a man in a passing car, which now slowed down. It was Bertie, looking happily surprised. He hastily pulled his car to the curb, and leaned out at us, beaming.

"Good ole Jer!" he said. "I knew you'd come to my party. But you didn't have to make a special trip to London on my account, did you? Hate to be the one to interrupt your jolly gap summer!"

Jeremy, looking a bit guilty, said, "No, no. Mum had a slight accident—nothing too bad in the end."

Bertie, looking instantly and sincerely sympathetic, said, "Is she in hospital?"

"No, she's home, a broken ankle."

"Ah, too bad," Bertie said. "Terribly fond of her. You say hallo to her for me, will you? And tell her she was the prettiest mum of all."

I had to smile. I knew Aunt Sheila would like that, even if she waved if off. And Bertie said it with a great deal of fondness in his voice.

"Can I drop you somewhere?" Bertie inquired. Jeremy told him we had a few more errands to run nearby, and Bertie twinkled at me as if he knew that we wanted to be alone on a lovers' stroll. "Lydia says she's so glad Jeremy found himself a nice, old-fashioned girl," Bertie said genially.

Coming from Lydia, I knew that wasn't a compliment. I just looked at Jeremy.

"Gotta dash, Bertie," Jeremy said hurriedly.

"Right. See you at the bash, then," he said, and nodded jovially to me before he drove off.

With a sinking heart, I realized that there was now no way that we could avoid attending his party. So, I decided to earn a few brownie points, and be magnanimous, since I had no other choice.

"Well, that's that," I said with my own version of English stoicism. Jeremy saw right through me, of course.

"I tell you what," Jeremy said. "I'll clone myself, and make the clone go to the party. Then we can go back to the Riviera."

"As long as you don't get mixed up, and I end up with the clone instead," I said. "How will I know the difference? Let's see. We should make up a password, so we can always test each other and be sure. What'll it be?"

Jeremy actually went along with this, as if considering it deeply. "How about *Temps Joyeux*?" he said. "Know what that is?"

"Of course," I said. "It's what Aunt Pen named her villa." We always thought it was a funny name which sounded better in French than its literal English translation, "Happy Times."

"Okay, that's fine," I said. "We can use it as a code at parties, too. It means, *May-Day. S.O.S. Help!*"

Jeremy smiled. "Okay," he replied. "We could just put in an appearance at the party, and when you give me the signal, I'll say we have to dash back to France."

"Well, that's all very well," I said. "But, from a fashion point of view, it's no easier to 'put in an appearance' than it is to stick around for the whole shebang. I still have to look good because this is the first time I'm meeting your old crowd, and you know how people are." I was still brooding over this "old-fashioned" business.

"You always look good," Jeremy said, as if he meant it.

"You are possibly blinded by love," I said. "What exactly does one wear to a 'bash'?"

Jeremy pondered this. "Somehow I never noticed," he confessed. "Some nice top, I guess, with some nice pants. Or skirt. Nice, but not completely formal."

I groaned. "I don't know why I even asked," I said.

"Actually, Mum will know," Jeremy said. "She's up on the latest fashion, even if she is older than us, and she knows where the younger women shop because of all her charity parties and stuff."

Aunt Sheila, still propped up in bed but surrounded by the magazines and books we'd left her with, listened with bright, alert eyes as Jeremy told her about the party, and how I'd need something new to wear. When he finished talking, Jeremy picked up the tray of food he'd left her for lunch—and he noted with satisfaction that she'd eaten everything.

"Anything else I can get you?" he asked.

"A cup of tea would be nice, there's a dear," she said. But I got the feeling she was just trying to get rid of him. When he was out of earshot, she turned to me and said, "Lydia's behind all this, isn't she?"

"How did you know?" I asked, intrigued.

"She telephoned here night and day when you two left town," Aunt Sheila said. "Always on one legal pretext or another, 'needs his advice,' that sort of thing. In fact, she telephoned one morning so early that I thought it was Jeremy with a problem, and I jumped up with my reading glasses still on, and went running to the phone to answer, and that's when I fell, because I misjudged the step."

"That figures," I said. "Why does Lydia seem to wreak havoc wherever she goes? Even when she's trying to act nice, I keep thinking she's going to spring up and scream and attack somebody. Probably me."

"She's always been that way, it's not just you," Aunt Sheila said, not without some sympathy for both of us. She paused, then added, "I think there's a few things you might want to know about Lydia."

She patted the bed, and when I sat beside her, she said, "I know it's a cliché, but Lydia had a fairly wretched childhood, even with all that privilege. We all knew her father had been a bit 'difficult'— drinking, carousing with other women; but, when he died, Lydia and her mother found out that he'd not only kept a mistress in another part of town, but had a whole other family with her. *And* left them half the money, too. Lydia got very jaded after that, acted out and was shunted off to a very strict Swiss boarding school."

"Oh, no," I said. "Now I'm going to feel like a rat for disliking her."

"Well, she can be quite destructive," Aunt Sheila allowed, "but that also means that she ends up being her own worst enemy. She had a nervous breakdown once. It doesn't excuse her meddling with you and Jeremy," Aunt Shelia concluded, "but your feeling that she's always on the verge of hysteria isn't far off. It was a terrible tyranny for Jeremy, of course. Weak people sometimes do end up manipulating those that are healthier. I just thought you'd like to know where she's coming from."

"I just want to know where she's going," I groused.

Aunt Sheila smiled. "If Jeremy gives you any trouble," she said, "just refer him to me and I can always send him to bed without supper."

I smiled, but I felt faintly gloomy. Aunt Sheila and Jeremy's friends were all from the same orbit, and they knew exactly how to interpret each other's signals. I, on the other hand, had been raised in America, by two high-end hermits who didn't bother much with social conventions and tribal customs. My friends were people who worked hard at top speed, like Erik, who used to joke that he'd have a nervous breakdown if only he had the time. But now, plunged into the world of privilege, I felt more than a little unsure of my footing in this rarefied atmosphere.

If Aunt Sheila sensed my thoughts, she didn't let on. She just picked up one of the fashion magazines and said briskly, "Now, let's see what I can show you as an example of what you might want to wear. We'll clip a few pictures and you can take them to Monsieur Lombard, a French designer I know. He's donated his help to our charity benefits. He just opened an outpost of his *atelier* here in London. His prices have gone up since I used to shop there. But tell him I sent you; I'm sure he can help."

Chapter Twenty-nine

So there I was, standing on a big satin pink tuffet like Miss Muffet, trying on and discarding one fluffy dress after another while three women with pins in their mouths tried to convince me that each dress was *parfait*. Well, not for me, they weren't. I'm not the fluffy ruffled type, even when the ruffles are young and insouciant and tongue-in-cheek fashion statements worn by the hippest rock stars and models. Besides, I didn't want to look like the "nice, old-fashioned girl" that Lydia had branded me. Plus, I was panicking at the prices, because habits die hard, and I can't help it, I just think there is something slightly immoral about a dress with a price tag that could feed a family of four for a year . . . and buy them a car. (And those weren't the most expensive ones, either.)

As dress after dress piled up, the ladies grew less patient with me. They kept reminding me that most of their clients ordered their clothes months in advance, so what did I expect now, so late in the season?

"Something simple, very simple, and modern," I said, but this only produced a slew of black dresses with metallic studs and street-tough zippers, placed on parts of the anatomy where zippers aren't required or even feasible, really.

Furthermore, I had not once met Monsieur Lombard, nor did these ladies seem to think that I deserved to.

"Impossible. He's very, very busy with the upcoming fall collection," said the frosty English girl who seemed to be in charge of this pack of jackals.

"Well, would you just let him know that I am here, and that Sheila Laidley recommended him to me?" I asked. "It's rather important."

She smiled at me patronizingly. "*All* our clients are important to us," she said, as the front doorbell tinkled and new customers came in. She turned, and then swept off with cries of false delight to welcome some regular client and her two daughters; all three of whom were stick-thin, artificially tanned, and left a cloud of perfume in their wake as they commandeered the rest of the fitting rooms and all the best mirrors.

The flock of pin-ladies fluttered off to attend their favorite customers. That left me standing there in my underwear, surrounded by piles of tulle and silk and chiffon. I glanced at myself in the mirror in annoyance. Why did I suddenly feel I needed a complete overhaul?

I climbed down from the tuffet, and wrapped myself in one of the black-red-and-white silk kimonos provided for customers, which said *L'amour et Lombard!* all over them.

"Did you find something you liked?" the frosty one called out aggressively to the back of my head. Something in her imperious tone grated on my nerves.

"No, I did not," I said. "Since I am neither a hooker nor a senator's wife nor an actress at the Academy Awards, I guess that lets me out. Thanks anyway."

"So-orry," the girl, who was only half-listening anyway, sang out as I headed for the dressing room where my own clothes were waiting for me to crawl back into them.

At that moment, a very short, wiry man in an unassuming black suit, and eyeglasses with thick black frames, came out of a back room, looking preoccupied. But when he heard the last exchange he frowned.

"May I be of service, mademoiselle?" he inquired.

"I doubt it," I said, "unless you know Monsieur Lombard."

He smiled. "Oh?" he said. "And how is it that you know Monsieur Lombard?"

"I don't," I said. "Sheila Laidley does. Might you be he?"

He bowed. "At your service. Do you have a particular occasion or color in mind?"

"All I want is something simple, modern, elegantly casual, for an evening dinner party," I said desperately, brandishing the torn pages from the magazine that Aunt Sheila had sent me in with. "And I *know* that your customers usually order ahead of time, and I know it takes years to get one's style right, but I don't have years, I have hours. What is the occasion, you ask? Only that I have to meet my boyfriend's old school chums and their gaggle of wives, who can't figure out how I, out of everybody they know, managed to 'capture' this great guy I love, okay? *That's* the occasion."

Monsieur Lombard took this all in with Gallic serenity, then spun ever so slightly on the balls of his feet, and fixed a severe look on the frosty girl. "Bring me everything we've got in her size from this week's samples," he said.

The woman blanched. "From—fall?" she said as if she could not believe it.

Monsieur Lombard said, very curtly, *"Oui,"* as if that one word were a dart that hit her straight between the eyes.

And suddenly there was another very different kind of flurry—one with absolutely no chatter. All those chickens silently scurried and hurried, and the next thing I knew, they hauled a rack of clothes out of the vault from the upcoming autumn collection, and Monsieur Lombard selected three beautiful dresses—a maroon silk taffeta, a pink crochet with delicate beading, and a blue knit with matching jacket.

I thought any one of them would do, right off the rack. But Monsieur Lombard frowned and fussed and then decided that the maroon was *le plus chic*. He crooked his finger at one of the gals-with-pins, who immediately began to fit the dress for me. He murmured to someone else, and a pair of maroon pumps appeared; then, a diaphanous long gold scarf followed, which worked as a shawl or could be wound around the head and neck for late night strolls on the veranda. Or yacht deck.

"Anything else?" Monsieur Lombard asked briskly. "Would you like to look at sketches for fall?"

I knew that this was one of life's rare moments, where I had the personal attention of a fine artist willing to listen and help. "I do need a few everyday items," I said hesitantly. "Nothing outrageous, just subtle and lovely."

"Bring her the book," he said. And he sat right down on the little satin pink sofa, and they cleared off the coffee table for him, and he opened up the big book that held his sketches for the fall collection, and he got some tissue paper to put over them and retrace them with an alteration here, a fix there, all in a quick line or swoop or squiggle; and he asked me a few calm questions now and then, the way a doctor does when he's checking to see what you're allergic to, and finally, *zut alors!* In less than an hour, he had made my own personal "book of suggestions" from his more moderately priced line, mapping out an everyday wardrobe (that Jeremy had assured me was "upkeep" for the year). Some well-chosen pants, skirts, blouses. A decent raincoat. A winter coat. A few good jackets, and pairs of shoes. A pair of boots. And *voilà*. It's done. Stop worrying about your clothes. Go out and enjoy your life.

"Look these over," he said. "You can e-mail or call me if you have any questions, about fabric and colors and so on. Then you can place your final order if you wish." I could have kissed him. Instead I thanked him in English and in French, and he smiled.

"Sheila is an old friend of mine," he said. "I hope to be yours as well."

One of the pin-girls came over, carrying a garment bag and another bag for the accessories. "Your dress for tonight is ready, mademoiselle," she said respectfully. "Would you like it sent or shall you take it with you?"

Nobody had asked for my credit card. I didn't know what to say.

"Um. I'll take it with me. Will you send me the bill?" I asked.

Monsieur Lombard patted my hand. "Wear it to the party and see if you think it's right for you," he said. "Then you let me know. I have been trying to get Sheila to wear my clothes to parties for years. She doesn't like to attract attention away from her charities. Have a good time."

And I went off, and the doorman hailed me a cab, and when I returned to Aunt Sheila's building I floated up in the elevator, carrying my garment bag that said *L'amour et Lombard!* all over it. I couldn't wait to show it to Aunt Sheila, and when I reached her bedroom I flung myself on her and hugged her.

"Ah," she said in her droll understated way, amid my squeals of happiness. "I take it you found something to wear?"

Chapter Thirty

"You look beautiful," Jeremy said as we walked up the steps. "And to think I owe it all to your mum and Monsieur Lombard," I said.

"You owe it all to your folks," he said. "They created Penny Nichols."

"That's *Penelope* Nichols, to your crowd," I said with mock hauteur.

Bertie's party was in a swank duplex, outfitted with all the latest gadgets and gizmos that modern money can buy. You know how it is when a divorced man is on his own: he buys all kinds of electronic equipment, the latest in TV screens, computerized players, souped-up speakers, hot new music DVDs, furniture in leather and chrome, crazy kitchen apparatus, enormous bedrooms with bordello-sized mirrors and beds covered in black silk; and bathrooms with big tubs, showers and sauna fit for an emperor.

There was an iron spiral staircase that made you go round and round in a dizzy tizzy, just to get from the living room to the "entertainment room" upstairs where jazz music was playing. Bertie immediately hustled Jeremy off to the bar, where all the men were clustered around a hired bartender.

The women were on the other side of the room, in chairs grouped around a low table. They had been chattering gaily, but the minute I walked in, they all clammed up.

Then one of them, a green-eyed brunette, said in a low, poshly accented voice, "You're Jeremy's girl, aren't you?"

"Penelope Nichols," I said.

"Love your dress," she said. And she introduced me to the others, only none of them said who *they* belonged to. Jeremy returned with Bertie and a couple of other men. Jeremy introduced me to them, and they all smiled in that frank way that guys do when they're meeting their friend's girlfriend for the first time. Jeremy passed me a drink.

"Harold and Rupert are here," Jeremy murmured to me in warning. These were his closest associates from his law firm.

"So, Penelope," said Bertie, "heard you work for television."

A few other guests did, too, so we exchanged some polite Q&A. I was a little out of practice; in France it was considered a *vulgarité* to charge right in and ask people what they do for a living; however, these folks had no such qualms. But soon enough they got right back to talking about their own world. Occasionally somebody stopped to politely attempt to explain the jokes about obscure politicians or friends who weren't there. Bertie especially turned out to be as sweet as Jeremy had told me, by trying to expand the conversation to include topics I could chime in on, like the latest movie or global warming or international politics or gossip about famous people.

And once the men got wind of calling me Penny Nichols, that old joke kicked around the table awhile. Small stuff, I'm used to that.

Just as Jeremy started looking furtively at the exit, a male cook in a white shirt and black pants came out and spoke in Bertie's ear, and Bertie announced that dinner was ready.

"He didn't bother to tell us it was a formal sit-down dinner party, did he?" Jeremy murmured out of the corner of his mouth to me. "I'm afraid there's nothing for it now."

Bertie's dining room was actually a large glassed-in alcove with big skylights overhead, so when you sat there you felt as if you were floating in a bubble, hovering over London. I was seated across from Jeremy, midway down an enormous table, and it really wasn't easy for us to hear each other. But that was the idea. You were supposed to talk to the people on either side of you, but you could still keep an eye on your mate to make sure he wasn't getting too chatty with his dinner companions.

I had a perfectly nice guy on my right, good-looking but accustomed to listening instead of instigating conversation. On my left was an older fellow, who made little jokes about his friends to make me laugh and relax; but he stopped talking every time a new plate was served, when he acted as if eating was a very serious task requiring all his concentration. Jeremy had the green-eyed brunette on one side; she had taken off her evening wrap to reveal a set of enormous breasts, scooped up and displayed as if on a serving platter. On Jeremy's other side was an older woman (the spouse of my older guy) who wore eyeglasses that twinkled in the light of the candles before us.

We progressed through course after course, harmlessly enough, with the wine flowing so endlessly that soon the men's laughter grew more boisterous, and the women's giggles more shrieky. The conversation ran the gamut from money-and-investments, to money-and-education, to money-and-the-second-house, to money-and-divorce.

But at one point I caught Lydia staring at me, and then she looked at Jeremy and made a small shrug, with the tiniest but unmistakable gesture of NOCD (Not Our Crowd, Darling). Jeremy knew what it meant, too, because he frowned at her, and glanced away and didn't look back.

Then he did a sweet thing, and looked at me and mouthed,

Temps Joyeux. He waggled his eyebrows at me questioningly, as if to say, *Well, I've had enough, how about you?* I nodded, and felt immediately better.

However, Lydia, alert as a hawk, saw this little exchange, and she didn't know what it meant but she bloody well knew what it *meant*, if you know what I mean. And when I saw the look that crossed her face, I knew we were in for trouble, even before she said, loudly and brightly, "So, Jeremy, do tell! Are you embarking on some sort of new career now?"

"Ooh, what is it?" one of the wives cried.

I shot a look at Jeremy, who appeared genuinely shocked, and shook his head. We'd both agreed that we would not mention the Lion to anyone we knew, not yet. I glanced over at Rupert, Jeremy's junior associate, who seemed embarrassed. Had Lydia wheedled something out of him? But Rupert always looked mortified whenever he sensed trouble, whether or not he'd caused it.

"Jeremy's working on an 'investigation' of some sort," Bertie said, as if he thought it were all great fun. "But he won't tell me what. Top secret, and all."

"Is it a murder? A robbery? Do tell!" one of the women cried out.

"What's that?" asked the green-eyed woman, turning to Jeremy. "Darling, you haven't become some sort of policeman, have you?" They all laughed uproariously.

"Jeremy a copper!"

"Maybe he's an international spy!"

Maybe he's joined MI6!"

I tried to tell myself that this was just good-natured ribbing, prompted by curiosity and a bit of pique that they had somehow been excluded. Jeremy must have sensed this, too, because I could see him searching for a way not to snub his friends while at the same time telling them to mind their own business.

Jeremy cleared his throat. "It's really just another inheritance dispute. Trying to help someone recover a lost item from an estate."

"Well, your girl here must know all about *that* sort of thing!" one of the men said.

"If you can suspend your summer vacation to work on that, then perhaps you can look into that little matter in Frankfurt I was telling you about," Harold said, looking peevish.

"From what Rupert tells me, it's coming along fine," Jeremy replied.

"But you're back in London to stay now, right?" someone asked, confused.

"No, no," Bertie said, "he's taking a gap summer. Like in school. We only hope that it doesn't turn into a gap year and a gap life, and we never see him again."

One of the women glanced slyly at Lydia and then said, "Jeremy, I heard you're going off on a yacht to explore your soul and come up with a Five-Year Plan."

"Good God! Like Stalin?" somebody asked, and they all roared.

"Huh!" said the older man next to me, who looked up from studying his plate. "Well, it's all very well to enjoy one's leisure, but, Jeremy, a serious fellow like you wouldn't want to make a lifestyle of it. People who go off to 'find themselves' usually find themselves bloody bored!"

The others nodded in agreement. I had a sudden flash of insight, as I looked at their stricken faces. They were terrified. Something was happening, some little thread was being tugged out of their crowd and they were afraid the whole thing might come undone. As long as everybody was doing pretty much the same thing, then nobody was getting ahead, and nobody was falling behind. I glanced at Jeremy, who looked embarrassed. I couldn't imagine what Lydia thought she'd gain by instigating this.

Until afterwards—when we took coffee and dessert in the living room. Most of the men wandered off to a billiard table in the back of the duplex. Harold and Rupert had pinned Jeremy in a corner and were talking urgently to him, and Jeremy's face took on a slightly perturbed expression that lingered even after the game ended, and the men deigned to rejoin the ladies.

I had been listening with dutiful attentiveness to one of the women who was very, very pregnant, and who advised me that if I was contemplating having children, then the thing to do was to have them all at once, one right after the other, no matter what people said about spacing them apart.

"It makes no difference to the kids if you space them out," she said positively. "So you may as well get it all done, just like a dog with a litter."

Jeremy came over to me and said, "Penny, I think we'd better be going. We have an early start tomorrow." Good, I thought wearily. By tomorrow we'll be back at the Riviera, back on the case.

"It's raining," Jeremy noted. "I'll go get the car." We'd had to put it in a car park down the street. "You wait here," he said, "and I'll phone you when I'm right in front of the house."

I went upstairs again in search of the "ladies' loo" which was a powder room with a big mirror and purple chairs, and a lockable door that led to a private water-closet with a toilet and its own sink. Both rooms were empty. But just after I'd washed my hands and was drying them on a purple towel, I heard Lydia and a couple of other women come into the adjacent powder room.

"So?" Lydia said cunningly. "What do you think?"

"She's cute!" one of them said, as if to deliberately stick it to Lydia.

"Jeremy always liked redheads, didn't he?" said another. Somebody giggled.

"I think she's just charming," Lydia said firmly, "but I have to say, I do worry about the influence she's had on him. Do you know he simply walked out of the office one day and never came back? *She's* the one who's making him take a gap year!"

"Why?" someone asked.

"Can't say, really. But people think it's a bad move. Jeremy's a company man at heart; so, without a sound business plan, well . . ."

"He'll come out of it," another woman said. "He's always been so sensible."

Lydia said in a low, conspiratorial tone, "Well, the fact is, he's losing clients. Some will wait for him to see the light, but some are gone for good!"

"Doesn't *she* care about his career?" someone asked, as if she'd been cued by Lydia.

"She took the lion's share of the estate right out from under his nose," Lydia said in a confidential tone. There was a general murmur of disapproval.

"Well, American girls certainly know what they want and they know how to get it!" one woman declared, as if she half-admired that sort of bitchiness.

"Oh, I like her!" somebody replied, and I felt a little better. Until I realized that was Lydia again. "It's just that she's all wrong for Jeremy, and I *worry*, that's all."

At this particular inopportune moment, my cell phone rang. Loud. They all stopped talking. Then there was furtive whispering and rustling, as some of them quickly slipped out the door so I wouldn't see that they'd been part of it. Having been "outed" in this way, I walked into the powder room, and took the call.

"Penny?" Jeremy said. "I'm out in front."

"Hi, Jeremy," I said. I smiled brightly. "What charming friends you have," I continued, while beaming at them all. "Won't we miss them when we're out there on our yacht? Yes, of course, darling, I'm on my way."

You could have heard a pin drop. I certainly heard a few gasps. They all froze.

I hung up and slipped the phone in my purse even as Jeremy was still saying, "What on earth—?"

"Cheers!" I said to the gals, and waltzed out.

Jeremy had the rental car waiting as if he were the driver in a bank robbery requiring a hasty getaway. I raced through the raindrops and ducked into the car.

"Well?" he asked after I'd closed the door and we roared off.

"Oh, nothing much," I said. "Just Lydia trying to organize the I-Hate-Jeremy's-New-Girl Club."

Jeremy sighed heavily. "It won't last," he said gloomily. "They do that with everybody's new girlfriend."

"Do they always make fun of people who want to do something different with their lives?" I asked. Jeremy grinned.

"Can't you tell garden-variety envy when you hear it?" he asked. Then he said, very seriously, "Look, I wish we hadn't had to come back to London, but we did, and it looks as if there really is trouble going on with a client in Frankfurt. I have to go there for a couple of days and straighten it out."

"So, who invited the guys from your office?" I said. "Don't tell me, let me guess."

"I've been getting frantic e-mails and phone messages from that client in Frankfurt all along," Jeremy said. "This would have come to a crisis, with or without the party."

"You never told me that," I said.

"Well, I didn't want to spoil our fun, did I? Been trying to hold them off without bothering you about it. I just can't 'phone it in' anymore. Harold and Rupert have been doing us a great many favors all along, you know, fielding all those calls and acting as a filter for us," Jeremy was saying defensively. "I can't very well tell them that I'm too busy working for strangers, or gazing into my navel trying to contemplate the true meaning of life." I sat there quietly, trying to comprehend what had been going on tonight.

"Jeremy, are you losing clients because of me?" I asked.

"No, of course not," he said. "Oh, some will go off in a huff, but frankly those are the ones I'd just as soon see the back of. No, what concerns me is more basic. I mean, exactly who am I supposed to be, anyway? Some bloke on permanent vacation? Are we going to spend the rest of our lives chasing after yacht-jackers or antiques thieves, at the behest of some senile old Count? What kind of a life is that for a man? Have you ever seen what Private Investigators look like after years of doing that sort of slogging? What's next, tailing some guy's wife who's having an affair?"

So, I thought. Lydia's arrows had met their mark, after all. "We're not a PI firm," I reminded him. "We are dealing specifically with a missing antique. With your international legal expertise and my art research experience—those were your words, remember? This is a test case. If we decide to continue doing this line of work afterwards, we can build a good client list of people dealing with the settling of estates, auction houses, museums, etc. It's an experiment, Jeremy. Nothing is set in stone. But you have to try different things before you know what you want."

"You're used to this nomadic, seat-of-your-pants way of doing things," Jeremy said. "I admire you for it. I just don't know if I could make a good partner for you, Pen." He looked really, truly concerned.

"Wait a minute," I said. "Are you the real Jeremy, or the clone? You sound like the clone. Because the real Jeremy would never let envious chatter get him down. Come to that, who told Lydia about our Plan?"

"I certainly didn't," he said, a bit testily.

"Maybe she picked up the extension that time we talked on the phone and she was in your apartment," I said. At the look on his face, I knew that he realized this could be a distinct possibility. But he wouldn't admit it.

"Oh, God, Penny," Jeremy said, sounding irritated. "You see Lydia behind every tree and under every rock. Well, suppose she did. What's the difference?"

I turned and faced him squarely, feeling ornery. "The difference, as I've been telling you all along, is that she knows how to ring your bells and push your buttons," I said. "So how long are you going to let her keep doing this to you, and, therefore, to us?"

"It's really got nothing to do with you—" he mumbled, as if this would reassure me.

"That's just the problem!" I exclaimed. "She yanks you right back into the past, where she knows I can't follow. Meanwhile, I'm trying to create a future for us. But you can't keep going back and forth, you know. At some point you have to pick which fork in the road you want, and go with it. It's called commitment, Bub."

Jeremy had that stunned, stricken look a guy gets when a woman reads him the riot act. For a moment he didn't speak or even make a sound. Then, he regrouped.

"There's no point in arguing," he said. "I have to go sort out Frankfurt."

"We're supposed to check on the townhouse tomorrow," I reminded him. "It won't be ready, but we should make sure it's progressing as it should."

"Well," Jeremy said, "I guess you'll have to do without me."

Chapter Thirty-one

It had sounded pretty ominous when he said it, and it felt even worse the next day when Jeremy flew out to Frankfurt and I had to "do without" him.

When the taxi arrived to take him to the airport, and he waved goodbye, I had the feeling that, although he'd return, I would never again see my buddy, my partner, the one who wanted to explore what the world had to offer before buckling back down in a law firm again.

I didn't like the way he'd ridiculed his own soul-searching. It was one thing if a couple of fuddy-duddy friends made jokes; quite another if he let it deter and dishearten him. But perhaps the men had said even more negative things to him over their cigars and brandy, to make him come away feeling foolish about it. At any rate, I felt I ought to face the fact that when Jeremy came back from Frankfurt, he might already have gone right back to his old life again. And it might very well be where he wanted to be.

I told myself, fine, I'll do it alone. I'll keep researching the Beethoven Lion all by myself, without that man. After all, I'd spent my entire working life doing research without the help of some guy, right? And I'd whip that townhouse into shape, too, because

Jeremy wasn't the sort of fellow who functioned well with bits of plaster falling on his head. And, fine, if I had to, I'd go into business all by myself. And fend off all those crazies all by myself. And go back to cooking dinner all by myself . . .

But, damn it. I missed that pain-in-the-ass man, and his dumb jokes, and the fun we'd had doing the research together. And what good was *Penelope's Dream* if it turned out that it was no longer Jeremy's Dream?

At any rate, Jeremy was stuck in meetings for days, and just when he was scheduled to return, he sent me a cryptic e-mail: *This is going to take longer than I thought. Going to have to miss dinner with your folks. Sorry, please give them my apologies. Jeremy.*

Well, I couldn't just slog around London feeling sad. So, I went over to the townhouse to check in with the workmen, and we figured out all kinds of complicated stuff about flooring and windows and security systems. Then Claude sent an e-mail saying that the yacht was all repaired and refueled and spruced up and ready to go. Did I think we'd be using it this week? I told him I'd have to get back to him.

At suppertime I locked up and went out to meet my parents for dinner on their last night in London. They weren't the least bit offended that Jeremy had to rush off to Frankfurt. They had been enjoying their vacation, but were ready to go home.

"You look *très belle,* Penn-ee," my father said. Bless 'im. He was wearing a fine grey suit with a nice blue and grey linen shirt and a blue tie; and my mother was in a pretty red dress with matching jacket. They were both so cute and dressed up. Every outing they made, they exulted in, as if just happy enjoying each other's company.

"Thanks," I said morosely, trying to pull myself together and resume being a grown-up again. We had gone to a new restaurant with a French/Vietnamese cuisine, and my father kept exhorting me to try different appetizers that he'd ordered.

"Well, you're right, this is very good," I grumbled, poking around with my chopsticks. "Jeremy doesn't know what he's missing."

My father said knowingly, "You have to be patient with young men. They are not so good at explaining their worries to the women they love. They want you to admire their strength."

"Oh, he told me what he's worried about, with work," I said glumly. My father looked at me with gentle humor, as if I were his idiot child who required extra patience.

"Not work, that's nothing," he said with a wave of his hand. He put his hand over his heart. "It is what's in here that he finds hard to tell you. But," he added with a chuckle, "always remember that you have my French blood in you."

"Oh?" I asked, intrigued. "What's that supposed to mean?" I glanced at my mother, and she looked amused but did not contradict him.

"You can charm him whenever you want to," my father said with utter confidence. "Using lightness and humor."

While I sat there trying to imagine how a glamorous French woman would handle the situation, the main course arrived in several platters which my father passed around to us. Seeing how distracted I was, my father scooped things up he thought I should try, and deposited them on my plate. It was what he used to do when I was a little girl, and he wanted to teach me the fine art of appreciating well-prepared food.

"It can't be easy," my mother said, "meeting your boyfriend's first wife and all her chums. Don't get stuck on trying to win their approval. The minute you don't care, that's when they'll give it to you."

"It's not that," I said hesitantly. Now, look. I'm not the kind of girl who calls her mother up every five minutes and tells her the minutiae of my life. In fact, with my own English blood, I'm not much at confiding in others at all. Too embarrassing. So I only said, "It's just that they have too much influence on him. They make him feel bad for wanting to go out on his own, that's all. And I think he's caving in."

"Really?" my mother asked crisply. "And what have you offered as an alternative?"

I didn't quite get her point at first. "I can't *make* him want to stick with our Plan," I said. "I can't *make* him want to build our own enterprise. It wouldn't mean anything if he didn't decide he wants to do it on his own."

"Well, I must say, that's not necessarily the best strategy to take."

"Strategy?" I asked. "What do you mean?"

"My advice is, you have to fight for your man," she said, "so long as he doesn't make you do it all the time."

As her words sank in, I said, "But you didn't have to fight for Dad . . . did you?"

"Why, of course, darling!" she said, as if it were the most obvious thing in all the world. My father, who was refilling our wineglasses, beamed.

"Wait a minute," I said in a deadly tone. "All my life you've told me that you and Dad fell smack-dab in love from the very moment that you 'clapped eyes on each other.' Those were your exact words!"

"That's right, dear," my mother said serenely. "Love at first sight is all very well. But it's second and third and fourth sight where you have to show your mettle."

"Wha-a-a-at?!" I said, feeling slightly betrayed. These two always acted as if they were perfectly fitted pieces of a puzzle that just automatically clicked together.

"Certainly," my father said in that low chuckle of his. "Smoothing out the rough edges is half the fun."

I sat back in my chair. Then, in a more hushed, awed tone, I said, "So what should I actually do?"

"Well, darling, I really couldn't say," my mother began with her usual disclaimer, "but if it were me, I certainly wouldn't hang about waiting for a man to sort out all his problems so he's the perfect mate. Meanwhile, you can't put off your dream while waiting for him to do it for you," she added incredulously. "If you want to start an enterprise, go ahead, but always leave him an open door, and share your enthusiasm with him, so that it's so contagious that everyone around you just wants to jump aboard. And do listen to what he's trying to tell you. Otherwise even the best of men might get the wrong idea, and think you didn't care."

"Yeah, but sooner or later he has to decide to make a commitment to one thing or the other," I said crossly.

"Of course. And he will. In any event," my mother said, "it helps to be pleasant. Life is only worth living when you've found people you can be pleasant with. Don't let anyone take that away."

After we'd hugged and kissed, I gazed at them as they walked back to their hotel. Tomorrow they'd return to the States, and tell each other how good it was to be home in their happy hermit existence, gardening and going for long walks together in the Connecticut woods when autumn made the tree colors riotous; then, come winter, they'd go south to their Florida bungalow.

All along, they'd be laughing and cooking together, as always. Mom was a children's book illustrator, and she and Dad launched their own picture books series. I remember, as a kid, seeing them lay out sketches and pages on the kitchen table after supper, their heads bowed, close, as they leaned conspiratorially over their work, very serious, yet telling wry jokes. They made it seem so easy. But I was beginning to get an inkling of what an accomplishment their lives truly were.

Before heading back to Aunt Sheila's, I stopped at Great-Aunt Penelope's townhouse. The workmen were gone, of course, but they would return tomorrow, so they'd left all their tools lying about downstairs, and even on the stairwell. I stepped over every-thing and went into Aunt Pen's second-floor apartment, and over to the locked desk where I'd left my computer this morning. I'd set myself up here, answering a few e-mails that had stacked up, be-cause the second floor had needed the least amount of work, so it was a good place for me to hang out, while still being accessible to the workmen when they had questions or decisions for me.

Aunt Pen's apartment always has a calming effect on me, and even now it still felt like an elegant oasis of serenity. Whenever I was in the library in particular, I felt like a heroine in a 1930s movie set. And I always found myself imagining how my great-aunt would handle these sticky-wicket situations I often seemed to get myself into. Sometimes I even felt as if her spirit lingered over me, offering guidance. Yes, she would have known all about being a single woman, alone in a big city, fending for herself with a can-do spirit.

I switched on the light, and got to work with a large writing pad on the desk, and became deeply engrossed. The meditative atmo-sphere induced me to think about the case in a slightly different light. It was as if I was trying to build a bookshelf with a do-it-yourself kit that was missing the instructions, and I had all these pieces lying about that simply had to fit together somehow; so I was placing them all out in some kind of order. I kept going over and over the fragmented anecdotes from the Count, and Kurt, and

Claude and everybody who had anything to do with it, but still there was something missing.

Finally my mind rested on one piece of information, and a question which, in all the confusion, I'd forgotten to ask. I picked up the phone and called up the photographer who'd taken the picture of the Corsican holiday celebration. There was no answer at his office, so I called his mobile number that was on the back of the photos.

"Hullo!" Clive shouted over very raucous background noise of loud music, loud laughter, and lots of clinking and banging. "Who is it?"

I had to say my name three times before he really heard it. "Ah, Penny," he said in a friendly way. "I just stopped in for a beer. Fancy a drink?" And he named a pub that was not far from me. I hesitated, but realized that we couldn't possibly carry on a telephone conversation, so I told him I'd stop in.

Chapter Thirty-two

The pub where Clive told me to meet him was very unassuming from the outside, apart from clumps of people standing around on the sidewalk, some just arriving, some trying to decide where to go next. They were youngish, very expensively dressed, and the girls were possibly drunker than the boys. They looked as if they had good jobs, and had stopped here to blow off steam after work.

Inside, there were a lot of reflecting mirrors, and balloons tied to the backs of chairs and barstools. It was dimly lit, and the dance floor beyond was also decorated with balloons and mirrors and bouncing lights, so the whole effect made me feel uncertain about whether I was stepping into another room or about to smash against a mirror instead. Gingerly I picked my way through the crowd, and found Clive seated at the bar with other men his age, all watching sports on a large TV overhead. Some of the men were eating their dinner at the bar.

"Penny, hi, sit down," Clive said, sliding off his barstool and letting me sit there. A fat guy at the end of the bar raised his head, looked me over, decided I probably wouldn't unduly disrupt the men's zone, and went back to watching the TV. Clive stood next to me, ordered another beer for himself to replace his empty glass, and asked if I'd have one. I picked a Belgian ale that Jeremy often ordered.

"What can I do for you?" Clive asked.

"I'm wondering about this family in Corsica who had that shepherd's hut," I said. "Did you talk to them at all?"

"Not that night," Clive said, remembering, "it was pretty noisy, with the festival and all. But a few weeks later, when the thing went missing, Donaldson wanted me to arrange a meeting with the family, but they wouldn't do it. Wouldn't even let him near the site. They were very upset, and felt that they shouldn't have allowed me to take a picture of a relative's grave, so they didn't want any more strangers prowling about. Well, you can imagine how tough it was for them to have a bunch of greedy foreigners clamoring to see them."

"So, you never got a chance to ask them about what the artifact was, and how they came to have it?" I asked, disappointed.

"We-e-ell," Clive said. After a brief pause, he said, "Look. She told me not to tell anybody about this. I mean, you're not going to write some article or start an expedition, are you? These people will know you got it from me, and they don't forgive a betrayal."

I assured him that I would be discreet, and was only trying to help someone who thought he'd purchased the Lion and had been misled.

"Okay, well, there's a young woman in the family, she's cool, and very smart. She's quite educated, won a scholarship to university and all that. She's studying medicine and genetics; such research is done on Corsica because, you know, it's a contained community and they can track people more easily."

"What's her name?" I asked. Clive started to fish around in his pockets. Being a photographer, he had lots of pockets. While he searched he continued, "Anyway, she became the spokesperson for the family, to handle all the attention they were getting. She protects them. She talked to me once. She's in her late twenties, I'd say."

"What did she tell you?" I asked, watching him still fishing in his pockets.

"Oh, you know, after the uproar I asked her what the thing was, and she said it was a family treasure which had been stolen many years ago and then recovered. Most of the time they kept it out of sight. Once a year they take it out for this ceremony. They've done this for many years. But this particular time, it got stolen. They say it's because of my photo. But," he said defensively, "somebody told me the thing is cursed. Certainly seems surrounded by bad luck."

"But—whose grave was it?" I asked.

"An ancestor," Clive said. "Of—oh, Lord, what *is* her name?" He found his mobile phone at last, did some rapid finger work and then said triumphantly, "Ah! Diamanta."

"I'd really like to talk to her," I said as calmly as I could.

"I only have an e-mail address for her, no phone. But look, you must promise me that you won't hound her if she doesn't reply. As I said, she'll know you got it from me."

"Sure, no problem," I said, and he let me look on his phone and copy it down.

"Anything else you can tell me about it?" I asked. Clive shook his head.

"She's your best bet. But she doesn't live with the family year-round. She's at the university. So don't be surprised if it turns out to be a dead end."

I slid off the barstool and thanked him. Clive looked at me with interest. "Would you like to pop round somewhere quieter for a bite to eat?" he inquired.

That's when it dawned on me that, without Jeremy by my side, my snooping could inadvertently help a guy get the wrong idea of why I so urgently wanted to see him, and how excited I was by what he was saying. I sort of forgot about that stuff. I thanked him nicely and he took it with good humor. Then I headed out on my own.

At night, the streets of London can be very changeable, even in the best neighborhoods. Roads that hum with life by day can become totally deserted and shut down in the evening; and a street that's busy and well-lighted at night might still be right next to a dark, deserted one. So when I turned the corner, searching for a cab, I ended up walking down streets more dangerous-looking than they were when I'd first set out earlier. And, suffice it to say that even when lots of people are out and about to keep you company, well . . . binge drinking is never a pretty sight, especially when someone's either getting sick, curbside, or is staggering around in a volatile state, becoming suddenly belligerent and aggressive with strangers. I saw two girls physically slugging it out over a guy. Nor is it so great to walk past crowds of emboldened, loud men who bump into you on purpose when you pass them.

I found the taxi stand, but it was empty. I heard another pair of footsteps echoing behind my own. I went faster. So did they. I crossed the street and tried to make a quick turn unexpectedly, but whoever was behind me seemed to anticipate my every move. There was nobody else about. I made a few more test-moves, and decided that yes, I was being followed. A glance over my shoulder told me the guy was wearing a hooded sweatshirt, his hands thrust in his pockets. I peered way ahead at the next corner, and I saw a lone car approaching.

There comes a moment, in times like this, where you have to abandon all pretext of fearless normality, and run like hell, even if it means finally letting your stalker know that you are terrified. I reached that moment right now. I took off, running madly in the direction of the car ahead, hoping I could at least get someone to witness my murder so that they could tell the police. The feet behind me began rapidly running, too. I put on a fresh burst of desperate speed and, just as I reached the corner where the car was approaching, I was seized with a mad inspiration. I waved at it and shouted as loudly as possible, "Officer! Over here! Officer, help!" as if it were a police patrol car that I was flagging down. The car slowed, and I ran right up to it, and banged on the hood.

Well, it worked. I guess whoever was behind me was so freaked out by the idea of police that he simply vanished, seemingly into thin air. I looked back only once, and the street behind me was eerily empty. The startled driver of the car, a man, steered away from me, accelerated and drove off. I ran the whole rest of the way back to the townhouse, flung myself inside, locked the door, and leaned against it, panting.

"This really sucks, working on this case alone," was my first thought, which I said aloud. My own voice sounded phony-brave, shaky. For a few minutes I didn't dare move or even flip on a light, waiting to see if my stalker had diabolically resumed his pursuit. But the street was silent. I found myself wishing that those elderly tenants were still around. I fumbled for my mobile phone, thinking I'd call for a cab back to Aunt Sheila's.

However, oddly enough, Aunt Penelope's telephone started ringing. I hadn't used this line in months. The answering machine wasn't connected, so it just rang and rang. I turned on the hall light, and picked my way over the carpentry tools on the stairs as I went up to the second floor. At first, I stood there, staring at the phone. The caller could be any one of assorted nuts. It rang again. Finally, I picked it up.

Chapter Thirty-three

I t wasn't Jeremy. But it was another familiar voice.

"Penny?" Rollo boomed. "That you? Good Lord, been searching for you everywhere."

I had visions of Rollo sitting on the yacht, drinking all Jeremy's wine and driving the crew crazy. "Where are you?" I asked.

"London. Been chasing after ole' Mortimer and the trail went cold three times. But now I've got some information for you that will knock your socks off, dear girl!" he cried, sounding enormously pleased with himself.

Oh, God, I thought to myself. *I'll end up in business with Rollo instead of Jeremy.*

And then, in the background of Rollo's call, I heard a familiar voice which could make your blood curdle. It was Great-Aunt Dorothy, saying to Rollo, in a scolding tone of contemptuous disbelief to her son, "For God's sake, Rollo, why on earth are you *helping* that girl? She robbed you blind of your inheritance!"

"Hold the line a moment," Rollo told me in a tense voice. There was a muffled sound, as if he were trying to cover the phone, but I could still make out every word when he retorted hotly, "Stay out of this, she's my *friend* and she has faith in me, which is more than I can say for you!"

I was astounded. Who would have thought that Rollo would even remember what I said to him on the yacht, much less care? But apparently it meant something for him to be, if not entirely trusted, then believed, at least now and then. It dawned on me that if his mother was yelling at him, then maybe he really did have some good information for me.

"What have you got, Rollo?" I asked.

"Sorry for the delay," he muttered as he returned to me. "But I thought you'd want to know that I heard on my grapevine that, just as I expected, it *was* old Mortimer Jones who sold that Lion to your Count."

"Was it really *the* Lion?" I asked.

"Darling, who can say? My sources didn't actually see it. But the point, dear girl, is that Mortimer is back in Corsica now. I've a notion of how we might flush him out, and find out for sure if he ever really had the right lion. But, Penny, we'll have to hurry. I have some other business to tend to tomorrow, but I can meet you at the yacht day after that, and you must be ready to go."

"Go?" I echoed.

"Corsica, darling!"

It crossed my mind that I shouldn't exactly let Rollo master-mind my fate. But I thought about what my mother said about full speed ahead on a dream. And at this point, all roads seemed to lead to Corsica.

"Okay, I'll phone the captain and tell him to make sure the crew is there and ready," I promised.

"Good work," Rollo said, and we hung up. Then I fired off a nice, friendly e-mail to Diamanta.

When I returned to Aunt Sheila's apartment, she was on the

telephone chattering with friends. I waved to her and went into the living room, gazing out the big window at the lighted boats going up and down the Thames, while I talked to Claude on my mobile and asked if we could make a voyage to Corsica. He assured me that the crew would be ready and waiting, with plenty of provisions.

As soon as I hung up, my phone shrilled and vibrated and nearly leaped out of my hand.

"Penny!" Jeremy said, sounding excited. "Where the hell have you been? Every time I call somewhere they tell me I just missed you. First Mum, then your folks; and your line's been busy whenever I tried it."

"Well, I'm a very popular woman," I said wearily. "What did you expect?"

"No time for jokes," he said briskly. "You won't believe what I've found out! First of all, the Count isn't as cuckoo as everybody thinks. There *was* an auction in his grandfather's time, 1890, to be precise. And there *was* a lion aquamanile listed as 'The Beethoven Lion.' And you can't believe how they make those aquamanilia. I can tell you all about it when I get back because I've actually *seen* some of the tools they use!"

My mind wasn't working fast enough at first, so I couldn't believe my ears. Yet, while my brain was still struggling to process all this information, I was feeling a surge of delirious happiness, a warm rush of delight.

"Jeremy," I said, still afraid to believe it, "what have you been up to, out there in Germany?"

"Research, of course," he said impatiently. "Guess who I actually had a little sit-down chat with? Kurt's sister." When I didn't reply right away he demanded, "Did you hear me? The Count's daughter. And boy did she have a lot to say."

"Whah—but—I thought you went out there working for one of Harold's clients," I said.

"Oh, that?" Jeremy said dismissively. "I wrapped that up straight away. Then I started picking up the trail of the Lion. Didn't you get my e-mail that I needed more time out here?"

"Well, you never said you were working on *our* case!" I shouted joyfully.

"Naturally! We can't just let it drop," Jeremy said. "I e-mailed Kurt before I left, asking if I could meet his sister. He sent me back a two-word e-mail, *Good luck*. But I charmed her into seeing me." He paused for breath. "Any news on your end?" he inquired.

"You bet! Clive told me about that family in Corsica that the Lion was stolen from!" I said excitedly. "Wait till you hear what he said, and I even got him to give me the name of a girl in the family who might be able to help us. I sent her an e-mail."

"Clive?" Jeremy said. "Oh, the photographer. He was an odd duck. How'd you get new information out of him?"

"I had to meet him at a bar and then I nearly get mugged," I said frankly. "Some guy followed me back to the townhouse. You're right, we do need security."

"Good God," Jeremy groaned. "You can't be traipsing about London alone at night when you don't even know where you are! Are you mad?"

"Steady on, m'boy," I said. I told him all about Rollo's call, and how I'd alerted Claude to get the boat to take us to Corsica. But, I didn't bother to mention that I had also been preparing to go it alone . . . for the whole rest of my life, *sans* love.

"Right!" Jeremy said. "I might as well just fly down to Nice directly from here. I do have to meet with Rupert here at lunchtime, though, to hand this thing off to him."

"Great, let's meet at the villa," I said.

"I'll be arriving in Antibes in the evening," Jeremy said, sounding as if he'd just checked a plane schedule.

"I'll be there," I said.

"See you soon, babe," he said. "And," he added, "don't go out for drinks and carrying on at all hours of the night with strangers."

"Hurry home, darling," I said sweetly. "I *do* get into so much trouble when you're not around!"

Aunt Sheila probably knew something was afoot, because, the next morning, I was ridiculously cheerful as I hurriedly packed my bags. But she said nothing, just watched me in that alert, droll way of hers. She told me that my parents had stopped by last night, and my father had fixed a bunch of gourmet eats for her, that could be easily assembled into various meals, so she shooed me away.

The plane couldn't get to Nice fast enough for me. I took a taxi straight from the airport to Antibes. I'd telephoned ahead to Celeste, who was now cleaning the place once a week. She'd picked up a few things at the market for me.

Still, it was a little spooky, waiting for Jeremy at the villa alone. The wind rattled through the trees, and the house creaked a bit, but apart from that, it was pretty quiet, especially as the birds grew drowsy when the sun sank below the horizon. The weather was very hot now, so the night was filled with the sound of crickets, cicadas and a strange owl which kept saying plaintively, again and again, *Who—oo-OO!*

I ate my dinner listening to him. Then I climbed into bed and lay there in the dark, trying to decide if I should let myself fall asleep (I was totally exhausted by now) or stay up so I could figure out if the car that finally pulled into the driveway and crunched the gravel was Jeremy's or an axe-murderer's (that thought kept me awake). While I was still trying to make up my mind, I finally dozed off.

Moments later I heard a key in the lock, and I stirred drowsily, rousing myself enough to call out, "Jeremy?" so that he'd know he could turn on the lights without waking me.

"Penny?" Jeremy's strong voice was so reassuring that I drifted into sleep again. He came up quietly in the dark, and undressed.

"Hi, Jeremy," I murmured, as he slipped into bed behind me.

"Hi, babe," he whispered, snuggling up against me and putting a reassuring arm around me. "Go back to sleep."

"Mmmm," I said contentedly, "welcome back."

Part Eight

Chapter Thirty-four

In all the fracas, I really hadn't had time to imagine what it would be like to actually have a yacht at my disposal. Sure, we'd been working toward this all along, and at times it had seemed as if *Penelope's Dream* was destined to remain only that. But now, when we drove down to the harbor where the open sky and sea awaited us in the pale early morning sunlight—there she was, our dream boat, all spiffed, ready and waiting to take us wherever we wanted to go.

And there was our crew, proudly lined up to formally receive us for our first big voyage: Claude, the captain, with his rugged tanned face and salt-and-pepper hair; François, the elegant steward, tall, dark and lean; Brice, the blond-haired first mate; Gerard, the gruff, barrel-chested engineer; and two young deckhands. They all looked so impressive in their matching navy and white and gold, standing there so proud of the beautiful job they'd done.

Jeremy and I walked up the gangway together. The yacht had looked lovely when we first saw it, but now, after all the work the crew had done, it shone like a finished gem. The brass railings and fixtures gleamed so brightly in the sunlight that you could see yourself in their reflected polish. The elegant staircase, panellings and flooring glowed with burnished elegance. We now had all our "mod-cons" with the latest in computer and communication technology, but still, the antique chronometers and lamps and furnishings lent a romantic, old-fashioned aura of timelessness to the boat, as if she had floated serenely through one century and would continue to do so for another, as long as her owners cared for her.

"Jeremy, it's just so beautiful," I said, stunned. His vision had finally been realized, and he looked pleased and happy.

"Well, maybe it wasn't so stupid to bid on the old tub after all," he said.

The crew's care and attentiveness made me feel as if any path I chose to walk had been smoothed for me, so that every move I made was as easy as gliding down a sliding-pond. Not a single bump on the road, no obstruction. This sudden new taste of freedom was as exhilarating as the salty air and as bracing as the cool sea, and I felt that nothing could stop us now.

We sat down with Claude in the pilot house to pore over maps and review our course. Then François informed us that breakfast would be served on the aft deck as soon as we were out at sea. So Jeremy and I went out on deck, sitting on the teak steamer chairs with their long striped cushions, so comfortable that I almost dozed off again, yawning sleepily. We were getting an early start, for, depending on the wind and tide, it would take most of the day to reach Corsica.

"I knew Rollo couldn't get up this early in the morning," Jeremy commented. "Well, we'll just have to shove off without him."

"We can't," I said. "We need him as our guide to the underworld."

A taxicab came screeching around the corner and roaring down the quay. A moment later, Rollo bounded out and up the gangway. I saw one of the deckhands direct him toward us.

"Wonder if he won or lost at the roulette tables," Jeremy murmured, referring to Rollo's inevitable stops at Monte Carlo.

"Judging by the spring in his step," I said, "he didn't make out too badly."

Rollo was out of breath when he reached us, but smiled as he took off his hat. "Got here as fast as I could at this ungodly hour," he panted, dropping into the seat next to mine, and setting down a leather suitcase he'd been carrying. He paused, taking a deep breath now, his nostrils wheezing, as he surveyed the spiffed-up boat, and it apparently met with his approval because he then said, "Well, what say we bag ourselves a Lion?"

There was a sudden silky roar of the engine. The crew was running about on deck, dealing with anchor, ropes and everything else that keeps it tethered to its berth.

"Onward!" Rollo cried.

As we pulled out of the harbor, the Mediterranean Sea was cool and calm under a pale blue sky with puffy white clouds. It was easy to see why van Gogh, and Gauguin, Matisse, Picasso and Cocteau were so enraptured with the light of the "Midi." It both softened and heightened the colors of everything—sea, sky, fishing boats, pastel houses, and flowering shrubs in a riot of color—pink, magenta, blue, purple, violet, yellow.

We began to pick up speed as we left the harbor behind, and the sea opened up. *Penelope's Dream* sliced through the water like a sharpened knife.

"Coffee," Rollo murmured in gratitude as François arrived with the breakfast tray. "Excellent."

Jeremy, Rollo and I got down to business. The plan was to head straight for Calvi, a main town on the northwest coast of Corsica. That's where the family who'd had the Lion lived, and where, according to Claude, the Count had gone to pick up his mysterious package. Clive had told me where we'd find the sailors' bar near the harbor.

"That's also where, I wager, we will find Mortimer," Rollo informed us, "and, I daresay, the Lion as well."

"You think Mortimer stole the Lion from the boat?" Jeremy demanded.

"I do," Rollo said positively. "Not personally, of course, he wouldn't risk being seen. But it wouldn't be the first time he hired some—shall we say, unsavory fellows willing to sneak aboard a boat in the dead of night?"

"But why did his guys steal the whole boat?" I asked.

Rollo shook his head. "Not sure they did," he replied. "Could have been someone else entirely, kids, even, like the police seem to think."

"Rollo," Jeremy said, after studying him carefully through all this, "is this a working theory of yours, or do you actually have some proof?"

"What I have is a plan, to obtain the proof," he said. "And, hopefully, the Lion as well. People have been talking, and my sources have been listening. The consensus is, Mortimer was behind the original theft of the Lion. But, he really didn't know beans about the true value of it; he only knew that a photographer was chattering about it, as if it were a nice find. So Mortimer tried, through locals, to buy it, but when the family who owned it refused, he arranged for it to be 'stolen,' possibly with the aid of a neighbor. Once the deed was done, he had to get rid of it. Tricky business, that, because he had to wait long enough for the uproar about it to die down again, yet, every week that he held onto it was a liability. So Mortimer was only too happy when the Count was eager to buy.

"Now, here's the really interesting bit: Did you know that there might be something hidden *inside* the damned thing? Nobody knows for sure what it is, but they say it could make the Lion worth ten times what the Count paid for it. When Mortimer found this out, he felt he'd been burned by the Count. My guess is that when Mortimer heard about the sale of the yacht, he 'arranged' to have the Lion stolen again. I think he's still got it, and is holding on to it until the 'heat' is off. But as I said, Mortimer's too smart to hold onto something hot too long. So, I think I can talk him into selling it to me."

"And what are you going to use for money?" Jeremy asked.

"Nothing," Rollo said dismissively. "Not when I have this."

He reached into his jacket and pulled out a very large pen. He clicked it, and said, "Testing, one-two-three," and fiddled with it, and then we heard his recorded voice come back hollowly with, *"Testing, one-two-three."*

"This is the real thing," he boasted. "Professional spies use it. You can blackmail Mortimer with it and make him give you back the Lion."

Rollo sat back, looking quite pleased with himself. "Do excuse me," he said, "I wish to use the washroom." And he rose, stretched his legs, and went below.

"Well, what do you think?" I asked Jeremy in a low voice.

"I think he's barking mad, to imagine he can pull this off," Jeremy said, "but I have to admit that I've actually heard a few things in Frankfurt which support some of what he said."

"Keep going," I said excitedly.

"Kurt's sister is named Marthe," Jeremy said. "She was a bit defensive at first. I guess her family blames her for being too quick to sell the yacht. Besides, you know, she's one of those aloof, old-fashioned European aristocrats who only talks to her own kind."

"What's she look like?" I asked, intrigued.

"Like a female Kurt, except with red lipstick," Jeremy said. "With lots of little white dogs yip-yipping at my ankles the whole time. I think Kurt must have suggested to her that she should see me," Jeremy continued. "Anyway, she eventually warmed up, and explained that she'd originally had no idea why her father went to Corsica, and he didn't tell her about the Lion until long afterward, because it took months for him to recover his memory."

"Yeah," I said, "once he found out the sale of the yacht went through."

Jeremy shook his head. "No, according to Marthe, it wasn't just the sale of the yacht that triggered the Count's memory. Apparently he got a very nasty call from an Englishman that upset him very much. She seems to think the man was demanding money from the Count, who soon refused to take any calls from the guy."

"Mortimer?" I said excitedly. "Then Rollo *is* on the right track."

"Maybe," Jeremy said. "Marthe also confirmed, as the Count told us, that his collection of aquamanilia had been in the family for years, and he was obsessive and wanted to retrieve the one missing piece that was stolen from the family's collection. But she knew nothing about the Beethoven connection, so she assumed the piece had been lost when her parents left Germany during the second World War."

"But on the phone you said the Count's grandfather really did find the Beethoven Lion in an auction. How do you know this?" I demanded.

"Because," Jeremy said triumphantly, "after I talked to Marthe, I went to the auction house in Frankfurt and spoke to their archivist. In 1890 they had a big auction with lots of important pieces for sale. So they kept a copy of the original brochure on file. The Lion is listed, but there's no record of its actual sale because the 'anonymous collector who owned the piece withdrew it.' Apparently you can do that, even at the last minute. She made a copy of the brochure for me, because she knows who you and I are from all the press about us. The catalogue was printed in German, English and French. Feast your eyes on this."

He handed me a shiny sheet of copy-paper. I peered at it.

> *The Beethoven Lion. Aquamanile in the form of a lion. Vienna, circa 1804. Copper alloy, eyes inset with almandine garnets. Copper inlays with incised details. Fine detailing on eyes, teeth and mane. (23.1×12.0×24.5 cm. Weight, 2391 g.) Anonymous owner.*

"Hoo-ee!" I cried, staring at the faded print. "It sounds beautiful," I added, then, "Oh, no—the metric system again. How big is it?"

"Almost nine inches tall," Jeremy translated, "nearly ten inches long and about four inches wide, and it weighed about five and a quarter pounds."

I studied it some more as Brice stopped by to tell Jeremy that we were steady on course. I then brought Jeremy up-to-date on all I'd learned from Clive about the Corsican family, and their daughter Diamanta, with whom I was hoping to make personal contact while we were in Calvi. But so far, I hadn't received a reply to my e-mails. In the last e-mail, I'd shamelessly told her all about the press coverage that Jeremy and I got for retrieving a lost work of art. I figured I might as well make the most of that dumb newspaper story. I also explained that I understood about the pricelessness of family heirlooms and that we would be very discreet.

"I told her we would come to see her in Corsica, and how to contact Claude on the boat," I said. "Still haven't heard back yet."

"Okay. By the way, I've got a bunch of aquamanilia info in the salon," Jeremy said.

"Ooh, let's see it," I said.

We entered the main salon and Jeremy spread out the photographs and illustrations he'd collected, on the round terrestrial-map table. Rollo had been wandering around the decks but now rejoined us, a glass of scotch in his hand from the bar.

Jeremy said, "I went to a workshop in Germany where modern artisans re-create aquamanilia in the traditional way, which is called the *cire perdu* or 'lost-wax' hollow-casting method," Jeremy explained. "They even use a lot of the old tools to do it. It's an arcane process, like alchemy, that was perfected in medieval times."

I gazed at the illustration, a reproduction of a woodcut, showing simple figures of aproned craftsmen working with stone ovens, big iron pots of melted metal, and other obscure tools.

"They start with a 'core' of a model made of clay—some of the clay even used to have dried dung in it. The clay is formed into the basic size and shape of the animal, but it has none of the details. That's where the wax comes in," Jeremy said. "They used beeswax, which was considered superior to all other waxes, so it was expensive. The artisan molds a layer of wax over the clay core, and since the wax is malleable, he can carve all those beautiful details, right into the wax layer—the animal's whiskers, eyes, teeth, the strands of fur and the lion's mane."

"But," I said, intrigued, "how do those details get put onto the metal?"

"Well, that's where it gets really wild," Jeremy said. "They have to actually build a system of wax tubes, extending from the model.

These tubes will eventually be the means for pouring in the molten metal."

"Wait a minute," I said. "You can't pour liquid hot metal into tubes made of beeswax. It will melt the wax!"

"Hang on. You don't pour the metal just yet. You next have to add what they call an 'investment,' which is essentially another layer of clay that goes over the wax. It's actually a mixture of clay, sand and stone. This has to be placed on very carefully, because it will pick up all the details that you just carved in the wax. Once that dries, what you've got is a sort of clay sandwich—clay on the outside, clay model on the inside, and the beeswax in between."

"What about all those wax tubes?" I asked. Rollo was peering over my shoulder.

"They're still there, and now they, too, are covered with a coat of clay investment," Jeremy said, pointing to a picture of something that looked like a ball of clay with tubes sticking out all over it.

"Once dry, the next step is to melt out the wax. The whole clay sandwich is placed upside-down near a heat source, like a fireplace," Jeremy continued. "That's so they could collect the valuable melted wax as it drips out, to use again another day."

"Hence, the 'lost wax,' " Rollo proclaimed. "Not lost to the maker. But lost to the aquamanile."

"Right. So now what you have is an empty space between the two layers of clay," Jeremy said. "But before you can pour the hot melted metal where the wax once was, you have to bake the clay in an oven until it gets red-hot, so it will become hard enough. Then you take it out with metal tongs, and bury it in packed earth, all the way to the top. The only thing sticking out are those tubes, which now, like the rest of it, are made of hard clay: one tube for pouring in the molten metal, and the others to allow the hot gases to escape so the whole thing doesn't crack.

"After the metal is poured into the clay sandwich, it all has to cool down. Next, they dig it out of the earth, and the outer layer of clay—the investment—is broken away and removed, and you also break off those tubes, and plug the holes with brass. Remember the X-rays that Kurt showed us? That's really the only way you'd notice the holes, because the entire aquamanile gets polished and finished with a patina. And, *voilà*—you now have a metal lion with all those details."

"Sounds like a ton of work," I said.

"It is. Very skilled work, too," Jeremy said. "One false move and you make a flaw—lop off the lion's ear or a nose."

"Wait—what about the original clay model inside?" I asked.

"That all gets scraped out by reaching into the largest opening—the mouth or the top of the head—because after all, the final product has to be hollow so you can fill it with water," Jeremy concluded. "Then you make a brass removable stopper for that filling-hole, like a kettle."

François arrived and paused politely at the door to the salon. "Lunch will be served in the dining salon."

"Fabulous!" Rollo cried. "This sea air really gives one an appetite. I'm so hungry I could eat a lion."

Chapter Thirty-five

A day upon the sea soon develops its own rhythm. You slow down, and your mind opens up to new possibilities. Plus, it helps if your chef is French.

And Rollo was right—walking about on the decks, breathing in the briny, salty air, was so invigorating to every cell in mind and body, that we were all famished by noon.

When we entered the dining salon, the table was laid with the yacht's china and tableware and linen napkins. Seeing this, I recalled what I'd heard about sudden storms springing up at sea, which could remove a whole crew with one big wave by washing them right off the deck, leaving behind a "ghost ship" with nobody on board—to be discovered later with its dining table still set for a meal that nobody had survived to eat. I thought of the Count, who'd encountered a storm on this very journey. Resolutely I put all this out of mind.

Brice pulled out a chair for me at one end of the table, and Jeremy took the one at the other end, and Rollo sat in the middle. Happily, not all of Jeremy's wine collection had been destroyed. Many choice bottles actually survived the boat-jacking. Brice served me first. François had already consulted with me in advance over this menu. So I knew what was coming, and I watched in delight as Jeremy and Rollo responded to each course.

For starters, François had made a lovely curried mussel soup as an *amuse bouche*, which was served with a dry rosé champagne, and we all clinked glasses to toast *Penelope's Dream*. This was followed by a first course of real Dover sole, baked atop a fresh bay leaf, accompanied by a chilled white wine called Vermentino, which comes from the Mediterranean and its islands. Then François, wanting us to taste some of Corsica's specialties, sent us a plate of grilled lamb medallions, served with a sauce of tomato and peppers, accompanied by one of Jeremy's hand-picked burgundies, and a fresh garden salad. I smiled to myself, thinking that when Jeremy imagined sharing his wine cellar with guests, he probably hadn't envisioned Rollo as his first formal dining companion.

When François arrived with dessert, we complimented him on his selections of fresh food for our trip, and he was pleased, but he told us mournfully, "I am afraid that the world's oceans and lakes no longer have the vast variety of fish that they used to. Twenty years ago, when a fisherman cast his net he might find twenty-seven different species; now he only sees about six. The warming of the planet, industrial farming and overcrowded aquafarms that dump horrible things into the water . . ." He frowned ferociously. "It is a sin!"

I thought of the beautiful sea that we were gliding across, and now I imagined the poor fish trying to survive in unnatural conditions in modern times. And then I remembered one of the charity organizations that had contacted me, back in London, who were working to preserve marine life. I brightened, thinking that perhaps I'd found a good cause I could really get behind.

"Ah, Paradise," Rollo said, as François served the dessert of fig tarte made with lemon, almonds, and chestnuts, and drizzled with prized Corsican honey, which, they say, tastes different in each season because the bees are feasting on whatever miraculous herb is growing at that time. This arrived with a small glass of Italian Sambuca that had a coffee bean floating in it, that lent its coffee aroma to the liqueur while you drank it; and, later, you ate the whole bean, which had soaked up a taste of the liqueur.

Feeling expansive, Rollo launched into a step-by-step plan of what he thought we should do to try to track down the dealer. I was surprised that Rollo had thought this all through so thoroughly. Jeremy started out skeptical, but after awhile he found himself thinking it was worth a try.

The idea was that, when we were close enough to shore, Rollo would have Brice take him out in the little emergency boat and drop him off at a secluded cove not far from town. This way, he would not be seen arriving with us when we docked at the harbor. Rollo would continue, on foot, to the sailors' bar in town, and he'd ask around for Mortimer, to see if he could convince him to sell the Lion.

And once he was able to make a recording of Mortimer admitting that he had the Lion, "Well, the rest is up to you," Rollo said. "You can buy the Lion, you can tell your French cops to have him arrested—but if you go that route I'm afraid I'll have to make myself scarce," Rollo said. "I don't like to be associated with the police. Personally, if it were up to me I'd make a trade with Mortimer—give me the Lion and I'll give you the recording."

I didn't know what to make of this. Rollo glanced at his big wristwatch. "We've got time for an afternoon nap," he said, perfectly serious. "See you on deck in a few."

And he shambled off to one of the guest cabins. Brice had been instructed by Jeremy to keep a sharp eye on Rollo, during this whole trip.

"Are we going with Rollo's plan?" I asked Jeremy.

"I say we let him make his recording and then meet us back at the boat and figure it out from there," Jeremy replied.

While we were pondering this, Claude came to me with a message he'd just received. He'd written it down. It was from Diamanta.

Yes, I will see you if you come. When you arrive in Calvi please telephone me at this number and I will send a relative to meet you and show you the way.

"That's it!" I cried triumphantly. "That's what I was waiting for!"

We were sitting on the steamer chairs on the aft deck under an awning that Brice had cranked open for us. On top of the mattresses he had laid out extra-long beach towels (so you didn't have to choose between having it only under either your head or your feet). We didn't plan to sleep, but eventually, with the splash-splash of the sea and the lovely salty air all around us, we both nodded off, anyway. Perfectly civilized, I thought drowsily.

And it worked, too, because, when, hours later, we could spot land ahead, I felt refreshed and ready. We all assembled on the fore deck to catch our first glimpse of the mysterious, majestic island.

Corsica is a whole world unto itself, looking like a great big rock sticking up out of the sea. Even today, Corsicans have a language of their own, called *Corsu*, which came from the Latin and is said to be similar to old Tuscan, akin to the language of the poet Dante. Although "owned" by the French, Corsica is really more Italian at heart.

Napoleon Bonaparte was born here, only a couple of months after the Italian city of Genoa sold the island to France. At age nine, Napoleon was sent to military school in France, and by the time he was a teenager, his father had died, so he was supporting his entire family. But, when civil war broke out in Corsica, Napoleon sided with France against the Corsica rebels—and became a condemned man. So, he had to sneak his whole family out of Corsica in the dead of night, back to France . . . and the rest, as they say, is history.

As *Penelope's Dream* floated closer to shore, I thought about Napoleon sneaking out, yet, thanks to Rollo, Jeremy and I were sneaking in. After being out at sea for so long, we were now eager to finally set foot upon our destination. The coastline of Corsica has miles of beautiful but fairly deserted beaches, and it's dotted with narrow gorges and other craggy watery nooks and crannies sheltered by towering walls of high-rising rock. We spotted a jagged-looking cove not far from the beach that led to town. It was here that Brice took Rollo out in the little emergency boat.

I couldn't help being a bit amused, watching Brice and Rollo put-putting toward the cove; and then seeing Rollo, with shoes and socks in hand, and pants rolled up, climbing out and wading to shore.

"That's the most energy I've ever seen him exert," Jeremy noted.

"I asked him why he was helping us," I replied, "and he said, 'Family honor, dear girl.' Apparently he has a reputation to protect, you know, *his* honor among thieves!"

"Plus," Jeremy reminded me, "we promised him a finder's fee. If we pull this off."

I peered over the bow of the boat, looking into the clear turquoise waters. "Look," I said, "the water's so transparent, you can see all those smooth rocks underneath."

"Good," Jeremy said darkly. "At least they'll be able to find our bodies."

When Brice returned with the little boat, it was full speed ahead to Calvi.

Chapter Thirty-six

Calvi is a bustling port town. High above it sits the famed citadel, a fortress that protected the city from pirates and invaders. People who live in the southern Mediterranean sometimes have the reputation for being stubborn or intractable, and this is mostly based on the pure willpower they demonstrate when they build forts, castles and whole cities on the edges of sheer cliffs and perilous rocks. You would think that the villagers are mountain goats themselves, to scale such heights and build dwellings on impossibly narrow ledges.

The two Italian cities of Genoa and Pisa fought like dogs over Calvi, and the Genoese won. Later, the British navy came meddling, by trying to help the Corsican rebels drive out the French; and it is here that England's Admiral Nelson was wounded in the eye and had to wear that famous eyepatch ever after. The citadel above Calvi still has one of Nelson's cannonballs lodged in it. The narrow streets of the main town lead to the port itself, and a coastline rimmed by a curving sandy beach. It's popular both with high-end celebrity vacationers—and with the French Foreign Legion, which is a pretty tough bunch.

Gazing at the picturesque shoreline, I reminded myself that the

Count had arrived here a dapper, vibrant man ... but after this adventure, ended up frail, wheelchair-bound and forgetful. This now struck me as fairly ominous.

We docked at the marina, where the crew would refuel and re-load. There was a promenade along the quay, with fashionable cafés and restaurants overlooking the harbor, and gift, souvenir and trinket shops. I used the ship's telephone to contact Diamanta. She was waiting for our call. I couldn't make out what she said when she first answered the phone. But when I told her my name, she said in clear, French-accented English, "Yes, I will send my brother to meet you. He will come to your boat."

Jeremy and I went below to freshen up. When we came back up on deck, Claude told us that a young man was waiting for us, in a car parked by the quay.

"Be careful," Claude cautioned, looking truly concerned. "If you need anything, please call."

The dark-haired, dark-eyed young man waiting for us was about eighteen years old, and the car he was driving was an old convertible that had probably once been expensive. He didn't speak English; in fact, he didn't speak a single word to us the entire time. We got in the backseat, and he drove through the town and up into the hills. The clustered village houses, some made of washed white granite from the majestic cliffs that towered over the sea, soon gave way to open fields, where the houses were spaced much farther apart, alternating with pockets of thick dense shrubs, and groves of trees that lined the narrow road.

We passed an old stone church, and then the road became dusty, unpaved, and bumpy with rocks. The air was fragrant with mysterious herbs, making the atmosphere hypnotic and somnolent in the blistering heat of the summer sun, which caused the trees to droop a little. I felt my eyelids fluttering closed. I had heard that many Mediterranean islands—Sicily, Sardinia and Corsica—have very modern cities and towns ringing the rims of the islands; but the moment that you penetrate deeper into the hills, you seem to go back in time, retreating into a quiet, medieval world.

The sound of a church bell, and the heavy flutter of crow's wings, made me open my eyes, suddenly alert. I started to feel uneasy. I mean, how did we know who this guy really was and where he was really taking us? He didn't glance at us or smile once.

"It better not be much farther," Jeremy muttered, just as we turned into a pebbled driveway leading to a fairly large farmhouse with an orchard, a planted field, and, to one side, a yard with a goat and a pig kept fenced beyond the house. The animals seemed to pause and look up at us inquiringly as we parked and walked past them.

The young man led us up the front steps and gestured toward the door. He walked away and turned a corner and disappeared from sight. Jeremy and I just looked at each other. Then we went inside.

It was cool and dark in the foyer. The adjacent parlor was empty of people; just some pieces of heavy old furniture, a chest of drawers with a small statue of the Virgin Mary atop it, and a little vase of fresh wildflowers set up as an offering to her. There were two armchairs, a sofa, and two small tables with lamps.

I heard the sharp tap of a woman's footsteps coming toward us from the dark hallway. A moment later, a tall, slender young woman with long dark hair appeared. She had a pretty face, with a high forehead and sharply chiseled nose and chin, but soft round cheeks that made her dark eyes seem to tilt upward at the ends. She wore a yellow-and-white flowered dress, with a pale yellow cardigan over her shoulders, buttoned only at the top button.

"Please, have a seat," she said, gesturing toward the sofa while she sat down on the upholstered chair opposite us. Her voice and speech had a modern tone, but she moved with an old-fashioned dignity, and had very slow and deliberate gestures, very formal manners. She told us that she no longer lived with her family, but spent only the summers here.

I made introductions and she said matter-of-factly, "Oh yes, I'd heard of you before you contacted me."

This surprised me and stopped me in my tracks. "From the press, or from Clive?" I asked.

"From my grandmother," Diamanta said. "She said you would come."

I glanced at Jeremy, whose face had that now-see-where-your-curiosity-has-landed-us-this-time look. "I beg your pardon?" I asked.

Diamanta smiled. "Grandmother said we would be visited by a red-headed foreign woman," she said, watching me closely. She was, after all, an educated girl who knew perfectly well that grand-motherly premonitions were not the predominant twenty-first-century mode of communication.

Great, I thought. In these environs, redheads were usually considered the troublemaking descendants of barbaric invaders, so they were pretty much viewed with suspicion.

As if reading my mind, Diamanta said, "Grandmother said that the spirits of this house condone your presence, and she believes that you were sent to end the injustices against our family."

Now I did gulp. That was a tall order from the spirit world. I doubted I was up to the task. Surely they must be looking for some other redhead.

Jeremy, ever one to get down to brass tacks, said in his calm way, "Diamanta. We are looking for a Lion aquamanile that we heard was taken from this place. Is this true, and how did you come to possess it?"

Diamanta said very simply, "It belonged to our family for many, many years, because the head of this house made it with his own hands for the woman he loved."

"Ohhhh!" I breathed. I turned to Jeremy. "The boy who made the aquamanile and fell in love with the German girl!" I turned to the girl. "Oh, what was his name?" I said. "Nobody I talked to seems to know."

Diamanta stood up. "Come," she said. "Grandmother wishes to see you."

She led us out of the formal parlor, past a few closed doors and into a kitchen at the back where four women were sitting: a very old lady, shelling peas into a basin in her lap; a middle-aged woman, stirring something in a big cast-iron pot on the stove, and two girls in gingham dresses, one slightly older who was braiding the hair of the younger one. The adult women wore black. From the way they looked at Diamanta, I could see that she was the pride of her family, the city girl who had made good, but came back to visit and help her relatives.

Diamanta gestured for me to approach the old lady. As I drew closer, I saw that the woman had strange bluish-white eyes that seemed to look permanently upward; and I realized that she was blind, and was performing her task by "feel" rather than by sight. This was the grandmother who had predicted my arrival.

"Here she is," Diamanta said softly to the old woman, who turned her head and then put aside the bowl she'd had in her lap. Diamanta gestured to the little girls, and they abandoned the kitchen chairs they were seated on so that Jeremy and I could sit by the grandmother. The old woman waited, her head cocked, alert, as if listening to the breeze that wafted in through the open windows of the kitchen.

"Talk to her," Diamanta murmured to me. "Just tell her your name, and why you came."

"Will she understand English, or . . . French?" I asked, hesitantly.

"It doesn't matter what you say. Just talk to her."

So in English, I said my name, and said that I had come to learn about the Lion, and the young people who, many years ago, had fallen in love but were parted.

"Please, tell us your family's story about the Lion, and what happened to your ancestor who made it," I concluded. Diamanta translated this question for her. The grandmother had been listening closely to the sound of my voice, and now she leaned forward, picked up my hand and placed it in her own. It was like being grasped by a gnarled old tree.

What happened next is somewhat open to interpretation. Jeremy told me later that, technically, he saw nothing out of the ordinary. But I felt something, like a distinct wave of energy, passing through me, as the grandmother uttered several words that I did not understand. The effect on the room was palpable, and even Jeremy admitted this later.

The grandmother continued to speak in a low rumbling murmur. Diamanta rapidly translated for us. I listened carefully, not only to Diamanta, but to the lyrical rise and fall of the grandmother's voice with its poetic inflections that spoke to me on another level.

"Our family goes back many, many years. The person you want to know about was named Paolo. He left Corsica when he was a very young man, to apprentice in Vienna for a German metalworker. His boss taught him to read and write. They say Paolo was greatly gifted with his hands, and could sculpt animals out of clay that were, how would you say, 'real enough to bite you.' Everyone wanted the things that Paolo made.

"One day, a fine German man asked Paolo to make a Lion for his daughter's piano teacher, who was a great musical *maestro*. Paolo fell in love with the rich man's daughter, whose name was Greta. Her father would not let her marry a poor boy, and the man was so displeased that he would not pay for the beautiful Lion when it was done, and ordered it to be returned. Paolo was fired from his job. But Paolo and Greta plotted secretly to run away together, until her brothers found out, and locked her in her room so she could not get out of the house! Then, one night, Greta's brothers went out to 'teach Paolo a lesson.' But Greta found a way to warn him, through a servant who was returning the Lion to him. The servant told Paolo to flee for his life, and said that Greta promised that she would find him again and they would be reunited before their son was born."

"Whoa," I said. "Their *son?*" This was more than Mr. Donaldson had known.

As the old woman continued, Diamanta kept translating. "Once back in Corsica, Paolo tried to get word to Greta, but she had returned to Germany and he could not find her. By this time Paolo had become gravely ill with pneumonia, but he kept hoping that Greta would appear at his bedside and present him with his son. But the girl never came, and he died."

There was a long silence.

"What a sad story," I said softly. I hesitated. "So, it was Paolo's grave that you made the procession to in November?"

Diamanta nodded. I had been mindful all along of something I'd learned from an art history teacher, years ago. When searching for family secrets, he said, *Tombstones speak.* Tentatively, I asked if we could see Paolo's grave.

Diamanta translated this for the older woman, who paused a long time. I held my breath, as the moment hovered over us. Then the grandmother murmured something. Diamanta said to us, "Come with me."

Jeremy had been watching the whole time, like a bodyguard, glancing round at everyone else in the room. As we moved to follow Diamanta out the kitchen door which led to the back of the house, the middle-aged woman at the stove suddenly looked up and spoke in an angry tone which even my ears knew meant something along the lines of, *What are you, crazy? Don't show her anything, look where it led the last time a stranger visited.* The two little girls stopped chattering and looked wary. The grandmother gave a short, decisive answer, holding up the index finger of her right hand, indicating that she had the last word on the subject.

"You must understand," Diamanta murmured when she saw my expression, "that we have always been a very private family. Only once did we allow a stranger in, and he took pictures that caused us to be robbed. But Grandmother understands that you are here to restore the balance that was disturbed. I will take you now to Paolo's grave."

Chapter Thirty-seven

Diamanta silently led us out the back door, beyond a fenced-in garden redolent of flowers, vegetables and herbs, through an arched wooden gate that led us up a grassy hill. The surrounding shrubbery was fragrant, and when I asked Diamanta about it, she told me that it was called *maquis*, a wild flowering variety that grew very tall and could be used as an herb in cooking.

We reached the crest of the hill, where, flanked on two sides by low stone walls and eucalyptus trees, was a small hut carved right into the rocky cliff. This, she told us, was a shepherd's hut which had been converted into a family crypt. I recognized it from Clive's photo. Diamanta had a key that unlocked it. We stepped inside. It was cool and damp, with an earthen floor. The walls were of carved rock.

As my eyes adjusted to the dark, I saw that the floor of the hut had three headstones in an area that was marked off by small round flat stones all around it. Diamanta had brought a flashlight, and now she pointed at the headstone in the center, which was the largest and most prominent.

"There Paolo sleeps," she said simply. I felt a slight chill on my skin, rippling up to my neck. But, I had come very far for these answers. I had to see it. Jeremy and I leaned forward intently, reading the name carved on the headstone. There was no birth date, only the date of his death. It said *Paolo Andria* on the biggest stone, followed by the words *padre caro, 1805.*

"Dear father," I murmured.

I asked Diamanta if I could make a rubbing of the tombstone. When I assured her that we would take care not to damage the stone, she agreed. I had brought my tools with me—a roll of white paper, and colored chalk. Jeremy held the paper against the headstone, while I carefully rubbed the chalk stick across the letters and numbers. When I was done, the tombstone inscriptions appeared on the paper as ghostly white writing against the colored background.

Jeremy nudged me, nodding toward the smaller gravestone on the left. As I peered closer, Diamanta aimed her flashlight at it. The letters were harder to read, so we traced them on the paper with the chalk, and I read them aloud as each letter emerged: G-R-E-T-A . . .

Greta von Norbert. 1834. Adorata.

"Von Norbert!" Jeremy whispered. "No wonder we've got two families telling the same story."

"Look." I pointed to the last stone, the one on the right, which bore the name *Aldo Andria von Norbert*, and the words *figlio amato, 1884.*

"Beloved son," I said. "Wow. This must be the child of Greta and Paolo. Is that right?" I asked Diamanta. She nodded. "But your grandmother said that Greta didn't show up," I reminded her.

"Years later," Diamanta explained. She led us out of the hut, and she sat on one of the low stone walls that flanked it. She had left the door to the hut ajar. Squinting a little in the sunlight, gazing up at us, she continued the tale of the Lion.

"You see, after Paolo died, his parents and brothers kept the Lion in the house. Meanwhile, back in Germany, Paolo's son, Aldo, was raised by his mother, Greta, as if he were the legitimate son of her rich old German husband. When Aldo grew up to be a young man, his mother told him the truth about his real father. Aldo insisted he must meet Paolo, so his mother agreed to go with him to Corsica. She did not know that Paolo had died so long ago, until she came to this house, and learned the truth. But, the voyage and the shock were too much for Greta, and she died here and was buried next to Paolo."

"And—the Lion?" Jeremy asked. "What happened to it?"

"Aldo, the son, asked to buy the Lion so that he could keep it as a memorial of his parents. My family was poor then, and Paolo's brothers agreed to sell it. Aldo returned to Germany, with the Lion."

"But," I said, "Aldo is buried here."

"Yes," said Diamanta, "because when Aldo went back to Germany without his mother, the von Norbert family blamed him for her death. And now that everyone knew whose child Aldo really was, his stepfather disinherited him. His rich stepbrother, Rolf, was always envious of the love that Greta had for Aldo, and he was heartbroken over her death. So, Rolf took the Lion, claiming it rightfully belonged to his family. Aldo stole it back from him, and ran away back here to Corsica, just as his own father had done."

"And the Lion was kept here ever since?" I asked.

"No," said Jeremy, "what about the auction in Frankfurt in 1890?"

Diamanta looked at him appreciatively. "You are quite right," she said. "Aldo married and raised his own family here. He had twin grandsons. They were restless young men, tired of being poor. They wanted to sell the Lion, even though the village *mazzera* told them it would be a terrible mistake, taking the Lion away from here, for it would be like stealing the soul of their grandfather, and they would both die within a year."

At the mention of the *mazzera*, Jeremy elbowed me. I had to ask.

"Diamanta," I said hesitantly, "is your grandmother a *mazzera*?"

"Oh, no!" she replied. "My grandmother has the second sight, but she is not a *mazzera*. There's a flower-lady, down by the pier, who is."

"Oh!" I said to Jeremy. I remembered that the Count had told us that a woman put a curse on him just before he left Corsica. Only he thought she was a beggar.

"But what happened to Aldo's grandsons in 1890?" Jeremy asked Diamanta.

"The twins ignored the *mazzera*'s warning, and took the Lion to a dealer in Frankfurt, who agreed to sell it at auction for them. But, that very week, one of the brothers was murdered in the streets for his pocket money. The other one took this as a sign, so he demanded the Lion back from the auction, and he fled, bringing the Lion home with him. Ever since then, once a year, on the night of the dead when our ancestors 'return' to inspect their graves, the family carries the Lion to Paolo's grave, to prove to his spirit that the Lion still resides here. They lock it in the crypt on that night, to appease Paolo's soul. The next morning, they unlock the grave and return the Lion to the house for safekeeping. But as you know, after that photograph came out, with all the publicity, the Lion was stolen right out of our house."

"You've seen this Lion?" Jeremy asked. Diamanta nodded.

"Oh, yes. It always had a place of honor in this house, with its own cupboard. I remember each year, dressing up for the procession from the church, with candles and flowers, and the eldest male in the family would carry the Lion from the house to this grave. And the next morning he would bring it back here."

"Did you ever look inside the Lion?" Jeremy asked. She shook her head.

"No, that was not possible, for it was sealed shut."

I reached into my purse for the sketchpad and pencil. "Diamanta," I said, "could you tell me exactly what the Lion looks like?"

Intrigued, she described it, watching the pad as I sketched it out. Little by little, it took a form and shape. Standing on all fours, big wild mane, tail, ferocious face . . .

"And don't forget the monkey," she said. My pencil stopped. I paused.

"What monkey?" Jeremy asked.

"Oh, it had a funny little monkey in its mouth," Diamanta said. "The body was sticking inside, so you really only saw the arms and the head and the face. You know of course who the monkey resembled."

As calmly as I could, I said, "No, who?"

"Why," Diamanta said, "Napoleon Bonaparte, of course."

I resumed sketching, following her instructions so that we ended up with the monkey sticking out of the Lion's mouth like a mouse in the mouth of a great cat. Diamanta said in amusement, "I was always told that the Lion was the Pride that had swallowed Napoleon, so that he lost his empire and was banished."

"And, the Lion itself?" I asked. "Did he look like anyone in particular?"

"I never knew who he was supposed to be until all that publicity from the photograph," she said. "It's Beethoven, isn't it? But I didn't have a chance to look at it again and see, because by then, it was gone."

Chapter Thirty-eight

Diamanta's brother was nowhere to be found when we were ready to leave. He had taken the car and disappeared. After conferring with her relatives, Diamanta told us that an elderly uncle would take us most of the way back to town; he lived halfway there and had a donkey cart that he used when touring his farm.

He was a very, very old man with a face like a wizened prune. He wore a straw hat and a rumpled suit. But he was cheerful enough as we climbed onto the buckboard, and soon we were bumping along the road.

"This," Jeremy said, "is what comes of not hiring a rental car wherever you go."

We had arrived in Calvi in the afternoon, so now, as we descended toward town, I could see that the sun was already beginning to slip into the sea. Diamanta's uncle hummed to himself until the road forked and he stopped the cart. After we dismounted, he tipped his hat to me and turned the donkey cart away toward his farm.

"Do you suppose that the Count knew he had a family connection here in Corsica?" I asked Jeremy.

"Who knows?" he said. "He apparently never contacted Diamanta's family. And why would he have bothered with Mortimer if he knew?"

"You know," I said, "the whole thing is finally starting to make sense to me. This Paolo, being a Corsican, might also have been disillusioned with Napoleon . . ."

"Well, judging from the fact that he made a monkey out of him," Jeremy said, "I vote that yes, this Paolo bloke was for Corsican independence."

We were passing by thick clusters of trees—lemon, juniper, myrtle, chestnut, and the prized strawberry tree that supposedly promotes longevity; and the air was filled with the scent of herbs like bay and rosemary. At times the shrubbery beside the road was so dense that I could hear crickets, even though it was still daylight. At other times there were wide open stretches of sand and desert scrub.

Jeremy was fiddling with his phone. "Can't get a signal at all," he said disgustedly. "I was going to tell Claude we're on our way—"

He was interrupted by a loud, popping sound that echoed across the open fields.

Now, look. I can't actually say I've ever been shot at before. Hell, I don't even know if I've ever really heard a gun go off, except on a movie set. And those are blanks. Even so, I can say that I knew right now, for certain, that someone not very far away had just fired a gun. And, I think it's a pretty good guess who the target was. Us.

Jeremy had the same idea, of course, because he'd dragged me off to the side of the road and into the shrubbery, then flung himself on top of me on the ground. I heard another shot, and another.

Then there was silence. We waited. A long time. During which I tried very hard not to think about scorpions, and about how if they sting you, you can die a very unpleasant death because there is no real antidote. I've never seen an actual scorpion, only on TV. But crouched there in the sandy soil in a dense thicket of prickly brush, I reckoned there was a distinct possibility of meeting up with one. Provided, of course, that a snake didn't get there first. Not to mention, of course, the gunman.

All of this crossed my mind while we lay there waiting. Jeremy was still on top of me. A grown man, even one you love, is a very heavy item.

"Penny," Jeremy whispered finally, "are you all right?"

And, idiotically, what I said was, "Yes. Hey, was that a gun?"

"Yes," Jeremy said. He waited, then decided it was okay to climb off me. He raised himself up and said, "Let's get out of here."

But when we returned to the road, another shot was fired. This one landed in the road ahead of us, judging by the dirt and dust spewing into the air. Jeremy grabbed me by the shoulders and this time we went plunging into the brush, away from the road.

"Run like hell," he said, pushing me ahead of him so he could keep me in his sights. "Head for the sea."

It didn't look that far away. And actually, it wasn't. However. Running on a dirt road is simple enough. Running through all manner of prickly scrub, shrubs and trees is quite another story. All along the way it seemed as if branches were grabbing at me and deliberately trying to slow me down so I'd be sure to get caught. My breath was coming out in wild gasps and my heart was pounding so hard that I thought my chest might explode. It was getting dark now, very quickly as it does on islands. I could hear the sound of cicadas filling the air.

I gasped with relief when we reached a paved road. And suddenly, there we were in the heart of the village, walking down a steep hill. With lots of people around us. But we must have looked like two maniacs.

For awhile, neither one of us spoke. It was enough of a heroic task just to recapture our breath. Panting, we studied each other. Clothes torn, faces smudged, hair insanely askew. Scratches bleeding on our arms and legs.

"You all right, Penny?" Jeremy asked, looking worried.

"Sure," I panted, trying not to think about how terrified I still was. Jeremy took out his handkerchief, and gently wiped my cheek and then my arm and leg, where I had scratches and cuts that were bleeding. I felt dazed and lightheaded from running pell-mell in the sultry heat.

"Who was shooting at us?" I demanded indignantly, as if I was talking about somebody stealing a parking space instead of merely trying to blow our heads off.

"Someone who wanted to scare us into never coming back," Jeremy said.

"Well, he succeeded," I said. "You think it was that neighbor that Diamanta told us about, the one she suspects stole the Lion?"

"I think it's whoever is in cahoots with Mortimer, and probably the same crowd that stole our yacht," Jeremy said darkly. "However, I am beginning to wonder if there wasn't also a more immediate member of Diamanta's family involved as well."

"Her brother?" I asked.

Jeremy said, "I guess we have to consider all possibilities."

We were trotting along a very narrow street now, built on a steep hill, just a short walk from the harbor. We slowed down as we approached a peach-colored stucco building that was so pretty, it was hard to believe that this was the sailors' bar. Several motorcycles were parked in front of it. Some tough-looking men were sitting on chairs at a table in front of it, playing cards and drinking.

The bar was the kind which has several doors that function like big windows and can be left open in the hot weather, so that the whole indoor area becomes visible from outside, and you can peer in and see people sitting at their tables or barstools. We hovered outside.

I whispered, "I can't believe our nice little Count came here to do business."

"Hang on," Jeremy said. "Do you see what I see?"

I peered in. A little boy was doing grown-up work, sweeping the floor with a broom that was taller than him. A worn-out looking woman was carrying a tray of glasses to the bar. A fat man was emptying a bag of ice into a bin at the bar. The chairs and tables were very simple, filled only with male patrons, some who appeared to be respectable locals, possibly the shepherds who came down from the interior; but there were also plenty of tough-looking sailors and military types.

"Over there," Jeremy said, "at that table by the street."

And there was Rollo, in his Panama hat, drinking beer with a brown-haired Englishman in a white shirt and hemp-colored linen trousers. I could not hear what they were saying; only the rise and fall of their accented English voices. It had to be Mortimer. The expression on his face was hard and unpleasant, even though he was smiling.

"You go back to the yacht," Jeremy said. "And tell Brice to fetch the first-aid kit. I'm going to sit at the other table and see if I can hear what they're saying. I just want to make sure that Rollo isn't double-crossing us."

"I'm not leaving now!" I said. The woman who was working at the bar glanced up, saw me and gave me a suspicious, disapproving look before she turned to serve another customer. "Splitting up is always a terrible idea," I objected in a lower voice.

"There are no women in there. You will draw the attention of everybody in sight," Jeremy insisted.

While we lingered there arguing, Rollo and Mortimer stood up and went into a back room together, behind the bar, disappearing from sight.

"Great. Thanks a lot," Jeremy said.

At that moment, one tough guy playing cards drove his fist on the table, then stood up and tore his cards in half, as if he'd been dealt a dirty hand.

Jeremy, sensing more trouble, said, "Come on. Let's get out of here."

François looked utterly horrified when he saw the condition we were in—disheveled, scratched, clothes torn. "My God, what's happened to you?" he cried. Jeremy explained, telling as little as possible. Brice got the first-aid kit, so we could clean and patch ourselves up. Claude listened gravely in silence.

"We must get under way now," he said warningly.

There was a shout from the pier. I looked up just in time to see Rollo running toward us. Two thuggy-looking guys were chasing after him. But when he hollered, they glanced apprehensively at the harbormaster's office, then veered off rapidly in another direction, expertly blending in with the milling crowd from the tourist ferry that was congregating at the harbor.

As Rollo came barrelling down the quay, a woman with dyed blonde hair, wearing a beige T-shirt and black skirt, carrying a large wicker basket of flowers for sale, reached out for Rollo, and plucked at his sleeve. Hastily, Rollo shook himself loose, and she called out something to him. She followed him, moving nearer to our yacht, close enough so that I could see that she had large, bulging eyes which were pretty but strange and compelling.

"Jeremy," I whispered. "The *mazzera*! Diamanta said so. She was trying to tell Rollo something. I wonder what it was?"

"Probably on the order of *Mind your own business, you bloody fool*," Jeremy said.

Rollo was charging up the gangway toward us like a snorting bull.

"Shove off! Let's go!" Rollo cried, unaware that the men had stopped chasing him, as he catapulted himself onto the deck and collapsed, gasping, leaning against the handrail. The yacht engine rumbled and a moment later we were pulling out of the harbor. But I looked back once more at the flower-lady, who had come right to the edge of the dock, staring with a hypnotic gaze, and, seeing my face, she raised the palm of her hand in what appeared to be a farewell gesture.

Chapter Thirty-nine

"Mortimer hasn't got your Lion," Rollo announced as we cast off from Calvi.

The moon had already risen in the cobalt-blue sky as we began our return voyage to the Riviera. Rollo, Jeremy and I assembled around the teak table on the aft deck, and François brought us cocktails. Not that Rollo needed any. But by now I sure did, to soothe my ruffled feathers.

"Say, did you hear me?" Rollo demanded. Jeremy nodded wearily.

"What happened to you two?" Rollo asked. "You look like the wreck of the *Hesperus*."

Jeremy closed his eyes. "Someone shot at us, thank you very much," he said. "Why do I imagine that your Mortimer fellow had something to do with it?"

"Well," Rollo admitted, "that's entirely possible, I'm afraid . . ."

"Rollo," I said, "the flower-woman. What did she say to you?"

Rollo said, "Who? Oh, Lord. What a strange creature! Couldn't say, she was talking something that sounded like tortured French to me."

Rollo took a swig of his gin. "As soon as I walked into the bar, I knew Mortimer was somewhere about, I could just smell it," he said. "So I sat there and played cards with the locals, losing just enough money to get them talking. That bar is the kind of place where information is exchanged on a regular basis and gossip spreads out to the village like wildfire."

"So?" I prodded. "How did you find Mortimer?"

"I didn't find him, I made *him* find me," Rollo said. "The old devil was in a back room with some of the other locals. So I flushed him out of his rabbit-hole," Rollo reported triumphantly. "I acted quite sozzled—but I had to actually stay somewhat sober to keep my wits about me—and soon enough, he came and sat down with me, and we got to talking. He said he buys and sells antiques, and I said, 'Well, well, it just so happens I am looking for a very rare item that I'd heard was found and lost in Corsica.' It wasn't the first time he'd been asked for it, let me tell you. He sized me up, then he said he didn't have it, but he thought he knew who did."

"So where the hell is it?" Jeremy asked.

Rollo waved his arm. "The best is yet to come, dear boy. After he drank a few more beers—" Rollo leaned forward keenly, "guess what the old devil admitted?"

"That he stole it off the boat!" I cried. Rollo grinned.

"Well? Is he the boat-jacker?" Jeremy demanded, looking ready to go back and find the guy and beat him up.

"Indirectly, but it was a botched job," Rollo explained. "He was hanging about the pier the night of your cocktail party, and he saw Kurt go aboard, so Mortimer realized what he must be looking for. Old Mortimer knew he'd have to work fast, so he hired a few bad fellows to go search for the Lion aboard your boat that very night. But when those idiots who ransacked the boat couldn't find the Lion aboard, they got frustrated, knowing they would not be paid for the night's work if they showed up without it.

"So the imbeciles couldn't decide what to steal off the boat, until one of them came up with the brilliant idea of stealing the entire boat to get money from the sort of person who would pay for a hot yacht," Rollo explained. "Only, not being professionals, they failed to notice that the boat hadn't even been refueled yet. They certainly couldn't even make it to Corsica, let alone Malta or Tunisia! So they lost their nerve, ditched in Villefranche, and cut their losses."

"Did you get all this recorded on your funny pen?" I asked.

Rollo looked uneasy. "I think I did," he said. "Can't say for sure."

"Well, let's hear it!" I cried.

Rollo looked embarrassed. "I turned it on and had it running the whole time," he said defensively. "Only, I suppose the conversation ran a little longer than the mechanism could handle. I was all set to go, shook hands with him and everything, when I bent to tie my shoe . . . and then the damned pen fell out of my pocket right smack on the floor and began saying out loud *Testing one-two-three* for all and sundry to hear."

"Good God," Jeremy said, disgusted.

"Afraid I had to hightail it out of there without looking back, *sans* pen. So there you have it," Rollo admitted.

"There we *don't* have it," Jeremy corrected. "No pen, no proof, no Lion."

"Where does Mortimer think it is?" I asked.

"He thinks *you've* got it!" Rollo chortled. "Thinks you took it off the boat the minute you bought it."

"Well, if Mortimer hasn't got it," I said, "and we know *we* don't have it, then who—?"

"Maybe the dotty old Count has it," Rollo said. "Unless the sly fox or his family sold it to someone."

"Hmm. I wonder how much the Count knows about the true origin of the Beethoven Lion," I said. "I mean, why didn't he tell us he had a family connection to it?"

"In any case," Jeremy said, "we should make one last search of this fine old boat. And if it doesn't turn up aboard, then it's back to Como."

As he spoke, a little wave literally leaped out of the Mediterranean Sea just like a dolphin, and catapulted over the handrail and splashed on deck. We all got wet, and laughed. At the sound of the cook's bell, giving us the twenty-minute heads-up for dinner, we went inside.

Jeremy and Rollo searched the main salon again. I went below to the master cabin. The closets and drawers had a nice fragrance of wood and lavender. I checked them again, but turned up nothing new. François had laid out two terrycloth bathrobes on the bed. They were white with the boat's name stitched in gold script on the pockets. On a bedroom chair just outside the bathroom door was a pile of navy-blue towels that matched the bed's counterpane. I picked up a nice big one and went into the triangular-shaped shower, which I'd stocked with my favorite Provençal soap and shampoo. It was fun, showering in the doll-sized toy shower. I was relieved to wash off all the dust and dirt of the day.

Then I went inside the dining salon for our light supper. Afterwards, we adjourned to the main salon, where Jeremy and Rollo opened up the box of chess pieces whittled by a sailor. They set up the board on that lovely round table with its terrestrial map. I put some music on the Victrola, and I curled up on the sofa with my pad and pen.

I wanted to record all the startling information we'd gotten in Corsica. You might say that family trees are my specialty. Pretty soon I had worked some of it out:

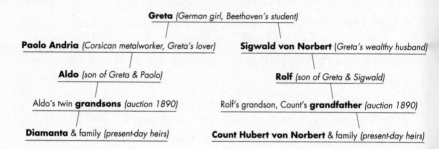

While mulling this over, I idly glanced at the chess pieces.

"You know," I said slowly, "this whole back-and-forth with the Lion, is kind of like a chess game being played between the two families. I mean, first Paolo brings the Lion to Corsica. Then his son, Aldo, buys it and takes it back to Germany, where it gets stolen by Aldo's stepbrother, Rolf; but Aldo steals it back, and takes it to Corsica. Then, decades later, Aldo's twin grandsons take it to auction in Germany, but one of them dies so the other twin panics and brings the Lion home again. That brings us to modern times, when the Lion is stolen from Diamanta's family. And the Count gets hold of it, so the von Norberts have it again," I concluded. "But not for long, because supposedly it was then stolen off this boat. The question is, by whom?"

Jeremy, without even looking up from the chess game, said, "Well, following that logic, then, it's the Corsicans' turn to get it back."

Rollo nodded sagely and dropped his voice to a stage whisper. "I wonder—if the Lion never got off this boat with the Count—then perhaps someone else aboard *Penelope's Dream* took it that night the Count came back from Corsica."

"Someone aboard it?" I asked. "Like who?"

"Like who?" he said. "Like your crew."

"What??" I said. "Like Claude or François? You must be joking. The police checked them out."

"Nevertheless," Rollo said, "when we land in Nice you might want to dig up the family connections of the people who worked on this boat the night the Lion disappeared."

"What a terribly suspicious thing to do," I grumbled.

Rollo shrugged. "You seem to be in the suspicion business, Penny dear," he said, as he rose to stretch his legs. François came up to ask if we required anything more. When we shook our heads, he and Brice cleared up the dishes. Rollo waggled his eyebrows at me and jerked his head significantly in their direction, and I frowned at him.

Even so, whenever Brice nodded to me or François smiled, I couldn't help momentarily second-guessing these sweet, agreeable people who had been gently looking after us the whole time. I found myself wondering if either of them, or Claude, could be one of Paolo's disgruntled descendants. It couldn't be . . . could it? Those warm smiles were genuine . . . weren't they?

At that moment my thoughts were interrupted when, totally without warning, there was a sudden rude bump against the yacht, as if a whale had slapped up against us. A moment later, the little curios in the cupboard started to rattle ominously, and some of the chess pieces keeled over. We all exchanged wary glances. Then Claude did something he'd never done before—he talked to us over the emergency loud-speaker, saying that we were heading into some unexpected rough weather, and might wish to go below to our cabins.

I got up and peered out the porthole at the sky. It was as if all the stars had been birthday candles but a big, impetuous child had blown them all out in one big breath. Now there was nothing but the darkness of the sea blending in with the darkness of the sky. And land-ho was still very, very far away.

Chapter Forty

Well, I'm guessing that Neptune himself was somehow displeased that night. I can't say for sure how it happened, but it was as if the wind had just hurled an insult at the sea, and the sea rose up to spit back at it. And suddenly, our big brave boat seemed very tiny indeed, as frail as the humans who made it, in the face of more powerful forces. I thought of the ancient Greeks, bravely setting out across the Med, making up stories about all the tough spots they passed through. Treacherous shallows, and rocky wind tunnels, and foggy shores and odd little islands, which in mythology became kingdoms ruled by giant bird-monsters or snaky-haired witches or fishy temptresses or one-eyed giants who had to be placated or tricked into letting Odysseus and his crew pass.

Now, I never thought of myself as a landlubber. But as the boat began to pitch and roll, this way and that, suddenly my stomach began to develop a curious rhythm of its own. And it wasn't a good melody. No, sir. That passed, but then I felt as if strange gravitational forces were pulling on my face, my shoulders, my knees, and that I was losing track of which end was up and which was down. I felt a sudden new profound urge to plant my two feet on dry land. *Now.*

"Penny?" Jeremy said, peering at me. I tried to speak but made only a strange little squawk. A second later I couldn't seem to see straight, as if I were looking through a photographer's lens that had been deliberately smeared with petroleum jelly, when they want to make everything blurry and surreal.

I heard Rollo's voice say, "Afraid she's had it. Better put her to bed."

Jeremy tried to help me walk but now my knees buckled as if they'd gone on strike. He actually had to carry me down to the master cabin, which wasn't so easy on the boat's narrow stairwell. I remember thinking that this could have been a wonderful romantic moment between us, if only I didn't feel so desperately like jumping out the porthole and swimming to shore.

"Don't worry, it will be all right," Jeremy's voice said above me as he tucked me into the bed. And there I was and there I stayed, for hours, buried under the nice blue counterpane.

"Poor baby. Want me to stay with you?" he asked.

" 'Druther you didn't see me like this," I said, still vain enough to care.

"Call me if you need anything, then," he said tenderly, pushing aside my damp hair from my face, looking worried. "You may have a bit of a fever. I hope you weren't bitten by anything." I moaned as he got up and made the bed bounce.

"No. I just need to be on something that's not moving," I said in a small voice.

"Soon," he promised, but I knew he was lying. We were still hours from port. I just had to wait it out. So, as Jeremy told me later, he had to kiss my little green face and leave me there.

With all the money rolling around the world, they still haven't really cured seasickness. I tried to tell myself that it was all in my mind. But trust me, it was all in my body. I didn't actually get sick, which in a way was worse. I simply felt too crummy to be sick. I just rolled around trying to make myself fall asleep, yet couldn't seem to, not really. I would doze off and then get yanked awake and be very sorry that I'd woken up. I told myself that soon I'd be sitting on the shore, looking back at this day and laughing at it. Someday. Not yet, though. I lay there, listening to the boat making creaking sounds, like a tree in a storm, or a haunted house.

And then, I must have slept, because I had a weird dream. Napoleon was marching up and down the coast of the Riviera, saying that someone had stolen his boat. Only he looked like Rollo. And Beethoven was conducting a symphony on the deck of the yacht, which I couldn't quite hear, except every now and then I heard the crash of cymbals. Loud. And Diamanta's blind grandmother was sitting on a chair by the side of the bed, shelling peas and speaking in that foreign tongue that I could not understand. Then she turned into the flower-lady *mazzera*, as she reached out to me with her gnarled hands clutching my arm, warning me in a strange, melodic voice, that *The heart of the Lion must not be destroyed.*

I woke with a start and sat up in bed, sweating and gasping. But now I saw something beautiful—the first pale light of dawn, peering through the porthole. And nothing was moving, rattling or shaking. Everything was calm and quiet.

Jeremy came down for one of his periodic visits to peer at me. As soon as he saw my alert face, he smiled. "We're about a half-hour from Nice," he reported. "You look a lot better. Last night you looked like a sick cat."

"I had a cat once," I said, more talkative now. "She hated being in the car, because the motion upset her little cat-gyroscope. She wouldn't stay put in her carrier cage, and she'd bust loose and scramble from one side of the back seat to the other, trying to adjust to every curve in the road. And boy, did she wail!"

"Is that how it was for you?" Jeremy said sympathetically.

I nodded. "I must be better, though," I said, still feeling tentative. "I no longer feel like I should be writing out my last will and testament."

"Feel well enough to come up on deck?" Jeremy asked. "The air might do you good. But don't push, if you're not up to it."

I threw back the covers and slung my legs over the side of the bed, and I wriggled into my little slippers. I tested my legs to see if they held when I stood up. They did. Then I noticed an indentation on the pillow next to me.

"Hey, were you here?" I asked. "Sleeping beside me?"

"Yep. For a bit, once you nodded off. I hung around awhile, just to keep an eye on you," Jeremy said. "You might want to change clothes, and put on a jacket. It's a little windy."

"Thanks. I'll meet you up on deck," I said, determined to make myself get my sea legs again.

When I climbed upstairs I saw that Rollo and Jeremy had been playing cards most of the night, waiting for me to get better. Rollo was alone, and said that Jeremy had gone to the kitchen to see if François would make some tea for me.

"Jeremy's been popping up and down like a jack-in-a-box to check on you all night," Rollo said. "I got to look at his cards any number of times. Couldn't get him to put money on it, though." He changed his tone when Jeremy reappeared. "Hullo, look who's here," Rollo announced, jerking his head in my direction.

Jeremy smiled at me. "François says herb tea with lemon will cure you," he said. "Are you warm enough?" I nodded, and Jeremy took a seat. Rollo began dealing a new hand of cards.

"Hey," I said suddenly. "It's a bum deal."

Jeremy said, "What is?"

"How come neither of you got seasick?" I demanded.

Jeremy and Rollo both grinned. "Darling," Rollo said, very matter-of-factly. "We're English."

"So am I!" I objected. "Half, anyway."

Jeremy and Rollo looked at each other and shook their heads.

"Definitely American," Rollo sighed.

"Sadly, yes," Jeremy agreed. Then, as an afterthought, he added meaningfully, "And French!"

"Whoa, worse yet!" Rollo howled in that idiotic knee-jerk way that the English sometimes put down the French.

François appeared with my tea, and set it down gently on the table. "Soon we are in Nice," he told me lightly, then left again.

"Case closed," I teased Jeremy. "The French are classier."

Rollo went below to gather his things. Jeremy and I went up on deck. The harbor seemed to welcome us with open arms. As we cut our speed and *Penelope's Dream* came gliding in to her berth, Rollo reappeared, with his suitcase all packed, and his hat on, ready to disembark the minute we anchored.

"Well, my friends, I'll say goodbye now," he announced. "I don't suppose you'd like to spot me a few quid for the tables, as payment for my excellent research work?"

"How much is a few quid?" I asked.

"Too much," said Jeremy. "When we find the Lion, Rollo, you'll get your fee, as agreed."

"Oh, very well," Rollo sighed. "But you might at least cover my bar tab in Corsica. Expenses, you know, while on-the-job."

I saw Jeremy slip him some money, "As an advance against payment," Jeremy said. Rollo accepted the money with stunning ease. And as soon as the gangway was ready for him, he went charging down to shore, and shambled off to a waiting taxi.

"How come you were carrying around that much cash?" I asked Jeremy as we went into the main salon.

"I figured we'd have to grease some palms along the way," he said. "Didn't know it would be Rollo's, but I might have guessed."

"Hey," I said. "What's that envelope on the table?"

It was addressed to both of us. There was a letter inside, on the yacht's stationery. Here's what it said:

Dear P & J,

    Hope you won't mind but I borrowed a little item from your curio cupboard. It's a small Chinese sailor clock which works as an excellent paperweight. I'm afraid it's a bit garish for your tastes, so I thought you wouldn't mind. Do let me know if you do. Yours faithfully, Rollo.

"I knew it," Jeremy said. "That old thief. What's this Chinese thing? It's probably worth more than the boat and the Lion put together."

"Take it easy, it isn't," I assured him. "It was among the items listed in the sale of the boat. It's worth about three hundred euros. And he's right, it's kinda scary-looking."

"Still, he stole it. I knew that leopard couldn't change its spots," Jeremy said, disgusted.

"Yes, he has changed," I said.

"How so?"

"When was the last time you ever heard of a leopard writing a letter of apology?" I asked.

Part Nine

Chapter Forty-one

We reached Lake Como at lunchtime, when the sun was high in the sky, and the birds were busily swooping around the twisty, gnarled trees in lush, fragrant gardens. The lake was a lovely aquamarine color, rippled by more boats now that the tourist season was up to full roar.

We drove to the Count's castle straight away. When we pulled into the gravel turnaround in front, there was a familiar car there, a large black BMW.

"Kurt's," I said. We rang the doleful doorbell and were ushered in, this time by the young servant girl who wore a white apron over her flowered dress. She led us to an elevator at the rear of the castle, that took us straight up to the Count's study.

The Count was seated in his upholstered wheelchair by the window, with his blanket across his lap. There was a wooden tray that fitted into the arms of the chair, so that the tray could hold his meals above his lap. He was using both hands to lift a big round bowl of soup to his lips. Kurt was standing in the corner, sipping his coffee from a tiny espresso cup. When he saw us he asked, "Would you like me to send for some coffee or tea for you?"

"No, thanks," Jeremy said briskly. He turned to the Count. "We have been searching for your Lion, but we cannot find it. We even went to Corsica to look for it. Where, I might note, we were shot at by an unknown assailant."

We watched as the Count widened his eyes. "So we need to ask you some questions," Jeremy said with a fairly stern expression.

The Count very carefully ate the last of his soup, then picked up a beige, cloth napkin and wiped his mouth. Kurt tugged on one of those old-fashioned embroidered sashes that rings a bell somewhere downstairs to summon a servant, who appeared shortly afterwards to clear away the dishes. Kurt gestured toward two other wing chairs, and we sat down to listen.

"Where did you go when you were in Corsica?" Jeremy asked.

"A perfectly dreadful bar in Calvi," said the Count. "Very common. And I had to go into a private room behind the bar to meet with that awful man. But he had it, all right. I saw it with my own eyes. I paid him, and he wrapped it up in front of me, and I went home."

"Is that all you did in Corsica?" I asked gently. "You didn't visit anybody else there?"

"I have no one to visit there," the Count said, sounding genuinely surprised.

"There was no one else you talked to while you were in Corsica?" I persisted.

The Count considered this carefully. "Just a beggar woman down by the pier," he said. "She had most peculiar eyes. She stared and stared, and seemed to look right through me. And she pointed a finger at me and cursed me. I cannot say why." The Count closed his eyes. I knew he really didn't want to answer any more questions, but I was fairly bursting with them now.

"We saw her, too," I said. "I am told that she is a *mazzera*, and if so, then she may have been trying to warn you, not curse you."

I was sitting on the chair beside the Count, and I leaned forward now and asked, "Could you possibly tell me the name of your great-great-great-grandmother?"

The Count looked surprised, but said to Kurt, "Bring me the family Bible."

Kurt went to one of the bookshelves and pulled down a very heavy, ornate volume. Inside the first pages of the Bible was a family listing of names, in faded, old ink. With a shaky finger the Count traced the names. "Beginning in present time, here is my son Kurt, my daughter Marthe, my wife Liesl and me; then my parents, my grandparents and my great-grandparents . . ." He paused, squinting at the faded names.

Kurt continued for him. "And your great-great-grandfather, whose name was Rolf," Kurt said. At that, I elbowed Jeremy. "And Rolf's father was Sigwald," Kurt continued.

"And what was the name of Rolf's mother?" I asked.

"Here she is," the Count said, pointing. "Her name was Greta."

"What else do you know about her?" I asked, watching his face.

But he only shook his head, and said, "Not very much at all. Only that there was a scandal because she ran away from her husband and family, and died abroad in disgrace."

I placed the family tree I'd worked on alongside his Bible. I could hardly contain my excitement as Jeremy unrolled the grave rubbings we'd made. He spread them out on the table for the Count to see. I pointed to the rubbing from Greta's tombstone. The Count leaned forward and studied the papers. Kurt gazed at them, too.

"We believe this is from Greta's grave," I said. "Which we found in Corsica."

Well, I must say that, considering the stunning information we had for them, Kurt and the Count were very cooperative. They bristled at first, not sure if we were trying to sully their family name or help strangers usurp their claim to a family heirloom. But gradually, bit by bit, we pieced it all together. The Count was a direct descendent of Beethoven's student, Greta, and her German husband, Sigwald von Norbert, and their son, Rolf. From generation to generation, they handed down their priceless collection of aquamanilia, and a story of the missing Lion. But they didn't tell their children about Greta's scandalous love affair with Paolo, the young Corsican who made the Lion, which resulted in a son, Aldo, and his long line of descendents who lived in Corsica, right up to Diamanta and her family.

And as family legends go, both sides of Greta's descendents believed that the Lion was rightfully theirs. The feud, the *vendetta* erupted because of this.

"What does it all mean?" cried the Count. "Did someone from Corsica take it away from me on the boat that night?"

Kurt said, "But who, Papa?" Kurt turned to us and said quietly, "Father couldn't really remember what happened on the yacht, because he lost consciousness on that voyage."

"I tell you, I didn't fall ill immediately," the Count insisted. "It was that storm. The worst weather I'd ever seen on the Mediterranean. Everything knocking about, sliding across the floor! I heard the door of the linen closet bang open; I must not have turned the handle properly to shut it tight. So I got up in the middle of the night and went out into the corridor to check my suitcase, and the Lion was still there," the Count said stubbornly. "I got dizzy then, so I went back to bed." I showed him the drawing I'd made of the Lion, per Diamanta's description.

"Is this what your Beethoven Lion looked like?" I asked gently. He stared at it, then glanced up at me with great excitement.

"Yes!" he cried. "This is the one I had. Did you find it, at last?" he asked hopefully.

Boy, I hated to have to tell him we didn't. He looked utterly crestfallen, and sat back in his chair, exhausted.

The nurse reappeared in the doorway. "The Count must rest now," she said.

"Father," Kurt said urgently, "is there nothing more you can recall?"

"No," said the Count, sounding defeated. "That is the last I saw of the Lion. And that is all I can remember."

Chapter Forty-two

"Gee," I said mournfully to Jeremy. "Our first engagement. A total bust."

Feeling fairly dispirited, we had filed downstairs, leaving the Count to take his afternoon nap. Out in the hallway, a servant was vacuuming the Persian carpet. In Italy, they vacuum all day. All morning and all afternoon. Even in the finest houses and hotels, for some reason, there is always somebody vacuuming a staircase or a hallway, droning away, leaving behind a long power cord that you have to step over.

Kurt led us into the "family kitchen" where he told us the cook would be sending up a few sandwiches and coffee for us. As we stood there, the cook's little grandson came tearing into the kitchen, being chased by his sister, the young servant girl in the braids, who was carrying clean towels in her arms.

"Pepi!" she cried in an admonitory, scolding tone, reaching out for the boy who'd just escaped her grasp and went tearing out of the room again. The girl straightened up, looking at us apologetically. "He is a wild one today!" she exclaimed, and, after she went out, I could hear her still scolding him. Jeremy told Kurt that we'd be leaving Lake Como this afternoon.

"But wait for the sandwiches. If you are in a hurry, we can wrap them up to take with you. I am sorry that we wasted your time on this chase. But I really don't see much hope of ever recovering this prize," Kurt said. This was a signal allowing us to give it up.

"Very hard to say what has become of it," Jeremy agreed reluctantly.

"I still don't trust that dealer," Kurt said bluntly. "And I know nothing of this Corsican family."

"The thief could be anybody," Jeremy admitted.

I felt extremely dissatisfied. "Oh, stop blaming the Corsicans," I said. "It's not them, it's not our crew, and it's not even Mortimer. These are all plausible theories, but they're all wrong."

They both looked at me. "Well, then, what's your theory?" Jeremy said, amused.

"For once," I said, "I don't have one."

Kurt sighed. "Well, perhaps the way to look at it is that my father paid for a dream. It was a nice dream, it made him happy. He can still imagine that he once owned that famous Lion. He even knows more about his family than he probably cares to. But I do not see the wisdom of spending more money on this dream."

I went out into the hallway in search of the ladies' room. A few doors down, the servant girl was putting fresh towels in a bathroom. She smiled, stepped out for me, and shut the door. The room seemed designed for female visitors, having a mirror rimmed with good lightbulbs for making up, and ample sink and counter space, and pretty white and gold tiles.

After I'd combed my hair and washed up, I turned to go out. As I reached for the door, I suddenly stopped dead still. I found myself in the thrall of a strange, sensory, somewhat Proustian moment. Only it wasn't a madeleine cake that triggered my memory. It was the door-handle. Not a knob, but a beautiful, curved, gleaming brass handle, with ornate curlicues. You had to turn the entire handle horizontally to open the door; and then make sure you turned it back vertically again to make the door click shut. The insight came into focus now.

"Hinges!" I cried aloud. I bolted out, and raced back to the kitchen, where Kurt and Jeremy were still waiting for me, with a newly arrived tray of food.

"I'm packing sandwiches for the trip home," Jeremy said. "Want ham or roast beef?"

"Kurt," I blurted out, "is there a closet in the hall outside your father's bedroom?"

"Penny! What's up?" Jeremy asked.

"Didn't the Count just tell us that, when he was on the boat during the storm at sea, he got up to check on the Lion and found the door of the closet hanging open?" I cried. "Well, that couldn't possibly have happened aboard the yacht. Because all the doors for the cabins on the lower level—including the door to the linen closet—have sliding doors. With no handles. Just those little circles you put your thumb into, to make the door slide. *Slide*," I emphasized, "not swing open or closed. However, there *are* handles on *these* doors. Brass handles . . ."

"Right!" Jeremy said, instantly on board.

But Kurt was less experienced in following me when I was on the scent. So he said a bit confusedly, "Do you want to look upstairs?"

"Yes," Jeremy said.

We followed Kurt into a narrow, wood-panelled elevator that took us up two flights. The door opened upon a section of the castle we'd never seen before. I was fairly jumping up and down with impatience behind Kurt's careful, methodical pace as we proceeded down the corridor. Finally he stopped at the end of the hall.

Kurt nodded toward the last door on the left, which was closed, and he said, "That is Father's bedroom. We must be quiet, as he usually sleeps at this hour."

Straight ahead was an open door to the bathroom, where the Count's silver-backed hairbrushes and comb, toiletry bottles and shaving equipment were all neatly laid out on a three-tiered silver-trimmed table with glass shelving, standing near a large white sink and huge claw-foot tub. There was another door in the bathroom which presumably led to the Count's bedroom. That left one other door at the end of the hallway, across from the bedroom.

"Closet?" I asked breathlessly. Kurt nodded.

"And every single one of these doors has a brass handle," Jeremy noted.

"Kurt," I said, "maybe what your father remembered about stashing the Lion in the closet, in the dead of night—happened here, with *this* closet and *this* corridor?"

Kurt reached out and turned the handle, and the door swung open. It was a substantial closet, with plenty of floor space for suitcases and trunks, which sat there in a neat row. Above were bed linens and towels, just like the closet on the yacht. Kurt reached in and pulled out each suitcase, one by one, and he and Jeremy opened and examined them. All were empty.

"Um. Are there any secret compartments in this closet?" I asked hopefully. Kurt shook his head, but he ran his hand along the cedar panels to make sure. Nothing.

"Who's out there?" came a voice that was strong enough to indicate that the Count had not been asleep. Kurt opened the door, revealing a large antique bed with thick heavy mahogany posts, and red draperies around it that could be pulled closed to shut out the drafts. The Count, still in his dressing gown, was sitting up in bed, with a book in his hands and his spectacles on his nose. He stared at us inquiringly. "Did you want to ask me something?"

"Sorry to disturb," Jeremy said. "But we need to be sure . . . that the last time you saw the Lion, it was in a closet where the door was hanging *open*?"

"Yes," the Count said patiently. "Because the handle was not properly latched. The storm probably made it fly open."

"Wasn't there also a storm here at Lake Como, the night you came home from the hospital?" I asked.

"Oh, yes. It makes me tired just to think of how weary I was when I got home after that long, cold, wet, miserable trip from the hospital in Nice," said the Count. "Yet, I slept very fitfully that night, because the wind kept making the shutters bang. But at least on land you know you won't drown."

"Are you certain that when you got up in the middle of the night on the yacht, to check the Lion—?" I reached out and turned the bedroom door handle, "it had a handle like this?"

A thoughtful look crossed the Count's face. "Yes. But there aren't any handles like that on the yacht," he said slowly, catching on. "All the doors on the cabin level are sliders."

"In that case," I said excitedly, "if the Lion made it back here with you, instead of being left behind on the boat, then the question is—who took it out of the suitcase in the closet, after you went back to bed?"

There was a long pause. Jeremy said, "Do you think we could speak to your staff?"

"Of course," said the Count. "Although we have questioned all of them before. But go ahead if you wish. They are all here today. The gardener, the cook, the girl, the butler, and that wretched nurse that Marthe has inflicted on our lives."

Kurt looked at his watch. "They would be downstairs having their lunch now," he said. "In the cook's kitchen."

Chapter Forty-three

All four of us couldn't fit in that elevator, so Kurt went down first with the Count, wheeling him outside to his garden for his daily breath of fresh air. When the elevator returned, Jeremy and I took it down to the basement, where the doors opened right into the cook's kitchen.

There was a giant black potbellied stove roaring away, a narrow wooden table, and a big pantry off the staircase with a swinging door, out of which came the cook, busily carrying a great big bowl of bread-dough. When the pantry door swung open, I could see rows and rows of shelves with canned and dry goods, boxed and bagged. The plump old cook went straight over to her work-table, where she set out busily thumping and kneading the dough. We nodded to her when we came in, and Jeremy told her that we were meeting Kurt down here. She glanced at us with polite interest, but then she went right back to her work, as if she had decided that we were none of her business and that she, therefore, was none of ours.

Seated in an alcove around the corner, at a larger, utilitarian wooden table, was the staff—the gardener, nurse, butler and the servant girl. They were having their lunch of cold meat and cheese with pickles and mustard, all set on plain sturdy cookware, with a small dark raisin cake in the center of the table, to have with their tea. A few minutes later Kurt joined us.

As gently as we could, we asked each of them to recall what they remembered of the night the Count returned from his long stay at the hospital. At first they defensively said that nothing out of the ordinary had occurred that night. The gardener, a cheerful, burly man, remembered the bad weather, and how he'd struggled up the stairs with the suitcases.

"Who unpacked them that night?" I asked.

The English butler, a thin old man, looked up with a slightly guilty expression. "Normally I would have unpacked everything for him," he said, appearing a bit ashamed. "But it was quite late, and we were so very worried about the Count. He was terribly exhausted, and the nurse said he should get into bed. We did not want to make him wait for me to unpack every suitcase and put things away in his dresser drawers. I had already laid out a fresh pair of pajamas for him. And, since I did not want to keep him awake by thumping about with trunks in the hall, I asked his permission to let the unpacking wait until morning. Which he gave me."

Jeremy turned to the young servant girl. She said, "I was busy helping the nurse get settled into her room. It was her first day with us. The rain came down in sheets!"

The nurse nodded vigorously. "I made certain that the Count took his medicine. After he went to bed, I, too, retired, and heard nothing till morning."

They all looked innocent, yet uneasy, because Jeremy and Kurt were watching them so closely. I reached into my bag, and unrolled my drawing of the Lion. I placed it on the table and they all bent over it intently. While they were deeply engrossed, Pepi came bounding in, then stopped in his tracks, shocked by the sight of guests in the cook's kitchen. Only the cook glanced at him, and told him that he could have a cookie. He sidled over to a cookie jar, took one, and then drew nearer to us to see what we were all looking at.

Pepi peered curiously at the drawing, studying it closely. Seeing what it was, he smiled delightedly, and growled like a lion and said, *"Ah-wumph!"* and pretended to chomp on his sister's arm. The men reacted with mild amusement and strained patience, as men do when they are preoccupied, and a child has intruded on their thoughts.

"Leonhard!" he said.

"Pepi, go in your room and play quietly," his sister said absently.

He now saw that I was watching him intently. His smile quickly faded, and his face went red. Then he turned and bolted from the room.

Jeremy and Kurt were still questioning the servants about what happened the next morning. The butler vehemently denied ever seeing any Lion in the suitcase. He could not remember if the closet door had been ajar. But one by one, each said absolutely that they had never seen the Lion.

By now, however, I was hardly listening to them anymore. My thoughts had followed little Pepi, and I wanted to know where he had gone. So I slipped out of the kitchen in the same direction. Ahead, there was only a flight of cement steps leading upward and outdoors. But to the right was a small room off the kitchen with a swinging door that was still swinging. I peered in the door's little round window, then went in. In the old days, this had probably been where the cook slept. Now it was a kind of playroom and nap room, because there was a little cot, covered with a bedspread that had funny-faced clowns printed on it. There was a pajama case that was shaped like the head of a floppy-eared dog. Pepi was sitting, scrunched into a guilty little ball on the bed, nervously petting the head of his pajama-dog.

"What a nice room!" I said, in a light, encouraging voice that seemed to make him relax a bit. I glanced around. "You have some great toys here. Want to show me?"

Warily at first, he pointed out that he had some story books, and some balls, and some puppets, on a shelf near the bed. He was very pleased as I marvelled over each one, and this calmed him more.

Finally I said, "Pepi, what's your most special toy?" There was a long pause.

"Leonhard?" I whispered conspiratorially.

Pepi flushed again. He glanced toward the kitchen worriedly.

"It's okay," I said gently. "I'll tell them you were a good boy and showed it to me when I asked you to."

Well, a kid knows when the jig is up. So he got on his knees and reached under his bed, and he pulled out a wide wooden toy chest. And I watched, rooted to the spot, as he threw back the lid of the chest and pulled out a shiny metal object.

"Ahh!" I said softly. "Can I see?" He nodded, and gave it to me.

I took it gently into my hands, almost afraid it might vanish at my touch. But it was heavier than I expected. A shiny copper figure, about nine inches tall, and ten inches long, and four inches wide. It possessed a strange natural authority, in the way the Lion stood proudly on all four legs, his head fiercely alert, with glittering, jeweled eyes; his back straight, his tail aloft and curving over the back to form the handle. A bona fide aqua-manile, all right.

I looked straight into the face of the Lion. It was so remarkable that I caught my breath; for it had the characteristics of both the king of the beasts, and the great genius of music, in its regal, wild mane and intense, ferocious scowl. Yet somehow its creator had also managed to capture, in the lines of the face, Beethoven's intelligent humanity, vulnerability, and passionately generous heart. Then, I studied the tiny metal figure clamped in the mouth. Oh, yes, indeed. That little monkey's face bore a startling resemblance to a certain audacious, visionary French emperor, trapped in the jaws of his own destiny.

Remembering what I'd heard of its construction, I ran my finger over the stopper at the top of the Lion's head. It was sealed shut. It took all my effort to keep my voice calm, so that I would not spook the kid.

"The Count will be so happy that you found it!" I said. "Let's go tell him together, what a good boy you were, to find his Lion for him."

After that, it wasn't hard to fill in the blanks. Of course, we had to promise the kid that, as long as he returned the Lion, he wouldn't get in trouble with his father, who would be very angry if he thought his son had stolen anything from the Count.

We found the Count sitting in his wheelchair outdoors, in the side-garden, watching birds darting around the bird feeder he'd placed in his trees. I marched right up to him, and plunked the Lion in his lap. Startled at first, his face broke into a wide grin, and the years seemed to melt away.

"But—wherever did you find it?" he cried, grasping it with both hands and holding it aloft as if even he couldn't believe what he was seeing.

"Father," Kurt said wearily, "it appears that the Lion has been in the castle, all along!"

"Well," said the Count triumphantly, "I told you I had found it!"

Pepi's sister shoved the child forward, to tearfully apologize for the theft. The Count was very gracious, as the girl explained that Pepi had been up and about, ahead of the entire household, on that morning after the Count returned from the hospital, because Pepi's mother had dropped him off quite early that day, since she had to work on an early shift. Pepi was told to play quietly, because the Count was back home. The Count sometimes brought Pepi a little present from his travels, and gave it to him at Christmastime. So Pepi ran upstairs to see if the Count was awake yet, but found only an open suitcase with a toy that surely had been bought for a child. As there were no other children in the house, naturally it must be for Pepi.

And, with the logic of a kid, Pepi decided that, since the Lion was meant for him, they'd probably just forgotten to give it to him at Christmas, when the Count had been away. So he solved this easily, and took it downstairs in his room to play with. And when it was time for his lunch, he put it away in his toy chest, as he'd been taught to do with his favorite toys. (Besides, he had the funny feeling that if he left it lying about, somebody might take it away from him.)

It was many weeks later when another hubbub ensued, once the Count recalled that he had bought the Lion, but lost it. They turned the house upside down, to no avail. But Pepi was not around when this happened; he was away visiting his cousins. So he never really knew how important the Lion was. And everyone assumed that the Count had left the Lion on the yacht . . . if indeed he'd ever had it at all.

"Well," Jeremy said, after we'd pieced this together, "we've found the Lion. But, the question remains—is it the Beethoven Lion?"

The Count had been sitting quietly listening the whole time. When he saw his nurse coming purposefully toward him with a blood-pressure measurer in her hand, and a stethoscope around her neck, he said to her, very firmly, "You must take this Lion upstairs and X-ray it. Right away."

The nurse opened her mouth as if she were about to protest, but when she saw the look on Kurt's face, and then ours, she shut her mouth tightly and did not speak. Wordlessly, she took the Lion into the house.

Chapter Forty-four

"The suspense," Jeremy said, "is killing me."

We were standing in the back garden outside the castle, overlooking Lake Como. Kurt told us he'd call us the moment the X-rays were ready.

We gazed out at the rippling lake, which was far below us but still seemed to fill up the view, rising to meet the sky. We could watch, but not hear, the little speedboats chugging by, leaving visible white wakes as they sliced against the blue water.

Under a fine old chestnut tree, there was a wooden table near a bench. Pepi's sister had packed up our sandwiches for us in a wicker picnic hamper. We sat down and ate.

"Jeremy, look down there!" I said, pointing across the lake. "Isn't that the Isola Comacina where we had that great lunch? Where your mum used to take you as a boy?"

"Yes, it certainly is," Jeremy said, and there was something in his tone that made me slide over to sit closer to him.

"Want mustard?" I asked, teasingly.

He grinned, and said, "Penny. I just want to say, I'm sorry for all that kerfuffle with Lydia and the whole London crowd."

"Don't even speak of it," I said, "don't even mention her name, or she'll turn up again."

"No, she won't," he promised. "Not anymore."

"Are you sure?" I asked with mock skepticism.

"Absolutely. You see, the final straw was when she came clomping onto our boat in those wretched high heels," Jeremy declared. "Did you happen to notice all the little holes she made on that priceless deck? I thought Claude was going to cry. It looked as if she'd jumped up and down on a pogo stick all over the bloody deck."

"To tell you the truth," I said dryly, "I didn't notice. I was too busy watching her make lipstick marks on your collar."

"Well, she very nearly ruined *Penelope's Dream*," Jeremy said. "We can't have that sort of thing in our lives. No, sir."

"What about all your posh friends?" I asked.

"Not a problem," he added ruefully, "because they know this time it's the real thing."

I glanced up at him quickly. "You see," he said slowly, "block-head that I am, I finally figured out why I was willing to keep letting Lydia disrupt our lives."

"You felt guilty about the divorce," I said promptly.

"No," Jeremy said, "I felt guilty because I never loved her." He said this with genuine sadness, and there wasn't a trace of a put-down; he wasn't acting like a guy who was dismissing one woman to placate another. I could tell that it was something truly painful for him.

"And that's why," he said softly, "I couldn't face it until now. Nor tell her outright to leave us alone. I knew I'd caused her pain without even realizing why. I was just too stupid to understand. I must have deceived myself, too; sometimes you just persist in believing you can straighten things out without looking too closely at them.

I couldn't figure out what I was doing wrong. But it wasn't until you came back into my life that I could even begin to comprehend what it feels like to honestly be in love with someone, for keeps."

I had an unusual, joyous sensation of something very calming, very peaceful, very eternal, descending on me like a feather-light but protective cloak. I have never felt so serene and quiet in my entire life. I felt strong enough to reach out and embrace the entire world.

"Then," I said gently, "there's room for all your friends."

Jeremy looked at me with gratitude. But what he said teasingly was, "Well, of course, they're all utterly aware that I've got my hands full with this one particular woman of mine, who is more than enough for any mortal man."

"Humph," I said. "That makes me sound like a little trouble-maker. Like one of those dizzy dames."

"Not at all," Jeremy assured me. "It would be a most noble job to look after Penny-the-heiress, and I am willing to devote the entire rest of my life to it. Anyone can see what a full-time occupation this will be. It's bad enough that, already, I've had to fend off a Russian oligarch, a young French gendarme, a German count's son . . . Not to mention countless future suitors," Jeremy continued. "I can see it all now: a Swiss ski instructor, a Japanese international playboy, an Australian tennis pro . . . all chasing after the famed American heiress with the copper-colored hair."

"You'll be my bodyguard?" I inquired, deliberately misunderstanding. "I rather thought you were heading in a different direction," I said, "what with that serious tone and all."

He leaned closer to me, and took my hand in his.

"You fool," he said sternly. "I am trying to tell you, in my own torturous way, that I think it's time we made this rather *personal* engagement of ours official."

"Hmmm," I said playfully. "I can certainly see why *you* need *me*. What other woman could possibly put up with such a grumpy—albeit sexy—Englishman like you, for all eternity?"

I cocked my head, pretending to consider all my options. "Should I actually agree to a return engagement with you . . . when, after all, as you've pointed out, I now have all these interesting, tempting men at my doorstep . . . ? Hmmm . . ." I said, gazing skyward.

"You really have no choice," Jeremy warned. "You'll never get rid of me now. Wherever you go, I shall follow you, just like a bloodhound. If necessary, I shall hire a skywriter declaring that you are mine. If need be, I will have the police stop all cars and planes and boats, and put out a dragnet, and I will haul you in like a big fish."

"You still haven't quite said it," I noted. "Not in so many words. Not really. Therefore, I'm not really sure what you have in mind."

He put his hand in his jacket pocket, and he pulled out a little dark blue velvet box.

"Ordinarily," he said, "I wouldn't dare go out on a limb and try to make a purchase of this magnitude for a woman who clearly has her own personal tastes in fashion. But, you see, this ruby has been in my family, on my mum's side, for years. Her mum gave it to her when she was sixteen. It was a pendant, and she said her mum made her keep it in a vault, so she hardly ever got to wear it. She'd almost forgotten about it. For some odd reason, she gave it to me when we were at her place in London. I can't imagine why, can you? So, I had it made into a ring for you. If you want it."

I opened the box with slightly shaking fingers. Inside was a beautiful glowing ruby, surrounded by sparkling diamonds and set in that lovely antique gold which has the look of endless time.

"Jeremy," I said, too choked up to say what I really wanted to. "When did you do this?"

"In Frankfurt," he said. "I've been hanging on to it ever since then, waiting for the proper moment. Because it really does have to be a proper moment, doesn't it? The very second that you pointed to the Isola Comacina, I felt my life had come full circle, and that, when I was a boy, sitting there gazing across the lake this way, you were the one I was waiting for. You and I are a team, in work and life, and wherever you go I want to be there with you."

Now my eyes did fill up with tears, which I tried to wink away. Jeremy saw them, and said, "Penny!" and hugged me tightly, and kissed the tears away. "Will you marry me?" he asked.

"Yes," I whispered. "Oh, yes."

"Excellent," he said.

And as we sat there, the mysterious winds of Lake Como began to shift, stirring the blossoms in the trees to carry the bewitching fragrance of jasmine and roses to us. It was a soft, sweet wind, and it made us breathe deeply as I leaned my head against Jeremy's shoulder, watching the tide ripple in response.

"When the *breva* and the *tivà* winds shift like that," I told him, "legend says we must each make a silent wish."

"Who told you that 'old legend'?" Jeremy asked tenderly.

"Nobody," I said. "The wind just told me herself."

Chapter Forty-five

I can't say how long it was that we sat in the Count's enchanted garden. I can only tell you that the sun descended beyond the darkening Alps, and the stars woke up and rubbed their eyes and peered down at the twinkling gems on my finger.

Then we heard a distinct *Boom!* coming from the window of the Count's study in the castle. Jeremy and I just looked at each other.

"Cocktail hour!" said Jeremy.

A few moments later, Kurt came walking toward us, smiling knowingly and a trifle apologetically. "Pardon me," he said, "Father was hoping to have your professional opinion on these X-rays. It is all really quite astonishing, and we are not sure what to think."

The entire household was waiting for us in the Count's study. And, spread out on a light-table before him, was the X-ray of the Lion.

"We can have an expert try to authenticate it," Kurt was telling us. "But Father is fairly certain that this is, indeed, the Lion he's been looking for. He thinks there is something very surprising inside it. Take a look."

My first impression was that the X-ray of the Lion made it look like an elaborate, very elegant piggy-bank.

"You can see various plugs and marks visible in the X-ray, and not to the naked eye when gazing upon the finished figure," Kurt said. "All this is perfectly normal."

"But," interjected the Count, sounding excited, "it appears to contain an unusual cylindrical *something*. That is not a joint or a supporting rod. I cannot say what it is. And, believe me, I have looked at so many of these. I have never seen anything like it." His words were understated, compared to his tone.

"What do you think it is?" I asked. The Count looked up at me, his blue eyes sparkling.

"I don't know, exactly, but it may be a tube with something in it," he said excitedly.

"Ohmigosh," I said, catching my breath. "It can't be . . . can it?"

"The fragment of the missing autograph?" Jeremy had to say it aloud to even consider it. "The long-lost 'Eroica' original?"

But the Lion didn't yield its secrets right away. It took weeks for Jeremy to get those experts from Frankfurt—the ones who actually knew how to do the complicated process of making aquamanilia—to come to Lake Como. They were eager to try to "operate" on the Lion, but Jeremy had to do some convincing to make them bring their tools and do the deed at the Count's castle, because the Count emphatically was not going to let the Lion out of his sight.

Meanwhile, I had to get hold of Diamanta so that she could come and witness the event. At this point, all the legal stuff kicked in, about who owned it, and where it would be kept. That took more time and wrangling, but we finally got both sides of this remarkable family to agree that the Lion would spend six months each year at a museum in Lake Como, and six months at a museum in Corsica. Donaldson's little museum in London would conduct the sale of it, so that various cultural institutions in Corsica and Como could put in their bids. Donaldson would therefore get a one-time, one-month premiere exhibition. The money from its sale would be split up between the two families, after the payment of legal fees . . . plus a fee for the firm of Nichols & Laidley (which meant Rollo would get his finder's fee from us.) But first, of course, the Lion must be opened, and its value established.

Finally, the Big Day dawned. Word got out about the Lion, so select members of the press were invited to attend. Including our photographer-friend Clive, whom we didn't tell until the last minute for fear he'd spill the beans again. And a famous Beethoven scholar attended, accompanied by a world-renowned concert pianist who parked himself on stand-by in the Count's castle at his grand piano, ready to play whatever music might be on any fragment discovered inside.

It turned into such a big deal that we all agreed to televise the event. Out of all the news organizations vying for the assignment, one production company who submitted a proposal was selected to do this great big-budget TV special.

That's right. You guessed it. Pentathlon Productions.

"This could really put us back on the documentary map," Bruce said to me ecstatically, as we all assembled at the Count's castle. Bruce went off to check in with the sound-man.

Erik rolled his eyes and said, "Now you've done it! You'll drive us all into the poorhouse if Bruce makes the changeover from drama to doc. No sets to design! Are you crazy?"

"Why should she care?" Tim asked. "She's stinking rich."

"Not to worry," I said. "Bruce's wife told me that the world will always want those bio-pics, so she'll keep writing them and she'll make sure that Pentathlon keeps shooting them."

I must have been gesturing, because Tim seized my left hand.

"What is THAT?" he cried. I hadn't told anybody yet. I'd wanted to keep it to myself a little bit. But Erik whooped so loudly that the whole crew heard him. Then he picked me up and slung me over his shoulder and carried me around and wouldn't put me down until I promised to let him help me plan the wedding.

"Okay, okay!" I cried.

"Excuse me," Bruce said in a strained tone. "Might I interrupt to say, ROLL 'EM??"

Chapter Forty-six

The opening of the Beethoven Lion took place in a garage on the castle grounds, just beyond the stables. "Garage" was hardly the word for such a grand structure; it was a carriage house, built in the days when the transition from horse to auto meant that the car simply went where the carriage had been parked. It was a big stone and stucco affair, with a mechanic's windowed office, and an upstairs apartment with a potbellied stove. Bruce converted the mechanic's office into a control room. The aquamanilia artisans from Frankfurt used the rest of the entire first floor to set up their metalworking shop, and they even made use of a stone oven/barbecue area in the nearby side garden. Amid much clanging and banging, the highly delicate operation on the Beethoven Lion was now about to begin.

"Poor guy," I muttered about the Lion, "I hope he comes through all right."

They planned to cut a hole on the Lion's head by following the circle around the plugged-up filling-spout. The pianist was stationed inside the castle, in the music room, which I'd seen for the first time—a beautiful rococo blue, white and gold salon with marble floors and great acoustics. Bruce's crew had rigged an elaborate network of lighting, camera and sound, set up in the castle, and in the carriage house, and outdoors, all strung together by a complicated system of cables and computers. The Count's household was terrified that one yank on a cable could bring a priceless urn crashing to the floor, so there was more than the usual flurry amid that slight boredom that sets in while waiting for the lighting and sound guys to do their maddening checks.

At Bruce's signal, the intro was taped outside, establishing where we were and why it mattered. The Beethoven expert was a bemused-looking German in his sixties, with a fastidious little beard, who spoke English tinged with a Bonn accent. He was interviewed by a garrulous English TV personality who usually did travel specials that aired on both sides of the Atlantic.

Then, a hush fell over the crowd. The excitement in the air was suddenly quite palpable. I gazed at all the expectant faces—from Kurt and his sister (who made the pilgrimage from Frankfurt, and did indeed look as if she could be his twin, although she was older than him)—to Diamanta, and her moody brother, who now looked like an excited, and slightly abashed, teenage boy fascinated with the mechanics of the show. Rollo was there, surreptitiously taking an occasional swig from a flat little antique silver-plated thermos, and Clive was watching him, until Rollo offered him a swig. Mr. Donaldson was accompanied by a middle-aged female museum worker who handled delicate restoration. Erik and Tim had spiffed up the carriage house, placing anything interesting they'd found as background props—an old carriage wheel, a pitchfork, horseshoes, lanterns. It looked great. The Count was waiting in his castle, playing chess with the pianist, because both were so nervous that they couldn't bear to watch.

The aquamanilia artisans adjusted their metal headgear, which looked like a cross between a mask and a helmet, with a light on the forehead like a coal miner. They bent over the Lion, then one of them gave a thumbs-up of readiness.

"And—ACTION!" Bruce cried.

Zzz-zzz. Zzz-zz—whirrr—whee-whish. . . .

The delicate operation had begun. This took a long time, and was very dramatic, with sparks flying all the while.

"You do realize," Jeremy murmured to me as we watched, "that there could be anything in there—a certificate from the workshop, or, hell, even just a bill for services rendered. Or a grocery list belonging to an ordinary nineteenth-century metalworking guy. Something his wife gave him. 'Bring home bread, eggs, milk . . .' "

"Shush," I hissed. We were standing in the back of the control booth. I listened to Bruce's commands to cut from one camera to another. I found it oddly comforting, being back on a set again.

Finally, the artisans laid down their cutting tools. One of them began working with his hands, and then I heard a small metallic clink. The brass plug had been pulled out of the Lion's head. It meant the Lion was finally opened up . . . after all these centuries.

A spontaneous "Ahhhhh!" came from the crowd of invited onlookers, all grouped reverently in one corner of the garage, because they were part of the show and were allowed to react. One of the workmen took off his headgear, picked up a pair of long metal tweezers, and reached in. This took a number of attempts, until he determined that he couldn't get the cylinder out that way. After a momentary murmuring among the artisans, they decided that they would have to cut into the Lion's belly if they had any hope of dragging the cylinder out.

Everyone took a break as the lighting crew swooped in to adjust the lights. The caterers had laid out a food spread in the upstairs apartment over the garage, and the smell of coffee revived everyone.

I hung around the operating table, glancing apprehensively at the Lion.

"He'll be all right," one of the metalworkers assured me. "He'll always have some stitches on his head and belly," he said, perfectly seriously. "But I think we might actually manage to get Humpty Dumpty back together again."

Then we were all called back to watch the next phase. More sparks flying. But this time, the artisans were able to pry the cylinder, ever so gently, out of the Lion. Jeremy, who couldn't stand it anymore and had gone outside for air, came racing back into the garage, just in time to see them gently lay the cylinder on a piece of chamois cloth.

Now the remaining task was to open up the cylinder without destroying its contents. After some discussion, it was agreed that they should slit it down the side. They did this carefully. One of the metalworkers peered in as we all held our breath.

"There's something inside!" he announced. "Looks like paper to me."

"Oooh," cried the crowd.

Bruce called out, "Okay, let's have the museum guys now."

I heard Mr. Donaldson snort at that, as he stepped forward with the female restoration expert, who was all ready with gauze gloves and another pair of even more slender tweezers to gently pull out the old, delicate document. Once again we had to wait for the lights to be adjusted, very carefully, so as not to hurt the paper when it came out.

Because there definitely was paper inside, all curled up. I watched, wide-eyed, as the tweezer-lady pulled it out—softly, softly, softly. Then, very reverently, she laid it on a special pad on the table.

"Just like a message in a bottle from a castaway on a desert island!" I whispered to Jeremy. A second later, the TV host said the same thing on-camera. Gently, gently, it was unrolled, and lightly flattened, just enough to see it. Mr. Donaldson and his worker bent over it. From Bruce's video monitor, I could see a close-up of hand-written scripting in faded black ink.

"It appears to be written in old French," Donaldson announced. "Can anyone translate?"

Diamanta stepped forward. Haltingly at first, she began to translate, picking up speed as she went. Clive wrote it down, helping her adjust the English:

> *Beloved,*
> *This is my promise which I do send,*
> *I will be yours until time should end,*
> *I will be yours till the stars all die,*
> *I will be yours till the oceans run dry.*
> *And if, by chance, these should come to be,*
> *Bury my ashes along with thee.*
> *Bury our hearts beneath a tree,*
> *Cast our bones into the sea.*
> *And you and I shall wash the shore,*
> *And flowers spring up where there were no more.*
> *And when the new world these flowers see,*
> *They'll know what became of you and me.*

"It is addressed *To Paolo*," Diamanta said. "Signed by *Greta*."

There wasn't a dry eye in the house. Even the cameraman sniffed.

But one unsentimental person was blatantly disappointed. "Well, that's it, then," said the Beethoven expert.

The TV host took this as his cue, and turned to the camera and said, "At long last, the secret of the so-called Beethoven Lion has been revealed. It does not appear to be a musical fragment at all, but a love poem. Written many, many years ago, to a metalworking artisan from his beloved girlfriend, who was once a student of the great Maestro, Ludwig von Beethoven . . ."

Meanwhile, Bruce spoke in a low voice to a member of the documentary crew, who in turn spoke via walkie-talkie to the music crew and pianist that were on stand-by inside the castle, giving them the message that it was a poem, not a musical fragment. We knew exactly when this message reached them, because we could hear them all groan at the same time, *"Awwwhoa. . . ."*

Only Jeremy wasn't listening. He had been peering intently at the fragment the whole time. Now he asked the museum woman with the cotton gloves and tweezer to turn the paper over, so he could examine the underside of the curl.

"Look," Jeremy said. "There's something written on the reverse. See . . . here . . . doesn't that look like . . . musical notes and . . . maybe, numbers?"

"Yes!" cried the woman. I crept closer, and peered over Jeremy's shoulder. He stepped aside so I could draw nearer. The paper was beige-colored, with brown music composition lines, on which the composer had written, in a strong, confident hand, black musical notes, faded now, but which looked as if they had been powerfully jotted down in a tearing hurry. Some were hastily crossed-out, smudged and redone. Above the notes were numbers: 4, 2, 4, 1, 7 . . .

"What does it mean?" I asked in hushed awe.

Bruce ordered the cameras back on, and the Beethoven expert came running over to examine it under a magnifier. For what seemed like an interminable pause, we all waited. Finally, he stepped back and looked up triumphantly.

"It's a fragment," he declared, and the ruckus started all over again.

"Push in closer!" Bruce commanded his cameraman. "Closer, damn it!"

"But what are the numbers?" Jeremy demanded.

The Beethoven expert was nearly dancing with glee. "It looks to me like an autograph fragment in Beethoven's hand, written as a fingering exercise!" he cried, ecstatic. He glanced up at the crowd, expecting a response, but when he saw the baffled looks on all the faces, he realized he'd have to explain it.

"Don't you see," he began, stumbling with excitement, "fingering. Fingering!"

A clear, firm voice rang out from the crowd. "Not only did Beethoven write the notes, but he added numbering above them to indicate which fingers should play them." The Count, sitting in his wheelchair, had been quietly brought into the room by his valet, who wheeled him closer now. I noticed that the Count had formally dressed for this important occasion in his life. He wore a navy suit, was well-shaved, and I think he'd even gotten a haircut.

"Stay on that guy," Bruce instructed his cameraman.

The Beethoven expert, far from feeling usurped, seemed glad to at last find someone who spoke the language of music. "Precisely," he beamed. "Most likely, he did this for a student," he continued. "Beethoven was a great believer in the value of learning impeccable finger-work. He was a stern taskmaster, but generous enough to do this for his students."

"You mean, these are music scales that he wanted his students to memorize?" the program host asked, confused.

"No, no," said the Beethoven expert excitedly, studying the notes. "This is no mere exercise scale. I believe it is an original piano variation. The theme is quite recognizable as the Master's. But this particular variation . . . I'm not sure I've ever seen it before."

He wanted to dash into the castle with the fragment, and have the pianist play it, but Donaldson got all upset and said adamantly that the paper was too fragile to be taken anywhere. So the Beethoven expert got out his lined paper, copied the notes, and handed it to a member of the crew, who rushed into the castle to give it to the pianist.

"Stand by," said Bruce.

And it seemed to me that everybody—the crew, the experts, the mountains, the birds, the fish in Lake Como, and the whole universe, in fact—held its breath and waited to hear the first of those notes come floating out on the air from the open windows in the castle.

Da ... DA ... da ... Da. ...
Da-da-da, da deedle-deedle Da ...

As soon as it reached my ears, I felt a physical sense of what I can only describe as "uplift." It was a charming, playful, sweet melody, from far away and long ago. I imagined the great Beethoven, with his wild hair and unkempt clothes, painstakingly jotting down the numbers; and then standing watchfully over his student at the piano—Greta, who, sitting very upright and proper, earnestly plinked out the memorable, contagious little tune.

Da ... DA ... da ... Da. ....

But then there was a pause in the music. I looked at the video monitor, and saw that the pianist had leaned forward, scrutinizing the notes.

"Isn't that the theme from the last movement of the 'Eroica' symphony?" Jeremy asked. "The finale, right?"

We all turned to the Beethoven expert, who had been sitting in a chair with his head cocked, eyes shut, listening so attentively that he swayed slightly with each shift of sound. When the lull occurred, he opened his eyes and smiled at us.

"It is a variation on that theme, young man," said the expert.

"Beethoven wrote over a dozen such variations. They are known as the 'Eroica Variations, Opus 35', although actually, the theme originated earlier in his ballet called 'The Creatures of Prometheus.' "

"That's right, that's right," Jeremy said excitedly. "Some of those variations make you laugh out loud, because they are like musical jokes, playing around with all the possibilities."

"However," said the expert, "this particular variation is quite new to me. And, apparently, to our pianist . . ."

Which explained the pause. But now the pianist resumed playing, this time something more developed and complicated. Yet there was still that persistent melody, underneath all the trills and thrills, which even my untrained ears could pick out, as the earlier tune in the exercise:

Da . . . DA . . . da . . . Da. . . .
Da-da-da, da deedle-deedle Da . . .
Deedle-oodle-daddle-oodle-da, da deedle-deedle-deedle-deedle-DA . . .
Deedle-oodle-daddle-oodle-da, da deedle-deedle-deedle-deedle-DA . . .

Everyone fell silent, listening, enthralled, as it went on. But then, as it was building to something very beautiful indeed, suddenly, it all came to an abrupt end. I saw on the monitor that the pianist had sat back, his hands in his lap.

I glanced at the expert, who, sophisticated man that he was, nevertheless had a misty look of regret in his eyes. By now, the silence was deafening.

"Oh, no!" I cried. "It can't end there."

The Count smiled at me sadly.

"Yes, my dear," he said. "I'm afraid it does."

Chapter Forty-seven

The Beethoven Lion fetched quite a bit of money. These things usually do. Two and a half million euros, to be exact. It was divided up just as we'd all agreed. Now, every year, the Lion makes his annual pilgrimage from six months in Corsica (where Diamanta's family gets it for the night of their procession) to six months in Lake Como (including one night at the Count's castle). I guess the Lion was just destined never to keep still for very long.

Accompanying him, and placed at his feet like a majestic carpet, is the Beethoven fragment, still a bit curly but quite legible, for all the world to see. Subsequent analysis by musicologists throughout the world led to a fairly general consensus that the fragment was indeed from a work-in-progress, in the Master's hand, of a previously unknown version of the "Eroica Variations."

I was glad that Diamanta's family and the Count were very philosophical about the whole thing. They realized that some treasures are too beautiful to be locked up in one person's house. Maybe that's the only way to end a vendetta and take the curse off both houses.

Jeremy and I headed home; first to Antibes, where we were only too happy to kick back and relax. Jeremy said he was going to spend this little hiatus just floating on his back in that pool. Me? Well, I had our new offices to outfit, and a children's charity auction to organize, and an ocean institute to promote . . . and, a wedding to plan. Not that the wedding was a big secret any longer. The headlines were already screaming their slight misinformation:

LEGENDARY ARTIFACT FOUND ABOARD ANTIQUE YACHT

The Beethoven Lion, a source of many myths about music and antiquities, was discovered on the Mediterranean Sea aboard "Penelope's Dream", a vintage yacht belonging to an American heiress and her boyfriend. True to its reputation, the Beethoven Lion contained another treasure hidden inside—a fragment of a Beethoven symphony. The world of music is agog. But where is Penny Nichols now? Rumor has it the American heiress is to wed her English lawyer in St. Tropez. Or have they already eloped to Tahiti?

You can't blame us for wanting to lay low for awhile. Just to revel in our good fortune, celebrate finding each other, and enjoy what lovely pleasures life had to offer . . . even to a girl like me, whom the world had previously written off as, well, a woman of few prospects. Surprise, surprise. Even two dopey kids like us could luck out sometimes.

But when the yachting season was done, we eagerly returned to the townhouse in London, which was now all ready for us to set up shop. I will never, ever, forget how it felt to walk up those steps and see, for the first time, the engraved brass plaque now officially established near the front door, proclaiming to all and sundry:

NICHOLS AND LAIDLEY, LTD.
DISCRETION GUARANTEED.
INQUIRE WITHIN.

"Well," said Jeremy one cozy night, looking up from his newspaper as he sat in his leather easy chair by the fireplace in our brand-new study, "you finally did it. You wanted our lives to take place in a 1930s movie set, and hey-presto, here we are."

"But it's better than a movie," I said, from the depths of my wing chair opposite him, "it's real life now." I was looking at some sketches that Monsieur Lombard had sent me, for wedding dresses, and a groom's outfit that I might want to talk Jeremy into wearing.

"I have only one question," Jeremy said, leaning forward to poke the fire in the fireplace. "Where's the Great Dane?"

"You don't just buy a dog like a carpet," I replied. "I have to do the research. Certain dog personalities may be better suited to the job he'll have in our establishment. I can't yet decide if, in the end, we may want a collie. Or a spaniel . . ."

"Okay, okay, get back to me when you have the info," he said, rattling the pages of his paper as he set it aside. It was then that I saw what he was reading. *The Yachting Gazette.*

"Next summer, maybe I'll enter *Penelope's Dream* in a classic motor yachts race . . ." Jeremy continued.

"Mmm," I said, "And I think we should—"

Sail all around the Med like we wanted to, I was about to say. But I never got to say it, because just then the phone rang. It rang and rang.

"I guess we'd better pick it up," Jeremy suggested.

"Make a note to hire a personal secretary," I said as I reached for it. Jeremy later told me that he watched my face go from mildly curious, to surprised, to stunned . . . and then I sat bolt upright.

"What's up?" he asked. "Who is it?"

Odd, how one little phone call can set your feet on an entirely unexpected path. Jeremy's feet, too. Naturally, because now we're a real team, pattering around the world together.

Still, in retrospect, I wonder if I should have just let the phone keep on ringing.

But that, I'm afraid, is entirely another tale.

THE END

ACKNOWLEDGMENTS

Special thanks to my husband Ray, for his generous spirit and spot-on advice. And to Margaret Atwood, for her guidance and friendship. To the unsinkable Jennifer Unter, and to Scott Gould and all the folks at RLR Literary. I also wish to express my appreciation to all the wonderful people at Penguin, particularly the admirable, ever-positive and unflappable Kara Cesare; and Rachel Kahan, Kara Welsh, Claire Zion, Lindsay Nouis, and all the good people in Penguin's art, sales, marketing, copy, promotion and production departments. Special thanks to Ro and Umberto Marcenaro, for their help with all things Italian and beautiful. I would also like to thank Ginger Barber, and Elizabeth Corradino, for their professional advice and for their enduring friendship. And finally, my thanks to all those readers who wrote me such lovely letters and e-mails from far and wide.

A Rather Curious Engagement

❧

C.A. Belmond

A CONVERSATION WITH
C.A. BELMOND

Q. The word "engagement" in the title and in the story itself refers to the hero and heroine's love life as well as careers. Was that your original intent?

A. Yes, because with Penny and Jeremy, the path to love and the path to their future careers have continually intersected. For me the title always comes right out of the story. As a matter of a fact, the "curious" refers to Penny's natural inquisitiveness as well as the "curio" or the antique artifact that motivates so much of the story.

Q. The heroine of this novel is someone who unexpectedly inherited a lot of money and property, and the hero has an interesting family background. When did all this happen?

A. This book is a sequel to one called *A Rather Lovely Inheritance*, which set up the story about Penny's great-aunt who died and left her a surprising legacy. The entire family tree is revealed there. Many readers wrote to me asking what was to become of Penny and Jeremy after they got their "lovely inheritance." Fortunately, I was already at work on the answer, because I wanted to know, too!

Q. The hero and heroine make a determined effort to manage their new-found windfall responsibly. Even their "Splurge" is carefully thought out. Other characters are obsessed with lost treasures. Are you using material possessions as a metaphor for a bigger picture?

A. Yes, definitely. It all begins with the question, "What would you do if you inherited millions of dollars, a villa, a flat, and a car?" In other words, once your day-to-day concerns are met, what then? Do you just become a perpetual shopper, or are there new responsibilities, and the freedom to be able to make a difference? Of course, Penny's life is always a bit of a romp—because her "nose" for family secrets, buried truths and lost history will always lead her (and Jeremy) into unusual adventures and sometimes dicey situations. But she's actually attempting to do much more than find a treasure. Underneath it all, she's really trying to figure out what's important in life. Along the way, she's intrigued with the people she meets and what motivates them.

Q. This book involves yachts, boats, and the sea. What inspired this?

A. I love vintage yachts; they're floating time-machines of old-world elegance, a special universe unto themselves. Being on any boat gives a new perspective and a feeling of great possibilities without obstruction. However, when you're not tethered to the shore, there's always the chance of being swept away! So, when I put my characters literally "at sea" I find great opportunities for unusual conversations, events and insights. The dream that Penny has aboard the yacht on the return voyage from Corsica to Nice is very seminal in helping her connect all the impressions, clues and discoveries she's made.

Q. What made you think of the Beethoven artifact? Are you a music-lover?

A. Yes, I love music, particularly Beethoven and Chopin, my favorites. Beethoven's music is so heroic, all about triumph over adversity through perseverance; so, no matter how tired and dispirited one might feel at the end of the day, Beethoven's symphonies always restore that exultant feeling of hope, and the pure joy of being alive. As for the artifact, well, I always thought that Beethoven had the face and attitude of a lion; and lions are a very common motif, particularly in medieval art.

Q. Do things like aquamanilia really exist?

A. Oh, yes. And there are plenty of lions, as well as dragons, horses, even unicorns. Aquamanilia date back to antiquity, and they were both functional and beautiful. After all, many of them were made before people had running water in their homes, and there were rituals that revolved around hand-washing, cooking, dining; and around religious ceremonies involving oil, water, wine and incense.

Q. There are some unusual new characters in this book—the Count and his son, the family in Corsica, Jeremy's circle of London friends—along with the reappearance of some original characters from the first novel—Rollo, Aunt Sheila, Jeremy's ex-wife, Penny's parents, her old coworkers. Is it easy or difficult to reprise earlier characters, and put them together with new ones?

A. I think of writing more in terms of "natural" than "easy." It was very natural to write again about the main characters, Penny and Jeremy, because I felt that they were already off and running on a new adventure and I could see it very clearly. The "supporting" characters come back into the story when the circumstances are right and they will interact well with anybody new. It's fun when a familiar character does something unpredictable; and you can have very touching moments when they reveal an unexpected vulnerability. In writing as well as life, I find it's best to remain open to being surprised by people, to allow my impressions of them to develop, deepen and alter as I get to know them better.

Q. What comes first for you, the character, the locales, or the plot?

A. For me, they really are inseparable, but of course you've got to see them all distinctly in order to get them down on paper. I'd say it begins when characters hover in my mind. I carry them around with me during the day; and at night, something might occur to me that I'll jot down on a bedside tablet. Images start to form, then the locale comes into focus, and other characters emerge from the background. Questions arise: What is the heroine doing here? But even the process of answering those questions is more of a meditation than a concentration; that is, I'll follow the thread to see where it leads, instead of trying to turn the thread into a pair of reins to take control too quickly. I trust that I'll get there.

Q. Do you make outlines of your stories before you begin?

A. Eventually I make outlines, but by that time I've already gone through the process we just talked about. So it's pretty far along in my mind. I'll outline just what I need for continuity and practicality, such as a family tree; and when was a character born, where did he start out, how old would he be now. That sort of thing. I might do a story outline eventually, too, just enough to capture the tone and flavor along the way, possibly incorporating the little scribbled night-time notes I've made. But even then, I like to leave room for surprises, and the kind of inspiration that can only occur when you're really in there writing, and the characters are galloping along, just being themselves, which always clarifies the situation.

Q. This novel takes place in England, France, and Italy. Have you travelled to all these countries?

A. Yes, it began when I was awarded a writers' residency, which gave me time not only to write but to become immersed in European culture, and involved with people who live there. Then my work in film and TV brought me back. Now it's very much a part of my life.

Q. Your novel made me hungry because it has such great meals in it! What is the significance of food in the story?

A. I use such details when they help illustrate the locale and the dramatic situation. A cuisine tells you a lot about a region, and the experience that the characters are having. It's all very much a part of the history of a place—with the actual sun, soil and water that nurtured such food, prepared by people whose families have been growing and cooking it for centuries.

Q. The heroine of the novel uncovers ancient rituals, superstitions, and legends. What makes you interested in such things?

A. I love to discover the mythologies that each country or community tell their children to provide them with a link to their ancestors and lost civilizations. Yet, certain universal themes and metaphors often emerge, reminding us of our shared love of the landscape and the sea, the planets and stars, the seasons. I like the contrasts to present-day, too; for example, earlier civilizations had a different concept of time, a way of looking at a year as something cyclical, returning and regained, as opposed to the current view of a year progressing in a straight line and then vanishing on New Year's Eve. Primarily it's the connection to nature that seems so vital now in the twenty-first century.

QUESTIONS
FOR DISCUSSION

1. The hero and heroine of this novel have inherited a windfall. What would you do if you received such a legacy? Would your life change? How? What things would remain constant?

2. Jeremy's ex-wife threw down the gauntlet in the previous novel, and now Penny must cope with this challenge. How does she deal with it? How does Jeremy respond? Does the situation change their understanding of each other? Does it deepen their commitment? What were the key turning points?

3. Why is the London townhouse so important to Penny when she talks to the accountant? Does it come to symbolize something important in her life with Jeremy? The characters go back and forth to London. What does London itself represent?

4. Penny links the purchase of the yacht ("The Splurge") to something that she calls "The Plan" which was Jeremy's idea about taking some time off in order to figure out their career options. She believes that this interlude is a rare opportunity, and she is very

protective of it. Why? Does it turn out to be as significant as she believes? What factors contribute to this?

5. The theme of family feuds recurs in the novel. Penny refers to her own family and their previous quarrel over the inheritance. The Count's family and Diamanta's family have a history of feuding. What similarities and differences can be found? What do these quarrels reveal about the characters involved? Are you reminded of any personal experiences of families and friends involved in such disputes?

6. The Lion aquamanile means different things to different people, thus revealing unique aspects of each character. What does it symbolize to the Count, Kurt, Penny, Jeremy, Rollo, Pepi, Clive, Diamanta and her relatives? What does it reveal about each person? What do you think is its ultimate value?

ABOUT THE AUTHOR

C.A. Belmond has published short fiction, poetry and humorous essays. She was awarded the Edward Albee Foundation Fellowship and was twice a Pushcart Press Editors' Book Award finalist. Belmond was a writer-in-residence at the Karolyi Foundation in the South of France, and her original screenplays were shortlisted at Robert Redford's Sundance Institute and the Eugene O'Neill Playwrights Conference. She has written, directed and produced television drama and documentary, and has taught writing at New York University. Her debut novel, *A Rather Lovely Inheritance*, launched the original story of Penny and Jeremy.

Visit the author at her Web site, www.cabelmond.com.